TOTEMPOLE

Sanford Friedman

1984
San Francisco
NORTH POINT PRESS

To Richard Howard

HORSIE

weetheart, why have you taken your pajamas off?"

"Dadda."

"Come on now, let's put them back before you catch cold."

"Dadda no jamas."

"But little boys must keep warm—even in the summer."

"Horsie no jamas."

"Who, darling?"

"Horsie."

"Come on now. First little leggie . . . that's the way: in it goes. Second little leggie . . . that's my pet. Back you go now, under the sheet. There we are. Little boys must have their sleep."

"Momma jamas?"

"No, darling, momma has a nightgown. Stephen and dadda and Roggie have pajamas."

"Stephen no jamas."

"Stephen goes bye-bye now. Good night, my love."

Harriet Wolfe bent down into the crib, kissed her son on both cheeks, switched off the overhead light and left the room, closing the door carefully behind her.

Stephen listened alertly to the clop-clop of his mother's mules growing fainter and fainter until, at last, it was terminated by the click of her bedroom door.

"Horsie," Stephen said out loud, sniffing the manure smell wafting in through the open window. Standing up straight in his crib, he crossed the mattress to the bars at the opposite end, closer to the window. He tried to push his head through; he strained to squeeze his body through—through the bars, through the screen, through the open window, into the daylit summer night, across the street to the red wooden walls of the Seaside Riding Academy— but the bars prevented him. Slowly, he turned his head, sniffing the air. The smell was here, here in the room, here in the crib—but where was horsie? "Where horsie?" he said out loud, searching under his monkey, Oscar, and crawling under the sheet. Across the

9

street, in the Riding Academy, a colt whinnied into the night, as if in answer to his question. "Horsie laugh," Stephen said and laughed himself, hearing the sound and smelling the horse-smell under the sheet. His fat fingers pulled at the elastic waistband of his pajama bottoms. "No jamas," he said, kicking them off with the sheet. The manure smell seemed stronger now. "Horsie . . . Dadda . . . Stephen . . ." he said, almost in a reverie, thrusting his legs against the side of the crib and fondling himself in the twilight.

"Saul," Harriet said to her husband, as she gently closed their bedroom door, "do you know what he's done? He's kicked off his pajamas."

"Do you blame him? It's too hot," Saul sighed, rolling over and stretching out flat on his back. With her back to her husband's naked trunk, Harriet sat down on her side of the double bed and lit a cigarette. "Come on, Hattie, how many times do I have to tell you not to smoke in bed?"

"Shhh. You'll wake—"

"Don't shush me."

"But I'm not *in* bed."

"Put it out."

"It's out. It's out," she said, nervously stabbing her cigarette into the ashtray. Harriet stared vacantly at *The Good Earth,* which was lying on her night table, but she just wasn't in the mood for all those famines and plagues. The cigarette smoke rose slowly toward the ceiling and gathered there like a patch of mildew, hanging motionless in the warm air, until a breeze from the sea unsettled it and sucked it out the open window.

Smelling the manure from the stables of the Riding Academy, Saul said, "Damn it. There it is again: that fresh salt air Seaside is so famous for. I'll be damned if I'll take this house again next summer. I'd rather swelter in the city, than have to smell those horses every night. If we can't get a place closer to the ocean next summer, we'll stay in the city. But I'll be damned if I'll commute for *this*."

"We're only four blocks from the ocean."

"That's four too many."

"You know how expensive it is on Ocean Avenue."

"Then we'll stay in New York. We have no business being here in the first place—not with a depression going on. I'm not about to pay a thousand bucks again to live across the street from a stable."

"It's not a stable; it's a Riding Academy."

"I don't care what it's called; it's full of horses that shit all night."

Harriet could feel herself blushing, and she got up and walked to the window.

"You and your bright ideas," Saul continued, "renting the one house in Seaside that's next to a stable."

"Me? It wasn't *me!*" Harriet retorted. "You were the one who refused to take the house on Ocean Avenue."

"We couldn't afford it."

"Oh, yes we could! Pop offered to pay the difference. He offered you the extra five hundred, but *you* refused. You wouldn't take it. Not as a gift, you said. You and your pride!"

"You're damn right. I don't take charity from anyone. Not anyone, you understand? Least of all your father."

"What's the matter with my father? Isn't his money good enough? Where do you suppose the money I paid toward the rental of *this* house came from, if not my father?" To emphasize her point, Harriet removed the screen and slammed the bedroom window with a sharp crack like the blade of a guillotine.

"What in hell are you doing, Hattie?"

"Closing the window. You said you couldn't stand the smell."

Without speaking, Saul swung his long legs to the floor, charged toward the window, yanked it open again, replaced the screen and returned to bed. "You want to suffocate me!"

It was dark now. Harriet stood at the open window, staring at the sign across the street: SEASIDE RIDING ACADEMY. It was lit from above by three large lamps that poured down golden light like honey, attracting swarms of insects. Harriet scratched at her scalp through her coarse hairnet until her fingernails were flecked with blood. For a moment she inhaled the manure smell with pleasure, remembering the horses in the square in front of the Plaza. Unconsciously, she turned and stared at Saul. Seeing his half-naked body, she began to question her enjoyment of the manure smell. Wasn't it unladylike, filthy, even disgusting of her to be standing there, sniffing in that stench as if it were perfume? Annoyed with herself, Harriet frowned and turned back to the window. The manure smell embarrassed her now, and the silence between her and Saul made her uneasy. "So that's what the baby meant," she said, staring at the Riding Academy.

"What?"

"He kept on saying, horsie, horsie. He wanted to go and see the horses." Harriet covered her nose to protect herself from the repugnant smell. "Saul, I don't want that baby running across the street by himself. He'll get run over."

"I've told him, Hattie. You've heard me tell him a hundred times. What should I do, lock him up?"

"Why can't he play on the beach with Roger and the other children? Why does he have to cross the street? What does he want over there anyway?"

"He likes the horses."

"What do you mean, he likes the horses? He's only two. What does a baby know about horses?" Suddenly, hearing the pounding sound of the surf in the distance, Harriet exclaimed, "He'll be trampled! He'll be trampled! You've got to talk to him, Saul. You've got to talk to him again. Sternly, Saul. Not the way you usually do—not all sugar and honey and letting him do just as he pleases. No wonder he pays no attention. He knows you'll let him have his way, no matter what he does. He knows he can wrap you around his little finger. You've got to be stern with him, Saul. You've got to forbid him once and for all to go near those horses. Then, if he still disobeys you, you've got to punish him."

"All right, Hattie. All right," Saul said. "I'll have another little talk with him in the morning. Let's go to sleep."

Harriet watched her husband stretch his large hand toward the Baby Ben and pull out the alarm, which was permanently set for 6:15. Deliberately, she fixed her eyes on his pajama tops; deliberately, she avoided glancing at the firm flesh of his exposed buttocks and long, muscular legs. Nor did she dare wait to watch him roll onto his back, but seized *The Good Earth* and hurried into the bathroom.

Saul stood in front of the shaving mirror, whipping up the lather on his face, while Stephen amused himself by scrubbing out the toilet bowl with his father's back-brush and flushing the toilet again and again. "Bad! Bad! Bad b.m.," he said, slopping the water onto the floor tiles.

"Don't do that, sweets." Saul put down the toilet lid. "Sit down here and talk to daddy." Stephen responded obediently, sliding his rump around the toilet lid in an exaggerated ritual, like a hen preparing to lay, until he finally settled. "Sweetiepie," Saul said, picking up his razor, "you know, it's very dangerous for little boys to cross the street alone; a car could hit you."

"Car," Stephen repeated with delight.

"Yes, you know."

"Stephen drive?"

"Sure you can—when we go to the station," Saul said, always delighted by his son's interest in motoring. "But only if you promise not to cross the street alone. You understand?"

"Stephen drive?"

"I don't want you running over there to see the horses by yourself, you understand? Horses can be even worse than cars. They don't have any brains. They can't see little boys under their feet. They can kick little boys and not even know it. Horses can hurt little boys."

"Horsie," Stephen said, jumping down off the toilet lid.

"Yes, yes. You know what I'm talking about."

"Horsie," he said, staring at the bald mound of dadda's knee-cap. Bald, like dadda's head. Bald foot, bald knee, bald popo, bald head . . . but then a billion furs, like momma's black fox in the other closet . . . Leg furs, thigh furs, ding-dong furs . . . bushy black ding-dong furs . . .

"I want you to promise me you won't go near the horsies by yourself anymore."

"Horsie," Stephen said, staring, stretching all of him to reach, to touch, to pet dadda's ding-dong.

"Damn it! Don't do that! Can't you see I'm shaving!"

Harriet called in from the bedroom, "What's the matter, Saul?"

"Nothing."

"What did he do?"

"Nothing. It's nothing. I just nicked my chin."

"Stevie dear, come out of there and let daddy shave. Now, now, there's nothing to cry about; daddy didn't mean to shout."

"Of course not, honey. You can stay and watch me shave."

"Come on, angel, let's go visit Clarry; your breakfast must be ready." Harriet took Stephen by the hand and led him out of the bedroom. When she returned, Saul had finished shaving and was getting dressed. He already had his shoes and socks and garters and underwear on, and was putting on his shirt now: buttoning up the front, buttoning the cuffs, buttoning the button farther up the sleeve, turning up the collar in preparation for the tie.

"Goddamn it! There's too much starch in this! Can't you ever get it right?"

"I'm sorry, darling. I'll tell her again."

"If she's too dumb to do it right, do it yourself!"

"Oh dear! Look at your chin," Harriet commiserated, changing the subject. "It's still bleeding." The tiny piece of toilet paper Saul had applied to the cut was saturated with blood. "Let me change it for you," she said, walking into the bathroom and returning with a fresh piece. "Just hold still a second, darling." Gingerly, she began to pick at the used patch, her inch-long fingernails fluttering around Saul's chin like the elytra of a firefly.

"Stop fussing at me, will you, Hattie!"

"How did the baby do it?" she asked, ignoring her husband's request.

"Stop it, I said," Saul ordered, jerking his chin away. "And let me get dressed," he added as he folded his shirttails neatly over his crotch and tucked them in between his legs to keep the shirt from blousing.

"What did he do?"

"What did *who* do?" Saul asked impatiently, seizing his trousers and holding the left trouser leg in his left hand to keep it from losing its crease or gathering lint on the carpet, while he stepped into the right leg.

"Stevie."

"Nothing."

"But he must have done *something* to make you shout like that."

"Like *what?*"

"Loud enough to make him cry."

"I wasn't shouting at *him*. I shouted because I cut myself."

Harriet watched her husband step into the left trouser leg and check the arrangement of his shirttails. . . . It isn't only neatness, she suddenly realized after five and a half years of watching Saul's shirttail performance, it's a means of self-defense . . . "But what did he do to make you cut yourself?" she persisted, watching him button his fly.

"Nothing," he said and picked up his black leather belt off his chifforobe where he had neatly coiled it like a lariat the night before.

"But he must have done *something*."

Saul picked up the beige summer tie he had laid out next to his belt the night before. "I said it was nothing."

"Why are you being so mysterious, Saul?"

"Stop nagging, will you." Saul folded the starched collar over his carefully knotted tie, and began to return his wallet and handkerchief and car key and business keys and lucky piece and loose change—all of which had been lined up like surgical instruments on top of his chifforobe the night before—to their habitual places in his various pockets.

"What's the matter with you, Saul?" Harriet held up his jacket as high as her arms could stretch.

"What do you mean?" he asked, stooping slightly to put his long arms through the sleeves.

"Why won't you tell me what he did?"

"Damn it, Hattie!" Saul exploded, whirling to face his wife. "I said it was nothing!"

"Well if it was nothing—"

"All right. All right! If you must know, he pinched my balls."

"He what?" Harriet gasped.

"You heard me," Saul said proudly, crossing to the door.

"Wait a minute. Don't go down to breakfast yet."

"I'm late."

"But, Saul," she pleaded, following him into the hall. "Saul—"

"What is it?" he asked, descending the stairs.

"Maybe, dear—maybe you ought not to walk around like that."

"Like *what?*" he demanded, stopping halfway down the staircase.

"I mean, maybe you ought not to walk around the house that way."

"What way?"

"In just your pajama tops. At least not in front of the baby. Maybe you ought to make a point of wearing your bottoms as well—in front of the baby, I mean. That's why he kicked off his pajamas last night. Don't you see? He was imitating *you.*"

"What are you talking about? If I can't walk around my own house dressed the way I want—"

"I don't mean that, darling."

"—I'll go and live in a hotel. That's what I'll do: I'll move to a hotel. Don't expect me home tonight."

"Now don't be silly."

"Who's being silly? Just wait till you get to the train tonight and I'm not on it—we'll see who's being silly then. If you're too modest to see a man in his birthday suit—"

"I didn't say *me!*"

"Well, that's what you meant!"

"No."

"There are plenty of women who'd give their eyeteeth—"

"I only meant if you wore your bottoms as well, it might not seem so conspicuous to him, it might not attract his attention so much."

"It, it, it! Say what you mean."

"You know what I mean," she hedged coyly. "You might avoid what happened before, if you wore your bottoms."

"Who said anything about before? Did *I* make an issue of it? No! It was *you!* You! Busybody had to know what happened. Well now you know. It's all *your* fault in the first place."

"What's my fault?"

"If you hadn't dressed him like a girl when he was little, he wouldn't be doing things like that. *Roger* never did. If you'd just leave your hands off him and stop babying him, he'd be all right. That goes for all of us—all the men in this house!—just leave us alone!"

"Stop shouting, Saul."

"Don't tell me to stop shouting! This is still my house! I don't care if you or your father or God Almighty paid half the rent, it's still my house, and I'll walk around it any way I damn well please. I'll walk around it stark naked, if I please, and I don't want to hear you open your big mouth about it."

"Don't you talk to me that way," Harriet sniveled. "Don't you dare."

"I'll talk to you any way I goddamn please!" Saul bellowed, stamping off the bottom step, into the hallway.

"Yes! So I see!" Harriet pursued him down the stairs. "So I see! It doesn't matter who's listening. It doesn't matter how you degrade me in front of the servants—how you degrade yourself—" Suddenly, spotting Stephen behind one of the lower panes of the glass dining room door, Harriet added ferociously, "In front of the children! He's watching us! Watching us right this minute, listening to every word!" she explained in a hoarse whisper, taking out her handkerchief and blowing her nose. "Come and have your breakfast, Saul."

"I haven't time. I'm going to miss my train."

Crossing to the dining room door, Harriet tapped on the glass and made eyes at Stephen. "Peekaboo, I see you. Come on, sweetheart, daddy's late."

"Dadda."

"Come on, *süsse*," Harriet said, opening the front door and stepping outside.

"Dadda."

"There he is. There's my angel." Saul lifted his son in his arms and hugged him tightly. Stephen poked at his father's cheek and rubbed his beard against the grain. "What's that, sweetheart? What's it called."

"Beard," Stephen grinned.

"That-a-boy, that's my baby," Saul boasted, as if there was someone else in the hall. "Come on, baby, let's go, baby; the flivver's waiting; daddy's going to take his baby for a spin," he crooned, putting on his Panama and dancing out the front door, carrying Stephen toward the Chevy parked at the end of the front path. Harriet was already inside, sitting next to the driver's seat. "Now I want you to be a good little boy and don't go near the horses today," Saul said as he stepped onto the running board and transferred Stephen to Harriet's arms.

"Stephen drive?" he asked his father.

"Don't annoy daddy when he's driving, dear," Harriet said.

"Sure you can. As soon as we get going," Saul said, settling himself in the driver's seat and starting off in the direction of the station.

"Hi ya, Stephen. How you today?" Charlie enquired with a big grin. "Come to look at your pal, Chestnut?"

"Horsie."

"There he is—over there on the other side of the ring," he said, pointing toward a chocolate-colored three-year-old being ridden by a teen-age girl in a new habit. "Just you be patient, now, my little equestrian, and he'll be round. He'll be round to see you, but don't come in the ring."

"Questrian." The word made Stephen giggle.

"Yes, siree, that's what you called: eeequestrian," Charlie said. Stephen giggled again. "My, but you're a smart little devil. My-my," he said, shaking his head and walking off toward the stable.

"Questrian," Stephen said, giggling as Chestnut advanced at a slow trot. "Horsie," he said, clapping his palms against the white fence post, seeing the big, parchment-colored teeth, the loose, dangling flesh of the neck, the long, tan line of the belly like the capsized boat on the beach, the keel of the capsized boat on the beach, horsie's big, dark, ding-dong keel. He clapped the fence post harder as the horse-smell filled his nostrils and the mountainous rump paraded past his ogling eyes. "Dadda," he panted, pushing the full length of his body up against the post, hugging the post and salivating as Chestnut's slightly raised tail thrashed past him into a cloud of dust. "Horsie," he cried, wrapping his legs around the post and crushing his forehead against it fiercely.

"What a lousy day," Saul said as he took off his tie. "Ninety-one-point-nine in the shade; you could have fried an egg on the sidewalk. And not an order—not a blessed order all day long. I'd have been better off on the beach," he moaned. "Where's the baby?"

"In the yard," Harriet replied.

"What have we got for dinner?" Saul asked, crossing to the window overlooking the back yard.

"Salmon, darling. Nice cold salmon."

"Oh, God," Saul groaned, squinting through the screen. "Wouldn't you know. I had it for lunch."

"Oh, God," Harriet groaned, "how does it happen? Every time."

"Stevie. Stevie. Stevie," Saul called out through the screen. After a moment, he turned back into the room. "He isn't there."

"He must be in the kitchen," Harriet said.

Saul took his copy of *The Sun* from the wicker table in the hall and strode into the kitchen. "Evening, Clarry."

"Evenin', Mr. Wolfe."

"Where's the baby?"

"Ain't he in the yard?"

"Stevie! Stevie!" Saul heard his wife on the floor above. And then again: "Stevie!" as she mounted to the attic.

"Stevie! Stevie!" Saul shouted, standing on the front steps, shading his eyes with the newspaper.

Hearing his name, Stephen turned away from the riding ring, toddled through the timothy and buttercups in the empty lot, and lurched out onto the macadam road.

"Watch him!" Harriet shrieked, thrusting her head out of the attic window. "Watch him!"

"Careful, sweetheart," Saul called, running down the front path and almost colliding into his son.

"Dadda! Dadda!" Stephen exclaimed joyously.

Saul squatted down in front of Stephen. "Hi ya, sweets. Give us a kiss."

"Dadda. Dadda," Stephen repeated and hugged his father's bald head.

"Saul! What are you doing, Saul?" Harriet called from the attic window. "Remember what I said last night."

"Now look here, sweetheart," Saul began. "I thought you made me a promise this morning. I thought you promised never to go and see the horsies again—unless you go with me or mommy."

"Horsie."

"Now listen to me, sweetheart, I'm not fooling anymore. It's very dangerous. If you go over there again, I'm going to have to give you a licking. You understand? Licking!" Saul illustrated the word by smacking the newspaper resoundingly against the palm of his left hand. Stephen looked bewildered. "You understand?" he asked, with affected sternness.

"Dadda lick Stephen?"

"Only if Stephen is bad and goes to see the horsies alone."

"Questrian," Stephen giggled.

"What is it, honey?" Saul said, standing up and taking hold of Stephen's hand.

"Questrian."

"Yes, darling, I understand. What is it, what's the question?" Stephen wrinkled his nose in perplexity and looked up at his father.

"You can go if I go with you, but not alone. You understand? If you do, I'll have to give you a licking. Come on now," Saul said, leading Stephen up the path, "let's go and have dinner."

"You've got to, Saul! You've simply got to."

"I wish you'd let me handle this in my own way, Hattie."

"No! He's got to be taught a lesson."

"I told you, I'm not going to beat that child."

"I didn't say beat him, I said spank him. There's a difference. What's the point of threatening him if you don't intend to go through with it? What was the *point* of that little demonstration yesterday?"

"What demonstration?"

"Slapping the newspaper across your hand—if you don't intend to go through with it?"

"I wish you'd let me bring up my sons in my own way, Hattie," Saul exclaimed with exaggerated patience.

"No! I've seen what you've done with Roger. I can't say a word to that child without his running to you. He's a brat! A brat! Wild and willful and spoiled. And *you've* done it to him, Saul. You've done it to him. It's all your fault. Always letting him have his way. Always contradicting *me!* Always reversing whatever I say. Well, I'm not going to let you do it to Stephen!"

"Then why don't you go and spank him yourself," Saul barked.

"Of course! Let *me* do all the dirty work! Let me be the one who always says no! Let me be the ogre, the one they hate—" This idea was so painful to Harriet her voice broke and her eyes filled with tears. "And you be the *gute Mensch!* No!" she cried. "For once *you're* going to do it! You're going to punish him, not *me*. It's not my place."

"Not your place," Saul repeated scornfully. "It's not your place to spank the baby. Not your place to fire maids. Not your place to bathe the children. Not your place to nurse them. Not your place to come to bed when I do—" Saul stopped and looked at his wife with loathing. The corners of his mouth were stretched to their limit; his lower lip was ragged and protruded like an open wound. "What exactly *is* your place?"

Harriet's normally large eyes bulged even larger and her lips turned into a tight, thin line as she took her throat in her hand dramatically. "I wonder, Saul," she said desolately. "Sometimes I wonder—wonder what I'm doing here—what it's all about." Harriet drew two short, quick breaths and hurried on. "Sometimes—" but she checked herself. Saul watched the blood drain from her face and a lunatic blank come into her eyes as if she were planning to strangle or drown him, as if she herself were being strangled or drowned. "Please, Saul," she muttered, "do as I say."

"All right, Hattie. You win," Saul sighed, walking out of the bedroom and down the front stairs.

Harriet rushed after him. "Don't hurt him," she cried, clutching the banister. "Don't hurt him, Saul."

"Stevie darling," Saul called gently, holding open the porch screen door. "Come here a minute, sweets."

Stephen scurried across the yard, up the two huge wooden steps as fast as his legs could climb and in through the open door. "Dadda."

Saul closed the door, took Stephen by the hand and led him to the glider. "Come on, darling, sit down here."

"Side, dadda?"

"Yes. That's right. Up you go," Saul said, helping his son onto the glider.

"Swing?"

"Not now, honey."

"Swing!" Stephen commanded, and his father obeyed.

"Listen to me, honey," Saul whispered. "We're going to play a trick on mommy."

"Trick?"

"Yes. We're going to play a game."

"Piggy-back?"

"No, a much better game than that."

"What?" Stephen whispered conspiratorially, imitating his father.

"We're going to pretend I'm giving you a spanking."

"Spanking," Stephen grinned.

"Licking," Saul explained.

"Licking," Stephen grinned.

"Come on now," Saul said, lifting up his son and laying him face down across his lap.

Stephen liked lying there, feeling dadda's warmth and the softness of his body and sniffing the sweaty, loamy smell of dadda's trousers —the ones he wore to work in the garden on weekends. He dug his chin into dadda's thigh, wriggled around against dadda's loins, revolved his smiling face and looked up over his shoulder. "Game."

"That's right, darling. Now, I'm going to pat you on the popo, and I want you to cry. I'm not going to hurt you," he added quickly, "I just want you to make believe. You understand? That way we'll fool mommy." Saul stiffened his right hand and started to deliver a series of love taps: pat, pat, pat, pat.

Stephen adored the game and began to twist and squirm licentiously. "Game," he giggled.

"Yes, darling," Saul whispered, resting his large hand on Stephen's buttocks. "But I want you to pretend to cry. When I do that, I want you to pretend to cry." Pat, pat, pat, pat. "Cry, sweetheart, cry," Saul coached. "Cry."

"Onnng, onnng, onnng . . ." Stephen began to purr, to hum, to growl like an electric motor, gritting his teeth and twisting his body, thrusting his legs against the end of the glider.

"No, darling, cry."

The motor sound grew louder now, more and more intense, high-pitched, unrestrained, terrible and deafening, like a buzz saw cutting through the heartwood of a walnut tree, until, at last, it could not be contained and burst from Stephen's throat: a long, sustained savage croak. Simultaneously, in the middle of this paroxysm, Stephen started weeweeing, and rammed his elbow into dadda's ding-dong.

"Ow!" Saul roared. The impact of the blow was painful. For a moment he sat in a state of confusion, not knowing what had struck him but feeling the pain; feeling the warmth rapidly spreading over his thighs, not knowing what it was but feeling it spread like the heat of a flame, until he recognized the smell of urine. Now, without thinking, but reacting instead almost in reflex, in self-defense, Saul tore down Stephen's cotton pants and underwear in a fury and began really spanking him.

The shock of this knocked the breath out of Stephen, made him yelp and then scream, "Jamas!"

"You're not to do that ever again! You understand!" Saul shouted. "I'll walk around any way I goddamn please—with or without my pajamas on—but you're not to do that ever again. Never again! You understand? You're never to touch me there again."

"Jamas!" Stephen bawled. "Jamas! Dadda! Horsie!"

"You're never to go near those horses again!" Saul shouted uncontrollably, smacking Stephen's naked body. "Never! Never! Understand? No more horses! Say it! Say it!"

"No more horsie!" Stephen howled, sucking in his saliva and mucus and gasping for breath. "No more horsie!"

"Never again!"

"Saul!" Harriet screamed from the living room.

"Never, never—"

"Stop it, Saul!" she shrieked, rushing out onto the porch and grabbing her husband's arm.

"Never—"

"STOP IT!" Harriet commanded in a voice so powerful and authoritative Saul's arms fell to his sides and he stared down dumbly at his son. "Have you taken leave of your senses?" she hissed.

"Horsie! Horsie! Horsie!" Stephen screamed hysterically.

"Shhh, shhh, shhh," Harriet said, picking up her son and cradling him in her arms. "Shhh, shhh, shhh," she repeated, as she comforted and caressed Stephen. "Mommy's here. Mommy's here. He won't hurt you. I won't let him, ever, ever. Shhh, shhh, it's all right now. Everything's all right. Mommy's here."

OCEAN

The center of Seaside's social life was not the public beach, but the Casino on Ocean Avenue. There, on top of the low clay cliffs that lined the Jersey coast for miles, the summer residents pursued their pleasures as if the beach and ocean did not exist. The Casino's facilities included bathhouses, a restaurant, a lounge, a card room, an outdoor dance floor and bandstand, and a fifty-foot pool.

Stephen had received his first swimming lessons in the pool when he was three, but now, at the age of six, he had very mixed and complicated feelings about it. On the one hand, he adored the pool just because it was made of water. That in itself was saying a lot since Stephen loved the water more than almost anything in the world—not more than Clarry, of course, and not more than his marine collection, but more than Mommy sometimes, and more than Daddy at others, and certainly a whole lot more than his brother, Roggie. The other thing he liked about the pool was the fact that you could jump into it whenever you liked, providing of course you had waited an hour after lunch. There was always someone around to keep an eye on you—like Mommy right this minute: "Three bam"—that was its one advantage over the ocean.

But whatever its advantages, the swimming pool just didn't compare with the ocean. In the first place the ocean, salty or not, wasn't filled with this irritating chemical that burned your eyes. In the second place there weren't all these grownups eating and knitting and gossiping and playing mah-jongg and Michigan rummy and backgammon and bridge, and whispering about the Lindbergh baby—at the ocean you could get off on your own. In the third place there weren't all these older children—including Roggie— showing off by plunging into the water an inch away from your nose, trying so hard to blind and drown you. The ocean didn't need to be churned up artificially, it had a way of churning itself up—of making its own stir, its own splash and spray and waves,

27

wilder than any kicking children or galloping horse could make.

And yet, for some reason, the ocean's wildness—the feature that attracted Stephen most—made the grownups nervous, and they forbade him to go into the water alone. That hateful rule created awful problems for Stephen, not only because no one trusted Bruce, the lifeguard, to rescue him if he should drown, but also because Mommy was suffering from something a little bit like chicken pox called neurasthenia that made her skin break out and itch terribly, and she wasn't supposed to set foot in salt water. Stephen had a theory of his own that the water would wash away the sores and scabs that covered Mommy's back (and stained her sheets and nightgowns), but Mommy had explained that brine was an irritant. Clarry had a problem, too, about going into the ocean: she claimed she couldn't swim. But Stephen knew it wasn't all *that* simple because once, when he asked her why she stayed in her uniform instead of putting on a bathing suit when they went down to the beach, Clarry laughed and said, "Cause they don't make 'em big enough for me"; and another time, when Stephen asked her why she refused even to wade, Clarry said, "What's the matter with you, sugar? These folks don't want my kind messin' up their water." That left only Daddy, but Daddy had to work in New York five days a week and could take Stephen into the ocean only on weekends and Friday afternoons when, like today, he came back from the city early, at four-fifteen. Stephen looked up at the big clock on the white wall outside the members' lounge: two o'clock. It would be hours and hours and hours before Daddy's train arrived.

But even so, even though he was not allowed to go into the water except on weekends, Stephen preferred the ocean to the pool, the beach to the Casino—at least there was the sand. Not only could you embrace the sand and eat the sand and drool your saliva into it, and punch and pat it, and roll and run and turn somersaults on it, and flop and jump and stand on your head on it, and let it trickle through your fingers, and dribble it between your daddy's toes, and throw it into your brother's eyes and pick it out of your belly button; but also, down by the water's edge, when the tide was low, you could dig pits and pools and caves and caverns in the sand; you could build bridges, moats, canals, towers, temples, castles, kingdoms in the sand.

As a matter of fact, Stephen Wolfe had quite a reputation for his sand creations on the Seaside public beach. Grownups and chil-

dren alike admired his patience and imagination, and stood enthralled while Stephen patty-caked pies and cones and domes in
the sand, let the sand drip from his fingers like paraffin, creating
pagodas and minarets, mounded and molded the sand into
Pueblo huts and Moroccan hovels, amassed great piles of sand and
made them into ziggurats, sliced through others with a stave from
an orange-crate and produced Assyrian palaces, Egyptian pyra-
mids, and Rockefeller Center, transformed the stave into London
Bridge, scooped out giant reservoirs and filled them with water
piped from the sea, engineered a system of canals and waterways
through a city the size of Bruges, and spent entire days reconstructing Babylon, Jerusalem, and Carcassonne.

And yet, no matter how arduously he labored, how deep he dug
his moats, how high he flung his bulwarks, how much he reinforced his walls, at some point in the night the sea came in and
stole his castles from him. At first Stephen had thought Daddy was
the culprit, and then he decided that it was Roggie who sneaked
down to the beach and trampled his creations, until one day Clarry
made it clear to him. "There's a war goin' on between them two
—between the ocean and the land. Has been since the beginnin' of
creation. That old ocean's on the warpath 'cause it come first and
the land come after. It jealous now 'cause the land is so much
larger. Jealous 'cause the land has got itself collected—sittin' cool
and pretty—while's the ocean, it always on the go, restless and
rampagin'. Sort of like the difference between a man and woman.
Yes, sir," Clarry chuckled, "that what it remind *me* of: the
natural, born-in difference between a man and woman. Why that
old ocean's like a starvin' animal, lappin' at the land. Ain't nothin'
gonna satisfy it till it's licked us all way."

Stephen agreed. The trouble with the ocean—its only drawback
—was that it wanted to gobble up everything in sight. But on the
other hand, it gave things back. It gave back all those treasures
that he had been collecting now for three successive summers—his
great marine collection that was resting right this minute safe and
sound at home on the radiator box in front of his bedroom
window. . . .

"Stevie, kitten," Mommy called.

Quickly, not in answer to his mother's call but in order to
escape it, Stephen submerged, swam under water and came up on
the other side of the pool. Holding onto the tiled conduit, Stephen
hugged the side of the pool and held his breath, hidden from

sight—or so he thought—listening to Mommy and the girls playing mah-jongg.

"Two bam. One crack. Six dots, Pung! Flower. East wind. Soap. Kong!"

"Come on, kitten," Mommy called again. "I can see you there. You've been in for over an hour."

"Green. Four bam. Four dots. South. Red. Flower. Five crack. Mah-jongg!"

Stephen peeked over the side of the pool and saw Mrs. Tishman press her jeweled fingers down and move the rest of her row of tiles up like linotype onto the top of her rack.

"I tell you she's been to the stable today," Aunt Ida remarked.

"She stepped in it good!" Aunt Fanny corroborated.

"Up to her knees!" Mrs. Kanig added.

As always, this puzzling commentary was followed by a din as familiar to Stephen as the sound of the milkman loading the empties into his wagon: the ladies were mixing the mah-jongg tiles.

"Excuse me, girls," Harriet said. "I'm going to get that child out of the water before he turns into a fish."

Hearing this, Stephen pushed off from the side and swam toward the center of the pool.

"Come on, Stevie, come out now. I'm not fooling with you anymore."

"Oh, Mommy," Stephen pleaded.

"Come on now."

"Just five more minutes?"

"No! You heard me: out!"

"But Roggie's—"

"I don't want to hear about Roger. If you expect to go in the ocean with Daddy later on, you'll come out *now*—right this minute!"

"Oh, Mommy," Stephen complained, ascending the semicircular steps at the shallow end of the pool.

"Look at you! Look at your eyes, they're bloodshot. You won't be happy until you turn into a fish. Come on now," Mommy said, taking Stephen's hand and leading him toward the mah-jongg table. "I want you to go inside and change your suit. Come, I'll give you the bathhouse key."

"There he is! There's my angel," Aunt Ida glowed. *"Umbeschrieblich,* Hattie, is that a doll!"

"Stevie," Mommy coached, "give Aunt Ida a kiss."

"Hello, Aunt Ida," Stephen said. "Hello, Aunt Fanny."

"Huhwo, wuffie," Aunt Fanny gabbled, her mouth, as always, packed with pralines.

"What about *me?*" Mrs. Tishman asked. "Don't *I* get a kiss?"

"Hello, Mrs. Tishman. Hello, Mrs. Kanig."

"All right, darling," Mommy said. "Here's the key. Now go and change your suit."

Stephen did as he was told: took the key and trotted around the pool toward the bathhouses. As he did so, Aunt Ida repeated the word *umbeschrieblich,* and Stephen thought: there are just too many words like that—like pung and kong and mah-jongg—that don't make any sense. As he entered Row A of the bathhouses, Stephen slowed down to a walk to protect his bare feet from the splintery boards. He loved this part of the Casino. Its long, narrow, east-west streets, intersected by shorter, broader avenues, constituted a city for him—a city in which he could explore and hide and chase around for hours without ever really getting lost or run over. Occasionally, among the million, identical, gray wooden doors (each with its six-inch diamond cut way above the level of a grownup's eyes) Stephen would discover one that wasn't locked—a bathhouse that had not been rented for the summer!—and appropriate it for himself, turning it into a tower or dungeon, a place in which to think his private thoughts, hold dialogues with imaginary friends, store treasures and eavesdrop on his neighbors. It was in one of these dark cells that he had first overheard the words: "Hauptman," "F.D.R.," "tits" and "Kotex," before some officious attendant evicted him and made sure the door was locked for the remainder of the season.

When Stephen reached the end of Row A, he turned right briskly, padded past B and C and D Streets, took a left at E Street, until he reached the door marked 97, and inserted the key. Once inside, he ignored the two turkish towels hanging on separate hooks on the right-hand wall, ignored the first one on the left and pulled down the second. After locking the door behind him, he walked to the end of E Street, turned left and meandered toward the men's shower. On the way, between E and D Streets, he came to the wall marked WOMEN. As always, as he passed, Stephen tried, surreptitiously, to catch a glimpse of the women inside, but the barrier obstructed his view. He knew what lay beyond was identical to what lay beyond the wall marked MEN: one enormous room without a ceiling, one long, green wooden bench, one clothes wringer and three unpartitioned showers with rusty chains. After the showers came a little house with a cement floor, two white sinks, two silver mirrors, two white urinals, three gray booths, and three white toilets. Long ago, when he was little, Stephen had gone behind the wall marked WOMEN almost every day with Mommy, except when Roggie took him behind the wall marked MEN. On weekends, of course, he had always gone behind the wall marked MEN with Daddy, and that's the way it had been for years and years until one summer when Mommy announced he had grown too big to continue coming with her anymore. When Stephen had asked her to come, instead, with *him,* Mommy only laughed and said she couldn't. That had left him slightly confused. Not only had he grown accustomed to going to the WOMEN's, he considered it his proper place—until, that is, Daddy explained that it was much more fun and natural "for the boys to get off on their own" and "keep the girls out of their hair." After that, the whole thing had seemed much more reasonable, and Stephen didn't mind being restricted to the area behind the wall marked MEN—as a matter of fact, he considered it a privilege. The only thing that bothered him about the women and made him try to peer beyond the barrier every time he passed was that Stephen didn't know exactly what it was he had seen when he was little that he was supposed to have forgotten now that he was big. . . .

After crossing D Street, Stephen came to the wall marked MEN, casually tossed his towel over his shoulder and strolled around the barrier. Inside there was an old, old, fat man, taking off his bathing suit in front of a long, green bench. As Stephen approached, the old, old fat man said hello. Stephen said hello in return and sat down in the sunshine to watch the man disrobe. As always with grownups, under his bathing suit, the old, old man wore one of those silvery pouches that looked like a horse's feed-bag over his peepee-er. Stephen had not yet figured out the purpose of those pouches . . . did they keep the grownups warm? Or were they more like Mommy's hairnet—that awful brown web she wove around her head at night before she went to bed. Was that the reason little boys didn't have to wear them, because they didn't have any hair to keep in place . . . ? Stephen watched the old man roll down over his enormous belly the elastic, supporting the silvery pouch, until the whole thing—elastic and pouch together —turned into a figure 8 around his bloodless ankles and he stepped out of it clumsily. When he bent over to pick up both his bathing suit and the figure 8, the old man's belly sagged like the underside of the hammock when Daddy was lying in it. Also, the old man's peepee-er looked like the neck of a dead chicken, and Stephen had to chuckle.

"What's the matter with you, sonny?" the old man asked. "Ain't you ever seen your father? What are you doing anyway, sitting there like that? This ain't a peep show." Stephen could tell from the harshness of his voice that the old man was angry and he turned away guiltily. A moment later he heard the old man exclaim, "Oooisch!" and Stephen turned around again, only to be confronted by the chicken neck bobbing up and down as the old man cowered and cavorted under the icy shower. "Look here, sonny," he grumbled, releasing the rusty chain and stopping the flow of water, "ain't you got anything better to do than sit there staring at me?"

"Can I run your bathing suit through the wringer for you?" Stephen asked.

"No, you can't," the old man answered curtly, donning his terry-cloth robe to protect his modesty. "You're Sol Wolfe's son, ain't you?" he asked, collecting his belongings. "The younger," he added sardonically, as he moved toward the exit—his clogs clattering over the floor boards—and disappeared.

The ambiguity in the tone of these last words left Stephen puzzled and staring after the old man, but his concern was only momentary. A second later he hopped off the bench, pulled down his bathing suit and ran to the first shower. Standing on tiptoes, stretching his left arm until the muscles ached, Stephen was just able to reach the rusty ring and pull it down. Taking pains to keep the freezing water from spattering his shoulders, he doused his bathing suit, released the chain and skipped over to the wringer. Carefully, he inserted a corner of his bloated, blue wool bathing suit—black now from the water—between the ivory-colored rubber rollers and began to turn the crank. Almost as if they were synchronized, Stephen's tongue emerged from his mouth at the same rate of speed as his bathing suit from between the rollers, so that by the time the garment was completely wrung-out, flat and dry and blue again—some of the surface hairs even silver in the sunlight—Stephen was licking his nose. Indeed, he loved the clothes wringer so much that when he was finished with his bathing suit, he repeated the entire process with his turkish towel from dousing through cranking. As a little boy, Stephen had tried, without success, to run his fingers and even his tongue between the rollers, and he still looked forward to the day when he would be tall enough to experiment with his peepee-er.

When he was finished, Stephen wrapped his damp towel around his waist, wandered back to E 97, changed into his red wool bathing suit, put on his orange water wings and waited impatiently for Daddy to come.

By the time Saul arrived, an unpleasant wind was blowing out of the southeast and the sky was overcast. The ocean didn't look the least bit tempting—after all, it was September 7, the summer was over and this was to be their last weekend before moving back to New York—but Saul knew how disappointed the boys would be if he canceled their dip, and he got into his bathing suit. "Come on, kids," he said. "We better hurry. There's going to be a storm."

"In that case, Dad, let's go down by the wooden steps," Roggie suggested.

Before Saul could answer, Stephen exclaimed, "No!"

"But Roggie's right, *kleine* dear. Look how much time we could save."

"No!"

"All right. We'll go the way we always do."

"No fair!" Roggie objected. "Why do we always have to go *his* way?"

"I'll tell you what, sweetheart, why don't *you* go down the wooden steps, and Stevie and I'll go down the main one, and then we'll all meet on the beach."

"Why can't you come with me and let him go by himself, if he's so stubborn?"

"Because he's too little. You know he can't go by himself."

"Why can't Mommy take him?"

"Because Mommy's playing mah-jongg."

The question settled, Stephen turned to his brother and made a nefarious face like Dr. Fu Manchu about to pull the switch that would annihilate the whole white race.

"Look at him! Look at him!" Roggie shouted. "Stinker!"

"I'm *not* a stinker!"

"Listen, kids," Daddy intervened, "either we go this minute or we don't go at all. Come on now, Roggie. Let's see who'll get there first."

"Are you kidding, Dad?" Roggie scoffed.

"All right. On your mark, get set—" Even before Daddy had a chance to say go, Roggie tore away across the dance floor, around the bandstand, toward the narrow wooden stairs that scaled the cliffs from the beach to the Casino. At the same moment Stephen took hold of Daddy's hand and tugged him in the opposite direction: out of the Casino, down the gravel driveway, onto Ocean Avenue, toward Seaside's stellar attraction: the promenade and Grand Stairway, two blocks south.

Construction of the Grand Stairway was begun in 1888 and completed in 1891, at a time when Seaside had hopes of contending with Newport and Southampton for favor as the foremost resort on the Eastern seaboard. Built of red sandstone in the shape of an "X," the stairway could be approached from either the north or south—it made no difference which, since its two broad descending flights were symmetrical and converged onto a central landing halfway down the side of the cliffs before they branched off toward the beach in opposite directions. But in the forty-six summers that had passed since the ribbon-cutting ceremony, the elements—the merciless wind and spray—the bathers' clogs, and toy, tin shovels had taken their toll of the stately stone newels and Victorian bas-reliefs, the ornately carved balusters and rails, and had left the Stairway a ruin, just as the years had ruined its earliest users—lovely young ladies with pink and yellow parasols—who sat, now, gray and withered dowagers, all bundled-up on stiff-backed benches along the promenade. And yet to Stephen the Stairway still retained its former grandeur. He considered it the most splendid in the world—except, perhaps, for the one in Central Park leading down to the fountain and the row-boat pond—and always insisted on using it.

When they reached the stairhead, Stephen saw the red flag flapping on Bruce's lifeguard pole, he saw the waves and whitecaps and the darkness gathering in the southeast. Instead of deterring him, these signs of storm only excited and spurred Stephen on, and he practically dragged Daddy after him, down the two long flights. At the foot of the south flight, stretched out on the sand, his head of curly black hair pillowed on his palms, was Roggie, trying for all the world to look completely casual, despite his heaving chest. "What took you so long, slowpoke?"

"I am not a slowpoke!"

"I've been waiting here an hour."

"You couldn't have. We only—"

"Come on, kids," Daddy interrupted. "Let's go in right away, before it gets too cold."

There were very few people left on the beach. Even those who had not been scared away by the oncoming storm, were leaving now because of the hour, straggling toward the Stairway, dragging their towels and umbrellas, toys and thermos bottles, backrests and inner tubes across the littered sand. As Stephen ran toward the water, he spotted the old, old fat man he had seen in the shower earlier that afternoon, and he slowed down and waited for Daddy.

When their paths crossed, Daddy stopped and greeted the old man cheerfully. "Hello, Max."

"Hello, Sol."

"Boys, say hello to Mr. Strauss, the toughest pinochle player in New Jersey."

"Hello, Mr. Strauss," Roggie said, shaking hands.

"That's Roger, Max, my older boy," Daddy explained with pride. "And this is Stevie, the younger one. *Kleine,* say hello to Mr. Strauss."

"There's no need, Sol. The youngster and I have met," Mr. Strauss said insinuatingly. "Ain't we, sonny?"

Stephen looked blank.

"Have you, Max? Where was that?"

"In the shower room, this afternoon. I must say, Sol, the boy has got a most peculiar habit."

"Peculiar, Max?" Daddy said defensively. "What do you mean?"

"Come, Sol," Mr. Strauss suggested, taking hold of Daddy's arm. "Walk me to the stairs a minute."

"Boys, you stay here and play, but don't go in till I come back. And no roughhouse."

"Okay, Dad," Roggie said, wrapping his arm around his brother protectively. "I'll take care of him."

When the grownups were out of earshot, Stephen whispered, "Roggie, what exactly does peculiar mean?"

"Peculiar! Well now, let's see. . . . Peculiar. That means kind of . . . oh, you know . . . kind of— I think I could tell you better by saying it in a sentence. Let's see now: 'the old lady . . . the old lady was very, very peculiar.' You understand?"

"Not exactly."

"Wait a minute. I'll think up another one. 'Ickes is a most peculiar name.' "

"Who's Ickes?"

"What's the matter with you? Don't you know *anything?*"

Suddenly, startled by the breaking of a very large wave, Stephen exclaimed, "Gosh! Did you see that one? Let's go down and see what it's brought us."

"That's all you think the ocean's there for—don't you, Stevie?—to bring *you* presents."

Stephen raced down to the tide line and waited impatiently for the leisurely surf to recede from the shore and reveal its store of treasures.

"You heard what Daddy said: you can't go in till he comes back."

"I'm not going in," Stephen answered, ankle-deep in water. "I'm just looking," he explained, feeling the wave's ebb tow at his heels, eroding the sand under his feet—his feet sinking deeper and deeper into the softness as he watched the stampede of stones and shells and sea wrack rush headlong back into the ocean. "Ohh!" he gasped, suddenly seeing a piece of green glass among the rubble and snatching it up before the next wave broke. "Look, Roggie. Look! An emerald!"

"You act like it's the first green you ever found. You must have two hundred greens by now."

"No I don't. I have thirty-six—thirty-seven with this one."

Suddenly, despite the noise of the surf, despite the fact that Daddy was well over a hundred yards away and the wind blowing in his direction, the boys recognized their father's voice, roaring in the distance. Together they turned and saw him standing at the bottom of the stairs that led to the Casino, shaking his fist at Mr. Strauss who was hurriedly mounting the steps. Automatically, Stephen began to gnaw at the cuticle of his thumb. "What is Daddy mad about?"

"Don't ask me," Roggie said, sucking his lower lip and turning away discreetly.

Taking the cue from his brother, Stephen turned away, too, and began to examine the emerald, but his ears remained fixed on his father's voice. None of the words, only the anger was intelligible to Stephen. Listening intently, he looked up from the piece of glass at the ocean. A comber was moving toward the shore, mounting steadily: ten, twelve, twenty-five feet high—or so it seemed to Stephen—a tidal wave like Daddy's voice, looming up, crashing down, splashing his thighs with stinging brine, spattering his face with foam, dragging, dragging at his ankles. But Stephen stood his ground.

"Look! A zeppelin!" Roger exclaimed. Stephen looked up and smiled at the silver cucumber, floating through the sky. "Someday I'm going to fly in one of those."

"Can I come, too?"

"I don't know. We'll see."

"Oh, Roggie, please, please let me come, too."

"We'll see," he said. "We'll see how good you are from now on."

"I'll be good. I promise."

"Here comes Daddy."

"Look, Daddy, look," Stephen shouted, pointing at the zeppelin, but Daddy didn't look.

"Come on, kids," Daddy said, putting his arms around the shoulders of both his sons. "Let's go in. It's getting late."

"Wait a second, Daddy," Stephen said, storing the emerald inside his bathing suit for safekeeping.

"No one criticizes *my* boys and gets away with it," Daddy went on. "Not while *I'm* alive, they don't . . . careful now, it's kind of rough. Come on, *kleine,* take my hand . . . that-a-boy. Roggie, don't go out too far; better stick near us."

"I'm okay, Dad. It's not *that* rough," Roggie said, stroking and kicking with all his might, trying for Daddy's sake to demonstrate his best form. "Watch me! Watch me!"

"That's very good, Rog. Very good. Just be careful," Daddy said, lifting Stephen in his arms and holding him for one thrilling moment above the crest of a wave.

"Yipeeee!" Stephen screamed. When they got beyond the breakers, Daddy let go of Stephen. With his water wings on, Stephen floated easily, while Daddy's head and shoulders broke the surface like a bust resting on a mantel. "Is it over my head?"

"Sure it is."

"Is it over yours?"

"No, sweetheart. I can still touch bottom here. Let's see how well you swim." Stephen lay back lackadaisically, kicked his left leg and flung his right arm out perpendicular to his body. "Come on now, you can do better than that. That's not the way you were taught. Look at Roggie. You remember," Daddy coached. "Stroke, kick, breathe. Stroke, kick, breathe. Just like in the swimming pool."

. . . But the ocean *wasn't* like the swimming pool—everyone knew that!—What made Daddy always say it was? The swimming pool was nothing but a great big box—eight feet deep at one end, two feet at the other—whose water was piped in through a spout and drained off at the sides, whose only sign of life was what you, the swimmer, brought to it. *That* was the all-important difference! In the ocean you didn't need to bother swimming, the ocean did it *for* you. The ocean was alive! "Daddy."

"What, *kleine?*"

"Let's play zeppelin."

"Zeppelin?"

"You know, instead of playing boat."

"All right," Daddy said, and he submerged obligingly.

Stephen scrambled onto Daddy's broad back and wrapped his arms around Daddy's neck and his legs around his tummy. The contact of their lubricated flesh reminded Stephen of Clarry's soapy hands in the bathtub, and he deliberately wriggled and squirmed and coiled his limbs around Daddy's body. "Mmmmmmmmmmmm!" Stephen imitated the motor of a zeppelin, as Daddy did the breast stroke. "Faster!" he commanded, and Daddy obeyed, swimming parallel to the shore. In his excitement Stephen forgot about the zeppelin and began to jog up and down on Daddy's back. "Giddyap!"

"Hey! I thought I was a zeppelin," Daddy said, spitting out a mouthful of water.

"No, a horse! A horse!" Stephen squealed, sitting upright and straddling his daddy, holding onto Daddy's bald head with both hands like a stirrup, moving it from right to left, manipulating it like a joystick, like a rudder, like a steering wheel. There, now, between Stephen's thighs, Daddy had become his horse, his plane, his boat, his car, his engine, steaming through the ocean. Almost in a state of rapture, Stephen vised his mount and pounded on its back, as if it were nighttime and he were squeezing and pummeling his pillow.

"Easy, fellow, easy," Daddy cautioned.

Stephen was too enthralled to pay attention. "Mmmmmmmmm-mmmmmmm-uh!" he exclaimed. The sound articulated and released all the energy and tension, all the exaltation in Stephen's body, but in his delirium he accidentally ducked his father's head. All of a sudden Daddy reared. At the same moment a huge wave swept Stephen off Daddy's back, lifted him up to a dizzying height, dashed him down into the depths, pulled him under and pounced on him with all its weight, winding him and flooding his lungs, rolling him along the bottom, heaving him over stones and cutting shells, dragging him toward drowning death, engulfing him in heavy, hurling, airless, black-death black . . .

When, at last, Stephen recovered consciousness, even before he opened his eyes, he felt someone's hand holding his hand, someone's fingers stroking his cheek, and he heard Daddy saying, "Don't be silly, Rog, he isn't dead, he's only winded. There's nothing to cry about. Look! Look! He's opening his eyes. What did I tell you? Hello, sweetheart. How do you feel?"

Daddy's face was white as milk; his eyes were big and red and bulging, and his brows were raised. Roggie was crying. The sky was very, very dark. "What time is it?"

"Ten past five."

"I thought it was night."

"That was some mean wave, huh, sweetheart? Thank God you had your water wings on."

"Why did you do that, Daddy?" Stephen asked, blinking his bloodshot eyes.

"What?"

"Drown me."

"Drown you! Me? It was the wave, sweetheart. The wave! It rolled you—all of us! Roggie, too. It's a lucky thing any of us are still alive."

"Hello, Stevie," Roggie sniveled. "How do you feel?"

"Hello, Roggie."

"He's all right," Daddy reassured himself and Roggie. "Aren't you, fellow? Imagine thinking it was *me!*"

Stephen reached inside his bathing suit.

"What's the matter? What is it, darling? Does something hurt you?"

Almost immediately Stephen found what he was looking for —the emerald!—and he smiled and clutched it in his fist.

"What is that?"

Stephen was not, as yet, convinced that Daddy *hadn't* tried to drown him, and he didn't feel like revealing his treasure. "Nothing."

"All right, then. Let's go back to the Casino. Mommy'll be worried. You think you can make it, *kleine?*"

"Sure."

Mommy was terribly upset when Stephen reported what had happened. After thanking God it was the last weekend of the summer, she asked Daddy a lot of questions about himself and

Bruce, and criticized them both severely. That made Daddy furious, and he began to shout about Mommy playing mah-jongg all the time instead of looking after her children, and Mommy shouted back something about her neurasthenia, and Daddy said he didn't give a good goddamn, it was her responsibility to keep the *kinder* out of trouble, and did she know what had happened with Mr. Strauss that very afternoon, whereupon Mommy screamed that Mr. Strauss was a bum, and Daddy screamed that *Mrs.* Strauss was a tramp, and they went on fighting all the way home in the car, until Mommy began to sob, and Stephen squeezed the piece of green glass so tightly it almost cut his palm.

When they reached the house, the first thing Stephen did, as always, was to run to the kitchen to show Clarry the treasure he had found. "My, that's a pretty one, sugar," Clarry smiled. "Lemme see, that makes thirty-six, don't it?"

"Thirty-seven, Clar."

"Thirty-seven! My, my: thirty-seven emeralds. What we need more of now is some sapphires, ain't it, sugar?"

"I know, Clar. But they're awful hard to find."

"Course they hard to find. You don't find precious gems lyin' in the gutter. That's what makes 'em precious. Now, I tell you what, sugar: before we go back to the City next week, you and Clarry is gonna go down to that there beach and scour it until——" Suddenly, hearing Mr. and Mrs. Wolfe upstairs, continuing their fight, Clara interrupted herself and asked, "What's the matter with your eyes, sugar? You been cryin'?"

"My eyes?"

"They're all bloodshot," Clarry said, and she stopped sprinkling the calves' liver and wiped her big floury hands on her apron.

"Oh, I forgot," Stephen exclaimed. "I was drowned."

"What do you mean?" Clarry chuckled. "You was drowned."

"I'm not kidding, Clarry."

"If you was drowned, sugar, you wouldn't be here to tell the tale."

"I mean it, Clar," Stephen stated earnestly. "Daddy drowned me, in the ocean and I was dead for a long time."

Clarry laughed. "Listen, sugar, once you dead, you *stay* dead. There ain't no comin' back."

"I'm telling you I *was*," Stephen insisted. "Ask Roggie if you don't believe me. Ask anybody!"

"All right, sugar, have it your way. Tell me, how do it feel, bein' dead?"

"It was horrible. I was so scared, Clar," Stephen reported

weakly, his face contracting with pain. "I don't ever want to die again."

Clara lifted Stephen up and set him down on the sturdy, unpolished, marble-topped table. Now Stephen was on a level with Clarry's compassionate eyes, and he could feel her warm breath against his cheek. "Course not, sugar. And you don't have to. You don't have to. Not whiles Clarry's around. You don't have to worry, sugar," she said, drawing Stephen's head to her shoulder, nestling her soft cheek against his forehead and stroking his hair. "Clarry'll look after you."

Though he could no longer see her eyes, Stephen heard the catch in Clarry's throat, he felt her bosom heave, her strong arms hug him tightly, and he knew that she was crying. "What's the matter, Clar?"

"Nothin', sugar. Nothin'. Clarry'll look after you."

"Is Rosie dead?"

"Rosie! What's the matter with you, sugar? You know Rosie's in Chicago. I've told you that a hundred times: my baby's in Chicago."

"But if you never see her, isn't that like being dead?"

"Course it ain't. It seem like that sometime," Clarry said, staring straight ahead of her, looking right through Stephen just as if he wasn't there, "like Rosie gone forever, but it ain't. It ain't like that. I dassent let it be. Come on, now," she continued in her normal tone of voice, returning Stephen to the floor. "You better put that emerald away 'fore it's time for dinner."

Stephen ran upstairs. For a moment he stopped to listen outside of Mommy and Daddy's door, but there wasn't a sound. Realizing that their fight was over, he hurried along to the radiator box in his own room where, much to Mommy's chagrin, Stephen had succeeded in re-creating the seashore's smell and sound and texture. Scarcely an inch of the cream-colored radiator lid was left exposed by his multifarious marine collection. Among its many treasures were a desiccated starfish, a perfect pear whelk, the feather of a tern, a piece of driftwood the color of smoke, two withered skate egg cases, the spooned carapace of a calico crab, a blue crab claw, a silver-streaked horse mussel embossed with several barnacles, a kidney-shaped piece of coral, fourteen periwinkles, five ashtray-size clam shells, three rough limpets, scallop shells, slipper shells, cockle shells, blue mussels, razor clams and the immaculate remains of a broken sand dollar. Crowded next to these, like the

minerals and gems in the Morgan collection at the Museum of
Natural History, were the hundred-fifty-odd pieces of surf-sanded
colored glass that Stephen had collected over the years—sapphires
from Vicks and Noxzema jars, emeralds, zircons, and aquamarines
from ale, beer, and Coca-Cola bottles, moonstones from baby-oil
jars, rose quartz from an unknown source, and one rare piece of
onyx from a bottle of My Sin.

Before adding it to his collection, Stephen studied the newly-
found emerald. Now that it was dry, it began to show tiny deposits
of salt in its pores, and its surface felt pleasantly powdery. Held
one way, it looked like a piece of candy corn, held another, it
became the head of a tomahawk. Compared with the other
emeralds, it had a poster-paint quality; it was greener, gaudier, the
color of a lime. Placing it was no simple matter. Like a master
jeweler creating a lavalière, Stephen moved it here and there, seeking an aesthetic balance, studying its form and color in relation to
the other gems.

As he was doing this, a gust of wind came through the screen
and blew the tern feather to the floor. Stephen picked it up,
smoothed its barbs and returned it to its proper place, between the
teeth of the blue crab claw. The dogwood tree on the front lawn
was being bent to the right so violently, it looked as if it were
about to snap. The wind tore off some of its leaves and whirled
them upward. Stephen watched them ascend into the menacing
gray-black sky, and wondered when the storm would break. He
feared lightning and thunder more than Mommy and Daddy's
fights or his own semiannual visits to Dr. Rosenstrock, the dentist.
Almost the first thing he ever did upon entering a stranger's house
was to inquire about its lightning rod. The image of the skewered
onion planted on a gabled roof was as meaningful to Stephen as
the crucifix on her church was to Clarry. He understood nothing
about their workings except for the one vital fact that lightning
rods kept the firebolts away from his body by conducting them
into the cellar. What fiendish fries ensued down there, Stephen
preferred not to think about.

For some reason the storm held off all through dinner and
through his bath, so that by the time Stephen was ready for bed he
had almost forgotten about it. After Mommy had kissed him good
night, and the soft but monumental security of Clarry's bosom
relinquished him to the dark, Stephen lay in bed musing, as always, over the ocean. He listened to the pounding surf, smelled the

brine, and searched for the grains of sand that invariably material-
ized in his hair, his belly button, his bed. He did not question how
they came to be there; Stephen knew—knew that he was part of
them, the sea and sand, mixed with them, a blend of them the way
green is a blend of yellow and blue. As on every other night, before
he was able to fall asleep, he had to get out of bed, tiptoe to the
radiator, and examine his marine collection one more time. He had
to seize the whelk and take it back to bed with him and hold
it to his ear, uncertain in his somnambulation whether the roaring-
rush he listened to emanated from the shell, the ocean, or his
heart.

At some point in the middle of the night a lightning-crack
awakened Stephen to tears. Even without looking, he knew the
house had been struck and rent in two. Someone had taken the
lightning rod off the roof and stuck it through his open window;
some evil executioner, armed with electric currents, was standing
in his bedroom, trying to electrocute him. The whole house quaked
as the bolts flashed and crackled before his hand-covered eyes and
the thunder detonated inside his eardrums and the rain deluged his
marine collection. But it wasn't only the rain, it was the ocean,
too. The ocean was angry. It had come onto the land, exactly as
Clarry had predicted it would. It was just outside his window
there, trying to get in, trying to reclaim all the treasures he had
stolen—all the shells and gems and creatures. The only way to
save them was to shut the window. He had to shut the window!
And yet Stephen knew that if he did, if he got out of bed, the evil
executioner would spy him and hurl a bolt of fire smack into his
face, so he helmeted his head in his pillow and dived under the
covers, where, lumped together like a pull of toffee, he eventually
cried himself to sleep.

The next morning, when the family came down to breakfast,
Clara greeted them with a barrage of communiqués. "Miz Wolfe!
Miz Wolfe! Disaster! Catastrophe! Worst ever! Five hundred
drowned: women 'n children. Right down here, here in our own
backyard, right off Seaside! Ocean liner, comin' home from Trinidad: burnin' and drownin'—flames a hundred foot high—"

"The *Conte di Savoia?*" Mommy exclaimed, clapping her hand
to her breathless bosom.

"Now, Hattie, don't get hysterical. Your father isn't due back
from Europe for another week. Anyway, she said it was coming
from Trinidad, not Naples." Daddy turned back to Clarry.
"What's its name?"

"Name, Mr. Wolfe?"

"The name of the ship."

"I think the radioman say it called *Tomorrow's Castle.*"

. . . I knew it! Stephen thought. *Tomorrow's Castle* struck by lightning in the night and burning on the beach. Flames a hundred feet high, burning women and children, burning the wall marked WOMEN with children inside: burning—but not the MEN . . . *Tomorrow's Castle* battered by the waves, wearing-it-away waves, washing-it-away waves—all of my constructions drowning and burning in the waves of MEN with children inside . . . "I knew it!" Stephen exclaimed intensely.

"You don't know anything, stupid!" Roggie said in his most superior manner. "As usual, Clara's got it wrong. The name of the ship is the *Morro Castle,* capital M-o-r-r-o, not t-o-m-o-r-r-"

"That's my little professor," Daddy said proudly.

"Oh, I've heard of that! It goes on Caribbean cruises. Thank God it's not the *Savoia,*" Mommy sighed.

"The number of dead is estimated at two hundred-fifty, not five hundred," Roggie continued. "It was coming back from Havana, not Trinidad, and it's anchored off a place called Shark River Inlet, not Seaside. May I have my eggs now?"

"How do you happen to know all that, Roger dear?" Mommy asked, as a deflated Clarry slunk from the room.

"I heard it on the radio before the rest of you were up. Did you think I was telepathetic?" Roggie's insolence made Daddy chuckle.

"Don't be fresh, Roger! And don't you encourage him, Saul."

"Who's encouraging him? I was laughing at his mistake," Saul lied.

"The word is telepathic, darling," Mommy said icily.

"I am *not* stupid!" Stephen growled, making a bulldog face and landing a brutal kick on his brother's shin.

"Damn you!" Roggie shouted, hurling his napkin ring at Stephen's face.

"Roger, don't you dare curse like that in front of me!" Mommy admonished him.

"Stephen, stop that! Put down that napkin ring!" Daddy said.

"But he threw it at *me!*"

"I saw you kick him first," Daddy said.

"He called me stupid."

"Sticks and stones will break my bones—" Roggie chanted.

"Damn you, too!" Stephen yelled, slinging back the napkin ring.

"Did everybody see that?" Roggie asked threateningly, sliding back his chair. "No one can say I started it *this* time!"

"Mommy!" Stephen cried, as Roggie turned the corner of the table, his fist prepared to inflict a series of eggies.

"Sit down, Roger. Roger, sit down!" Mommy shouted, leaping up herself and grabbing Roggie's arm. "Sit down, I said!"

"Here we are," Clarry said, smiling as she pivoted her big body through the swinging door and found herself in the middle of the tug-of-war and spilled the platter of eggs all over the carpet. This made Stephen laugh hysterically, and Clarry's eyes bulged from their sockets like a French bulldog's.

"Goddamn it!" Daddy roared. "Why the hell don't you watch where you're going?"

Stephen stopped laughing and clenched his fists. "It wasn't Clarry's fault," he said timidly.

"Who asked you? The whole thing's *your* fault in the first place!"

After the eggs were wiped up and a new batch cooked and eaten, Daddy and Roggie retired to the front lawn to have a catch, and Stephen went upstairs to play with his marine collection. He was standing in front of the window, holding the whelk to his ear, thinking about the destruction of *Tomorrow's Castle,* and watching Daddy throw the hardball—projecting his arm its full length instead of throwing it from the wrist the way he, Stephen, did—when Mommy entered the room.

"What are you doing, sweetheart?" she inquired tenderly.

"Playing."

"You know, my love, we have to think about packing soon. We're going home on Wednesday—remember? You ought to start sorting out your collection."

"Sorting?"

"I mean, for instance, you don't want to take something like this, this old mussel, back to New York, do you?"

"Yes."

"But it smells. So do these devil's purses. Don't you want to leave them here?"

"No."

"All right, darling, do as you like, but find a box to put them in." Harriet smoothed down Stephen's golden hair. "You know, my love, no matter what anyone says, Mommy knows you aren't stupid." Stephen squeezed his mother's hand between his cheek and shoulder, as they watched Roggie dash across the lawn to catch a high throw. But just as the ball was about to nest into his mitt, Clarry appeared on the front steps and he fumbled it.

" 'Scuse me, gentlemens. I just thought his royal highness would like to know the burnin' hulk of the *M-o-r-r-o Castle* is bein' towed toward Sandy Hook."

"What did Clarry say?" Stephen asked.

"Saul, what did Clara just say?" Mommy called through the window.

"I don't know. Something about the *Morro Castle.*"

"Pay no attention. She was only taking revenge on me," Roggie said, tossing the retrieved ball back to Daddy.

In the course of the day interest in the fate of the burning vessel intensified. By noon the Seaside Ladies Conservation Committee had rallied its forces and was making a door-to-door collection of rough-wear for the victims of the disaster. Emergency first-aid stations were set up at Point Pleasant and Sea Girt for the care of the survivors suffering from shock. In the afternoon a fisherman in Belmar discovered the body of a drowned woman floating near the shore. All along the Jersey coast solemn crowds gathered in hopes of catching a glimpse of the burning luxury liner or any of its passengers—dead or alive. While the Coast Guard combed the sea for casualties and the merchant marine responded to the *Morro Castle's* repeated distress calls, the governor surveyed the scene from the cockpit of an airplane.

By three o'clock Stephen had finally convinced Mommy to let Clarry take him down to the beach. When they reached the balustrade of the Grand Stairway, Stephen gasped. "Look, Clarry! Look!"

The ocean was like an enormous cauldron of boiling rice: as far as the eye could see, its surface was covered with churning foam. Closer to shore huge walls of dirty green water rose to the height of trees, before crashing onto the beach. The beach itself looked brand-new, swept clean, without a sign of human traffic; there wasn't a footprint or a piece of paper anywhere, only the unbroken sand crust, looking as it must have looked before life became amphibious.

"Mean," Clarry muttered.

"Let's go down!" Stephen urged excitedly.

"Uh-uh, sugar. It too dangerous down there. You get swept away like the *Morro Castle.*"

"Where is it, Clar? Where *is* it?"

"Where's what, sugar?"

"Tomorrow's Castle."

"It in someplace called Sandy Hook."

"Where is that?"

"Got me, sugar."

"But I have to see it, Clar. I *have* to."

"Maybe we can see it tomorrow, sugar, when it clears. Come on now, let's go back. It ain't nice down here."

Stephen acquiesced reluctantly. Hand in hand they lagged the long blocks home. On the way he confided to Clarry how the ocean had tried to break into his room the night before.

By five o'clock the flaming *Morro Castle* had broken away from its tow. After drifting several hours, the surf grounded it on a sand bar off Asbury Park. When Stephen heard the news, he refused to go to sleep until he had wrested a promise from Mommy to take him to Asbury the very next day. "And can we play miniature golf?"

"Yes, darling, yes. Now go to sleep."

As if it were Christmas or his birthday, on Sunday morning Stephen awakened at 5:55, restless with anticipation and excitement, eager to get under way. His room was filled with a fugue of bird-sounds and, gradually, as the day began to dawn, lovely bright sunlight, every trace of Friday night's storm was gone. But by the time the family piled into the Chevrolet—Stephen in the back seat next to Mommy, Roggie up front next to Daddy—it was 11:25 and everyone's nerves were slightly frayed. Because it was Sunday and the weather so good, every car, truck, trailer, bus, motorcycle, bicycle, beach, and station wagon within a radius of two hundred miles was on the road, heading for Asbury Park.

For awhile, as the Chevvy moved along unimpeded by the traffic, the brothers played a lively game of license plates. Stephen spotted one from Tennessee—his favorite state, not because it counted more than any other but because the plate itself was visually onomatopoetic—and one from California which counted fifteen points, and gave him a comfortable lead, until Roggie claimed he saw a foreign plate from a country called British Columbia, which, according to the rules, counted twenty-five. Since Stephen did not see the plate himself and had never heard of the country, he accused his brother of cheating, and the game ended in a fray that required the intervention of both parents.

As they approached Allenhurst the traffic began to jam, making Daddy slow down and stop and stall and start again every other second—something which always angered him. "You and your bright ideas," he grumbled, glaring at Mommy in the rearview mirror. "I said we should have left right after breakfast. I said—"

"We couldn't leave Clara stranded in church."

"Then we shouldn't've come."

"But we promised the children." Mommy smiled and petted Stephen's head.

"At this rate we'll be lucky if we get there in time to come back." Daddy wrapped his right arm around Roggie's shoulder. "Another one of your mother's brainstorms!"

Stephen studied Daddy's pinky. The straight black hairs looked like mermaid's hair matted under his chunky gold signet ring. "Sit back, darling," Mommy said, laying her hand on Stephen's shoulder. Suddenly her fingers clamped his flesh painfully and Mommy gasped. "That's a red light, Saul!" The abrupt stop nauseated Stephen.

"Who's driving this buggy, you or me?"

"You are, Saul."

"Then just sit back and keep quiet—unless you want to walk."

Now that they were standing still, the smoke from Daddy's cigar, mixed with the smell of gasoline and the exhaust from other cars, was sickening. Stephen tried to roll his window lower, but the rear wheel prevented it. Honk! Honk! Honk! He turned around and saw the man in the car behind, honking his horn impatiently. "Roggie, look! It's a Pierce Arrow."

"What's the matter with *you,* you bastard!" Stephen heard Daddy shout. "Can't you see it's red?"

"It's green, Saul," Mommy corrected.

"Goddamn it! Whose side are you on?" Daddy demanded, as he pulled his head back into the car and stepped on the gas. "That imbecile began to honk before it changed. Or didn't you notice? It's always *my* fault, isn't it? Never the other guy—always me! No matter what happens—"

"I didn't say—"

"Could you get us there any better, brain trust?"

"Don't call me—"

"Then shut up, damn it, just shut up!"

"Don't you dare—"

Stephen sat forward on the seat in an effort to get more air. He watched the orange signs go by and tried to read their message. On the first and second he made out the words *she, the* and *by*. On the third and fourth he was able to read *She . . . it was her . . .* The fifth, of course, he knew at sight: BURMA SHAVE.

"—any more of your Goddamn lip!" Daddy roared.

Turning away from the window, Stephen saw Mommy squeezed into the opposite corner. She was watching the scenery. At the same time, her white-gloved hand groped blindly for her beaded bag, located it, and fished out an embroidered handkerchief. For a moment Stephen smelled her strong gardenia perfume until the heavy cigar smoke overwhelmed its sweet aroma.

"What are you crying about, anyway?" Daddy asked.

"Nothing," Mommy answered, almost voicelessly, her shoulders quivering as she raised the handkerchief to her nose. Empathically, Stephen reached toward Mommy's bare, freckled arm and stroked her vaccination. In response Mommy turned around, pressed Stephen's hand endearingly and tried to force a smile, but her chin was as flat and pocked as a cooking pancake, and her mascara trickled down the sides of her nose, silently staining her cheeks.

"Then stop it!" Daddy said.

Mommy turned back toward the window. Stephen could hear her muted whimpering and the tears welled up in his own eyes. Suddenly Daddy stopped short again, and Stephen gagged, his mouth flooding with saliva. "Daddy!"

"Stop it, I said," Daddy repeated, driving on, "before I really give you something to cry about."

"Daddy!"

"What is it, *kleine?*"

"Will you stop a second? I'm carsick."

By the time they reached Asbury it was one o'clock. There were seventy-five thousand people there looking at the liner, and Daddy had to park eleven blocks away from Sixth Avenue and the boardwalk, off which the *Morro Castle* was grounded. Because Stephen had been carsick, Harriet thought he should have some chicken broth, but no one else agreed, so they gulped down hot dogs and pressed toward the boardwalk. Daddy, running interference for the family, had several verbal battles with strangers along the way but managed by a combination of height and brawn, charm and tyranny, to get within a quarter of a mile of the disabled vessel.

"There it is! There it is!" he shouted. "Will you look at that: still smoking."

"Where? Where? I can't see!" Roggie and Stephen cried in unison.

"Come on, fellow, up you go," Daddy said, hoisting Roggie onto his shoulders.

"Tut! Tut! Tut!" Mommy clucked, seeing the wreck and straining to lift up Stephen by his waist.

"Higher, Mommy! Higher!" Stephen pleaded. "The man's hat's in . . ." But suddenly it was there—the gigantic, red-streaked hulk swerving in the lively surf as if it were on a pivot, its broadside parallel to shore but listing slightly toward the sea, its lifeboats all scorched and askew, dangling from their davits, and other fallen rigging hanging down across the rows and rows of portholes, charred and smoking still after thirty hours—*Tomorrow's Castle* —bigger than the whale in the Museum of Natural History, bigger than an apartment house, and stronger than an armory, but dying now, lying on its side, coughing smoke and bleeding lead, destroyed and dying in the ocean—awful, awful ocean— Stephen reached out his hand to console the ship, but Mommy, unable to support his weight any longer, lowered him into the forest of trousered legs.

The next day Stephen begged Mommy to take him back to Asbury Park, but she refused. "You know how carsick you got yesterday. You know how bad the traffic was. I'll take you to the beach, sweetheart. Maybe you'll be able to see the *Morro Castle* from there."

When they reached the stairhead Stephen looked toward Asbury, and down on the beach below he looked again, but from neither place could he see *Tomorrow's Castle*. To ease his disappointment, Mommy suggested he build something big—a fortress or a castle—so the beach would have something to remember him by when he went away for the winter. Stephen thought Mommy's idea a good one and decided to build the biggest castle in history. He surveyed the sand and chose a spot ten yards from the water's edge. He cleared the site of stones and shells, and set to work carrying handfuls of wet sand up from the water and mixing them with the drier sand, creating a kind of cement. By noon, when Mommy came to take him to lunch, he had amassed a solid block of sand the size of a steamer trunk.

"Oh, Mommy, I can't stop now. Can't you bring me back a sandwich?"

"But isn't it finished, darling? It looks finished to me."

"Oh, no! I have to put the turrets on. I have to build the wall. I have to dig the moat."

When Mommy returned with his lunch, Stephen was still working feverishly, setting jagged fragments of shells around the perimeter of his castle's roof. He could scarcely spare the time to gobble down his sandwich before he began to build the walls. Harriet turned her backrest toward the sun and watched Stephen as he scurried to and from the waterfront, carrying scoops of dripping sand—doing in a single day and alone the labor an army of Egyptians at Gîza had taken several generations to complete. Had it been earlier in the summer, he would by now have attracted an audience of envious children and grownups to watch him consummate his colossus, but on this September afternoon there was almost no one on the beach. Stephen was glad. He didn't need or even want an audience to urge him on. He wasn't building it for *them*. He was building it for himself, this mausoleum—for himself and those women and children who had died aboard *Tomorrow's Castle;* he was building it as a monument to them and as a resurrection of the ship itself, to stand against the ocean. No wave in all of the Atlantic was big enough or brave enough to trespass this far up the sand; even if there was, he would see to it his walls were thick enough to repulse the worst assault. . . . I must make them higher, thicker, he thought, anxiously glancing at the sun to see how much time he had left.

At half-past four, long after Mommy had called to say they must be going soon, Stephen was down at the water's edge on one of his countless missions to collect wet sand, when something in the water distracted him from his purpose. At first he couldn't even distinguish the shape of the thing, or rather, the thing kept changing its shape as it floated there a foot or two beneath the surface. The only fact he felt fairly certain about was that the thing was white. A fish, he thought, but dead and floating on its back. He watched with fascination as the tide brought the fish's underbelly closer to the shore. No, it's like that thing underneath a cow where the milk comes out, he thought, as he began to discern four inflated upright fingers. Fingers! All of a sudden his heart beat uncontrollably, his flesh tingled, and he lost his sense of hearing as he breathed the one word "hand." . . . It's a hand, he thought, unable to move. A hand! A hand! A woman's hand, and he plunged into the ocean.

"Stevie! Stevie! What are you doing? It's much too cold!" Har-

riet shouted, leaving her backrest and hurrying toward her son.
"What's the matter with you? Have you taken leave of your
senses? Come out of there before you catch pneumonia!" she
scolded.

"Ohhh, Mommy—"

"You heard what I said, come out of there this instant!"

"Ohhh, Mommy—"

"I'm going to tell your father on you, and you know what'll
happen then."

"But, Mommy," Stephen conspired, "I found a hand."

"What? What on earth are you talking about? Come out of
there, I said!"

This time Stephen obeyed and began to emerge from the ocean,
holding the white hand by its wrist. When Mommy saw it she
shrieked and covered her eyes.

"Shhh . . . Shhh," Stephen said, not wanting anyone to over-
hear or see them.

"What is it?" she asked in pain.

"A hand," he confided, still holding the dripping thing.

"Oh, you're awful! Simply awful!" Mommy said, after she uncovered her eyes. "You're worse than your brother, to play a trick
like that on me! Throw that stupid glove away!" she said, more
annoyed than relieved.

"It's a hand."

"It is *not* a hand! It's a glove. And I'll thank you not to scare
me like that ever again."

At last Stephen examined his catch. Mommy was right, it *was* a
glove, a woman's white cotton glove exactly like the ones Mommy
wore. Anyone could see that, now that the water had drained out
of it, leaving it hanging there, limp, between his fingertips. But
what in the world was a woman's glove doing in the ocean?

Harriet was just as troubled by the question as Stephen. She
thought about the Lindbergh baby. She thought about the dirigible
—what was its name?—that had crashed a couple of years ago,
killing seventy-five boys—the *Akron!*—off this very coast. "Oh how
silly of me," she said, ejecting her pent-up breath as she realized
the truth of the matter. "It's from the *Morro Castle.*"

Tomorrow's Castle . . . Stephen hurriedly turned to look at
his construction. It was still intact, untouched by the tide.

"It must have belonged to one of the passengers. How terrible
—terrible," Mommy said, wondering whether she ought not to

keep the glove and turn it in to the authorities. "No. Throw it back, dear, throw it back, and let's go home. We're late enough as is."

With all his strength Stephen hurled the glove back into the ocean, but it didn't travel very far. As he watched it sink out of sight, it turned into a hand again.

The following day, the last Stephen ever spent in Seaside, Mommy and Clarry were up at dawn. He could hear them clattering in the kitchen. After breakfast Mommy said, "Clara and I have a lot of work to do today. Do you think you can play by yourself? Or with your brother?" she added as an afterthought.

"But I have to go down to the beach and say good-by to my castle," Stephen said.

"That's all right, if Roger'll go with you. Otherwise, I want you to stay around the house. Oh! And find a shoebox for those shells and things. I don't want to have to be worrying about them at the last minute."

Stephen knew, before he asked, that Roggie would refuse to take him to the beach, so he put on his bathing suit, sneaked out of the house, and went by himself, running all the way. When he got to the stairhead, he looked for his castle, but he couldn't find it. He rushed down the steps toward the spot where he had worked all the previous day, but the spot had disappeared. Both the castle and the sand on which it stood had disappeared. Half the beach in fact had disappeared, and Stephen was frantic. He knew he had built it to the right of the stairhead, and he searched farther and farther south but found nothing. He retraced his steps and ran toward the cliffs—back and forth between the ocean and the cliffs—but found nothing. Finally, at the water's edge, he discovered the ocean lapping at a little gray amorphous mound of sand and recognized the bits of seashell he had used for turrets. He sat down beside the shapeless ruin, supporting his chin in his hands, but he couldn't cry. It demanded something more than that, the ocean, more than tears, he thought. . . . Maybe once a woman wept the ocean and then it turned into a man . . .

Suddenly, not five feet from his toes, creeping up the pebbles, he saw that hand again, the hand of the woman who had drowned aboard *Tomorrow's Castle*. So it wasn't a glove after all. It couldn't be! It was still alive, trying again and again to crawl out of the ocean, but the tide refused to let it. That was the trouble with the ocean: it wouldn't let go of your hand—even after it had eaten your entire body.

Stephen raised his head and gazed out to sea, where the ocean seemed to overflow into the horizon. He looked at the shifting whitecaps. He singled out a special wave and tried to observe its progress as it traveled toward the shore, but halfway in it drowned or got mixed up with another wave, and he lost sight of it. He tried again, but the same thing happened, until finally he settled for watching the general movement of the incoming tide. He watched it crash on the beach in front of him and eat away the sand beyond the spot on which he sat. He watched it ebb back into itself, taking with it yet another portion of his already unrecognizable castle. Tomorrow there won't even be a trace of it, he thought. By tomorrow the ocean will have taken all of it, even the turrets, giving me back in exchange a broken shell, a blue crab claw, a little piece of coral—all sorts of unfair things! Nothing like a sea horse or an ocean liner. No! That would be too valuable. The most I can expect is a dead or dying fish . . . a woman's hand. . . . "But where's her body?" Stephen cried aloud. "What have you done with her body?"

The tide had reached its flow now, and Stephen was sitting up to his waist in water. Feeling it caress his limbs, Stephen had to weewee. Cautiously he glanced up and down the beach. There wasn't a soul in sight, not even Bruce; the summer was over. As it flooded out of him, his weewee hot against his thighs, Stephen felt a great release. He loved the idea of sitting there in his own water, mixing his own water with the ocean's, mixing the ocean with himself. How many times had Mommy said "You'll turn into a fish"? Well, now at last the time had come. Who cares? he thought, lying back and letting the tide tow him into the sea. Who cares about the things onshore? As if he were going to sleep, Stephen shut his eyes deliberately. Deliberately he abandoned his resistance. He longed to be unconscious now, longed to leave the world behind and turn into a fish. More than anything, he longed for the ocean to work its will and ravage him the way it had ravaged *Tomorrow's Castle* until there was nothing left of him but a little brittle fingernail lying on the sand. Who cares about those dead and broken things when there is this—the turbulence, the touching . . . ! "Good-by, Clarry! Good-by, Mommy!" Stephen cried as he drifted out to sea. "I love you, ocean, love you!" he confessed, feeling the water under him.

Stephen's lover responded vigorously, pulling him down, rolling him over, spilling him out onto the sand. Stephen paid no attention. As soon as he had wiped his eyes, he scrambled to his feet again and ran back into the water, abandoning himself like something inert until his lover tossed him out a second time. It's like a game, he thought, lying on the cold soft sand. No matter how many times the ocean kicks you out, the sand is always there to welcome you, dead or alive, and to give you back again, until the ocean's had a chance to tear you into little pieces and turn the pieces into sand—until the sand itself is eaten by the ocean, and the land becomes the sand, and there are no more houses anywhere, and no more people left on earth . . .

After surrendering himself for the third time, Stephen staggered to his feet and stumbled out of the water. He was exhausted and exhilarated. He filled his lungs with the clean sharp air. He stood and stared up at the Casino perched on top of the cliff. For a moment he remembered the wall marked MEN and the wall marked WOMEN. He almost toppled over as he threw back his head and gazed into the sky. . . . . Mommy is the land, he thought, Daddy is the ocean. "No, that's not right," he said aloud. *"I'm* the land and Roggie's the ocean." No, somehow that wasn't right either, and Stephen mulled it over in his head and made it into jingles as he straggled home:

> *Daddy is the ocean,*
> *Mommy is the land.*
> *Roggie is the ocean,*
> *Stevie is the sand.*
> *Stevie is the ocean,*
> *Daddy is the land.*
> *Mommy is the ocean,*
> *Roggie is the sand . . .*

That night, before he went to sleep, Mommy questioned Stephen about his marine collection. "What's the matter with you, darling? I thought I asked you to pack these awful shells and things. That's not like you, to disobey me."

Stephen propped himself on his elbow and deliberated for a moment. "I don't think I'll take them with me."

"What?"

"I think I'll leave them here."

"Oh, thank goodness! That's my angel child," Mommy said, switching off the light and leaving the room.

In the dark, Stephen lay down in bed and lullabied himself to sleep:

Daddy is the ocean,
Mommy is the land.
Roggie is the ocean,
Stevie is the sand . . .

SALAMANDER

Stephen stood with his ear pressed like a suction cup against his bedroom wall, listening to his parents fight. This evening, as always, the instant he heard his father raise his voice Stephen had been pulled toward the wall as if he were a scrap of iron caught suddenly within a magnetic field. The power that pulled him and held him transfixed was never simple curiosity, it was a pressing need to protect his mother. And yet Harriet had far better means to protect herself than Stephen understood, and it was Stephen—paralyzed by his father's fury, tortured by his mother's mewling—who invariably suffered the brunt of his parents' battles.

"For God's sake, Saul, please read his letter carefully."

"I have."

"Well don't you see how mercenary . . . how despicable he is? He isn't fit to run a camp . . . to handle children. First he lists a dozen reasons why a child six years old—"

"Stephen's seven."

"—shouldn't be sent to camp, and then he turns around and decides to make an exception. Why? Why? For the money, of course! He needs the money. Well, send him a check for three hundred dollars—if that's what he wants—but don't send him my baby."

"That's it! There it is, right there, the whole thing in a nutshell. Your *baby!* Baby, my eye! He's seven years old—"

"Six!"

"Well, he'll be seven in June. He's a boy now—a boy!—not a baby anymore, and he better start acting like one. He's got to start playing with other children. He's got to start taking an interest in sports—and *you've* got to let him. You've got to stop babying him—you and Clara. That's just why I want him to go away: to get him out of the clutches of you women. He's been around you women too long. It's just about time he became a man. A man!"

"How do you expect a six-year-old to act like a man?"

"You know what I mean."

"But I don't. I don't! He's a baby!"

"What the hell are you getting so hysterical about?"

"I—I just won't let that child go away to camp."

"Now wait a minute, Harriet."

From his slow, deliberate, threatening tone, Stephen knew his father had reached the turning point and would soon pull out all the stops and start to roar. Unconsciously, Stephen grabbed himself by the groin and squeezed.

"I want him to spend one more summer—just one more summer, Saul, at Seaside, with us."

"I wouldn't go back to Seaside for all the money in the world. I've had enough commuting to last me a lifetime. I said he's going to camp and that's all there is to it!"

"I'll take him to Seaside myself."

"Like hell you will!"

"You can come on weekends."

"Like hell I will! I don't want to hear another word—"

"Or we could come—"

"Not another word!"

As if it were visible instead of audible, Stephen covered his eyes to protect himself against the deafening outburst. For a moment there was silence until his father broke it by asking in a completely different tone of voice, "What have we got for dinner?"

"Tongue."

"That's all I've had all day." Stephen didn't understand his father's pun. It was followed by another short silence, which, in turn, was broken by another shocking outburst. "Goddamn it! Stop that scratching. You know what Dr. Ginsberg said about your allergy." Stephen envisioned his mother scratching. He could see the tiny crimson scabs that pocked her back and shoulder blades, the bloodstains on her sheets and slips and nightgowns, and he dreaded the thought of her being sent away again to Arizona or New Mexico. "Stop it, I said!"

"You think I want to scratch? You think I enjoy it—enjoy being miserable like this?"

"Then stop it, if you don't."

"I can't. I can't," she whimpered, and the tears trickled down Stephen's cheeks.

Unlike Stephen, Roger tried to do everything in his power to ignore his parents' fights. If, as now, he happened to be reading, instead of allowing the fracas to distract him, he would hold his book up like a shield and intensify his concentration. No matter how much it unnerved him, he was old enough to realize there was nothing he could do about his father's shouting. But his brother's sobbing was another matter. "Damn you!" Roggie said, slamming down *The Mystery of Cabin Island.* "Can't you let me read? I'm going to tell Daddy you were eavesdropping."

"Oh, don't. Please, Roggie," Stephen begged.

"What'll you give me?"

Stephen searched his pockets. "A penny."

"The Indianhead?"

"Oh, no!"

"Then I'm going in right now and tell."

"No, no. I'll give you my magnet," Stephen blurted out. He knew that Roggie had coveted the stumpy Swedish magnet ever since he had bought it in Atlantic City the winter before.

"O.K.," Roggie said, "fork it over."

Stephen went to his toy chest and lifted up the lid. Why hadn't he said the magnifying glass, the pureys, the pearl-handled pocket-knife Grandpa had given him, the shriveled chestnut, or one of the stuffed animals—not, of course, his monkey, Oscar, or the yellow bear or the black bear or the prone lion with the furry mane. . . .

"Come on! Quit stalling," Roggie said impatiently.

Why did it have to be the only *living* toy he had? Well, not the only one; there was still the vial of mercury, but those were the only two—the magnet and the mercury—that had a life of their own.

"How about the mercury?" Stephen asked.

"You said the magnet."

"All right!" Stephen slammed down the lid. "Here," he said begrudgingly. "Wanta know a secret?"

"What?"

"*I'm* going to camp too," he announced with spite.

"Wanta bet?" Roggie said.

"Bet I am!"

"Oh, boloney, they don't take babies at Potawatomi."

"Wanta bet?" Stephen said.

"O.K. for you, wiseguy," Roggie said, his pupils the size of ice-pick points. "We'll see who's going to camp," he cried as he charged out of the room.

"No fair!" Stephen complained, chasing after him into their parents' bedroom.

"Daddy, is Stevie going to camp with me?"

By this time Daddy had quieted down and was sitting in front of the magnifying mirror, tweezing ingrown hairs out of his ballooned-up cheek. "Who said that?"

"He did!" Roggie grumbled, pointing an accusing finger at his brother.

"Of course he isn't," Mommy interjected. "He's much too little."

"Pay no attention to your mother, Rog," Daddy said contemptuously. "You know we don't do things by halves around this house, we don't play favorites here. Whatever's good enough for one of my boys is good enough for both. You know—"

"Don't worry, Roggie dear," Mommy interrupted, "it isn't settled yet."

"What's the matter with you, Harriet, trying to mislead the child? Rog, you know who to listen to, don't you, kid? You know who your pal is, who tells the truth around this house? I said it was settled, and that's what I meant: Stevie goes to camp!"

"Yipeeee!" Stephen squealed, elated by his triumph, and Roger clamped his lips together as if he were crushing his brother to death between them.

"That pleases you, doesn't it, Stevie dear?" Daddy beamed.

"Oh, yes," he answered, grinning at his brother.

"Good boy," Daddy said. "Now go inside and get washed up for dinner." As the boys filed out of the room, Saul followed and laid his hand on Roger's shoulder to detain him.

"What is it?" Roger asked resentfully.

Saul raised his forefinger to his lips and waited until Stephen was out of the room. Then he crouched down and pulled Roger into the space between his spread knees. "Don't frown like that, sweetiepie, there's something you don't know."

"What?"

"When you get up to camp, Stevie's going to be with all the babies in tepee Number One, but you're going to be in tepee Number Three with the big boys." Roger's features relaxed and regained their normal appearance. "And you know what else?" Saul continued.

"What?" Roger asked eagerly.

"Next year, when Steve is still a Papoose, you're going to be a Brave. You know what a Brave is? That's the next thing to a Warrior."

"A Warrior!" Roger exclaimed, swelling with anticipation and pride.

"Yes siree. Now tell me who your best pal is."

"You are, Dad." Roger smiled and kissed his father on the cheek.

"Go and get washed up now," Saul said, sending Roger out of the short hallway created by his and Harriet's closets. When he walked back into the bedroom, Harriet was in the bathroom—he could hear the water running—so he lit a cigarette, sat down in his easy chair, and glanced again at the letter he had received from Major Fischer, the director of Camp Potawatomi for Boys in Northfield, Maine.

> . . . As you know, it is not our policy at Potawatomi to accept children under the age of eight. From past experience we have discovered that such children are too immature to adjust to camp life.
>
> However, we sometimes make exceptions in the case of youngsters who have older brothers already signed with us. Since your younger son, Stephen, fits into this special category, we are pleased to inform you that we have decided to accept him at Potawatomi this coming season.
>
> Obviously, because of the difference in their ages, we cannot assign your two boys to the same "tepee" (actually, they are sturdy, wooden cabins!). Stephen will live in tepee Number One with our youngest campers, and Roger will live in Number Three, but both boys will be classified as "Papoose," the designation (Algonquian) we give to our eight- and nine-year-olds. (Please remind Roger that next year, of course, he will be promoted to the class of "Braves.")
>
> Naturally, despite his age, Stephen will be required to dress in strict compliance with all rules and regulations of Potawatomi, and to that end I am enclosing a duplicate copy of our *Minimum Uniform Requirements* for the benefit of Mrs. Wolfe, who may by now have mislaid the copy we forwarded last month when Roger was signed up.

"Harriet," Saul said as soon as he heard the water stop, "what exactly did you do with that first copy of *Minimum Uniform Requirements?*"

After a moment of silence, the bathroom door swung open with such velocity that its knob smashed against the bedroom wall and gouged the wallpaper. "You think I've lost it, don't you?" Harriet hissed. "You think that imbecile of an army man knows what he's talking about, don't you?"

The intensity of his wife's response made Saul burst into laughter. "No."

"Well, now I'm going to show you both!" she said triumphantly, rushing toward her bureau.

"I just wondered if you still had it. There's no need to show—"

"Oh, yes there is!" she said as she ripped open her top drawer.

"I believe you." The fierceness with which Harriet seized her sewing kit made Saul laugh again, but he stopped abruptly as soon as he noticed her frenzy had been paralyzed. "What's the matter, darling?" he asked, staring at her hunched shoulders.

"I had it here this morning—right here, under my sewing kit. I had it in my hand, I tell you!" she cried, her hand arrested in mid-air, where it looked like the snout of a pointer spotting a game bird. "Oh, now I remember!" she exclaimed, her hand bounding toward Saul's chifforobe. "I put it with the letter."

"Harriet, what in the world are you doing?" Saul said as he watched her ransack his papers.

"Where is it? Where is it? I left it here this morning. I had it in my hand."

"I didn't see—"

"No! No! I must have put it—" Harriet whirled around, facing the center of the room. "Where? Where?" she cried, and rushed back to her bureau.

"What's the difference?"

"No. No. I had it here, here in my hand. I tell you I had it, just this morning—I swear I did," she wailed, almost unintelligibly. "Oh God, where is it?" she screamed, flinging her sewing kit to the floor. "What have I done?" she cried, flipping through her handkerchiefs and tossing them aside, moving about her boxes of costume jewelry like a lunatic medium moving planchettes, overturning her bottles of nail polish and polish remover, disarranging her bank statements and bills, her emery boards and orange sticks and knitting needles until they looked like a pile of kindling wood someone had kicked apart. At last she ripped out the drawer entirely, dropped it on the bed as if it were burning her fingers, rushed back to the bureau and got down on her hands and knees to see if the papers had slipped down in back or stuck to the bureau's top.

Suddenly Saul heard a terrible, high-pitched yelp. It took a moment for him to realize it had come from the boys' room and not from his wife. "Jesus! What was that?" he said, leaping out of his chair.

Roger had Stephen pinned to the floor and was sitting on top of him. Stephen's hands were scotched under his brother's knees, and Roger was using his own hands, as well as his chest, to hold a pillow down over Stephen's head. "Lousy little Papoose! Papoose! Papoose!" Roger repeated hoarsely, as Stephen flailed his legs and kicked his heels against the parquet floor in an effort to tell his brother how close he was to suffocation.

"Roger!" Saul roared. "Stop that! Stop it!" he shouted, taking Roger by the arm and dragging him off his brother. "What's the matter with you? Do you want to kill him?"

"No," Roger said, almost voiceless with guilt.

Stephen moved his head slightly, enough for Saul to see his tousled hair and ruffled brows, his frightened eyes and flushed cheeks. "Yes he does."

In the middle of the night, Stephen was attacked by a hoary monster that was half-tree and half-man, and he sprang up in bed to escape it. In the silver-blue moonlight, he could see his brother lying asleep in the next bed and listened to his breathing. Hadn't he given Roger the magnet to keep him from snitching? And hadn't Roger snitched anyway? Stephen slipped out of bed and crept across the room to the chair where Roger habitually draped his knickers. His heart pounded as his fingers stole into the right-hand pocket and touched a handkerchief, a marble, one, two, three coins. He thrust his hand into the other pocket and felt the solid lump of cold steel.

"Donwayah," Roger mumbled, turning over in his sleep.

What was that? Was Roggie . . . ? Stephen, who had been about to take a step, froze in the shadows like a heron. After waiting an eternity, he let out his breath, tiptoed to the door, turned the knob, and stepped arthritically into the hall. At least it's winter still, he thought, noticing that the door to his parents' room was closed. What if it were June and they had left it open for the breeze? Stephen clenched the magnet in his fist and moved catlike through the dark. He listened to the castanets in the living-room radiator, the pipes wheezing inside the walls, the distant, wrenching rumble in the elevator shaft, a sudden screech of automobile brakes in the street, and then, right behind him, a floorboard creaked and he knew for certain he was not alone. For a long time he

stood perfectly still; the corners of the foyer were filled with eyes
and hands and lurking bodies. He could feel stares on the back of
his neck; he could just make out bony hands reaching through the
darkness to clutch him by the throat. Finally, he couldn't stand the
strain another minute and fled from the foyer, through the dining
room, into the kitchen. As always, Clarry had left her door ajar
and he could hear her heavy breathing. Cautiously, quietly,
Stephen poked his index finger against the door and it swung halfway open. He could see the big mounds of Clara's blanketed
body.

He liked Clarry's room more than any other in the apartment,
not only because it was out of the way but because it was small and
had only one window overlooking the rear courtyard of the building, which made it very dark. He liked the greasy feel of her chintz-
covered easy chair and the bouncy spring of her army bed. Most of
all he liked the worn snapshot of her plump daughter Rosie, who
at the age of fifteen had run away to Chicago with a trumpet player
and broken Clarry's heart—poor Clarry.

"Clarry," he whispered almost inaudibly. "Clarry!"

The mounds stirred. "That you, sugar?"

"Yes. Can I come in?"

"Come ahead, honey. What's the trouble?"

"I had a nightmare."

Is it any wonder, she thought, with such carryings-on round here
tonight. "Come on, sugar," Clarry said, raising her bedding like
the wing of a swan, "crawl in here with me. There's plenty room,"
she said, shifting her big body toward the wall. The great humidity
of Clarry's bed, together with the heavy, sweet smell of her cologne
made Stephen think of the jungle as he rolled into her hot arms.
"Know why we have them awful dreams at night, sugar?"

"Why, Clarry?"

"So's we learn to appreciate the daytime more," she said, adjust-
ing the pillow. "Now you just lay your pretty head up here, whiles
Clarry sings you a song." The airlessness of the room and the
softness of Clarry's fleshy arms made Stephen succumb to her
suggestion easily. "That's the way," she said and began to hum
"You're My Everything." The song, which resounded through
Clarry's ribs and the thin cotton of her nightgown, vibrated against
Stephen's cheek and communicated its meaning to him—despite
the absence of its lyrics—before it lulled him to sleep.

The next morning, when Saul opened his bedroom door at 7:15, he noticed the door to his sons' room was ajar, and he poked his head inside. Roger was still asleep, but Stephen's bed was empty and his bedclothes a tangled knot. Up already? Saul wondered as he tiptoed into their bathroom, but Stephen wasn't there. He walked into the dining room and rang the bell.

Clara appeared, smiling and holding a bowl of oatmeal. "Morning, Mr. Wolfe," she said.

"No, I haven't drunk my orange juice yet," he said, gesturing to her to take away the oatmeal.

"Oh, I thought I heard the bell."

"You did. Where's Stephen?"

"He's in my room."

"What's he doing *there?*"

"Sleepin'."

"What?" Saul's amazement disfigured his upper lip. "What do you mean, 'sleeping'?"

"I mean . . ." Clara searched unsuccessfully for a synonym, "sleepin'."

"In *your* bed?"

"Yes, sir. Jus' like a bug in a rug."

"Take that oatmeal out of here!" he ordered in a loud voice, and Clara obeyed.

Saul's command awakened Stephen and filled him with alarm. "Clarry," he called as she came through the swinging door, "what's the matter?"

"Don't ask me, sugar. You go on now and get yourself dressed."

Stephen adjusted his pajama bottoms and started back to his bedroom. But instead of going the most direct way, through the dining room, he went around by way of the foyer. However, this alternate route did not eliminate the necessity of his crossing his father's line of vision, it simply postponed it. As he approached the open double doors between the foyer and the dining room, Stephen could hear Daddy turning the pages of *The New York Times,* and paused for a moment like an actor preparing to go on stage.

"Stephen," Saul said, seeing his son scurry past the open doors.

"Morning, Daddy."

"Don't I get a kiss?" Reluctantly, Stephen entered the dining room and kissed his father on the cheek. "Where are your slippers?"

"Inside."

"What are they doing there?"

Stephen knew Daddy meant they should be on his feet. "I forgot them."

"Stephen," Daddy said, pushing back the carved, cumbersome Spanish chair that reminded Stephen of the Frog King's throne, "tell me something: did you sleep with Clara last night?"

"Yes."

"Have you ever done that before?"

"Yes."

"Why?"

"Why?"

"Why did you sleep with Clara?"

"I had a nightmare," Stephen said.

"But why don't you come into Mommy and Daddy's room when you have a nightmare?"

"I don't know."

"Wouldn't that be the logical thing to do?"

"Logical?"

"All right," Daddy said, giving up and ringing for his oatmeal. "Go inside and get dressed. And don't walk around barefoot."

In her semi-sleep Harriet overheard Saul's second outburst of the morning. What was it this time? The oatmeal again? Had Clara forgotten to put in the pat of butter? Harriet opened her crusted eyes. She was clutching her pillow as if it were a piece of cargo and she the victim of a shipwreck. The bloodstains on the sheets depressed and exasperated her. She closed her eyes again, but the uproar in the dining room was deafening.

"Take it away! Take it away, I said!" Saul shouted.

"Saul! Saul, what's the matter, darling?" Harriet asked as she hurried into the dining room, tying the sash of her robe.

"I don't want that woman in my house—not another minute!"

"Saul, please, what are you saying?"

"You heard me!"

"You know how hard it is to get a decent—"

"I don't want her here!"

"Schweig!"

"Don't tell *me* to be quiet!"

"What did she do?" Harriet asked, regaining her patience.

"The oatmeal was like ice."

"I'll have her reheat it."

"Never mind."

"It'll just take a minute."

"No, I said. If you got up in the mornings like you're supposed to and saw what was going on in this house—"

"I'm sorry, Saul. Let me—"

"Do you have any idea where your son slept last night?"

"What do you mean?"

"In there!" Saul said, pointing through the dining-room wall to the iniquitous bedroom. "With her. Stephen! In the same bed with the *schwartze!*"

"What?" The thought of the smell of Clara's room turned Harriet's stomach and she sat down.

"And it wasn't the first time. He's done it before. And you wonder why I want to get the child out of this house and off to camp!"

"I'll talk to Clara. I'll talk to both of them," Harriet said, holding her forehead in her hand.

"No! I want her out!"

"But we can't get rid of her."

"Oh, yes we can. I don't care if we have to eat in restaurants the rest of our lives!" Saul smashed down his coffee cup to emphasize the point, went to the foyer closet and put on his overcoat.

"But she's been with us four and a half years," Harriet complained, trailing after him.

"I don't care. I want her out!" Saul said, crowning himself with his fedora.

"Oh, Saul, can't we wait until the summer? It's only three more months."

"No. I'm late. We'll talk about it tonight," he said, pecking her on the cheek and sweeping out of the front door.

Dejectedly, Harriet wandered through the unlit foyer, past the children's bedroom, into her own room. Leaning against the cold wall, she stared out one of the windows that overlooked Riverside Drive, twelve stories below. The Hudson was clogged with large chunks of free-floating ice that looked like garbage. From the comfort and security of her Wedgwood-blue boudoir she surveyed the irregular rows of clapboard and tar-paper shacks that uglified and obscured the riverbank—Hoovervilles. Why on earth did they call them that? What had Mr. Roosevelt done to make things any better? Nothing! No, the depression was still on. Despite all the fancy phrases and all those confusing abbreviations, the depression was still on . . . Harriet heaved a choked sigh, not for the victims of the depression, but for herself. She had asked Saul to wait until summer before dismissing Clara, by which she had meant until the boys went away to camp. She had accepted the fact of Stephen's departure, she had as much as admitted it, and the admission took her breath away and filled her eyes with tears.

After procrastinating for a month, Harriet finally took her sons to Dr. Loeb for their typhoid shots, which neither of them liked. The following afternoon she took them to the sporting-goods house recommended by Major Fischer—she was sure he got a cut on every item—and had them outfitted for Potawatomi. The camp's colors were green and gray. The latter was the basic color of all jerseys, windbreakers, bathrobes, blankets, sweat shirts, and sweaters; the green was reserved for the large capital P which initialed these items. The only other place the color appeared was in the campers' shorts and in the letters on their name tapes, which had to be specially ordered from Philadelphia.

In May, when the two rolls of name tapes finally arrived, Clara was assigned the task of sewing them onto every piece of clothing and personal property destined for Potawatomi.

Stephen was engrossed watching Clarry snip off the first inch of cotton tape. "Does that really say my name?"

" 'Course it do, sugar. Look here," she said, holding the tape between her broad beige thumbs and spelling it out, "S-t-e-p-h-e-n, Stephen, W-o-l-f-e, Wolfe."

"Why can't it just say 'Stephen'?"

" 'Cause that ain't all there is to your name. Just like Clara ain't all there is to mine—there's a Johnson come after it: Clara Johnson."

Stephen had not thought about his name that way. Until he had started public school, he seldom if ever considered the "Wolfe," and now that he had, he didn't much like it. "Why does there have to be the Wolfe?"

"What do you mean? Supposin' there's another Stephen up at that there camp?"

"What other Stephen?"

"I don't know, we're just supposin'. And just supposin' this second Stephen, he wear the same size socks as you, how you goin' to tell 'em apart 'less you have a last name too?"

"I thought the name tape was to tell me apart from *Roger*. That's what really matters, Clar."

Clara laughed heartily as she finished stitching the first name tape onto a white cotton sock and bit off the thread between her dazzling teeth. "There's sure some sense in that, sugar, but that ain't all of it. You see, there's two parts to every name: the last name and the first. The last name called the family name 'cause it tell what family you're from. You know what I mean? It tell us who your folks are. Supposin' someone say to you, 'My, but that's a fearsome temper you got there.' Then you say, 'Well, sir, that there's the Wolfe in me,' meanin' I gets my temper from my daddy. Or someone else, he say, 'My, but you sure got the prettiest hair.' And you say, 'Oh, that there's the Stern in me,' meanin' I inherit my hair from my mommy's side, since mostly all the Wolfes are bald but mostly all the Sterns, they has golden hair. See what I mean, sugar? That the sort of thing your last name tells: the things that comes to you by way of your inheritance, all them things you have in common with the generations of your folks."

"What about my first name, Clar?"

"Well now, that there's jus' the opposite. Your first name tell what makes you different from the other Wolfes—what makes you special in your own right, know what I mean? It tell what makes you one of a kind—the only one in all the world!—that why it called your Christian name."

"You mean there's no other Stephen in the world?"

"Sure there is. I told you that when we began. There are other Stephens and other Wolfes, but there ain't no other Stephen Wolfe. That's why we gotta have *both* names 'fore we know who a person is. It wouldn't do to have jus' one."

They talked the afternoons away until Clara had sewn on all the tapes—both Roger's and Stephen's—and Harriet packed the steamer trunks—carefully checking off their contents against the master list of *Minimum Uniform Requirements*—and the Railway Expressmen came and moved them out of the apartment, and the boys were ready to leave for camp.

Just before they did, Clara came into their bedroom to say good-by. "I sure am gonna miss you children."

"Aren't you coming with us, Clar?" Stephen asked as if the thought had not occurred to him before.

"Of course she's not, dumbbell," Roger said impatiently.

"Why not?" Stephen asked.

"Because she's not a boy, you ass."

"That sure the God's honest truth," Clarry said. "Can't you jus' see me in a pair of them little green shorts?" She laughed aloud at the notion and then took Stephen into her arms. "Now I don't want to see you poutin', sugar. I wants you to be a good boy and stay well and be happy and grow lots of inches and remember all the things I taught you, hear?"

"No," he said. "I'm not going."

"Come on now, what kinda talk is that? Clarry'll be here when you gets back. She'll be waitin' for you, waitin' at the door, with arms wide open. I swear I will, sweetheart."

"I'm not going," he repeated with fierce resolve.

Roger ran into his parents' room to report his brother's behavior. Harriet was putting on her hat. They had forty-five minutes before they were due at Pennsylvania Station, but Harriet knew Saul would be leaving his office now to arrive at the station half an hour early, and she knew better than to keep him waiting. She went into Stephen's room to hurry him along, but he refused to move. Realizing that Clara was the crux of the problem, Harriet took her aside and asked her to leave the room. As soon as Clara left, Harriet again tried to convince Stephen to put on his jacket, but he refused. She told him Daddy was waiting and reminded him how much Daddy hated to be kept waiting. She told him how awful it would be if they missed the train. She suggested he follow the example set by his brother, who had been ready for an hour. She explained that if he wanted to be treated like a grownup he had to act like one. She threatened to go without him. She took Roger by the hand and left the room and went into the foyer and called good-by and slammed the front door without going through it, but Stephen did not budge. After standing absolutely still for a moment, she left Roger in the foyer, returned to the bedroom alone, and tried to dislodge Stephen physically, but he held onto his chair with all his strength. She tried, finger by finger, to loose his grip, but failed. Finally, in desperation, she screamed at him, "Why did you wait until now? Why didn't you say so in March, when you were asked? It's too late now!"

"I'm not going."

"You are!"

"I'm not!"

"You must!" she screamed, losing her control and smacking him across the mouth with all the force of her fury and frustration. As soon as she realized what she had done, Harriet turned away from Stephen. The blood drained from her face and she began to gasp. She had never in her life struck anyone. Why, now, had she struck her baby, who mattered more to her than everyone? And for what? For wanting the very thing she herself had wanted most in the world. When she turned back to him to beg his forgiveness, she saw that Stephen had his jacket on and was waiting at the bedroom door. She began her supplication by calling him her darling-darling, but before she could get any further he left the room in silence.

For the second time, Clara heard the front door slam, but this time she also heard the elevator door open and close, and knew that they had really gone. She went into the living room and watched from the window as Frank the doorman hailed Mrs. Wolfe a cab. Even at so great a distance, Clara could see how stiffly Stephen was standing and how he kept turning his head away from his mother and brother. "Bye-bye, baby," Clara said, as Frank closed the yellow door and the taxi pulled away. "I'll be waitin' for you, sugar." All of a sudden Clara's sorrow erupted through her eyes and nose and mouth simultaneously, covering her cheeks and the palms of her hands with tears and saliva and shaking her body with sobs. "Oh, Rosie, Rosie—why did you do it?" she cried out against the closed window, supporting her weight on the window sill. "Why did you do it?" she implored the sky.

By the time Stephen and Roger boarded the train, were given their box lunches, and assigned to the same berth (it was Major Fischer's policy to sleep two boys in every lower berth and one in every upper), Stephen had forgotten how painfully he and his mother had parted. He had refused to speak to her from the moment of the slap, and when, after some coaxing from Saul, he finally relented and said good-by to her and marched away, he heard his mother's whines pierce the general clamor of the station. He tried not to look back because the sound was contagious and he was so susceptible to it that the tears had already begun to roll down his cheeks. As the campers crowded toward the black iron gates, Stephen could hear his mother calling, "Roger, take his hand! Take him by the hand!" but Roger had pushed too far ahead by then. Just before he passed through the gates and down the steps, Stephen broke from the ranks and turned to wave a last good-by to his mother, but all he could see was her back. His father had his arm around her waist and was helping her out of the station.

Roger was disappointed that he had to share his berth with Stephen. He would have much perferred to share it with some older boy—a Warrior or Chieftain, if possible—but that was the penalty of having a younger brother. Stephen, on the other hand, could not have been more excited. He stood agog before the dark green flaps that curtained off their already-made-up berth. He trembled as Roggie pulled the flaps apart and revealed the inside of an Arab tent, a pillbox in Manchuria, a private one-room house, a cave. He waited impatiently in the aisle until Roger had arranged himself and then scrambled into the berth and shut out the world behind them. "It's like a fly," he giggled as he buttoned up the flaps from inside.

"Here, let me do that," Roggie said. Stephen acquiesced and began exploring the light bulbs in their tiny, ornate niches, the upholstered shelf above the pillows, the monogram on the beige blanket, the green mesh hammock strung across the stiff green window shade. Then he noticed the brass clips and pinched them together two or three times before he cautiously raised the shade in its track. Through the window he saw two men in navy-blue uniforms standing among clouds of steam. He watched them look up and down the platform, call out " 'Board" and disappear. He heard the high-pitched whistle and was startled when the train lurched forward three or four times.

"We're moving, Roggie," he exclaimed, and his brother joined him at the window.

"This is my half, next to the window," Roggie decreed. "You sleep over there."

"O.K.," Stephen said.

Roger reconsidered his earlier conclusion and decided younger brothers had their compensations after all. If he had been put with a Chieftain he would have had to sleep on the outside of the berth.

"But can't I stay here now?" Stephen asked as the train settled into a steady forward-moving motion.

"If you behave yourself," Roggie said. The brothers knelt at the closed window and peered out into the dark. At first they accepted the blackness of the tunnel, but gradually, as the pressure mounted in their ears, it began to seem interminable and their hearts were filled with apprehension.

"Do you feel it?" Stephen asked.

"Swallow," Roggie said. Stephen obeyed and the pressure was temporarily relieved. For the first time in his life Stephen realized how much he really loved his brother. After all, who else could he turn to, now that Clarry and Mommy were gone? Who else did he know in this black and endless tunnel? Roger, too, felt an intimation of the same sentiment. Daddy was gone, and with him all recourse to higher authority. Roger himself had become the higher authority now, and this new status brought with it not only an increase in power but also a sense of protectiveness and compassion. They had only each other now, and somehow they both knew it as they huddled together in the dark, waiting to emerge from that unnerving tunnel. At last a sloping wall, a piece of twilit sky and a lamppost flashed before their window and the brothers breathed more easily.

After eating their box lunches, Roger and Stephen took their overnight kits and went to the washroom, where they met some of their fellow campers. But Stephen was much more interested in the shapely brass spittoon than he was in the other boys, and he spat into it three times. Even more fascinating was the toilet bowl that flushed onto the fugitive railroad tracks, and Stephen couldn't wait to whisper the news to his brother. But Roger had made his own discoveries. "Look at this," he said, pushing and pulling the little chromium lever that raised and lowered the drain in the washbowl. "And this," he said, spraying a squirt of green viscous soap into the cup of his palm.

When they finished their toilet, they returned to their berth, buttoned its flaps, and went through a series of mild contortions before they managed to undress and get into their pajamas. Then Roger lay on his back and stamped against the roof of the berth with his bare feet. Stephen tried to imitate his brother, but his legs weren't long enough. Suddenly someone in the upper berth shouted, "Hey!" and the boys giggled and got under the covers. Roger took his valuables—the silver dollar his father had given him at the station, his penknife and wrist watch—tied them up in his handkerchief and hid it under his pillow. Stephen thought this was a good idea and did the same. Then Roger switched off both lights and pulled down the shade.

"G'night, Stevie."

"Don't you wanta talk?" Stephen whispered.

"No. We have to get up at six," Roggie said, rolling over onto his side.

"Don't you wanta tickle me?"

"No."

"Are you sure? You have my permission."

"No. Go to sleep," Roggie said.

Stephen tried, but he was much too excited to fall asleep. He wished Roger hadn't pulled the shade down all the way. What was the point of sleeping next to the window if you were going to shut your eyes and pull down the shade? What wonders would he miss, passing in the night? He watched the shapes and shadows that sneaked in at the sides of the window-shade dance across the curtains and disappear. He wanted to raise the shade but restrained himself because he knew the light would fall on Roggie's eyes and wake him. He wondered what camp would be like, but that only reminded him of Clarry and his mother, whose absence made him miserable. He listened to the repetitive rhythm of the wheels. He squirmed and turned a hundred different ways. He was careful to keep to his own half of the berth, but finally, quite by accident, a moment came when his thigh happened to touch Roggie's hand, and his flesh goose-pimpled at the contact. Cautiously he took his brother's hand in his own and held it loosely until, much to his surprise, Roger's hand responded and their fingers entwined tightly.

"Aren't you asleep?" Stephen asked.

"Ummmm-humm."

Stephen held his brother's hand until perspiration spoiled his pleasure and he decided to release it. Then Roggie, who was only half-awake, kissed his brother on the shoulder and Stephen lay back in a reverie and listened to the wheels again and let the vibrations of the Pullman car lull him to sleep.

The next time Stephen opened his eyes, the train had stopped. Were they in Maine? He sat up, lifted the side of the shade and peeked out the window. It was still night and they were in a station. Unable to control his curiosity, he raised the shade a foot. On the platform two men were unloading some gray canvas bags. Another man was standing around in his shirt sleeves, holding a coffee cup. Suddenly, above and beyond the shingled roof of the platform, Stephen noticed a huge skyscraper. It was floodlit and loomed up in the midnight sky like a golden tower.

"Roggie! Roggie!" Stephen exclaimed, shaking his brother's arm.

"Whaa?"

"Look!" he said, pointing toward the skyscraper. "Isn't it beautiful?"

"Where are we?"

"I don't know," Stephen said. At that moment the train lurched forward with such force that it jolted Roger's overnight kit off the shelf and onto his head. Stephen giggled until Roger stood up and dropped the kit on Stephen's head to let him know what it felt like. When the train reached the end of the platform, Stephen spotted a black sign with gilded letters. "What does it say?"

Roger had some difficulty articulating the word. "Prov-i-dence."

"Where is that?"

"Don't ask me," he said, and they both went back to sleep.

In the morning the first thing Stephen noticed about Maine was the difference in its air. Not only was the air cooler than New York's, it was cleaner and lighter and fresher. There was no trace of exhaust or soot in it, and it carried no sounds of traffic. In place of the rush of elevated trains, the racket of garbage pails being emptied into sanitation trucks, the clinking of milk bottles, the clang of trolley-car bells, the honking of horns, the shrill of fire engines, there was silence, interrupted only by the chirp of birds. The countryside was cool and sunlit and silent, except for the chatter of the campers and the rattle of the sideboards on the truck that carried them along the rough dirt road to Potawatomi.

As Major Fischer had explained in his letter, Stephen was assigned to tepee Number One, two cabins away from his brother. At first this separation troubled Stephen profoundly and provoked a series of nightmares, but gradually, as his new surroundings absorbed him, he grew accustomed to it. Peculiarly enough, what interested Stephen least of all at Potawatomi were his cabin-mates: Johnny Auerbach, Frenchy Bloch, Billy Lowe, Harvey Glassbaum and Tubby Geist, all of whom with the exception of Harvey, who had been born in New York, came from other cities, such as Philadelphia, Detroit, Louisville, and Paris, but from almost identical family backgrounds. Aside from Billy, who became a relatively close friend, Stephen scarcely exchanged a word with any of them all summer long, and when he did it was only to ask to borrow the broom or pass the milk or refuse to participate in the frenching of Tubby Geist's bed. As for Uncle Dave, their counselor, a quiet, mild man in his early forties who wore steel-rimmed glasses and was in charge of the arts and crafts workshop, Stephen liked him well enough but not nearly so much as someone like Uncle Sal, the tennis coach, who looked like Sir Lancelot and was Roger's cabin counselor. Uncle Dave, for his part, liked Stephen a lot because he always did what he was told, kept to himself, never made trouble, and behaved in general like an inmate of a concentration camp.

He was the first to get out of bed in the morning, the first to make up his bunk and the first to sweep his area—if not the entire cabin. He kept his trunk as neat as a display tray at Cartier's, and his table manners were like those of a prince. One of Major Fischer's directives required every Papoose and Brave to write home at least once a week. It also required each tepee counselor to "peruse the aforementioned correspondence in order to catch and correct any serious error in grammar, spelling, or punctuation," but in Stephen's case Uncle Dave didn't have to bother. He knew Stephen wrote home at least twice a week without any prodding and could be trusted not to criticize the administration.

Before long everyone who was aware of his presence realized that Stephen was a model of docility. When he was told to run the hundred-yard dash, he ran it. When he was taught to swing a baseball bat or tennis racket, he swung it. When he was ordered by a Warrior to find a sky-hook, he found some reasonable facsimile. When his curiosity got the best of him and he sneaked down to the Chieftain's camp to spy on them and was caught and given a pinkbelly, he never breathed a word about it to anyone. Though his swimming habits were irregular—he seldom could be seen on the surface of the water—it was soon apparent that he was one of the best and most fearless swimmers in the Papoose class. His diligence in the crafts shop was exemplary, and within his first month he had produced a beaded Indian belt for Clarry, a hammered aluminum fruit bowl for Mommy, and a tooled leather cigarette case for Daddy, all of which pleased Uncle Dave a lot. Sometimes Stephen abandoned his own vernacular for days on end and spoke uninterruptedly in a Negro dialect which entertained and delighted all who heard him. This practice especially endeared him to Aunt Olga, the puffy, blowzy Russian dietician he had nicknamed "Cup Cake," because, despite her better judgment, she often kept him after meals to ply him with goodies. But Aunt Olga was not the only one who favored Stephen and found him precious; Uncle Doc did, and Nurse Williams did, and so did Uncle Tony, the dramatics director, who even broke a precedent and cast Stephen, a Papoose, in the annual minstrel show.

But as the summer progressed it became increasingly apparent that Stephen was the victim of a consuming passion which began to taint his record of good behavior. It was neither corrupt nor illicit, this passion of his, but it was truant and always resulted in his conspicuous absence from the baseball diamond or volleyball court shortly after the game had begun.

"Where in the world is our left fielder?" Uncle Vince would exclaim, setting off an outburst of complaints and groans among the players. "Has anybody seen Stephen Wolfe?" Then all eyes would scan the horizon until someone spotted a tiny figure crouching in the timothy on the hillside above the playing field. At first Uncle Vince and Uncle Pritch thought Stephen suffered from a weak bladder, and then for a while they thought he hated sports, until one day Uncle Vince decided to investigate the matter for himself.

"Stephen Wolfe, I see you up there. You aren't fooling anyone," he said as he approached the hillside.

"Shhh," Stephen objected.

"Come down from there, before I come up and get you."

"Shhh, you'll scare him away."

"Who? What?" Uncle Vince asked bewilderedly.

"The toad."

"Toad!" Uncle Vince exploded. "Don't you know seventeen boys are waiting for you to play ball?" The admonition brought Stephen back to the game, but after an inning or two he was off again, in pursuit of another toad or turtle or snake. That was always the pattern, and eventually his counselors recognized it and didn't even bother to start him in the games. It became common knowledge that Stephen Wolfe liked toads better than baseball or tennis or track. Nature was his enslaving passion, his hopeless malady, and one either accepted it or tolerated it or made a joke of it, but everyone knew it was futile to attempt to cure it. Even Roger, to whom it was a constant source of irritation and embarrassment, gave up trying.

The only person at Potawatomi who sympathized with Stephen's fervor was Uncle Alf, the nature counselor. He was a short, thin man in his late twenties, with a large head of unruly hair, midget eyes, and an abundant drooping mustache that gave his face a permanent expression of sorrow. Every day he wore the same shapeless brown corduroy pants, heavy knit sweater and dirty sneakers that made his body look much fuller than it was. Before speaking he always hesitated for at least a half-minute, as if he were translating his thoughts into a foreign language, and when at last he spoke, his voice was uninflected and monotonous, which gave the false impression that he was slow-witted. During the winter he worked as an Assistant Curator of Reptiles at the Philadelphia Zoological Garden, and despite his inability to communicate easily, he knew all there was to know about North American reptiles and amphibians.

"Uncle Alf, what's an ant-phibian?" Stephen asked.

Uncle Alf stared into space as if he were calculating some astronomical distance. After a moment he pronounced solemnly, "Frogs and toads, newts and salamanders." But Stephen wanted to know more. "Amphibians are the animals who, long ago, millions and millions of years ago, first ventured out of the sea, out of the slime, onto the land. Before that, all living creatures were different kinds of fish contained, of necessity, inside the sea. But frogs and toads and salamanders had a kind of wanderlust, like pioneers, and went exploring onto the land, where no living creature had ever set foot. As a matter of fact, before the amphibians, no living creature had feet. They had no need of them—hands or feet—under the sea. The sea was a substance that surrounded them, held them, handled them—you understand? They were inside of it the way a slice of banana is inside a cup of Jell-O. But when they crawled out onto the land, there was a new dimension suddenly: something outside themselves, something to hold, to handle, to overcome." Uncle Alf continued intensely, illustrating his words with groping, clutching gestures, "and so, as a consequence, these pioneers developed digits—"

"Digits?"

"Hands and feet and fingers with which to experience and explore and master this astonishing new dimension."

None of which would have made much sense to Stephen if there had not been living examples of these pioneers for him to examine and handle himself. In addition to the aquariums of turtles, frogs, newts, and sirens arranged on shelves and tables along the walls of the nature house, there were terrariums containing lizards, toads, and salamanders, cages of snakes, mice, chipmunks and moles, as well as a caged red squirrel. There were cotton-bedded, black-framed display boxes of butterflies and beetles, a collection of regional geological and mineralogical specimens, a group of Algonquian arrowheads, some tree fungi, a few porcupine quills, three fossils of ferns, and the rattle from a rattlesnake.

Outside, in a deep stone and concrete well, were two thirty-pound snapping turtles which frightened Stephen. Past these was a big wire cage built around and over the trunk and lower limbs of a slippery elm that had been stripped of its bark, and here Percy, the opossum, spent his time. The only other exhibit was a barred wooden box that confined Andy, a clownish raccoon. The snappers were nameless because no one except Uncle Alf could ever tell them apart—or, for that matter, wanted to.

Stephen adored all the animals and objects displayed in the nature house. He could stand for hours watching the chipmunks and mice running on their treadwheels. He could stare at a toad until he hypnotized himself. He was never tired of shaking the rattlesnake rattle or poking the points of the porcupine quills into his fingertips. He collected fungi and birch bark voraciously and spent rainy afternoons scratching Clarry's name or Roggie's or Uncle Alf's onto their delicate flesh and when they turned the color of cocoa he was even more delighted than he had been, earlier in his life, when he watched the invisible lemon-juice marks he had scrawled on a piece of paper appear over a flame. Although he had less patience for it, he also enjoyed making ink prints of leaves and ferns, and plaster casts of spoors. As a matter of fact, there wasn't anything about the nature house Stephen didn't adore—except for the cyanide bottles.

These four bottles, the size and shape of three-pound peanut-butter jars, were kept on the highest shelf, well out of the campers' reach, and were used by Uncle Alf to asphyxiate beetles and butterflies. The first and only time Stephen saw Uncle Alf drop a monarch into the bottle and screw on the lid, he sympathized so completely with the butterfly that he got a stomach cramp and had to lie down on the grass outside. Afterward Uncle Alf came out and explained to him that it was a painless death for the butterfly, but Stephen refused to believe him. He remembered the countless times Roger had tried to suffocate him under his pillow, and he thought Uncle Alf was cruel. But that was the only time he ever hated Uncle Alf or the nature house.

As much as his activities inside the nature house pleased him, Stephen liked his solitary field trips even more. The purpose of these trips was not to hunt and bring back specimens; Stephen never went armed with nets or traps—what he sought was the living encounter: to find, to catch, to hold, to touch, and talk to these wriggling, slimy, primeval creatures; to look into their lidless eyes and stroke their membranous skins and let them go.

Very soon he discovered that a specific species inhabited a specific area. Green snakes, for instance, preferred the tall, cricket-infested grass on the hillside above the playing field. Sometimes pickerel frogs and garter snakes could be found there too. Toads seemed to prefer the barren, dusty terrain around the track and tennis courts. Once or twice he discovered a box turtle in the mulch under the infirmary, and the place to look for a painted turtle, a wood frog or a water snake was along the trail leading to the Chieftains' camp. The only creature that eluded him consistently and seemed not to live in any of these places was the salamander.

"Uncle Alf, why don't I ever see a salamander?"

"Because they're nocturnal, Steve."

"What's that?"

"They're creatures of the night; they hide by day."

"Where do they hide?"

"Under rocks and stones, in secret crypts."

"But where?"

"By the sides of streams."

"What streams?" Stephen asked with impatience.

Uncle Alf hesitated. He knew the gorge was off limits to the campers, but he also knew the intensity of Stephen's passion. "Why don't you try the gorge?" he suggested. "Overturn some stones in the gorge, down at the end, near the lake."

"The gorge!" Stephen repeated, excitedly. He had walked across it a dozen times a day ever since he arrived at Potawatomi. He had looked down into it from the middle of the bridge where it seemed so deep and dangerous. Is that why it had never occurred to him to descend into it? So that's where the salamanders were.

"Be careful," Uncle Alf warned, as Stephen hurried out of the nature house. "Don't go down the bank by the bridge, go by way of the campfire." Stephen understood and ran up the hill, across the bridge and behind the Lodge until he reached the campfire. Then he waited and pretended to pick blueberries while he watched to see if anyone had noticed him. It was a sunny afternoon at the end of July and there was no one on the rear porch of the Lodge. He ducked into the bushes and crawled on his hands and knees through the underbrush until he reached the bank of the gorge. The gorge, which had once been a river bed but had since dried up, was shallower here than up above where the bridge spanned it. Nevertheless, the bank was steep and stony and after attempting to descend it standing up, Stephen lost patience and sat down and descended the slope in a sitting position, using his hands to ambulate like a legless man.

By the time he reached the bottom he had hurt his palms, scraped his right calf, torn his shorts, and provoked a small avalanche. While the stones were settling he looked up through the birches and beeches. The sun shone through their leaves like shattered ice: it had a broken brightness, but no warmth. The gorge was a catacomb, damp and cool and vaulted. When, at last, it recovered from his intrusion, Stephen got to his feet and walked as quietly as possible toward the lake.

Under rocks and stones, Uncle Alf had said. Stephen began overturning the countless gray and white, potato-sized stones that lined the river bed, but they revealed nothing more than centipedes, worms, and spiders. In the distance he heard the period bell ring.

As he moved on, overturning every stone in sight, he began to notice that the ground was becoming damper. There were mosquitoes now and gnats, but no sign of a salamander. After turning over thirty or forty stones, he decided to try some rocks, which were usually embedded deep in the ground. It took two hands and sometimes a stick to pry them loose, but once they were up their vacated holes immediately filled with muddy water before Stephen could see what they contained. At last, under the ninth or tenth rock he thought he saw a salamander's tail, but only for an instant. By the time he got the rock out and darted his hand into the hole, there was nothing but water. He sloshed his hand around in the mud, but found no trace of the creature. He searched the entire vicinity, but nothing stirred. Where had it gone? He heard the camp bell ring again. Was it three o'clock or four? he wondered, running on.

There were other salamanders now, none of them hallucinatory, but the same thing happened every time; he could only catch a glimpse of their glistening tails before they disappeared. Stephen took to moving bigger rocks, ten- and fifteen-pounders. He strained his back on one, which convinced him that it was *the* rock under which he was destined to catch his salamander, but it wouldn't budge and he had to abandon it. He scraped his pinky on the next and dropped the rock before he could see what was under it. His injury didn't matter, he thought, as he sucked the bruise and hurried on into the increasingly thick and gloomy undergrowth.

His moccasins were wet now. He was almost at the end of the gorge, where rain water and backwash from the lake collected in a stagnant basin separated from the lake itself by a narrow, bush-grown bank. As he approached this basin, Stephen saw some birds fly up into the trees that sheltered it. Two or three frogs leaped from the nearby shore and plunked into the water. A dragonfly hung motionless over its surface, but swooped away as Stephen came closer. When he reached its edge, Stephen stooped down and peered into the foul pool. Its surface was covered by an opaque film, like an eye cataract, across which skittered a multitude of waterbugs and whirligigs. He could see a leopard frog kicking its way through the slimy water to the opposite side, where it emerged like a submarine. He even saw a black snake wriggle away into a mat of dead leaves and vanish, but he couldn't find a salamander.

Exhausted and despondent, he sat down on a damp piece of shale that protruded like a seat from the side of a hillock. His right hand sank into a soft, spongy bed of reindeer moss and he stroked it as if it were fur. Far away he heard the camp bell ring again and wondered if it was dinnertime. He uprooted a fern and stripped it of its leaves, as he thought about the salamanders. Maybe if he waited until it got dark they would come out, but how would he manage to see them then? And what if he got lost? No, he had better go back while it was still daylight.

Stephen stood up and looked at the shale ledge he had been sitting on. Almost mechanically he lifted it up. As soon as he did, the Jefferson salamander twitched its tail and clumsily hobbled into the recesses of the cavity. A chill ran over Stephen's body and his heart beat violently. He didn't move—he didn't dare—he just stood and stared at the black, fleshy creature as it shrank into an S. Then he stooped and stared into the salamander's goitrous eyes. "Hello, salamander," he whispered, "are you blind?" but the salamander just stared back. He examined its voluptuously rippled, glistening black skin, its tiny, infantile toes splayed against the loam. Unconsciously, Stephen stuck his tongue out, but otherwise neither of them moved. "Don't you want to talk to me?" he asked. "I won't hurt you, I promise," he said, but the salamander didn't stir.

Stephen realized he would have to make the first move. With excruciating stealth he began to raise his right hand. His breathing intensified. His fingers seemed insensate, jointless as his hand came up. At last it reached the lip of the ledge and stopped, erect and poised like the tail of a scorpion about to sting. The salamander rested its snout flat against the loam and waited. Stephen hesitated, breathless. He could not bring himself to move his hand. "Please don't crawl away," he begged. He knew he would have to force himself, will himself to attack. Without a thought for strategy, he thrust his hand toward the salamander and seized it in his palm. He could feel its fat, slippery trunk squirming there, and he squeezed his fingers tighter. "I've got you! I've got you!" he exclaimed and hurried up the river bed until he came to a spot where the sunlight shafted through a gap in the trees. Then he stopped and cupped his left hand over his right and peeked through an aperture he made with his thumb. It was like looking through the little window in one of those toy Austrian Easter eggs. "Hello, salamander," Stephen said, before he realized that something was wrong.

Cautiously, he removed his left hand and looked with horror into the cupped palm of his right. It held a twitching black tail—a living tail, three inches long, but no trunk, no feet, no head, no eyes. What had happened? What had he done? For a moment he stood in a state of shock, staring at the spastic tail. "I've broken it!" he cried and rushed back to the hillock.

Stephen searched the cavity, he got down on his hands and knees and searched the reindeer moss; he pulled apart the bed of ferns, he kicked aside the pile of sticks, he overturned every stone in the area and examined every inch of ground, but he could not find the salamander's body. At last he gave up searching and looked at the hideous tail again. It had stopped twitching now and seemed glued to the flesh of his palm. Suddenly he remembered the cyanide bottles and shook the tail loose and threw it into the underbrush. The smell of his hands made him sick, and he went back to the pool and washed them in the slime. Then he wiped them on his handkerchief and stumbled back to camp.

Every day after that for seven days, Stephen returned to the gorge to search for the tailless salamander. He found a lot of others: spotted ones and marbled ones, but not the one he had broken. He never breathed a word of his crime to anyone, neither Uncle Alf, nor Roger, nor Billy Lowe; and when his parents came to visit him and his brother the first weekend in August, he didn't tell them either.

They brought a bounty of comic books and food with them, and tried to divide it equitably between their sons. Harriet was overjoyed to see her baby looking so well, and Saul was pleased because at last she admitted he had made the right decision. He was also pleased that Roger was in the same tepee with the son of Johnson Weintraub, an extremely successful Wall Street broker. And though they saw very different parts of it—since Stephen guided his mother and Roger his father—both parents agreed that Potawatomi was a child's paradise. Before they left, Stephen gave his father the cigarette case and his mother the aluminum bowl, as well as the belt for Clarry.

When he saw the belt Daddy laughed out loud. "It'll never go around her."

"Of course it will," Mommy said.

"It wouldn't even fit around her wrist," Daddy quipped. "Besides—"

"Schweig!" Mommy interrupted.

"You'd better give it to your mother," Daddy said.

"No," Stephen objected, "I made it for Clarry."

"Stevie," Daddy began in a different tone of voice, but Mommy interrupted him again.

"I'll give it to her, darling," she said. "Don't you worry. Come on, Saul. Good-by, Roger dear. Good-by, Stevie angel."

"Good-by, boys. It won't be long now and we'll all be back together again," Daddy said heartily. "In the meantime, remember the magic words: Take it easy and you'll last longer," he said, stepping on the starter. "Let's hear from you," he called out—just as if he had not already received a total of thirty-five letters from his sons—and he and Mommy drove away.

Stephen experienced a recurrence of homesickness as he watched their car drive down the dusty hill, and he asked if he could go back to Roggie's tepee with him and read comic books. But Roggie wanted to play ball, so Stephen went back to his own tepee and lay down on his bunk until he heard the dinner bell.

During the next two weeks Stephen was kept much too busy rehearsing for the minstrel show to think about his tailless salamander. At the same time most of the Braves and Warriors were going off on camping trips for periods lasting as long as a week. Their absence greatly relaxed camp routine and afforded the Papooses some special treats. They had their own showing of *King Kong,* and their own campfire at which Uncle Tony, dressed in a loincloth and ankle bells, did an authentic Algonquin tribal dance and Uncle Vince told a terrifying story called "The Monkey's Paw."

When the Braves and Warriors returned, all the campers, including the Chieftains and Papooses, were divided into two different teams, the Greens and the Grays, and the tribal war commenced. Stephen was a Green and Roger was a Gray, and after a week of strenuous battle the Grays defeated the Greens by a margin of twenty-seven points. Roger was elated and wouldn't let Stephen forget the shame of the Greens' defeat. He even blamed his brother for it because, during the decisive tug-of-war, Stephen thought he saw the tailless salamander on the playing field and had let go of the rope to pursue it.

On August 29, in an elaborate campfire ceremony, a tomahawk was buried and a peace pipe smoked by the leaders of the victorious and the defeated teams. The following night there were tablecloths on the tables in the mess hall, and ferns, and celery and olives and assorted nuts, and lobster Newburg was served. After the banquet was eaten, the annual awards were distributed. Stephen won a gold arrow for being the best craftsman in the Papoose class and Roger a brass arrow for being the third best all-around Papoose athlete. Then every camper was given a copy of *Tom-tom,* the Potawatomi yearbook, and Taps was blown before they went to bed. The next afternoon the rattling truck took them back to the depot in Northfield and they boarded the train for New York.

When the taxi came up the ramp from Pennsylvania Station, the roar of New York rushed into Stephen's ears as if he had suddenly cupped two seashells over them. It was all around him, everywhere, as if the city itself had been built inside a giant seashell. But this time the noise excited every nerve in his body, and he sat forward in his seat remembering P.S. 87, the piers along the Hudson, his trips to Staten Island, the Natural History Museum, the mammoth rock in Riverside Park, the Aquarium, Grant's Tomb, the trolley cars, a toy shop on Broadway called Levy Brothers, Woolworth's, Womrath's, his apartment, the kitchen, Clarry . . .

"Stevie dear, sit back in your seat," Mommy said, as the taxi turned west on Thirty-fourth Street. "Ooooh am I glad to have you two home again," she said, hugging her sons to her sides. She and

Saul had met the train at seven o'clock, after which Saul had gone on to his office. "What shall we do to celebrate? Shall we go to Schrafft's for lunch?"

"Can we go to Coney Island?" Roger asked.

"Not today, darling; maybe tomorrow," she said.

Frank was delighted to welcome the boys back. "Here they are, the wild Indians. My, but you grow big," he said.

"Haven't they, Frank," Mommy agreed.

"Yah. I won't be able to beat youse up anymore, will I?"

"You better not try," Roger said, punching the old man in the stomach.

"You little rascal," Frank said, laughing.

Once they were in the elevator, Roggie asked Leon if he could run it. "Sure thing," Leon said, stepping aside. Roger rotated the control handle all the way to the right and they went up seven floors and then he stopped the car and pushed the handle back to the left and they started going down again.

"Come on, darling, don't fool around," Mommy said.

"Come on, Rog," Stephen complained, almost simultaneously. He was impatient to get upstairs and see Clarry. By the time they reached the twelfth floor he had almost undone the stitching on his overnight kit. His mother had hardly inserted the key in the lock and opened the door when he pushed past her into the kitchen.

"We're home, Mae," Harriet called out, closing the front door. A moment later a young, attractive Negro holding a dust rag came out of the master bedroom into the foyer. "Mae, this is Roger, my older son."

"Hello, Roger."

"Hello, Mae."

"Glad to be back from camp?" Mae asked.

"You bet," Roger said, pulling off his jacket and running into his bedroom.

"Stevie," Harriet called out.

At the same moment Stephen charged into the foyer. "Mommy, where's Clarry?"

"Oh, there you are," she said. "Stevie dear, I want you to say hello to Mae, our new cook."

"Hello, Mae," Stephen said.

"Hello, Stevie. I've heard a lot about you. You're just as handsome as your mommy said," Mae remarked in a friendly but anonymous voice.

"Mommy, where's Clarry?"

"I'll tell you in a minute, dear," Mommy said with a certain embarrassment. "All right, Mae, you can finish up my bedroom now." As soon as Mae was out of the foyer, Mommy took Stephen's hand and led him into the living room. "I forgot to tell you, darling, Clarry had to go back to Nashville. Her daughter got sick and she had to go home."

"Rosie?"

"What, darling?"

"But Rosie's in Chicago."

"Who, darling'?"

"Clarry's daughter, Rosie."

"Oh no. She got sick during the summer and went back home to Nashville."

"When is Clarry coming back?"

"She's not coming back," Harriet said, as firmly but gently as possible. "Now I don't want you to hurt Mae's feelings asking for Clarry every minute. Mae's a lovely girl and a wonderful cook and I want you to be nice to her. She's made you a marvelous cake—it's chocolate—for dinner tonight. Want to come inside and see it?"

"No," Stephen said, and went into his bedroom.

That night, when the chocolate cake was served, Stephen refused to eat it. To avoid upsetting Mae, Harriet took Stephen's portion, broke it into small pieces and flushed them down the toilet. Saul was confused by his wife's behavior and his son's but dismissed the whole thing as part of the excitement of homecoming.

The next day was Thursday, Mae's day off, and in the afternoon Stephen sneaked into her bedroom to see if he could find any of Clarry's belongings. The chintz-covered chair was still there, and so were the bed and bureau and mirror, but otherwise there was no trace of the former occupant—the room didn't even smell of cologne.

By Saturday Stephen forgot his hunger strike, but for some reason he was unable to retain his food. He threw up twice during the night and on Sunday Harriet made him stay in bed. Even though his temperature was normal, she called Dr. Loeb and asked him to come over. Annoyed as he was to interrupt his Labor Day weekend, Dr. Loeb was even more annoyed after he examined Stephen and diagnosed his case as an upset stomach. He put his patient on a diet of tea and toast, and Harriet was relieved when Stephen managed to keep them down. By Monday he had recovered completely and on Tuesday Harriet allowed him to go to school, since it was the first day.

But that afternoon, when the boys came home, Harriet thought Stephen's head felt hot and took his temperature. She was alarmed to discover he had 102° and put him to bed immediately. This time, Dr. Loeb said Stephen had the grippe and prescribed aspirin, fluids, lots of rest and, if necessary, alcohol rubs. Before leaving, he suggested Roger sleep in the living room that night and said he would be back the following morning. At six o'clock Harriet gave Stephen two aspirins which he washed down with a little orange juice. He showed no interest in food. When Saul came home he was upset by the news and took Stephen's temperature again. This time it was 103°. He and Harriet discussed the possibility of calling in another doctor, but decided to wait until the morning. Harriet announced she would sleep in Roger's bed that night and let Roger sleep in hers, which he did.

Stephen passed the night fitfully. Not only did he thrash around and throw off his cover, but he mumbled and groaned in his sleep. At one o'clock he suffered a severe chill and woke up shaking from head to foot. Harriet ran to the cedar closet, unpacked the winter blankets and covered him up with two of them. His shivering continued so she made him some tea, which he refused to drink until she held his head and spooned it down his throat.

The following morning his temperature was down to 101.4°, and though Stephen complained about the aches in his joints, Dr. Loeb was pleased with his patient's improvement. "He'll be all right," he reassured Harriet as they walked to the front door. "Just keep him in bed and feed him plenty of fruit juices. It'll only take a couple of days." He came again on Thursday, by which time Stephen's temperature had dropped to 100° and Dr. Loeb predicted it would be normal the following day. That evening Stephen ate some soft-boiled eggs—his first real food since he had been sick—and Harriet was delighted. Nevertheless, she insisted on sleeping in his room with him again that night, because he still had a temperature.

Stephen fell asleep at nine o'clock, and Harriet covered the bed lamp with her bathrobe and read for hours before she finally switched off the light. At two o'clock she was awakened by screaming. She leaped out of Roger's bed and rushed over to

Stephen's, but his bed was empty. She switched on the light. "Stevie," she called as she ran to the bathroom door, "are you all right?" There was no answer. Harriet knocked on the mirrored door. "Stevie darling, are you all right?" she asked again, but still there was no answer. "Stevie!" she repeated as she opened the door, but the bathroom was empty.

"Give it back! Give it back!"

From inside the bathroom. Harriet heard him scream again. "Where are you, darling? Where are you?" she cried, running back to the bedroom. And then she saw him, sitting outside the window, on the window ledge, with only the metal safety bars between him and the street, twelve stories below. Even before the scream had escaped from her throat, she clapped her hands over her mouth, rushed to the open window and seized him by the shoulders.

As Harriet dragged him into the room, Stephen clung to the slender metal bars and screamed, "Give me back my tail! Give me back my tail!" Harriet broke his grip and examined his tear-stained face. Even though his eyes were open and he kept repeating, ". . . my tail . . . my tail . . ." Harriet realized he was sleepwalking and carried him back to his bed. After a moment Stephen awakened and saw his mother sitting on his bed, crying and stroking his head. "What's the matter, Mommy?"

"Nothing, darling. Nothing . . . now. Go to sleep."

"Why are you crying?"

"I guess because you frightened me."

"How?"

"You were delirious and walked in your sleep, my love."

"Delirious?"

"It doesn't matter, darling. It must have been the fever breaking. It's over now, thank God!" she said, closing her eyes. Then she kissed him and switched off the light. "Please go back to sleep."

Stephen obeyed, and the next morning, just as Dr. Loeb had predicted, his temperature was back to normal.

LOON

In 1937, when Stephen returned to Potawatomi for his third consecutive summer, he was just nine. Even though Roger had been a Brave for a year, Stephen was still only a Papoose and could not expect to become a Brave until he turned ten.

Just as the campers' age-groups at Potawatomi were designated by the words Papoose, Brave, Warrior, and Chieftain, a camper's swimming ability—that is, his endurance, not his form—was classified by the names of fish. If a camper could swim a hundred yards without drowning he was called a Minnow, if he could swim two hundred yards—the distance between the two waterfront docks—he became a Perch; swimming four hundred yards made him a Bass, while a Pickerel had to be able to swim the three-quarters of a mile across Micmac Pond; in order to achieve the supreme status of Dolphin the camper had to swim to the opposite shore of the Pond and back. During his first summer Stephen passed the Minnow test with no difficulty, but refused to try for Perch until the following summer, when he became one on his second attempt. Immediately thereafter, he tried for Bass. Roger had been a Bass since the first week of their second summer, and Stephen felt challenged to equal his brother's record, but failed repeatedly.

During his second summer, Stephen also became stage-struck. There were many reasons for this. He had achieved something of a personal triumph in the minstrel show his first summer and longed to repeat it by performing again. It was so hard to have to be constantly thinking up funny or brilliant things of your own to say—especially when vocabulary was not one of your strong subjects; it was so much easier to memorize someone else's—some famous playwright's—words. It was so much fun to smear on stripes of blue and beige and flesh-colored grease paint, apply lipstick and rouge and eyeshadow, add putty to your nose, combed-out curls of crepe hair to your chin or a brunette wig over your scalp. In a matter of minutes you could transform your freckled

97

face into a sunburned Adonis, a deformed dwarf, an irresistible flapper, a craggy old man, a middle-aged matron, a Cherokee Indian, or a Chinaman with a queue. And then there were the costumes: battered stovepipe hats, moth-eaten cutaway coats and spats, ebony canes and alpenstocks, decaying satin parasols, high-buttoned shoes and high-heeled pumps, heavy Scotch plaids and beaded chemises, diaphanous saris and scarves and veils, and dazzling rhinestone brooches. Of course, there was also that agonizing hour of stage fright before you ever set foot on the boards, but that was more than made up for by the whistles or cheers that greeted your entrance and the applause when the curtains closed. And afterward, after you'd packed on gobs of cold cream, removed your make-up and left the theater, there was always that noticeable increase in your popularity the following day. The other campers grew deferential; either they admired or envied you or found you amusing, and you were able to say and do things in the character you had acted the night before, things that you would never have dreamed of saying or doing as yourself.

Stephen soon discovered that actors were granted license—exceptional social license—forbidden to ordinary human beings. Sometimes he would hobble around wheezing and trembling like a palsied, asthmatic old man; he might perform a tantalizing strip-tease with his towel in the bathhouse or pretend to be crazy, and groan and pull his hair and kick the trunks of trees. His repertoire was infinite, but it seldom if ever included acting himself, except when he was alone on one of his nature hikes or swimming under-water.

Even though he felt less certain about it, the other activity Stephen became interested in during his second summer was riflery. Actually, the rifles themselves bothered him, not so much because they backfired with a terrible impact and noise or because he grasped the meaning of their deadliness, but because there were so many warnings to listen to, so many precautions to take and so many rules to follow before Uncle Leo would give the order to fire. What Stephen really enjoyed was the range. He liked reeling his target in and out, collecting empty cartridges, and lying prone on the tumbling-mats. He didn't much care if his strap was adjusted correctly or his sight was too low or if he breathed when he squeezed the trigger. He didn't even care whether or not he was able to perforate his target so long as he was allowed to keep his empty shells. But despite his indifference he became a Marksman in his second year and treasured his medal above all his other possessions.

Consequently, when he returned to camp for the third time Stephen's titles ranged from Marksman and actor to Perch and Papoose. He was assigned to tepee Number Four with his old pal Billy Lowe, as well as his former cabin-mates Harvey Glassbaum and Johnny Auerbach. Tubby Geist had been bullied out of camp by Glassbaum, and Frenchy Bloch's father had returned to Paris, taking Frenchy with him. These two were replaced by Lloyd Rosencrantz, whose father was a Milwaukee beer distributor and who, like Tubby, was another obesity case; and Teddy Baer, to whom Stephen was attracted not only because he was gentle but because Stephen liked his name.

Stephen's cabin-counselor, to whom he took an immediate liking, was new at Potawatomi. His name was Uncle Hank. When Stephen asked Uncle Hank what activity he was in charge of, he was surprised by his counselor's answer. "Totempole."

"Totempole? What's that?"

"Haven't you ever seen a totempole, Steve?"

"Sure, I have. In the Natural History Museum. But I never knew it was an activity."

"Oh," Uncle Hank reconsidered. "I guess I'm really in charge of arts and crafts."

"Where's Uncle Dave?"

"Who?"

"The *old* arts and crafts counselor."

"He isn't back this summer."

Uncle Hank's simple statement sent a tingle down Stephen's spine and saddened him, but only for a moment. After all Uncle Dave was pretty old and pretty ugly. As nice as he was, he had never been a favorite—not like Uncle Alf or Uncle Tony, both of whom were back! But even *they* were pretty ugly, pretty skinny compared to Uncle Hank. For a moment Stephen stopped making his bed to observe Uncle Hank. He had such a big nose, big eyes, big hands; his thighs and calves looked very, very powerful exposed, as they were, below his khaki shorts. He was almost as tall as Daddy and just as good-looking, but altogether different— much, much younger, stockier, not bald. There was something untamed about Uncle Hank; something about his trout-colored curls, his intense black eyes, his prominent cheekbones and wiry body-hair that made him seem savage. And yet, he wasn't. He was easygoing, soft-spoken, sensitive. Stephen knew intuitively that Uncle Hank would never have to raise his voice or slam things down the way Daddy did. Somehow you could sense his strength without his giving any demonstration of it . . . "Uncle Hank," Stephen confided, "I'm awful glad you're in the bunk next to mine."

"Thanks, Steve. So am I."

The first time Stephen spotted the huge, stripped white pine in the clearing behind the Lodge he became excited about it without even knowing what it was or that it bore any relationship to Uncle Hank. He straddled it and spurred its sides; he climbed up on it like a tightrope walker and balanced himself along its length until he heard Major Fischer's voice from the dark screen window: "Get down from there! Young man, get down before you dent that wood!"

As Stephen fled from the clearing he almost collided with Uncle Hank who was coming out of the Lodge. "Hey, Steve."

"Oh! Hi, Uncle Hank."

"Where are you running?"

"Nowhere." Uncle Hank was carrying a rust-colored canvas bag. "What's that?"

"Tools."

"For what?"

"To carve the totempole."

"The totempole," Stephen realized, looking back toward the white pine. "I forgot. Are you going to carve it?"

"I'm going to try."

"How long will it take?"

"I'm not sure: two . . . three summers. Just between ourselves, Steve, I've never carved one before."

"You haven't? Then how will you know what to do?"

"Oh, I'll manage. You see, where I come from, in Oregon, Steve, they have a lot of totempoles in the museum. The best collection in the country. I've been looking at them ever since I can remember."

"How old are you, Uncle Hank?"

"Nineteen."

"Nineteen," Stephen murmured, his eyes filled with wonder and worship. It was the best, most marvelous age he had ever heard of: old enough to do whatever you liked and young enough not to be old. "I wish I was nineteen."

"Why?"

"So I could carve a totempole."

"You don't need to be nineteen, Steve. You can do it now."

"I can!"

"Sure. You can come and help me or watch whenever you're free."

Stephen soon discovered that Uncle Hank worked on the totempole all morning, every day, and he saw to it that he was "free" much of the same time. By now most of the counselors were used to Stephen's cutting activities that didn't interest him. They knew it was pointless to look for him on the baseball diamond, wrestling mats, volleyball court or track five minutes after the period had begun; from past experience they knew he had sneaked off to hunt frogs and snakes. But this summer they were wrong, because Stephen began to cut even his beloved nature hikes for the sake of the totempole. Fortunately, most of the other activities he liked such as riflery, dramatics, arts and crafts, and fishing were scheduled for the afternoons. The only morning activity that he attended religiously was swimming, but that was not until eleven o'clock, which gave him plenty of time with Uncle Hank.

At first he only sat in the sunshine and watched Uncle Hank chop and adze away one side of the tree so that after two or three weeks he was left with a semicylindrical pole a foot through at its thickest point and twenty-five feet long. During that time, Stephen kept out of the way of the swinging tools. He played with the pine chips, studied the shifting muscles in Uncle Hank's body and spoke to him about becoming a Brave, a Bass, and a Sharpshooter. Sometimes he strutted about with the script of a play called *Freedom,* which was to be the season's première, declaiming the difficult lines of the eccentric Poet:

> " 'Bright with the loathsome phosphorescence of putrescence. Adroit as the slimy members of a specimen of saurian reptile. Agile as the senile, blue-bottomed gibbon gibbering ineptly to his idiotic mate! If I possessed handy to my tongue the multi-syllabled, parti-colored, blasting epithets—' "

"Stevie," Uncle Hank interrupted, "have you any idea what the hell you're saying?"

"No," he confessed, "but isn't it marvelous?"

Or sometimes he and Uncle Hank discussed intimate, private,

painful subjects such as bed-wetting. "If I were you, Steve, I wouldn't let Glassbaum ride me about that."

"Wouldn't you?"

"No. There's nothing to be ashamed of."

"Isn't there?" Stephen asked skeptically.

"Of course not."

"But only babies and sissies wet their beds," he despaired.

"That's a crock! I'll tell you a secret, Steve: I still wet *my* bed sometimes, even now."

"You do?"

"Sure. I like the way it feels, don't you?"

"No, I hate it! Especially here, here at camp with these flannel sheets: they never dry."

"That's not what I mean, Steve. Sheets can be laundered. That's what laundries are for. My father owns a laundry in Portland. You should see some of the sheets he gets—they're much worse than yours."

"Are they?"

"Sure. But what I meant was, it feels good while it's happening —while you're wetting your bed—doesn't it? Don't you enjoy that?"

Stephen hesitated. "I don't know. Doesn't it happen while you're asleep, Uncle Hank? I don't think I wake up until it's over. Then it's too late. It smells so bad and everybody knows you've done it. If only it didn't smell so bad. Don't you hate the smell, Uncle Hank?"

"No. Why should I? I hate the smell of vomit, not urine. Sometime you should try to wake yourself up while it's happening, Steve; you'll enjoy it."

Stephen took his counselor's advice to heart, and even though he didn't wake up the next time while it was happening, neither did he feel so ashamed of himself the following day.

One morning early in the summer Major Fischer came out of the Lodge to inspect Uncle Hank's progress. The Major lived in a suite of rooms to the right of the entrance hall and it was rumored that no one, neither counselor nor camper, had ever set foot inside except for the fifteen-year-old Indian girl named Poppy who kept it clean. After completing his tour of inspection, the Major stopped in front of Stephen and said, "Young man!"

Stephen leaped to his feet. "Yes, sir."

"At ease," the Major said magnanimously. "Aren't you scheduled for some activity this period?"

Stephen bit his nail.

"I had him excused, Major," Uncle Hank interceded. "I needed an assistant."

"Oh, very good. Carry on," Major Fischer said and strutted out of the clearing.

As soon as the Major was out of sight, Stephen ran over to Uncle Hank and took his hand. "Thank you."

"What for?" Uncle Hank asked. "You *are* my assistant, aren't you?"

Stephen beamed. That morning before lunch, he ran to the library in the Lodge, took down the dictionary and looked up *a-s-i-s-t-e-n-t* but the word was much too advanced and private to be found in any dictionary. During rest period he wrote a letter home:

"Dear Mommy & Daddy: I am Uncle Hank's asistent. We are making a totum pole. He is my favorite. Love, Stevie xxxxx"

When Stephen arrived at the clearing the next morning, Uncle Alf and Uncle Pritch were already there with crowbars, helping Uncle Hank roll the pine tree onto its other side. After they accomplished this task, Uncle Hank thanked them and they went away. "This is the side we're going to carve," he said to his apprentice as he began to adze the new side into shape.

"When can I assist?" Stephen asked.

"Soon. Soon."

Stephen sat down and tried to be patient. "Uncle Hank, are you gonna go to Lodge tonight?"

"What are they having?"

"Movies." Every night of the week some recreation, called Lodge because it invariably took place in that building, was scheduled for the campers. Movies were shown twice a week; on other nights there were songfests, plays, bingo games, boxing matches, or similar tournaments.

"What's it called?" Uncle Hank asked, aware that Stephen always ran up to the Lodge balcony where the projector stood to investigate the round, aluminum containers of film on the mornings of movie nights.

"Something *of Red Gap*."

"Sure. I guess I'll go," Uncle Hank said.

That night, after dinner, Stephen got his flashlight and put on his heavy gray wool sweater, but when he saw how Uncle Hank had simply draped his over his shoulders, Stephen took his sweater off and did the same.

Generally, the campers sat on folding chairs in front of the screen and the counselors sat on the balcony or under it, on top of the ping-pong tables, at the rear of the Lodge. "Uncle Hank," Stephen whispered as they entered the building "can I sit next to you?"

"I don't see why not," he said, and they sat down on the ping-pong table next to Uncle Vince and Uncle Pritch.

"Hi-ya, Hank," Uncle Pritch said. "Well, look who you've brought us—young Barrymore."

"Or Bernhardt," Uncle Vince suggested, and Stephen laughed with the rest of the Uncles. A moment later the lights went out and the campers flashed their flashlights, whistled lasciviously, groaned, or did bad imitations of Mae West before *Ruggles of Red Gap* began.

Stephen didn't like the movie much. He didn't understand what was so funny or what the Uncles found in it to comment about, but he was overjoyed to be sitting next to his favorite.

After the movie, the lights remained off and the bugler played Taps—the traditional ending of every Lodge—while the campers solemnly sang the words:

> *Day is done*
> *Gone the sun*
> *From the lakes*
> *From the hills*
> *From the sky;*
> *All is well,*
> *Safely rest,*
> *God is nigh.*

Stephen loved and hated Taps. Its mournful melody haunted him and the truth of its words troubled him. . . . *Day is done.* . . How did it happen? When you entered the Lodge it was still daylight outside and the shades had to be pulled down when movies were shown. By the time they were over the daylight had disappeared, the sky was black, the moon and stars were out, the woods were alive with noises, and there was a chill in the air. But the shiver that passed through Stephen's body came from more than the cold. It had to do with the fact that the dark in which this dirge was sung could swallow up a hundred and fifty boys and leave you standing all alone. If the dark could do that, then it could do anything: claim you or your mommy or your favorite Uncle, and the fact that *God is nigh* didn't seem to matter much.

Da-da-da-dooo . . . da-da-da-dooo . . .

There it was! The eerie call that came from across the Pond. "From the lakes, from the hills, from the sky" . . . like a fanfare for the night and the rising of the moon. Long ago Uncle Alf had identified it for Stephen—he said it was a loon—and ever since Stephen had been responsive to its call. Sometimes it sounded like a kettle steaming, high-pitched and tremulous; at others it was like a yodel, long and loud and cheerful; and there were times when it sounded like a wolf's howl, with a double trill before the bay: *Wuh-wuh-wooooo! Wuh-wuh-wooooo!* There was one other loon-call, the frenzy call, that Uncle Alf had told him about, but it was extremely rare and Stephen had never heard it himself. The calls always began at twilight, when the rasping of the crickets and the croaking of the frogs began—before the night crawlers came out—and lasted as long as consciousness. Stephen had no idea to whom or what the loon was calling—whether to the moon or stars—but soon decided it must be calling him. Even though he'd never seen one and didn't know how to answer it, he knew the loon was calling him to come away, give up his soft warm sleep, swim across the night-cold pond and fly away with it forever.

Wuh-wuh-wooooo . . . wuh-wuh-wooooo . . .

Stephen reached for Uncle Hank in the dark and touched his bare thigh, and Uncle Hank put his arm around his assistant's shoulders.

When Taps was over and the lights came on, Stephen was relieved to have someone to walk back to the cabin with for once. Usually he went alone, listening to his loon, expecting at every moment that someone or something would see him coming and rush out of the underbrush and grab him by the throat. In order to avoid such an ambush, Stephen would switch off his flashlight and grope his way through the dark, stumbling on rocks, tripping over roots, bumping into trees until he was in a state of terror. But tonight he had Uncle Hank, and they walked back together, talking about the movie and the totempole.

"Uncle Hank, I won't be able to work on the totem tomorrow," Stephen said as they neared the cabin.

"Why not?"

"I have to take my test for Bass."

"Oh, good. You'll pass that easily."

"Yes," Stephen said with self-assurance. "For you," he added as they mounted the wooden steps.

At eleven-thirty the next day, Stephen ran to the clearing behind the Lodge. He came in his bathing suit, his feet were bare and his hair was still dripping. "Uncle Hank! Uncle Hank!" he shouted as he approached. "I passed. I passed!" he panted, blinking his bloodshot eyes.

"Congratulations, Stevie."

Stephen stopped and stared. "Who's that?" he asked, pointing at the girl with the straight black hair.

"That's Poppy, Steve. Poppy, this is Stephen, my assistant," Uncle Hank said.

"How do you do," Poppy said shyly, smoothing down her orange skirt. Stephen examined her carefully. She was dressed in a man's shirt and sneakers. Except for her skirt and her long shiny hair, Stephen thought she looked like a boy.

"Stephen's just become a Bass," Uncle Hank explained to Poppy.

"A Bass?" Poppy pronounced the *a* broadly.

"That means he's a very good swimmer," Uncle Hank said and Stephen smiled. "Poppy's an Indian, Steve," he continued, acting like a host trying to create rapport between two tongue-tied guests, "but she's never seen a totempole. Of course, there's no reason why she should've. They weren't ever made by the Algonquins, only the Northwestern tribes."

"Are you from Gitche Gumee?" Stephen asked.

"Where?" Poppy said, turning to Hank for assistance.

Uncle Hank in turn asked, "Where's that, Steve?"

> " 'By the shore of Gitche Gumee
> By the shining Big-Sea-Water
> Stood the wigwam of Nokomis
> Daughter of the moon . . .' "

he chanted syllabically.

Much to Stephen's astonishment Uncle Hank was noticeably annoyed. "She doesn't live in a wigwam, stupid," he said, turning away from Stephen. "Where *do* you live?" he asked in a gentler voice.

"Across the pond. I live with my father and brothers. They work for Mr. Fowler at the mill. I have to go now," she said, and before Uncle Hank had a chance to say another word she disappeared into the Lodge.

"Poppy cleans the Major's rooms. She can't be more than fifteen," Uncle Hank said, as much to himself as to Stephen. "Isn't she nice?"

Stephen didn't answer.

After that Poppy came to the clearing frequently. She always wore the same orange skirt, the same pair of sneakers and a man's shirt, which she left unbuttoned at the throat, exposing her prominent shoulder blades. It wasn't long before Stephen began to feel less jealous of her. After all, she wasn't a boy, she wasn't a Bass, she didn't sleep in the same tepee with Uncle Hank, in the very next bed, she didn't sit on his right side in the mess hall morning, noon, and night, and she wasn't his assistant; she was only a girl who came to see the totempole once or twice a week . . .

When Uncle Hank had tapered the pole to the right shape, he marked it into five equal five-foot sections and stretched a string taut from one end to the other, dividing the pole down the center. "We're going to carve four figures on it, Steve," he announced.

"But, Uncle Hank, you've marked off five."

"The fifth one goes in the ground, thank God. That's all I need —I'd be at this forever. You see this string?" he asked, plucking it with his finger. "That's to keep the figures symmetrical."

"Symmetrical?"

"That means the same on both sides. Now," he said, conducting Stephen to the end of the pole, "our first figure, here at the top, is a fellow named Raven. You know what a raven is?"

Stephen thought hard. "Raven?"

"It's a big black bird, like a crow."

"A bird!" Stephen exclaimed. "At the top of our pole?"

"Uh-huh."

"Like a loon?"

"No, it's not a water bird."

"Couldn't it be a loon, Uncle Hank?"

"It *could* be a loon—"

"Oh, please! Let's make it a loon!"

"Except that the Indians never put loons on their totempoles. We have to keep some semblance of authenticity. You see, Steve, these animals were thought by the Indians to be their ancestors— that means their great, great, great-grandfathers. They thought they possessed magical powers. They weren't just animals; they were human beings like you and me, who had the power to metam—to change themselves into animals."

"Magically?"

"That's right. And they performed miraculous deeds. This fellow Raven, for instance, he turned himself into a bird and stole the sun and moon and stars from a greedy magician who kept them hidden in a box. After he stole them he hurled them into the sky in order to give light to the people on earth."

Stephen's mouth fell open and he pointed at the sun that was blazing overhead. "He did?"

"That's what the Indians say." Hank paused and thought for a moment before he continued. "I suppose we could call him Loon if you like."

"We can!"

"Sure. He has a beak and wings like a loon."

"What about his body?"

"Well, no, Raven has the body of a man. That's to show his double nature. But so would Loon, I guess, if he were Raven."

Stephen was slightly confused, but overjoyed by the prospect of seeing Loon. He took the patterns Uncle Hank handed him and traced Loon's head, eyes, mouth, and legs onto the tree. Meanwhile, Uncle Hank carved two two-foot boards into the shape of mummy cases and mortised them into the sides of the tree at forty-five-degree angles. These were Loon's wings. Then he carved another piece of wood, the shape of a big banana, and stuck it in the middle of Loon's face. On both occasions Stephen prepared the glue, poured it into the appropriate holes, pushed the wings and beak into place and drove them down with a heavy mallet.

Gradually, as Loon's features started to emerge from the wood, the rest of the campers began to take an interest in the totempole, and Stephen was always on hand to explain it to them. "That's Loooon," he would begin, drawling the word onomatapoetically, enlarging his eyes, pursing his lips, hunching his shoulders and letting his arms dangle stiffly from their sockets until he had transformed himself into the subject of his story. "Loon, who stole the moon from the shore of Gitche Gumee by the shining Big-Sea-Water where it was held prisoner by the ugly evil magician. Loon strangled the magician and stepped on his face and stole the moon and tucked it under his arm like a football and flew away with it into the sky. At the top of the sky, as far away as he could fly," Stephen chanted, pointing toward the heavens like an ancient astronomer, "he took moon out and hung it up like a Christmas ball—but what do you think?" Stephen paused dramatically. "Some of his armpit feathers stuck to the ice of the moon and that's why every night when the moon comes out Loon howls like a loon." It wasn't long, before everyone at Potawatomi, including Uncle Hank, referred to the top figure on the totempole as Loon instead of Raven.

When Loon was almost completely carved, Stephen took the patterns for the second figure, Bear, and traced them on the pole. The outline of Bear's head began immediately below Loon's human feet. As a matter of fact, Loon stood right on top of Bear's head like an acrobat, and Stephen wondered if that was what made Bear stick out his tongue and grit his teeth so ferociously. Bear had monstrous paws, ears that stood erect and a large, peculiar nose that turned up sharply at the end and touched his forehead. After Stephen finished tracing Bear, he and Uncle Hank changed places; Hank to carve Bear's savage teeth and Stephen to sandpaper Loon.

"Stevie," Uncle Hank said, driving his chisel into the wood, "you've been a Bass for over two weeks now. When are you going to try for Pickerel?"

"Pickerel?" The question troubled Stephen. He had given it a lot of thought. He wanted to become a Pickerel, but at the same time he dreaded the possibility of getting halfway across the pond and then, unable to take another stroke, sinking to the bottom and being eaten alive by the giant snapping turtle he imagined lived there. "Soon," he said and changed the subject. "You know what the next play I'm in is called?"

"What?"

"*The Bear*. Isn't that funny? I mean that I'm in a play called *The Bear* at the same time we're carving one."

"That's called a coincidence."

"Coincidence," Stephen repeated, committing the word to memory. "I play the part of Elena Ivanovna Popova," he continued, pronouncing the name perfectly.

"Wow!" Uncle Hank exclaimed with amusement.

"That's Russian, you know. I'm Russian too. I mean, my grandfather is. He says 'danks' instead of thanks, but I'm not going to talk that way in *The Bear*. I play a beautiful widow, and some awful man comes to collect a debt from me— Actually, he comes to collect it from my husband, but my husband's dead, so he tries to collect it from me, but I don't have the money in my house, so I ask him to come back after the weekend but he refuses to leave. That's when I call him a bear, because he's such a loudmouth and a slob. That's why he challenges me to a duel and when I accept he falls in love with me."

"Do you fall in love with him?"

Stephen stopped and thought about Popova. "I guess so."

When the curtains opened revealing Stephen as Popova and Ernie Rossbach as Luka, her ancient footman, the campers stamped and whistled automatically. It always killed them to see a camper portraying the part of the heroine; they enjoyed that as much as the play itself. But in Stephen's case it was different. He didn't achieve his effects by exploiting or even parodying the humorous aspects of the female sex. He never overstuffed his bosom, never pitched his voice too high or exaggerated the swing of his hips. He was too serious, too accomplished, too authoritative an actor for that—besides, it simply would not have occurred to him. He submerged himself completely in the character he was playing, the character dictated everything. It was this intense self-conviction combined with his own striking beauty that made it easy for Stephen's audience to accept the illusion of the dress and wig and jewelry he wore, to sit and watch him in engrossed silence as if he were not only an actress but a prima donna.

As Popova, Stephen wore an upswept, auburn wig and a full-length black velvet dress whose collar buttoned high, making him hold his chin up. His eyes were heavily shadowed with blue, enlarged and extended with liner. Around his throat he wore a large, gold cross and, dressed in deep mourning, looked starkly beautiful.

During the final love scene, when Marty Gross was supposed to say, ". . . I'm weak, I'm wax, I've melted . . . I'm on my knees like a fool, offering you my hand . . ." he went blank just before the word 'hand' and began to stutter until the audience howled over the suggestive implications of his memory lapse. After a minute, Stephen prompted him like a ventriloquist, and when Marty finally spoke the word the audience laughed even louder at the anticlimax.

The performance was a huge success. The actors had to take seven curtain calls, and Stephen and Marty each took a solo bow. When Marty took his he waved to his pal Frank Bloom, who was sitting in the second row, but Stephen was too professional for that, and even when the campers cheered he remained in character.

Uncle Hank found it hard to believe that Elena Ivanovna Popova was the same boy who slept in his cabin, ate at his table, and helped him with the totempole every day. As soon as the performance was over he rushed backstage. "You were marvelous, Stevie. Marvelous!"

"You really think so?" he asked without turning around but looking at Uncle Hank in the make-up mirror.

"Of course I do."

Stephen stared at the reflection of Uncle Hank and himself as Popova, almost head to head in the mirror. He admired his own complexion now that the make-up was covering his freckles. He admired the sweep of his eyebrows, the exoticism of his eyes, the sculptured delicacy of his lips, and he knew that he was much more beautiful than Poppy. "I thought we ruined the ending," he protested.

"Don't be silly. It was great."

By the time Uncle Tony and most of the campers had said the same thing, Stephen had quite a swelled head, and the following day, on the crest of his triumph, he decided to take his Pickerel test.

The day was bright and clear. You could see the pine trees on the other side of the pond. You could almost see their cones and needles and smell their fragrance. The water itself was as warm and calm as a baby's bath. Stephen plunged in and swam out to where Uncle Fred, the assistant swimming coach, was waiting for him in a rowboat.

"I want you to take it easy, Steve," Uncle Fred said as he began to row. "You can use whatever strokes you want—you can even float on your back or tread water, so long as you don't touch the boat. Don't worry about me. I'll keep up with you. I'll go as slowly as you want. There's no rush. We have all morning. The main thing is for you to gauge your energy, you understand?"

"Yes."

"If for any reason you want to stop—either because you get a cramp or run out of breath or whatever it is—just grab the boat and I'll stop rowing. But remember, if you do that, you're disqualified. Right?"

"Right," Stephen said and started doing the breast stroke.

"That was a swell performance you gave last night," Uncle Fred said as he rowed slowly past the float.

"Did you really like it?" Stephen asked, lifting his smiling face out of the water.

"You bet I did," he said, pulling in his left oar and leaning over the side of the boat, "but I don't want you to talk. I mean, I'm going to say a lot of things as we go across the pond, but I don't want you to answer me. Understand? Just save your breath and let me do all the talking."

Stephen understood and kept quiet. About a quarter of the way across the pond he turned over and did the backstroke. He knew they were entering deeper water now—he could tell by the change in temperature, the darkness and the density. He was apprehensive about that giant snapper that lived in the middle of the pond, and felt less nervous on his back. I would rather sacrifice my arm or leg or all of me, he thought, than have to meet that monster face to face. As he kicked and swung his arms he gazed into the sky. It was completely clear except for one cloud that looked like Uncle Hank in profile. Stephen watched it change into a sheep dog. He wondered if he would be able to see Poppy's house when they reached the other side. He wondered if he would see a loon. He wondered what a real loon looked like. . . . Would Uncle Fred wait and let him hunt for one? Where do you hunt for a loon? Up a tree? In the water? Under a bush? If loons stay awake all night and howl at the moon, then surely they must shut their eyes and go to sleep in the daytime. Like salamanders, loons must be nocturnal . . .

"We've passed the halfway mark," Uncle Fred announced. Stephen rolled over and looked at the opposite shore. It seemed as far away as it had been before they started. "Are you getting tired?" Uncle Fred asked, observing that Stephen had slowed down and was doing the side stroke.

"No," Stephen lied. He had wanted to say yes. He knew he couldn't go much further, he knew he couldn't make it to the other shore, but he felt abashed by the prospect of having to admit his defeat to Uncle Hank. How would he ever be able to face him and say, I've failed?

Suddenly a shadow passed over the surface of the water. Stephen noticed it but didn't look up; he assumed it was the cloud.

"Look! That must be a loon," Uncle Fred remarked. "I've never seen one before."

"Loon! Where? Where?" Stephen shouted, grabbing the gunwale and looking up into the sky. It was flying low and Stephen saw its long, yellow, pointed bill, its black neck, its white underbelly and webbed feet.

"Hey, Steve, you're holding onto the boat!" Uncle Fred said.

Stephen didn't remove his hands. He watched the loon's long gangly body fly into the distance. It was humpbacked. . . . What was it Mommy always said? You shouldn't laugh at humpbacks; if you touch their humps they bring you luck . . .

"Do you want to stop?" Uncle Fred asked.

The black and brown pattern on the loon's back looked like a waffle. Stephen watched as the loon split the surface of the pond into spray and landed near the opposite shore.

"Hey, Steve!"

"What?"

"You're holding onto the boat!"

"Oh, am I?" Stephen asked innocently. "I'm sorry."

"Don't you want to go on?"

"Oh, no," Stephen said righteously. "That wouldn't be fair." So Uncle Fred helped him climb into the boat and they rowed back to camp.

This time when Stephen reached the clearing he had his shoes and socks, shorts and jersey on, and his hair was combed. Uncle Hank knew from the way Stephen walked—slowly, weightlessly, with downcast eyes as if he were trying to make himself invisible —that he had failed his test. "Hi-ya, Steve."

"Hello."

"Want to help?" Without saying a word, Stephen picked up a piece of sandpaper and began sanding Bear's giant paws. "It doesn't matter, Stevie. You'll pass the next time."

"How do you know?" Stephen asked with alarm. "Did Uncle Fred tell you?"

"No. I just guessed."

"It wasn't my fault," Stephen explained. "It was the loon. A loon flew over. I saw a loon!"

"You did?"

"That's what made me grab the boat." Stephen shrugged his shoulders and pursed his lips. "And then I failed. You're not supposed to touch the boat. I didn't even know I was doing it."

"That doesn't matter. You saw a loon; that's what matters, Steve," Uncle Hank said. "How did you like him? What did he look like?"

"He didn't look much like ours. He has a humpback," Stephen reported, imitating the loon's deformity, "and his legs come out of his behind."

Uncle Hank laughed.

During the last two weeks Uncle Hank finished carving Bear and explained to Stephen, as well as to Major Fischer, who was growing as impatient as a phratry chief for the completion of this status symbol, that the rest of the totempole would have to wait until the following summer. The day before camp closed Stephen watched Uncle Hank, Uncle Alf, and Uncle Pritch wedge props under the pole and cover it with tarpaulin for the winter. For the first time Stephen realized that camp was over and that he was going to have to leave Uncle Hank. —Leave Uncle Hank!

He ran back to the cabin and flung open his trunk which was already neatly packed and tagged and labeled. He lifted out the tray and put it on his bed. At the bottom of the trunk, in a pair of cotton socks, he had hidden his Marksman's medal. He removed it from its hiding place, returned the tray to the trunk, slammed down the lid, and ran back to the clearing. Uncle Alf and Uncle Pritch had gone away, leaving Uncle Hank to fasten down the tarpaulin with pup-tent pegs.

"Can I help?" Stephen asked, slipping the medal into his pocket.

"Sure," Uncle Hank said. "You can hammer down some of these pegs."

Stephen took the mallet, the same one he had used to drive in Loon's wings and beak, and began to pound the tent pegs. Their heads were crushed to a pulp from years of being hammered, and Stephen felt sorry for them. He held the pegs tightly in his left hand, but hammered gently with his right, afraid he would smash his fingers under the mallet. The fourth peg he came to was loose. He had to replant it and start all over. At the first blow of the mallet he struck his thumb. "Ooow!"

"What's the matter, Steve?"

"I hit my thumb."

"Let me see," Uncle Hank said, stepping over the pole. Stephen held out his hand. Uncle Hank took it in his own and examined the thumb. "The skin isn't broken. It'll be all right," he said, massaging the sore spot.

The gentle but strong touch of his favorite's fingers made Stephen's heart throb. Just as Uncle Hank was about to withdraw his hand, Stephen seized it and whispered intensely, "Uncle Hank, I—I—"

"What, Steve?"

Stephen raised his head and gazed into his counselor's eyes. Not only were they filled with patience and compassion, they looked infinitely friendly . . . inviting . . . welcoming . . . Stephen lost his gravity, his corporeality, himself; turned into a vapor, floated up through the air and entered the Elysium of Uncle Hank's receptive eyes. "I don't want you to leave me," he avowed. "Ever. Ever."

"But I'll be back next summer."

"No! No! You mustn't go away." Stephen saw the tenderness and concern deepen in his counselor's eyes. He felt his counselor's hands gently envelop his own, and his heart leaped with anticipation.

"I have my work to do," Uncle Hank said soberly, "and you have yours. You have to go back to New York to school. Your mother and father are waiting for you."

"I don't care. I want to stay with you."

"I wish you could—"

"I can! I can!" Stephen felt Uncle Hank's hands disappear.

"No, Steve, that's impossible."

"Why? Why is it impossible?"

"Because—" Uncle Hank moved a step or two away.

Stephen followed, desperate to reestablish contact with his counselor's eyes. "Why?" he repeated fervently.

"Because, you have your life and I have mine."

"But why? Why can't we have each other's?" Stephen could tell that his question was confusing. He could see the perplexity on Uncle Hank's brow, and he knew of only one way to dispel it. "I love you, Uncle Hank!" he exclaimed, embracing his counselor's naked waist.

"I know that," Uncle Hank said simply. "I love you, too."

Like a caress of fur, the words made Stephen's skin erupt in goose flesh. They took his breath away and almost made him swoon. Never before had he experienced such ravishing sensations, and he longed for more. "I love you," he cried out passionately. "I love you as I never loved before. . . . I'm weak, I'm wax, I've melted . . . I'm on my knees like a fool, offering you my hand." Stephen looked up and saw his counselor smile sadly. "Please! Oh please don't laugh at me! I love you! Love you," he persisted, wanting Uncle Hank to respond, waiting for the magic words to consummate some miraculous fusion between their separate selves. But Uncle Hank only sighed and shook his head.

"I'm sorry, Steve."

"Why?"

Uncle Hank frowned impatiently. "There's nothing we can do about it."

"Why not?" Stephen implored.

"There just isn't!" Uncle Hank answered with finality.

Through his tears Stephen watched Uncle Hank turn away and walk toward the totempole. Like the polar bear at the Central Park zoo that has stood too long on its hind legs at the bars of the cage and drops on all fours and lumbers away, Uncle Hank's movements revealed his restlessness and discontent. He picked up the mallet and began to pound the pup-tent peg where Stephen had left off. But Uncle Hank's swings were much too powerful and violent for the peg: it split in two, and Stephen ran away.

Only after he returned to the cabin did Stephen discover his Marksman's medal still in his pocket. That night Taps seemed sadder than it had ever seemed before, and the loon called louder and more relentlessly than he had ever heard it.

When Stephen returned to camp in 1938, he was ten and became a Brave automatically. Much to his surprise he discovered that Uncle Hank was his cabin counselor again. Usually the campers were assigned a different counselor every summer, but when Uncle Hank agreed to return to Potawatomi he did so with the proviso that he be put in charge of his former cabin. As he explained to Major Fischer he could not possibly complete the totempole that season if he had to take the time to get acquainted with a new group of boys.

Stephen was disturbed when he found his trunk waiting for him at the foot of the bunk next to Uncle Hank's. The juxtaposition of their beds reawakened all the events and emotions he had tried so

hard to forget during the winter. Uncle Hank looked even hand-
somer, happier, more sympathetic than he had the summer before,
and Stephen could hardly restrain his impulse to fling his arms
around him and resume from where they had left off. But quickly
he remembered the humiliation, the hurt, the shame, the guilt his
love had cost, and he was cautious, resentful, even cold. When
Uncle Hank asked him to be his assistant again, Stephen said
no.

"Why not, Steve? What's the matter?"

"Nothing," Stephen answered breezily. "I've just got too many
other things to do. Uncle Tony wants me to play the lead in *Ali
Baba*. I have to pass my Pickerel test. I want to add some bars to
my Marksman's medal." Oh, how relieved he was not to have
made a fool of himself by giving the medal to Uncle Hank!

"Won't you even come and kibitz sometimes?"

Stephen tried to be charitable. "Sure I will."

After holding out eight or nine days, Stephen went to the clearing to look at the totempole. Poppy was there with Uncle Hank.
She was wearing the same skirt and the same pair of sneakers, but
instead of the shirt she wore a soft, blue sweater and Stephen could
see the rise of her small breasts. After they said hello, Uncle Hank
asked Stephen if he wouldn't change his mind about being his
assistant, but Stephen said he couldn't.

"Don't you even care who the new figure's going to be?" Uncle
Hank asked, pointing to the totempole.

Stephen took a guess. "Poppy?"

"Poppy? Poppy's not an animal," Uncle Hank said, and Poppy
laughed aloud, making Uncle Hank laugh, too.

"Oh, I forgot," Stephen said.

"As a matter of fact, though, it *is* a girl—well, partially," Uncle
Hank said, walking with Stephen down the length of the pole until
they reached the third section.

Stephen stared with repugnance at the penciled outline of the
ugly, squatting woman with the heavy eyebrows and enormous lips
who was holding a caterpillar between her thighs. "Why is she
hugging that caterpillar?"

"It's not a caterpillar, it's a woodworm," Uncle Hank explained.

"Woodworm?"

"That's a worm that lives in wood."

"Well, why is she hugging it?"

"Because it's her pet."

"A worm?" Stephen sneered. "She must be cracked! Why does she have a worm for a pet?"

"Well, now," Uncle Hank hesitated, "that's pretty hard to explain . . . but I'll try. You see, Steve, the Indians who carved these totempoles had a custom when young girls came to puberty to put them—"

"What's that?"

"What?"

"Puberty."

"Oh, that's when . . . someone reaches manhood."

"I thought you said they were *girls.*"

"They are. It doesn't matter. It's the same—"

Just then the period bell began to ring. "Oh! Excuse me," Stephen said. "I have to go and take my Pickerel test. 'Bye."

"Good luck!" Uncle Hank shouted after him.

When Stephen reached the waterfront, Uncle Fred was waiting for him just as he had the summer before. This time there was a haze over the pond, but otherwise it was just as calm and warm as it had been the last. Stephen dived in and swam underwater without coming up until he reached the rowboat.

"Anybody who can stay underwater as long as that," Uncle Fred said, "can pass this test in his sleep. It's a cinch," he added. "You would have passed last year if it hadn't been for that crazy loon. Remember?"

Stephen nodded. "I wonder if we'll see him again?"

"I hope not," Uncle Fred remarked. "This time we're going to reach the other side and nothing's going to stop us. Right?"

"Right," Stephen agreed and started swimming. He forgot all about Uncle Hank and Poppy. After a moment, he even forgot about the loon and concentrated on his strokes. He was determined to become a Pickerel. He had only seen a pickerel once, but he had never forgotten its elongated snout and tubular body that looked like a cross between an alligator and an eel. . . . If I swim and strain enough, he wondered, will my body stretch and turn into a pickerel's?

"Take it easy," Uncle Fred advised him, "we're just beginning, you'll wear yourself out."

Stephen slackened his pace and tried to take his strokes in slow-motion, like Stanley Weiss, the camp swimming champ. He tried to maintain his form and a steady rhythm, coordinating his arms and legs and breathing.

"That's the way," Uncle Fred said.

Stephen remembered the ocean and realized how different this was. In the ocean you were just a piece of driftwood carried on the crest of every swell, crushed beneath the weight of every wave. No matter how you strove against the tide, no matter how you kicked, the ocean always overwhelmed you and there was nothing you could do about it but submit. But in this pond, *you* became the ocean; it was you who had the power and control, and the pond that had to submit. It was forced to do your bidding, just as you had once been forced to do the oceans—or Daddy's or Roggie's. For the first time in his life, Stephen sensed what it was like to be a master.

But gradually his arms and legs began to tire, and his wind began to fail. And yet he refused to give in, he refused to turn over and float on his back, he refused to lose sight of his objective—the distant, pine-covered shore. "Have we passed the halfway mark?" he asked, breathing with an effort.

"Just about," Uncle Fred replied. "You want to tread water for a minute?"

"No," Stephen said firmly and began to swim underwater, advancing five or six yards at a breath.

"That's foolish, Steve. You'll wear yourself out that way."

But Stephen paid no attention. He pushed ahead in spurts like a frog. Sometimes he plunged too deep and it took all his breath just to come to the surface again. Sometimes he exerted all his energy in an effort to pass the rowboat, but every time he emerged for air the boat pulled up alongside of him and the race was never won. He listened to the monotonous creak of the oars and watched their silver blades slash and carbonate the water. He saw a sunfish dart between the bubbles and disappear. He watched the bubbles rise to the surface and turn into air. At last he came to the surface himself and stayed there, exhausted and panting. "How much further, Uncle Fred?"

"Another hundred yards or so," he said, "don't stop now."

Stephen had the will to go on, but not the energy. He could still manage to flutter his feet like the wings of a dying moth, but his arms had turned to cement and he could barely raise them.

"Keep going, Steve! Keep going, boy, it's only sixty yards."

Stephen noticed some shadowy purple plants in the water and realized they must be growing on the bottom. . . . If I can see the bottom here, he thought, I must be close to shore, and he began to stroke and kick with vehemence.

"That's the way!" Uncle Fred encouraged him, "but don't overdo it." Stephen splashed the water higher than he had when he first began and Uncle Fred had to pull the boat aside in order not to get wet. "Just thirty to go," he called out and Stephen heard him and thrashed his arms in a fury, straining every muscle.

All of a sudden his mouth went dry, his limbs stiffened and he lost his sense of hearing, sight, and touch. Instead of the creaking of the oars there was a ringing in his ears, instead of the tepid water there was only his strained muscles, instead of the pine trees there was blackness—a huge oppressing blackness that left him worldless and afraid. But even so, he went on kicking, stroking violently, his body taut. Like a victim of stereotypy his movements were fitful, frenzied, endlessly repeated—Thrash! Thrash! Thrash! Thrash!—the tension mounting rapidly, steadily, unbearably until his body was immobilized by tension.

At this moment, one remove from senselessness, from stone, Stephen suffered a paroxysm that shook his body from head to toe. Instantly the tension was relieved, reversed: began to flow spasmodically in the opposite direction, out of him, back to its source, the pond. He could feel his limbs and bowels that had been like bars of steel, melt and drain into the pond. It seemed as if all the fluids in his body—all the water, plasma, juices—were draining out of him, but pleasurably . . . pleasurably . . . and Stephen let them go.

"What's the matter with you, Steve? What's the matter?" Uncle Fred asked excitedly, turning Stephen over in the shallow water.

"Matter?" Stephen murmured.

"I was just about to give you artificial respiration. I thought you'd fainted, floating there like that."

"I felt . . ." Stephen started to say, but thought better of it. "Did I pass?"

"Of course. Look where you are!" Stephen turned his head and saw the pine trees just behind him. "Didn't you hear me calling you?"

"No."

"Come on now," Uncle Fred said, "let's go back."

Stephen stood up shakily and climbed into the boat, and Uncle Fred rowed him back to camp.

For days and days after that, Stephen thought about the new sensation he had had and longed to experience it again. He knew it had something to do with being in water and under pressure but he didn't know exactly what. He begged Uncle Fred to let him take his Pickerel test again, but Uncle Fred only laughed and said he had already passed it. Then one day toward the end of July it happened again of its own accord.

It was Stephen's habit to spend his entire swimming period from eleven o'clock to a quarter of twelve underwater. During those forty-five minutes he would dive for stones, pretend to be a crab and go around pinching his fellow campers' toes, or try to break his own record of turning eleven somersaults underwater without coming up for air. None of which bothered his counselors at all, since campers were allowed complete freedom at the waterfront. Only one rule was strictly enforced: when Uncle Cliff blew his silver whistle, everyone—Papooses and Chieftains alike—had to get out of the water. No exceptions were ever made to this rule and no excuses were tolerated. Anyone who disobeyed was punished.

On this particular morning Stephen was turning somersaults and when, at last, he came up for air he realized that the whistle must have already blown because most of the campers were straggling out of the water. He came to the surface close to the dock, almost under Uncle Cliff's bare feet, but Uncle Cliff was too busy shouting at Greenberg to take any notice of Stephen. "Greenberg, if you don't get out of there this minute I'll see to it you miss Lodge tonight!" Stephen knew it was a movie night—*The Invisible Man* was to be shown—and he didn't want to miss it, so he dived out of sight again. The wooden dock was constructed over a frame of steel supports secured in concrete blocks. Stephen dived down and grabbed one of these steel pipes with both his hands in order to hold himself under until Uncle Cliff moved away. He wished he had heard the whistle. He wondered if Uncle Cliff would catch him. He was worried how long his lungs would hold out. Suddenly, just as he was about to give himself up, it began to happen—that glorious sensation as if someone were titillating his flesh with a giant feather and causing his loins to laugh uncontrollably. He knew he was out of breath and ought to let go of the pipe before he drowned, but his knowledge only served to intensify the pleasure that was gushing out of him, causing his limbs to ripple and quiver. . . . At last, when it was over, he rose gasping to the surface and bobbed up and down under the planks of the dock. Then he swam the length of it, bumping his head on the cross-beams, reached the shore, crawled out from under the dock un-noticed, and ran to the bathhouse to change back into his uniform.

Every morning after that, Stephen remained in the water minutes after the whistle had blown, inducing the conditions of his ecstasy. At the risk of being caught, of missing Lodge, he hid under the dock, held his breath, grabbed the pipe, gripped it between his thighs and pressed against it with all his strength until he experienced the sensation he craved.

The first week in August Uncle Hank finished carving Woodworm and began work on the totempole's fourth and final figure, who was not an animal but a man. When Stephen remarked on this discrepancy, Uncle Hank explained that the figure was "a little innovation" of his own. Man had a squat, rugged body, a bold jaw, clenched fists, thrust-out knees and broad, hunched shoulders that bore the entire burden of Loon, Bear, and Woodworm.

During this period Stephen noticed that Uncle Hank was often late to meals, always absent from the arts and crafts shop in the afternoons, seldom at Lodge. The flesh under his eyes began to turn black, his cheekbones protruded, and he drank many more cups of coffee than usual. Stephen's curiosity was aroused by these changes, and one morning he decided to investigate their cause.

Instead of going directly to the clearing, he went into the Lodge and spied on his counselor from the window behind the ping-pong tables. Squatting alongside the pole, Uncle Hank was working feverishly. His naked back was the color of roast turkey; it glistened in the sunlight, basted by sweat. His shoulder blades and muscles were in constant movement as he tapped the chisel head. "Henry," someone suddenly said, "why do you work so much harder on this figure than the others?"

Even though he could not see her, Stephen recognized Poppy's voice. . . . But who was Henry? To whom was she speaking?

Uncle Hank rested his mallet on the pole. "I want to finish before the end of the summer. Besides this is the most important figure. You see, Poppy, the Indians read their totempoles from top to bottom. That makes Man the crucial figure—not Loon!—even though everyone thinks it's the other way around."

Stephen resented this remark. It made him angry and jealous. Since he regarded Loon as more or less his own property, he took the words as a personal rebuff and refused to speak to Uncle Hank for three whole days after that.

Because of the time pressure, when Man was finished Uncle Hank recruited Stephen to help him paint the totempole. At first

Stephen was reluctant to help, but gradually, as he became reacquainted with Loon and Bear, his old enthusiasm was reawakened. He pried the lids off all the cans, mixed the paint and, in those areas that did not require too much care such as Loon's breast, Bear's body and paws, and the bodies of Woodworm and Man, he slopped on coats of apricot, yellow, and red. Simultaneously, Uncle Hank went around with cans of blue and black and olive and painted in the faces and feathers and all the conventionalized elements of design.

The excitement of painting the totempole, combined with that of his daily indulgence under the dock, began to interfere with Stephen's sleep. Every night after Lodge he would go to bed with the tune of Taps still in his head, listen to the loon's call, shut his eyes and fall asleep just as he had always done, but now, at some point in the night, he would wake up again. The first time this happened Stephen sat up in bed to see if, by some chance, Uncle Hank was awake too and wanted to talk about the totempole, but he discovered that Uncle Hank's bed was empty. He sat and waited for his counselor to come out of the john, but Uncle Hank never did. Stephen was confused. He knew Uncle Hank had been there when he went to sleep—he had watched him turn out the light and get into bed—but where was he now? Was he working on the totempole?

The next morning when they resumed painting, Stephen noticed that the work had not advanced beyond the point where they had left off the evening before and concluded Uncle Hank could not have been working on the totempole. "Uncle Hank, where were you last night?"

"Where?"

"Last night, where were you?"

"In bed."

"I mean in the middle of the night," Stephen persisted.

"What makes you think I was anywhere?"

"Because your bed was empty."

"Don't be silly," he scoffed, "you must have been dreaming."

That night, to reassure himself, Stephen awakened deliberately and looked at Uncle Hank's bed, but much to his surprise Uncle Hank was in it. Two nights later, however, Uncle Hank was gone again. Stephen rubbed his eyes to see if he was dreaming, but when he looked the second time the bed was still empty. Stephen was mystified. The following night when Uncle Hank turned out the lights Stephen only pretended to go to sleep. After lying awake and listening to the loon for what seemed like hours, he heard Uncle Hank get up. Stephen watched him put on his shorts and sweater, tiptoe out of the cabin, and walk down the hill in the direction of the waterfront, but his destination was obscured from Stephen by the birch trees and their shadows. Stephen was intensely puzzled and curious about his counselor's errant behavior but said nothing more about it.

When the totempole was completely painted Uncle Hank began to dig a trench about fifteen feet long, gradually sloping to a depth of five feet. Since this was the last step before erecting the totempole, the entire camp grew increasingly excited. Major Fischer came and paced about nervously, licking the corners of his mouth and shouting orders: "Stand back there! Don't kick that dirt! Don't touch that paint, it's not completely dry! Poppy, what are you doing here? Go and finish my room!"

After the trench was dug, a block and tackle and a ten-ton truck were brought on the scene. The uncarved end of the totempole was rolled into the trench and a log was placed under its upper end. Several lines that had been run through pulleys were tied around Loon's waist and legs and attached to the rear end of the truck. Then all the campers were cleared out of the way and at a signal given by Major Fischer the truck drove off toward the Lodge, hoisting the totempole into the sky.

"It's up! It's up!" Stephen exclaimed, and everybody cheered.

When the pole was erect, Uncle Hank began heaving heavy stones into the deep end of the trench. "Wait a minute! Hold on there!" Major Fischer cried.

"What's the matter?" Uncle Hank asked impatiently.

"You have it facing the waterfront!"

"That's where it's supposed to face!"

"No! No! I want it to face inland, so I can see it from my window."

"Sorry, Major, it's too late now." Uncle Hank continued filling the trench with stones and some of the other counselors began shoveling the dirt, as Major Fischer walked away in a huff.

That night instead of Lodge there was a dedication ceremony. Even though the moon was full, a huge bonfire was built and lit, and Major Fischer, who was wearing a Chieftain's headdress, delivered a speech about peace and prosperity. This was followed by Uncle Tony's war dance, which all the campers had seen before and knew by heart. As soon as Uncle Tony was finished, Uncle Hank got up and said a few words about the Northwest Coast Indians and expressed his appreciation and gratitude to his assistant, Stephen Wolfe.

Instantaneously, Uncle Hank's simple words revived all of the love and passion Stephen had tried so hard to stifle, and he glowed with excitement and pride. He felt the flames of the fire warm his limbs and loosen them seductively. He watched the sparks explode and rush up toward the moon. He listened to the loon calling in the distance, more insistently than ever, and he yearned to fly away with it and take Uncle Hank along.

As soon as Uncle Hank sat down, a dozen cases of Moxie, which had been bought by the Major as a special treat for the campers, were brought out and served. After most of the beverage had been poured into the bushes, Taps was played and the ceremony was over.

As they walked back to the cabin together, Stephen suddenly turned to Uncle Hank and said, "Can I come with you?"

"Come with me?"

"Tonight!"

"Where?"

"Wherever it is you go."

"I'm not going anywhere."

"Oh, please take me along! Please!" Stephen pleaded.

"But I tell you I'm not going anywhere," Uncle Hank protested.

When they reached the cabin, Stephen tried to fall asleep, but couldn't. The loon was too insistent. It was shrieking at the top of its lungs in a shrill, maniacal, quavering voice that Stephen had never heard before.

Waaaa-waaaa-waaaa-waaaa-waaaa-waaaa-waaaa .

Stephen clenched his teeth and buried his head under his pillow. For the first time since he had started coming to Potawatomi he knew he was hearing the frenzy-call and he hated it and wanted it to stop. It made him want to scream out loud—louder than the loon! It made him want to strangle the bird. The shrieking drove him frantic. It filled his head with frightening voices, his heart with desperation, and he began to cry uncontrollably. He clutched his sheet and bit into his pillow but could not stop his tears.

"What's the matter, Steve?" Uncle Hank asked, sitting down on the edge of Stephen's bed.

"Take me with you! Take me with you!" Stephen cried hysterically, hugging his counselor's throat.

"Shhh. Shhh," Uncle Hank said, rocking Stephen in his arms. "You'll wake the others."

"Take me with you, please!" Stephen implored.

"I can't. I'm sorry, Steve," Uncle Hank whispered. "Now go to sleep."

Stephen laid his head down on his pillow. After his sobs subsided, he heard Uncle Hank tiptoe out of the cabin and close the door. As soon as Uncle Hank had been gone a minute, Stephen jumped out of bed, got dressed, and followed him. Because the moon was full, he had no difficulty finding his way down the hillside. When he got to the bottom, he hid behind the bathhouse and watched Uncle Hank untie a rowboat, push away from shore, fix his oars and start to row. As he watched him row across the moonlit lake, it suddenly occurred to Stephen where Uncle Hank was going. "Poppy!" he exclaimed and ran out onto the dock.

Waaaa-waaaa-waaaa-waaaa-waaaa . . .

The loon had not stopped and its cries sounded louder now than they had when Stephen was in bed. He strained to see the bird. He stared across the pond, but all he could make out was Uncle Hank's rowboat moving further and further away. Stephen considered swimming after it. He was a Pickerel, after all, and had done it once before. He took off his jersey and shorts. He unlaced his shoes and took off his socks. After placing his clothes in a neat pile, he lowered his naked body into the soft warm water. He could not remember ever having swum in the nude before, and the water's touch was excitingly sensual.

Waaaa-waaaa-waaaa-waaaa-waaaa-waaaa-waaaa . . .

Instead of following Uncle Hank, Stephen dived under the dock and held fast to the steel pipe. He could still hear the loon and see the moonlight through the water. He hugged the pipe between his legs and wondered what would happen if he were caught. Suddenly, he began to feel the sensation, and he tugged at the pipe ferociously.

After it was over he came to the surface and climbed up the ladder onto the dock. The air was colder than the water. He stood in the moonlight and started to dry himself with his woolen jersey. When he got to his groin he felt something sticky and massaged it between his fingertips. Suddenly he saw the totempole silhouetted in the moonlight, saw Loon's outspread wings. He heard the shrieking of the real loon and turned around just in time to see Uncle Hank's rowboat disappear into the dark . . . "Gone the sun, from the lakes, from the hills, from the sky . . ."

Stephen pinched the sticky stuff between his thumb and fore-finger and gazed up at the moon. "What is it?" he asked with perplexity. "What is it?"

And from across the pond, as if in response to his plaintive query, the loon cried out, *Waaaa-waaaa-waaaa-waaaa-waaaa waaaa* . . .

MOOSE

Stephen had been forewarned. Months before, his parents had revealed that they were going to send him to a different camp, a "better" camp, a camp where—as Daddy put it—he would be "treated like a big boy," where there would be a little more emphasis on athletics and less on theatricals, where they would work off some of that baby fat. Stephen had been told the new camp's name: Penobscot. He had gone with Mommy to the sporting-goods house. He had seen the new colors: blue and gray. He had watched Mommy sew on the new name tapes. He had heard her say how much more sensible the setup was at Penobscot than Potawatomi. He had listened to her explain that there were really *two* camps—junior and senior—separated by a lake, and that he would be a Junior and Roger a Senior. He had even agreed with her when Mommy remarked how much better that would be: no more teasing, no more tormenting, no more fights. For once Stephen would be away from Roger with children his own age or *younger,* since eleven was the oldest age at junior camp.

In order to go to Penobscot—just as to Potawatomi—you had to leave from Pennsylvania Station. At least that much was the same! So were the mob of parents and children, the white sleeveless sport shirts, the canvas overnight bags, the warm reunions between old friends. What was different was the faces: there wasn't one familiar face in the crowd—except, of course, for Mommy and Daddy who were about to be left behind. But even that was the same: these good-bys had always been unbearable . . .

Tearful and downcast, Stephen descended the black iron steps to the train. The steam from the engine smelled the same as it had previous years: sulfurous and stale. He had no difficulty locating Car 5049, Lower 6 to which he had been assigned by someone called Chief. The boy with whom he was obliged to share the berth—even that was the same as it had been at Potawatomi—was already there. He was very plump and wide-eyed, and introduced

131

himself as Marvin Klein. Stephen said hello, but did not disclose his own name until he was asked.

"Do you care which side you sleep on, Stevie?"

Stephen shook his head but did not speak. Nor did he speak when Marvin asked him if he had ever been to camp before, he simply nodded.

"You have? This is *my* first time. What's it like?"

Stephen shrugged, and opened his box-lunch. The contents were the same as always: two pieces of fried chicken, one white, one dark, a hard-boiled egg, two slices of buttered bread and one Sunkist orange, all of which he ate slowly but relentlessly, tasting none of it. He wished he knew where Roggie was so that he could trade his piece of breast for Roggie's drumstick, since Roggie hated dark meat.

When the train got halfway through the station tunnel Stephen began to feel the same old pressure in his ears that he had always felt and he relieved it by swallowing the way Roggie had taught him. The wheels of the train sounded the same as always and the same twilit scenery fled past the same sooty window. The inside of the berth was the same: its ceiling looked like the top of a cigar box, but darker: the color of a phonograph record—and Stephen closed his eyes.

During the night Stephen was awakened by the sound of Marvin crying. Instead of asking what was the matter, Stephen lay there listening, pretending to be asleep. He knew what Marvin's trouble was. He knew it was the same as his: homesickness—the most painful sickness in the world, the only sickness for which there was no medicine, no help, no cure. He knew he couldn't comfort Marvin and Marvin couldn't comfort him. They had only one recourse: to bury their heads in their pillows and sob themselves to sleep.

Like Potawatomi, Penobscot was situated in southern Maine. Both camps were built on the side of a hill overlooking a lake. Both had birch trees and wooden cabins. Both simulated Algon-quin social customs. Both began with the letter P. And yet, despite these similarities, Stephen spent his first day at Penobscot stumbling around as if he had never been to camp before, as if he were an ignorant, frightened, resourceless private who had fallen into the hands of the enemy. When he was introduced to his cabin mates he did not hear their names or see their faces or respond in any way. He said hello to Marvin Klein just as if they had never met. He made his bed mechanically as if he had spent all of his

previous life interned and doing nothing else. He ate his lunch in
much the same manner and when he was finished he could not
have said whether what he had just eaten was creamed tuna fish or
macaroni and cheese. During the rest period he buried his face in
his pillow and pretended to sleep but the convulsions of his back
betrayed the fact that he was crying bitterly.

In the afternoon all of the campers went to the infirmary and
waited to be examined. When it came Stephen's turn to be weighed
and measured, Dr. Siegel, who spoke with a heavy German accent,
said, "So . . . so . . . you're the tallest boy in camp till now."

Stephen pondered the doctor's remark. The first summer, when
he went to Potawatomi, he had been the youngest and the smallest
boy in camp and everyone had treated him like a mascot. In the
three years that followed he was oblivious to the number of inches
he grew or the amount of weight he gained. Even though he was
succeeded by younger campers, he still retained that initial impression he had of himself as the littlest boy at Potawatomi. Now,
quite suddenly, he was the biggest boy at Penobscot. How had it
happened?

"Yah, but even so," the doctor continued, nudging the counter-
weight along the chromium register, "you're overweight. From
your record here, I see you gain thirteen pounds this year. Ah, but
don't you fret," he added in response to the scowl on Stephen's
face, "we work that off in a jiffy."

For the first time Stephen looked around the room and studied
the slight hips, small buttocks, flat chests and stomachs of the
other naked bodies. Then he turned back and looked down at his
own: at the breasts that protruded like cones from his chest, and
his ugly, swollen belly. Where had his old skinny body gone—the
one he had had at Potawatomi? What evil cook had come in the
night and stuffed him like a hard-boiled egg inside this enormous
meatloaf? Unconsciously, Stephen seized his left breast and tried
to wrench it off.

"Step down there, please," Dr. Siegel said. "Next."

Stephen felt self-conscious about the perspiration trickling down
the insides of his arms and was relieved to put his shirt and shorts
back on. He pulled his braided leather belt as tight as he could,
causing his stomach to bulge abnormally.

As he came down the infirmary steps, a camper ran past Stephen and shouted to another boy who was strolling down the path
ahead of him, "Hey, Roggie, wait for me." The camper's name
struck Stephen with the impact of a batted ball. He jerked his head

up violently only to see a boy with a bush of copper hair and a rash of freckles who in no way resembled his brother. Stephen stopped and watched the two friends fling their arms around each other's necks and walk off toward the cabins.

"Roggie . . . Roggie . . ." Stephen whispered tremulously, trying hard to hold back his tears. But his tears would not be stopped, they broke through his nose with a snort and squeezed out from under his eyelids. He covered his face and ran away from the friends, away from the cabins, away from the camp until he reached the top of a hill and threw himself down in some timothy that obstructed everything but the sky.

At last he understood what was the matter, what was making him so miserable . . . it was Roggie! The absence of Roggie. Mommy had told him that Roggie would be at the senior camp and he would be at the junior one. She had told him the two camps were separated by a lake, but at the time her words had had no meaning. . . . It was one thing to be told about a lake and quite another for the lake to be there physically, irrevocably with you on one side and your brother on the other. What was the reason for it? At Potawatomi the Papooses and Braves had not been separated from the Warriors. At Potawatomi you could even reach the Chieftains' camp on foot; why not at Penobscot? Had that been Mommy and Daddy's purpose in sending them to this so-called big boys' camp—to split them up? Had that been their purpose this past winter when they moved to Central Park West and he and Roggie had been made to sleep in separate rooms and sent to different schools? But at least in New York you knew that Roggie was in the same apartment: you heard him in the bathroom every morning, you saw him at the dinner table every night; even when he locked you out of his sanctum sanctorum you knew that he was in there, you could see the light under the doorsill, you could plead with him to open up, you could pound on the door with your fists until you forced him to unlock it and sock you in the teeth. But even that—as much as it hurt—was better than this! It was much, much better to see your brother—even if it meant getting socked in the teeth!—than not to be able to see him at all.

Suddenly, lying there alone, it occurred to Stephen that he had become a part of his brother—an organic part—like a double cherry or a normal slice of orange that has another, smaller slice imbedded in its side, and he was seized by a terrible panic. Without Roggie he was will-less, he was on his back like a scarab beetle, helpless to get up. Without Roggie he had no understanding of anything, no interest in anything, and no one he could call his friend. Without Roggie he was no one, nothing. The only thing he knew for certain was that he was lying on his back, looking up at a cloudless sky and feeling very scared. But otherwise, he did not know who he was or why he was there or what he wanted—except to die.

At last Stephen sat up and stared down at the biggest, fattest body at Penobscot. It was even fatter now, in this sitting position with Stephen bending over it. He handled it the way a doctor handles a broken limb—cautiously and carefully, not knowing when the least amount of pressure will produce the most agonized response. Stephen couldn't believe these thighs were his—attached to him—and yet he saw his hand exploring them and felt its touch. He could not reconcile what he saw with the person who was doing the seeing. He knew the person who was seeing—he had known him all his life—but the person that he saw was new and unfamiliar. . . . Surely Roggie must have taken the old Stephen away with him across the lake, leaving only Stephen's former heart and brain inside this foreign body. No wonder his heart felt alone and lost, no wonder it felt afraid and crushed under all this excess, ugly flesh. He would have to go to Roggie in order to regain himself.

For the first time since he had flung himself down, Stephen stopped crying. He wiped his eyes, blew his nose, got up, brushed himself off and started on his quest. As he walked toward the cabin of the man with the balding head, the long face, the big, broken nose, trimmed mustache, and steel-rimmed glasses—the one who he had heard called Chief—Stephen rehearsed what he would say. By the time he mounted the wooden steps and knocked on the screen door, he was well prepared. "Chief?"

Chief turned his hound face toward Stephen, but its stony stare and broken nose made it seem more sinister than sympathetic. "Yes? Come in," he said, pushing his chair back from his roll-top desk. "Let me see now . . . Don't tell me! You're . . ." Chief's eyes penetrated Stephen's as if he expected to find a name tape sewn inside of Stephen's skull. After a moment of squinting Chief leaned back and wrinkled his brow. "No. I give up." Stephen looked puzzled. "Well, what's your name?"

"Stephen."

"Stephen who?"

"Stephen Wolfe."

"How do you do. I'm Chief. How is it we didn't meet on the train?"

"We did. You gave me my berth number."

"Oh . . . yes . . . Well what can I do for you, Steve?"

"I have to go and see my brother. It's his birthday today and I have a present for him."

"Where is he?"

"On the other side of the lake."

"At senior camp?"

"Yes. I have to go right now."

"Is your present wrapped?"

"No."

"Then I suggest you go back to your cabin— By the way, what cabin are you in?"

"I don't know."

"Well which one is it?"

"That one, over there," Stephen said, pointing across the quadrangle at the first cabin in the row.

"That's cabin Number Twelve, the leading cabin in camp. You're very lucky, Steve. . . . Now, about your brother, I suggest you return to your cabin, wrap your present and bring it back to me. I'll see that it's delivered in the morning."

"But his birthday is today!" Stephen lied.

"There's no one going over anymore today."

"That's why I have to go myself."

"Oh no, that's not the way it works at all. If your brother gets permission he can visit *you,* but Juniors are not allowed to go to senior camp."

"But it's his birthday."

"You should have thought of that last night. You should have given him his present when you were together at the station."

"But it wasn't his birthday last night."

"I've told you what to do—"

"Can't I take a boat—"

"No! The only thing you can do—"

"I'm a very good rower."

"—Is leave it here with me, as I suggested."

"Don't you understand, I have to see my brother?"

"It's *you,* young man, who doesn't seem to understand the English language."

"It's a matter—"

"I said No—"

"—Of life and death!"

"—And I meant No!"

"I'll die if I don't!" Stephen screamed, but his scream encountered a pair of outraged eyes, lost force, and dwindled into a whine. "I'll die," he repeated pitifully.

"Look here," Chief said, standing up, his face dispassionate and solemn as a crag, "we'll get along much better if we understand each other. I'm here to run this camp. I've been running it for seven years—successfully, I think, otherwise its owners wouldn't keep on hiring me. It's my job to control seventy-two campers —not just you and Jimmy Jones, but seventy-two of you. Now that's a big responsibility. It takes a little planning, a little discipline, and jurisdiction . . . just how much depends on *you,* on the amount that you cooperate. I can be tough or easy, whichever you prefer. You understand? When I ask you to do something— whether or not you agree with it—I expect you to comply. If you do, I think you'll find me a very fair and lenient person; if you don't—well, I have ways of dealing with boys who don't," Chief said, reaching across his desk and pulling out a long, narrow drawer. Stephen held his breath expecting Chief to produce a strap or cane, and he sighed with relief when he didn't. "I see from your file card you've come to us from Potawatomi. As far as I'm concerned, Potawatomi's a nursery, not a camp! We don't take the chill off your milk at Penobscot and we don't tuck you in at night. We don't expect any boy—much less one who lives in cabin Twelve—to be a crybaby or problem child. If you want to move to cabin One with the eight-year-olds, that can be arranged. But if you don't, I expect you to act your age, to set an example and act like a leader—not a spoiled brat!" Stephen resented that description even more than his father's favorite, which was prima donna. "Stephen, don't you know there's a war going on in Finland? Don't you know that children just your age—many of them younger— are homeless and starving, being wiped out like bugs, and you stand there crying about your brother. You ought to be ashamed of yourself. You ought to get down on your hands and knees and thank God you're not in Prague or Vienna," Chief sneered and crossed back to his desk. "That's all. You can go now. I'm glad we had this opportunity to chat. Next time I won't have to ask who you are, I'll remember."

Stephen pulled open the door, stumbled down the steps, and ran across the island in the center of the quadrangle, but before he reached the other side he heard his name called out stentorially and stopped dead in his tracks. "Stephen Wolfe, we've provided a footpath for that purpose; please keep off the grass!" Stephen recognized Chief's voice immediately even though it sounded mechanically amplified. For a moment he stood bewildered. He didn't know whether to continue in the direction he was going or retrace his steps and start all over, using the pebble footpath, but Chief, in a second display of omnipotence, clarified his question. "Stephen Wolfe, didn't you hear me? Come back across the grass and use the footpath, please!"

As soon as Stephen reached the sanctuary of his cabin, he rushed to his trunk. In the tray he found a new tube of toothpaste, still in its box. He dumped out the toothpaste and kept the box. On the bottom of the trunk he found a piece of tarpaper and pulled it out. With his pocketknife he cut off one of the drawstrings on his laundry bag. Finally, he seized his writing kit and carried it, together with the box, the string and tar paper, to his bed. After glancing around to make sure no one was watching, Stephen kneeled on the floor, using his bed as a desk, and scribbled a note to his brother: "Dear Roggie, they won't let me come see you. Please! Please! Please come see me as soon as you get this. If you don't I will die. Love, Stevie." Stephen folded the message four times, stuffed it into the toothpaste box and started to wrap it, but he soon discovered the tar paper was too unwieldy and so he substituted a piece of writing paper. After tying it up with the laundry bag string and making a quadruple knot, Stephen addressed the package in heavy print, put it aside and began to write a letter to his parents. He knew they would be visiting his Aunt Pearl and Uncle Morton over the Fourth of July weekend and decided to send his distress signal to Westchester, Special Delivery.

July 1, 1939

Dear Mommy & Daddy,

I am miserable. I hate this new camp. Why did you send me here? I hate it! No friends. No brother. Awful counselors. I want to come home. Please come and get me please. As soon as you read this letter please come and get me right away. I am waiting for you. I need you. If you don't come I will die. Hurry!

Love,

Stevie xxxxxxxxxxxxxx

P. S. Don't let any one know I wrote this letter. Burn it! They will kill me. Come quick!!!

When the letter was finished he took it and the package and started to leave the cabin, but before he reached the door he decided the package felt too light. Surely Chief would weigh it in his palm and grow suspicious. Stephen returned to his bed and attempted to open the knot he had tied, but failed repeatedly. At last he took it between his front teeth like a chipmunk and pulled it apart. As soon as the package was opened, he ran to his trunk, removed the tube of toothpaste, pushed it into the box and wrapped it again, retying the quadruple knot. Then he left the cabin, walked around the pebble footpath and delivered his salvation into the oblivious hands of the enemy.

"Oh good," Chief said, taking the package. "I see you *do* understand English after all. That always makes things easier. I bet I can guess what this is," he said, holding the package to his ear and rattling its contents.

Stephen's heart began to thump. "What?"

"A fountain pen."

"That's right!"

"And the letter?"

"Letter?"

"Does that go with it?"

"Oh no . . . no. That's just a letter home. I meant to put it in the slot."

"Oh, well just drop it in that box on your way out," Chief said, indicating a cardboard grocery box nailed to the cabin wall under the outside slot.

"Thank you, Chief," Stephen said, carefully placing his letter under the others that were already in the box.

As Stephen descended the steps he gazed up into the afternoon sky. It was the color of irises, and his heart flew out of him, joyously. He had taken care of everything; there was nothing more to do now but wait. Roggie would receive the package tomorrow, July 2, and come in the evening; the letter would reach his parents on the third or fourth and they would be here by the weekend at the latest. What did it matter now if the Penobscots beat their tom-toms, shrieked their war whoops, or shot their flaming arrows, the Federal troops had been informed and could be counted on to arrive in the nick of time.

The following evening after dinner Stephen ran to the dock at the waterfront and waited for his brother. At first there was no sign of Roger, and Stephen was despondent. He imagined someone had intercepted his package and he felt miserable and fearful of the consequences. But suddenly he saw a rowboat with a single oarsman in it half a mile out, heading toward the dock, gliding over the still, gray, twilit lake like a noble swan, and his heart revived. Even before it reached the shore, the sight of the oncoming boat made Stephen's panic subside and disappear. He forgot about Chief, the boys in cabin Twelve, his newly-acquired body. Stephen felt so overjoyed, so much like himself again he even forgot the reason why he had sent for his brother in the first place.

"Hi, Roggie."

"Hi, Stevie."

"Gee I'm glad to see you!"

"I got your birthday present," Roger said, securing the boat and coming ashore.

"Wasn't that tricky of me?"

"I guess. What's the matter, Stevie?"

"Nothing."

"I mean why'd you ask me to come?"

"I had to see you."

"What about?"

"Nothing special."

"Are you kidding?"

"No."

"Well, why'd you say you'd die?"

"I don't know."

"Come on, cut the kidding, will you? I have to be back before it gets dark."

"Can't you go to the movies with me?"

"No."

"I'll shine your shoes—"

"Will you stop acting like a baby! I had to give up a game to come over here. I had to get special permission from Mr. Bloomgarden—now what do you want?"

"Nothing—"

"All right, wiseguy!"

"—Just to see you."

"Like hell you did! You just wanted to torture me, like you always do. It kills you when I'm having a good time, doesn't it?"

"No!"

"You just hate to see me enjoying myself when you're not there, don't you?"

"No!"

"Just because you have no friends of your own, just because you're a fat, disgusting—"

"I just had to see you!"

"Well take a good look, wiseguy, 'cause you're never going to see me again."

Stephen felt his heart stop.

"I won't be fooled the next time. You can cry wolf until you're blue in the face—"

"I wasn't crying wolf!"

"Not much you weren't, shithead!" Roger snarled, leaping back into his boat and casting off.

"Wait!" Stephen shouted. "I wanted to tell you something."

"What is it?" Roger asked impatiently. "Well come on, what is it?"

Stephen opened his mouth, but no words came out: he couldn't think, he couldn't breathe.

"Jesus, you're the limit," Roger sneered, dipping his oars into the water.

As Roggie pulled away, Stephen felt his panic return. He felt the tug of Roger's oars in the pit of his stomach as if his brother had tied his guts to the stern and was dragging them out stroke by stroke. The more Roggie receded the more unhappy Stephen became; by the time the boat was indistinguishable in the dusk he was crying uncontrollably. The only thing that prevented Stephen from throwing himself into the lake was the letter he had sent his parents and his anticipation of their arrival.

In order to survive the next day, Stephen bypassed it in his imagination and projected himself into the Fourth of July. He saw himself hanging on his mother's neck, hopping into the car with her, driving back to New York City. He saw himself molting his new repulsive body, and with it his pain. He saw Penobscot Pond open like the Red Sea to facilitate his deliverance.

But in reality the Fourth was slow in coming—even slower perhaps than it had been for General Washington. When at last it did, Stephen found it painful—painful to prepare himself for the departure he had already accomplished so completely in his imagination. In order to leave Penobscot, he had to be there in the first place, which meant he had to bring himself back from his dream world and reestablish residence—if only for a day, but it was worth the agony. There was no humiliation too unbearable to suffer now that he was leaving, not even baseball.

For Stephen baseball was not a game, it was a tribal initiation. Ever since he could remember, he had heard men discussing baseball with a kind of reverence, partisanship, and passion they seldom brought to anything else, excepting love and money. Ever since he could remember, his father had tried to teach him to hold a bat and throw a ball, just as his mother had taught him to eat and toilet-train himself. Ever since he could remember, his father had taken him to the Yankee Stadium—always jammed with thousands of screaming fanatics—and had tried valiantly to indoctrinate him into the mysteries of baseball. And ever since he could remember, every autumn there was an unofficial national holiday that would last as long as a week sometimes during which every adult male, including the President, suspended work and went or listened to the World Series. But somehow, despite all this, Stephen was afraid of baseballs, afraid of being hit. To Stephen the crack of a bat connecting with a ball was as overwhelming as a crack of lightning and consequently he always struck out.

At Penobscot, as elsewhere, the obvious and only way to celebrate America's independence was to play a game of baseball. Since the game had begun, Stephen had come to bat twice and been struck out twice, but for once he didn't care; he knew this game would be his last.

At ten-thirty someone dressed in a butcher's apron came to the baseball field looking for a camper named Stephen Wolfe. "Here!" Stephen shouted in a voice that sounded loud and unfamiliar to the rest of the players who, up until that moment, had thought he was a mute. "Where are they?" Stephen asked, rushing up to the man in the butcher's apron.

"In the mess hall."

Stephen seized the words as if they were a baton in a relay race and started down the hillside. Just as he had known it would, his body lost its gravity and he flew over the ground, past the cabins, through the trees and into the mess hall. "Where is she?" he panted.

"Who?" asked the man in the white chef's cap.

"My mother."

"Mother?"

"Mrs. Wolfe!"

"Oh, you mean the telephone—"

"Telephone?"

"It's over there, through that door."

Stephen followed the chef's finger and found.himself inside a refrigerator the size of a bedroom. As soon as he saw the four dead cows hanging from their hooks, he turned to leave, but on his way out he noticed a telephone receiver dangling from its cord. "Hello—" he said in bewilderment.

"Hello?"

"Hello!"

"Hello, sir, is this Mr. Stephen Wolfe?"

"Yes."

"Stevie!"

"Mommy!"

"Hello, White Plains—"

"Yes, operator. Saul! I've got him, Saul!"

"—Your party's on the wire."

"Yes, yes, operator. Thank you."

"Go ahead please."

"Stevie, darling—"

"Mommy dear!" At last they were connected. Just as the plugs were plugged into the switchboard in Lewiston and White Plains, so now they were plugged into Harriet and Stephen. Each of them felt it enter his body, travel through his arteries, and penetrate his heart, and each of them received the connection avidly, like a blood transfusion. For a moment they were silent, they had no need for words—they had each other physically, biologically, symbiotically.

"Hello, sweetheart, how are you? I thought they'd never find you."

"Oh, Mommy, Mommy . . ."

"Tell me, darling. Tell me!"

Stephen surrendered to Harriet's voice. He let it cover him like a hot bath, relaxing every nerve and muscle, releasing every tension until his tears seemed to be issuing not only from his eyes but from his pores as well. "It's awful here, just awful—awful counselors, awful kids . . . they won't let me see Roggie. Oh, Mommy, Mommy I can't stand it here, I hate it here, I'm dying here, dying! Come and get me, Mommy; come and take me home. I love you, miss you, Mommy—"

"Ohhhh, my darling—"

"Oh, Mommy, Mommy, please don't cry!"

"Hello, *kleine,* how's my boy?" Saul interrupted from the extension in his brother-in-law's bedroom.

As soon as Stephen heard Daddy's voice he stopped crying automatically, as if some incompetent operator had disconnected him from his mother by yanking out their plugs. "Daddy?"

"What seems to be the trouble, *kleine?*"

"Wait a minute, Saul," Harriet complained tearfully.

"What do you mean? You've had your turn!"

"Please, Saul, I haven't finished yet."

"Do you mind if I speak to my son?"

"In a minute, Saul."

"No! Now! Now! Hello, Stevie?"

"Yes, Daddy."

"Darling, don't hang up when Daddy's done—"

"Harriet, will you please get off this line!"

"—I want to talk to you some more."

During his parents' exchange, Stephen began to feel cold. He had come to the phone so swiftly, purposefully—defying time and space—that he had not noticed the radical difference between the temperature on the playing field and inside the refrigerator. But now, quite suddenly, he became aware of it and wished his arms and legs were not exposed.

"Tell me, *kleine,* what's the trouble? Aren't they giving you enough to eat?"

"Oh, Saul—"

"Goddamn it, Harriet—"

"Oh, yes."

"What's that, Steve?"

"They're giving me enough to eat."

"Is somebody mistreating you?"

"No."

"You know me, I'll kill them if they are."

"I know."

"Well what's the matter, fellow?"

"I . . ." Stephen stopped himself, overcome by embarrassment and shame.

"What's that? I didn't hear you, Steve. This damn connection —you'll have to speak up."

"Nothing . . . I'm all right."

"Harriet! Did you hear that, Harriet?"

"Stevie, darling. Listen to me, darling, listen to your mother. You mustn't be afraid to tell us if there's something really wrong. You and your brother are all we have, all we care about, all that really matters to us in the world. You know that, don't you, darling?"

"What's the matter with you, Hattie? You heard what the child said, he's all right now, aren't you, fellow? He was just a little thrown by his new surroundings, weren't you, fellow? It takes a little while for anyone to acclimate himself, to grow into the swing of things. He only wanted to hear the sound of our voices, didn't you, fellow?" For the first time, Saul paused and waited for his son to respond. "Didn't you, Steve?"

"Yes."

"That's only normal, only natural. It can happen to the best—"

"Excuse me, please. The three minutes are up. Kindly signal when finished please."

"Mommy!"

"Don't be frightened, darling. I'm right here. That was just the operator. Daddy asked her to let us know when the first three minutes were up. You see, we're using Uncle Morty's phone—"

"Well, I guess we'll say good-by now, *kleine*—"

"Not yet, Saul!"

"—Just keep your chin up and keep on punching."

"Darling, we'll be up to see you at the end of the month—on Roger's birthday—just as we planned. That's not so far away, my love, only three weeks from tomorrow."

"So long, *kleine*. If you need anything just shout. You know where to reach us. Don't stand on any ceremony."

"Good-by, Daddy."

"Can I send you something, darling? Is there anything you want?"

"Come on, Hattie, say good-by and let's hang up. This is costing your brother a fortune."

"Good-by, sweetheart, don't forget how much I love you." Stephen felt his mother's words reactivate his misery and he remained silent in an effort to stifle his tears. "What's the matter, darling? Aren't you going to say good-by to Mommy?"

"Good-by," he said in a breathless falsetto that sent a poignant tremor through his entire system.

"Good-by, fellow."

"Good-by, angel."

Click . . . click . . .

"Oh, Mommy, Mommy, please don't leave me! Don't go yet. I love you, too; I love you, Mommy," Stephen cried into the dead receiver. "Don't hang up! Don't hang up!"

"Hello, Lewiston. Are you finished? Are you finished? Hang up please."

"Good-by," Stephen murmured into the receiver before returning it to its hook. "Good-by," he said again, like a muted echo of his own despair.

The refrigerator was freezing now and manifestly silent. Stephen leaned against the wooden wall and stared at the four dead cows in their suits of bloodless fat. He slid to the floor and sat in the damp sawdust, shaking, shivering, waiting for his flesh to turn colorless and numb. He knew his life was over now. He knew his mother and brother had abandoned him. He had no hope of ever seeing them again . . . this room was meant to be his tomb . . .

Suddenly the refrigerator door swung open. "What's this?" the chef demanded playfully, "A change in the menu? You want to be roasted for dinner tonight? Huh? Come on, you can't stay there, you'll catch pneumonia."

Stephen picked himself up and wandered out of the mess hall. . . . So it wasn't over after all. The Federal troops weren't coming to his rescue. He was going to have to stick it out alone, at the mercy of these savages . . . Stephen scowled. He realized that he didn't know anything about his enemy—who they were, what weapons they would use, what their strategy would be—except that they were all around him, everywhere.

Instead of returning to the baseball field, he went to his cabin and began to go from trunk to trunk, examining the stickers. *Freddie Blum:*—the tiny guy with the close-cropped hair, friendly smile—there used to be a guy named Freddie Blum at Potawatomi, I met his grandma once, she said she knew my grandpa— No wonder this guy's always smiling and trying to be nice, he must be the same Freddie Blum—No threat. *Jack Leftcourt,* the one with the glasses who walks like a freak, I wonder if he's crippled? —Can't see anything, always squinting, so grown-up and serious, never cracks a smile, never acts like a boy— His father must be a doctor— No threat. *Marvin Klein:*—the fat boy on the train with me—cried all night—what about? Mother? Brother?— No threat. *Dave Miller,* the athlete, all-star sourpuss—blond and pale like cream sauce, but powerful— Enemy. *Harold Herman*— which one's he? Oh, the clown, funny rubber face—could be wiseguy— May be enemy. Finally Stephen inspected the hand-made wooden chest that had *Uncle Clint* inscribed in red paint on its side. Stephen had no pronounced feelings about his cabin coun-selor except that he felt slightly contemptuous of his body-building equipment and wondered why anyone would want to spend all of his time standing on his hands, doing push-ups and lifting dumb-bells. —No threat.

Before lunch Stephen cornered Freddie Blum. "Didn't you go to Potawatomi?"

"Sure I did. I was beginning to think you had a twin, Stevie."

"Why?"

"You didn't seem to remember me."

"Course I do. How's your grandma, Freddie?"

"Oh she's fine. I wrote and told her you were in my cabin—"

"*Your* cabin?"

"You know what I mean, the same cabin. She'll be pleased. Don't you like it here? A whole lot more than Potawatomi? I do. I like being off by ourselves like this, away from the senior kids."

"You wouldn't say that if you had a brother over there," Stephen remonstrated, as if Roger were trapped in wartorn Finland.

"I'm sorry," Freddie said.

At lunch Uncle Clint asked his cabin if they had any good ideas what to call the weekly newspaper he was in charge of printing.

"Why don't you call it *Smoke Signal?*" Stephen suggested sarcastically.

"*Smoke Signal?*" Uncle Clint repeated, missing the point. Harold Herman illustrated Stephen's suggestion by covering and uncovering his steaming plate of chipped beef with a paper napkin and Freddie assisted by making whooping noises. "Oh! That's a great idea!" Uncle Clint said. "How would you like to write a column for us, Steve?"

"A movie column?" he asked eagerly.

"No, a kind of log—a daily log."

"No thanks," Stephen said.

"Well anyway, *Smoke Signal*'s a great idea. I think you deserve doubles on dessert."

When the rice pudding was served Stephen found it filled with too many raisins and offered his second portion to the boy on his right.

"Are you sure you don't want it?" Marvin Klein asked, unable to believe his good fortune.

"Sure."

"Gosh thanks, Stevie."

When lunch was over Marvin chased after Stephen who was walking back to the cabin alone and caught up to him. "Stevie, can I walk back with you?"

"I don't care."

"Thanks again for the rice pudding—that was awful nice of you."

"You're welcome."

"Didn't you like lunch?"

"I hate chipped beef," Stephen said. "It tastes like dead leaves —creamed. They only serve it to save money."

"You think so?"

"I know so."

"I didn't mean the food exactly, I meant I liked—" Marvin lapsed into silence, at a loss to express himself.

"The atmosphere?"

"Well not exactly, no. It was *you,* I guess. You never talked before. Hardly anybody in our cabin talks. Have you noticed that? All Jack cares about is reading books—"

"That's why he's going blind."

"Is he really?"

"Yup."

"Who told you that?"

"I have my ways of finding things out."

"How horrible!" Marvin exclaimed. "I guess that explains why he doesn't talk. And I don't talk and you don't and Herman just makes faces. Sometimes in the mess hall I would look around at the other tables and wonder what was the matter with us. We seemed to be under some kind of spell. But then, today, when you suggested *Smoke Signal,* something happened. Everyone began to talk and joke and kid around the way the other tables do. Didn't you notice? I think you broke the spell."

"Did I?"

"Yes, Stevie. You know, when we met on the train I liked you right away. And when I found out we were in the same cabin, I was so happy. I wanted so much to be your friend. I tried to be. I tried to talk to you a hundred times, but you were so unhappy you didn't even notice. Why were you so unhappy, Steve? Why do you cry every night?"

"That's not me, that's Jack."

"Jack?"

"Because he's going blind—that's what makes him cry," Stephen explained. "Like *you* were crying on the train," he added in retaliation.

"I didn't think you heard me."

"Oh, yes I did. What were you crying about? Are you going blind, too, Marvin?"

"No."

"Then what were you crying about?"

"I don't know," Marvin said, evading Stephen's suddenly-demonic eyes.

"Oh, yes you do. Tell me."

"I forget."

"No, you don't."

"It doesn't matter anymore."

"Yes, it does. Tell me."

"It's over now."

"No, it's not. Tell me."

"I said it's over."

"And *I* said tell me!" Stephen growled fiercely.

"What's the matter?" Marvin asked, staring at Stephen's bulging eyes.

"Didn't you hear my question?" Stephen paced his words slowly, tensely, turning them into a terrible threat.

"Yes."

"Goddamn it! I said tell me!" Stephen exploded, grabbing Marvin's chubby arm.

"What are you—"

"Tell me," Stephen panted and tightened his grip.

"You're hurting—"

"Tell me," he whispered almost without moving his lips, as if he were holding Marvin's forearm clenched between his teeth.

"I'd never been to camp before—I'd never been away from home—I was so afraid," Marvin cried, reproducing the tears he had shed on the train, but compounded now by the humiliating agony and indignity of his forced confession.

"Just what I thought," Stephen sneered with satisfaction, releasing Marvin's arm. "You're a crybaby, a lousy little crybaby. Don't you know there's a war going on in Finland? Hundreds of boys just your age are being killed like bugs, and you stand there crying because you're away from home." Marvin stood dumbfounded, massaging the red marks left by Stephen's brutal grip. His plump, normally relaxed features contracted with pain and his gaping mouth begged voicelessly for some explanation. "Stop it!" Stephen ordered. "Before I really give you something to cry about." As hard as Marvin strained to produce words, he was only able to gasp. "Stop it!"

At last, overcoming his fear and confusion and shock, Marvin asked, "Why did you do that?"

"Because you're a crybaby! A fat, disgusting, homesick crybaby," Stephen said, pulverizing his words and with them Marvin's spirit.

"Wait!" Marvin pleaded, running after Stephen.

"Go away, shithead! I hate your guts."

After that, Stephen and Marvin were inseparable. They went to and from the mess hall together, sat next to each other at meals and Lodge, went swimming and fishing together and took long walks. To their counselors and fellow campers they appeared to be the best of friends. In their cabin Stephen never let anyone borrow his comic books until Marvin had finished reading them first, in the mess hall Stephen invariably gave the desserts he didn't like to Marvin, and in the bathhouse whenever Marvin forgot his towel it was always Stephen who lent him his.

But when they were out of sight, when it was twilight and they were able to get off on their own, away from camp, away from the counselors, into the woods or out on the lake, alone, Stephen and Marvin behaved quite differently.

"Shall I drop the anchor here, Stevie?"

"Have you baited the hooks yet?"

"No."

"Well what are you waiting for?" Stephen asked, shifting oars and passing Marvin the can of worms.

"You know how much I hate to touch them."

"Just like my brother," Stephen sneered. "As soon as he sees a cockroach or moth—even a potato bug—he screams for help. 'Stevie! Stevie! Come and get it out of here. Get it out of here!'— just like you. Do I have to do everything?—find the worms, row the boat, bait the hooks, catch the fish!"

"No. I'd be happy to row if you'd let me."

"You! You couldn't row a walnut shell. Just bait the hooks."

"But I hate—"

"You heard me."

Marvin knit his brows in supplication. "But you do it so much better, Stevie."

"You heard me." Gingerly Marvin reached into the can, looking away as he did so. "Come on. Quit stalling. It's not going to bite you." From the sudden look of disgust on Marvin's face, Stephen knew his friend had touched a worm, and Stephen smiled. Squeamishly, Marvin raised the wriggling creature to the point of the hook and stopped. "Go on!" Stephen ordered. "Stick it in him." Reluctantly, Marvin did as he was told. "No, not that way! The fish'll steal it in a second. How many times do I have to tell you: stick it through its head. You have to work the hook through its body— just like when your pajama cord comes out— That's the way. Go on. Go on! You aren't hurting it."

By the time both hooks were baited it was dusk. The light was draining from the sky. A cloud of gnats drifted by like a tumbleweed. Except for an occasional jumping fish, the lake was still and silent. Marvin sat despondently, staring with revulsion at his blood-and-slime-stained hands. "Now," Stephen said softly, "you're going to lick them clean."

"What?"

"You're going to lick that stuff off your hands."

"No, Stevie."

"You heard me."

"No."

"I said you're going to lick your hands."

"Please, Stevie, please don't make—"

"Are you going to lick your hands or aren't you?"

"No," Marvin murmured without conviction.

"All right," Stephen said and started swaying his body from side to side, causing the boat to rock.

"What are you doing?"

"I'm going to tip us over."

"No! No!" Marvin exclaimed in panic. "You know I can't swim that well."

"Are you going to lick your hands?" While Marvin sat in silent terror debating between the alternatives, Stephen rocked the boat with increasing violence. "Have you ever seen a snapping turtle, Marvin?"

"No."

"They weigh a hundred pounds and they have teeth like a shark. They can bite a man's arm off, right up to here." Stephen pointed to his shoulder. "I've seen them do it. I've seen them chew a boy's fingers off like celery."

"Stop it! Stop it! Stevie, please!" Marvin pleaded, as Stephen tipped the boat so far to one side the water ran over the gunwale.

"There's one right here—a giant snapper—here in this lake. It lives right under us—under this very spot. It's waiting for you, Marvin, waiting to snap your arms and legs off."

"Please! Please!"

"If you don't start licking right this minute, I'm going to tip us over—"

"No!"

"—And you'll never see your family again, you'll never see—"

"All right!" Marvin cried, his usually plump, bright face contracted with pain. "All right," he surrendered, staring with abhorrence at his filthy hands.

"Go on!"

Closing his eyes, averting his head, slowly, jerkily, Marvin raised his right hand to his lips, opened his mouth and gagged.

"Go on!"

Tears the size of seedless grapes fell from Marvin's eyes, as his tongue came forth and licked the worm-slime.

"Mmmmm! Good, isn't it?" Stephen asked maternally. "Just like number-two."

Sometimes if they were lucky and happened to catch a fish, Stephen would spread its dorsal fin and use it as an instrument of torture. Or if they went into the woods, Stephen would break off a sapling and switch Marvin's bare legs and force him to walk blindfolded through a briar patch or make him take up a handful of mud and smear it over the seat of his own shorts. And afterward, if anyone happened to question Marvin about some new scratch or bruise or black-and-blue mark, he always had his answer ready, "I had a little accident." He was much too terrified to tell the truth about their secret rites. He knew that if he did, he would surely lose his life. Or if, by some miracle, he should happen to survive, he knew that Stephen would not hesitate to lie, to twist the facts, to accuse him of committing some atrocity much worse than any Stephen had committed. He knew that if it came to a showdown, Stephen would even go so far as to inflict a knife-wound on himself or break his own leg in order to furnish Chief with evidence of Marvin's guilt.

But that was not all, there was something else that prevented

Marvin from exposing his assailant. For some reason, inexplicable to himself, Marvin felt involved with Stephen in a way that made him something more than Stephen's victim. At first he reacted like a boy who's lost a fist fight and lies about it to conceal his shame. But gradually, as he saw himself helplessly, willingly return for more, Marvin began to feel like Stephen's accomplice. He began to feel as guilty of Stephen's crimes as if he had committed them himself—against himself. And finally, he began to feel much more afraid of being caught than he was hopeful of ever being saved.

At the end of July, just before Parents' Day, Stephen warned Marvin that he would kill him if Marvin told his parents anything about their little games. When their parents arrived both boys tried to act naturally; they introduced their parents to each other, took them on a joint tour of the camp, and lavished their praise on the campers, the counselors, and the food. Their parents were pleased by what they were shown and it made them quite congenial. The men discussed the comparative merits of their respective country clubs and the women discovered they had friends in common and spoke of getting together in the city.

As they strolled over the grounds, Stephen could not help but remember with incredulity that day three weeks ago when he had thought his very life depended on this visit from his parents. But now that it was happening, he felt indifferent, dispassionate, even slightly ill-at-ease. The words and kisses they exchanged were typical, traditional, but somehow now they felt mechanical and false. All of it—parents, presents, handshakes, hugs and kisses, cigars, and linen suits—seemed make-believe and false, an artificial ritual, what grownups meant by being civilized and courteous. As far as Stephen was concerned, Parents' Day was like a formal function that served no other purpose than to interrupt his *real* life—the one he lived at twilight with Marvin in the woods. And even when he and his parents drove around to senior camp to have lunch with Roggie, Stephen felt the same. He recognized his brother but for once the recognition didn't stir his heart, and he had difficulty thinking up things to say. As Stephen stared at the oilcloth-covered table, he suddenly remembered the birthday gift he had fabricated and realized that today was really Roggie's birthday, but today he had no present for him—nothing now: no need, no love, no longing. They weren't even brothers now; they were strangers. What else could you be to someone who was somewhere else? All of them were strangers now—mother, father, brother—and Stephen felt impatient for them to leave.

After lunch on Sunday, just when all the parents were preparing to leave and everyone was in the parking lot exchanging kisses and saying good-by, Stephen was startled to feel someone's hand fall on his shoulder. It was Mr. Klein. "Excuse me, Saul," he said. "Can I borrow this bruiser for a moment?"

"Sure thing, Herb," Saul said. "Anything *I* can help you with?"

"No, I just want to have a word with Steve," Mr. Klein explained, leading Stephen away from his father's car. "Steve, can you tell me what's the matter with Marvin? I know *something's* bothering him. Both my wife and I have noticed it."

Automatically Stephen assumed that Marvin had told his father everything. "Why ask me?" he said, squirming out from under Mr. Klein's paternal arm.

"Because you're his best friend."

"Am I?"

"Aren't you?"

"I don't know anything about it."

"But you do. I can tell by the way you're acting."

"Excuse me, Mr. Klein. I have to go and say good-by now," Stephen said, running back to his parents' car.

As both their parents drove away, Stephen and Marvin stood side by side in the parking lot, watching and waving good-by. "You told them, didn't you?" Stephen asked out of the side of his mouth. "Didn't you?" he demanded.

"No."

"I warned you what would happen," Stephen said, ignoring Marvin's answer. "I said I'd kill you if you told and now I'm going to do it. I'm going to kill you, Marvin," Stephen said, as he waved and smiled good-by to his parents. "Just you wait and see."

Marvin knew from the tone of his voice that Stephen wasn't kidding; he wasn't threatening or bluffing, he was really going to do it. Marvin hated himself for having been too much of a coward to tell the truth when his father had asked him what was the matter, where had his old smile gone. He wanted desperately to run after his father and escape in his car, but the car was out of sight. He knew his only hope was to keep out of Stephen's way. But how can you avoid someone with whom you live in the same cabin twenty-four hours a day?

Marvin soon discovered how impossible it was; the more he

tried to keep away from Stephen, the more ubiquitous Stephen became. In the mess hall, just when he was beginning to enjoy his food, Marvin would feel someone step on his toes—not heavily, but noticeably, just enough to remind him that he was sitting next to Stephen. At rest period when he wanted more than anything to forget it all and take a nap, Marvin was permanently conscious of Stephen lying on the cot across the aisle watching him—even when he shut his eyes and turned his back he could feel Stephen watching him. When movies were shown and Marvin took a seat, he knew even without turning around, that Stephen had managed to get the seat behind him, that presently he would feel a knuckle pressing in his ribs. Every day when he went in the water Marvin was torn by indecision—he knew that if he started to swim a hand would grab his ankle and pull him under, and if he stood still a stone would be brought down on his toes. And every night after the lights went out, Marvin lay awake afraid to breathe, afraid to move just listening, watching, waiting to be strangled in his bed.

But Stephen was in no hurry. He found it much too pleasurable to prolong his victim's agony. He realized how much more subtle and delectable it was to torture than to kill. And so he waited, waited patiently until the summer was almost over and he had driven Marvin almost insane.

On August 17, after all the other boys returned from their camping trips, the boys in cabin Eleven and cabin Twelve, under the supervision of their counselors and Dr. Siegel, set out for Maine's famous North Woods for an eight-day stay. In the morning they were trucked as far as Greenville, at the foot of Moosehead Lake, where they ate lunch before boarding the small tender which had been hired to transport them to North East Carry, another tiny harbor at the opposite end of the lake, forty miles away.

During the truck ride and lunch Marvin successfully managed to avoid Stephen by sticking close to the boys from cabin Eleven who, as Marvin knew, mistrusted and disliked Stephen. As soon as they boarded the tender Marvin infiltrated the group of excited boys collected at the bow and was relieved to notice that Stephen settled himself comfortably on top of a pile of poncho-covered sleeping bags on the portside. It wasn't long before the small craft had left the primitive little harbor and emerged into a vast, landless, choppy sea. At first the campers were thrilled by the whitecaps and responded to the pitching of their boat with choruses of "the worms crawl in, the worms crawl out," but gradually as the sky darkened and the swells intensified, they lapsed into silence, dispersed, and sat down on the deck with their backs pressed against the captain's cabin. Marvin knew immediately that he was going to be seasick, but he felt ashamed of the fact and tried to conceal it. After pushing his palms against the deck for several minutes and praying and perspiring profusely, he scrambled to his feet and rushed to the rail. Almost immediately he was joined by Dr. Siegel. "Thata boy. Let it out. Don't hold down. This lake is like a sea, worse than the Channel."

"What's the matter, Doctor?" Marvin heard Stephen inquire and he realized that Stephen must have been watching him ever since they left Greenville.

"Can't you see?" Dr. Siegel replied curtly

"*I'll* take care of him," Stephen said, moving around to Marvin's other side.

"No," Marvin moaned as loud as he could without lifting his head from the railing.

"He's all right," Dr. Siegel said. "I'll look after him."

Hearing that, Marvin felt better and stayed with the doctor for the rest of the boatride. When they reached North East Carry it began to rain heavily and everyone took shelter in an abandoned barn. After dinner, on the pretext of still feeling queasy, Marvin asked Dr. Siegel if he could sleep next to him and the doctor said of course. During the night a shrew darted over Marvin's hand; he shrieked so loudly he awakened everyone, but it didn't take long for the campers to fall back to sleep. The following morning the group rose early, ate breakfast, and hiked three or four miles east, through the woods, until they reached their permanent camp site on Lobster Pond.

As soon as Marvin saw Uncle Clint begin to distribute the pup tents, he went to Dr. Siegel and asked if he could share the doctor's tent. "Thank you, Marvin, but I must sleep under the lean-tent with the other counselors."

"I won't have another nightmare, I promise."

"It isn't that, but I must be where everyone can find me in case of emergency."

Marvin wanted to tell the doctor that *this* was an emergency but hurried over to Freddie Blum instead. "Freddie, can I share your tent with you?"

"Sorry, Marv, I promised Jack."

Finally, Marvin rushed up to Harold Herman. "Harry, can I share—"

"No, I'm sharing with Dave."

Marvin looked around him frantically. He knew that everyone from cabin Eleven would be teamed up with a pal, and he realized his fate even before he heard Stephen's voice. "Hey, Marvie, we're over here." Marvin thought of asking the counselors to let him sleep under their lean-to, but he knew they would want to know the reason why and he couldn't think up a credible excuse. "Is this your sleeping bag?" Stephen asked.

"Yes," Marvin answered listlessly.

"Come on," Stephen said, hoisting it onto his right shoulder and disappearing around a clump of alders.

When they reached their tent site, Stephen refused to let Marvin do any of the work. He cleared the ground, assembled the poles, pitched the tent, hammered down the pegs, dug the trench and padded the floor with pine needles all by himself as if he were building a home for his bride. Then he spread his poncho over the pine needles, unrolled their sleeping bags and laid them out with both heads facing the back of the tent so that he and Marvin would be able to talk at night before they went to sleep.

"Isn't it nice?" Stephen asked when he was finished. Marvin crawled into the tent clumsily like a baby bear and his swinging backside struck the front pole. "Careful," Stephen suggested sympathetically. For a moment Marvin thought his ordeal was over—Stephen had decided to be merciful—and he sighed contentedly as he flopped down on his sleeping bag. In the trees overhead some catbirds were scolding and the sunlight shone on the tan canvas. "It's like being inside a grocery bag," Stephen remarked.

"Yes," Marvin giggled. "I'm sorry, Stevie."

"For what?"

"Bumping into the tent-pole."

"Don't be silly, you couldn't help that."

"Sometimes I wish I wasn't so fat."

"It's only baby fat, you'll outgrow it."

"You think so, Stevie?"

"No, on second thought I guess you won't," Stephen said philosophically. "But it won't matter *then*."

"When?" Marvin asked with apprehension.

"When you're dead—it'll cease to be a problem then, so enjoy yourself. Enjoy yourself while you can," Stephen advised, stretching himself luxuriously and patting Marvin's cheek. "I want you to enjoy these last few days."

After that everything around them—the reindeer moss, the rocks, mushrooms, lichens, thistles, pine cones, lily pads, dandelion puffs, birch bark, blueberry bushes—everything looked brown or gray and connoted death. All the trees bore needles—the larches, spruces, pines, and firs bore needles that crunched beneath their feet like snow, sending shivers down their backs. The blazing, crackling campfires turned to ashes in front of their eyes, the metallic stars winked knowingly, the owls hooted hauntingly, and the long, cold nights left deposits of moisture and mildew everywhere. For both of them, Stephen and Marvin, the summer was over and the entire landscape had turned into a graveyard.

On August 22, their sixth day out, Uncle Clint announced at breakfast that they were going to climb Mount Spencer and everybody, except for Marvin, cheered at the news. Marvin knew this would be their last full day at Lobster Pond; tomorrow afternoon the group was scheduled to hike back to North East Carry, sleep overnight, and reboard the tender the following morning. He knew today would be the day Stephen was going to kill him—and what better way than by pushing him off the top of Mount Spencer?

Marvin dropped his mess kit and ran to Dr. Siegel. "I don't feel well, I have an awful stomach-ache," he gasped, holding himself and bending over as if he was in excruciating pain.

"Where is it, Marvin?" the doctor asked with concern.

"All over."

"Does it hurt you when I press you here?" he asked, applying pressure to Marvin's appendix.

"Yes."

"More than here?"

"No."

"You're sure?"

"It hurts all over."

"Maybe you had better not come with us up the mountain," Dr. Siegel suggested and he arranged with Uncle Clint for Marvin to stay behind and guard the camp until they returned in the afternoon.

At one o'clock, after everyone had been gone for hours and he had read every comic book in sight, Marvin decided to take advantage of the sun. He went and got his sleeping bag, dragged it into the open, and stretched himself on top of it, directly under the blazing sun. For the first time in over a month he felt relaxed and peaceful, he felt the sunshine bake away his tensions and bring a smile to his lips. He shut his eyes and fell into a half-sleep, oblivious to everything but the tweeting birds and the blistering sun. But after fifteen or twenty minutes, through his closed eyelids he saw the sunlight fade and felt its warmth disappear. Almost unconsciously he opened his languid eyes to look at the cloud that had come between him and his source of bliss. Stephen was standing in front of him.

"Thought you could sneak away from me, huh?"

"How?—"

"Well, two can play the same game as one. I pulled the same stunt you did."

It didn't occur to Marvin to reason with Stephen, not because he realized how futile it would be, but just because he didn't stop to think; he scrambled to his feet and ran frantically into the woods.

Stephen started after him. He knew that Marvin was a hopeless runner and that he would wind himself in a very short time, so he didn't rush. He had no idea what he would do to Marvin when he caught him—terrorize him more perhaps, maybe even punch him once or twice—but he realized that his pleasure lay in this pursuit, this chase, this stalking of Marvin through the woods—whatever happened afterward would be an anticlimax. And so he walked on slowly, keeping his eye on Marvin, watching him stumble over logs, thrash aside the underbrush, and crash between the trees.

As many times as Marvin tripped or fell he always managed to pick himself up again and keep on going. Stephen was astonished by the endurance of his quarry. He had no idea what direction they were moving in—whether north or east—but he sensed they were circling the pond. The sun was still overhead and very hot even through the trees, and Stephen began to feel tired and thirsty. He hated the cobwebs that kept taking him by surprise and breaking across his face and he wiped them away with disgust. He knew how susceptible he was to poison ivy and began to suspect every leaf he touched—whether brown or green, round or pointed—of carrying the poison, and his arms and legs began to itch. When he wasn't scratching, he used his arms to flail away the insects that were attacking him from every side. It wasn't long before Stephen's pleasure turned into complete discomfort and it was only his pride, like Marvin's fear, that drove him on.

After trailing Marvin for more than forty minutes, Stephen sat down on a bed of moss to remove a pebble from his shoe. In the time it took him to unlace his shoe, shake the pebble out, massage the irritated spot and put his shoe back on, Marvin disappeared.

Stephen leaped to his feet and ran in the direction he had last seen Marvin moving. After running a hundred yards or so, he came to a fallen maple and stopped and stood perplexed, not knowing whether Marvin had hurdled the tree or gone off at a tangent. He peered through the trees in all directions and listened intently, but neither heard nor saw a sign of Marvin. "All right, wiseguy," Stephen shouted at the top of his lungs, "you think you can get away with this? You think I don't see you hiding over there! You better come out now, before I come in and get you. You hear me, Marvin? I'm going to count to three and if you're not out here by the time I finish, I'm going to come in there and get you. One!" Stephen watched and waited, but nothing stirred. "You think I'm bluffing, don't you? Well, just you wait and see. Two!" Again he waited, but nothing stirred. "Three!" Once again nothing stirred. "All right, pusshead, I can wait as long as you can," Stephen shouted and sat down flamboyantly on the trunk of the fallen tree. "You can't stay in there forever. You'll have to come out sooner or later and when you do, you know what's going to happen? I'm going to take you by the hair and drag you to the pond and tie you to a tree and tear off all your clothes. And then I'm going to get a lot of leeches and stick them all over that fat, disgusting, body of yours—on your eyelids and in your ears and up your nose and in your belly button and over your balls, and watch them suck your filthy blood!"

Stephen went on sitting there alone like that, talking to himself, concocting more and more satanic tortures until the sound of a loud, resounding crack arrested his attention. Without thinking, he started running in the direction of the noise. As he ran he heard the noise again and he couldn't imagine what Marvin was doing or how he could be so stupid as to give himself away like that. Had he gone berserk? Was he beating the trunk of a tree with a stick? Suddenly Stephen realized that the noise had ceased. He had not heard it for a minute or more and couldn't be sure that he was running in the right direction. Had Marvin heard his footsteps? Stephen stopped, stood absolutely still and stared into a bed of ferns, a clump of juniper, a blueberry patch, some alder shrubs, straining to catch a glimpse of Marvin. As he stood, surveying the area, Stephen gradually became aware of another noise, a very different noise from the one he had heard at first. This one was sustained and sounded animal or human, a series of low grunting groans accompanied by other sounds—scuffling, thumping sounds that Stephen could not quite distinguish. Had Marvin been attacked by a bear? Was he being eaten?

At first Stephen thought of turning back, but the sounds were too arresting, too intriguing, and compelling to leave unexplored, and he got down on his hands and knees and began to crawl through the underbrush. In some places the ground was moist, a compost of mud and moss, dead leaves and pine needles; in others it was dry and scratchy, covered with lichen and sharp-edged stones, but Stephen barely noticed either. He was too intent on discovering the source of the mysterious coughs and grunts that were growing more intense the more he advanced through the underbrush. He could see a clearing now, thirty feet ahead of him —some grass, a hillock, trunks of trees—and he wriggled toward it cautiously, hypnotically, an inch at a time, not daring to make a sound.

As Stephen approached the clearing he began to be conscious of a foul aroma. The closer he came the more intense the stench became—musky, pungent, putrid—until, at last, it overwhelmed him, made him stop and shut his eyes and gag with nausea. When he recovered and was able to move again, Stephen opened his eyes and gasped audibly.

To one side of the clearing he saw two enormous, gray-brown beasts—bull moose!—their withers humped, their heads thrust low, their antlers locked, their hind legs braced—the one's against a heavy log, the other's against a pine tree—butting, shoving one another back and forth over two or three feet of disputed ground. As Stephen stared at their heaving flanks, their powerful, pugnacious shoulder blades, their bent and straining hindquarters, he wanted to run but didn't dare for fear of being noticed, charged, trampled. He didn't dare to budge or breathe.

Suddenly the moose that was braced against the log began to lose ground—the log began to slip! The animal was thrown off balance, backward, onto its haunches, but instead of trying to regain its balance it drew its hind legs together helplessly and began to urinate. In response the other moose began to grunt and hoof the ground, kicking up the sod and thrashing its antlers from side to side. Before the first moose had time to recover its stance, the moose on the offensive lowered its swinging head and charged, heaving its opponent into the air and gouging its breast with its antlers. Even before the assaulted beast began to bellow, Stephen clapped his hands over his eyes and gritted his teeth. The bellow was followed by a deafening din of crashing, cracking noises as if the entire woods were being stampeded and razed. Stephen waited, tense and trembling, until the woods was silent before he removed his hands and saw that the moose were gone.

When he got to his feet he felt unsteady. His head was light, his heart pounding, his legs weak, as he stumbled into the clearing. All the topsoil as far as the edge of the woods had been overturned and scattered. All of the brush had been uprooted, slashed, torn apart and trampled. Even some of the smaller trees had been broken or kicked over, and larger ones were scarred and running sap. Stephen stared around him at the devastation. Next to his shoe he spotted the point of an antler, six or seven inches long, and he stopped to pick it up. It was beige and gray and slightly sticky, stained with blood.—Stephen let it drop. Once again he smelled that pungent, putrid odor—suddenly connected in his mind with the urinating moose—and he traced it to a soggy shallow pit whose stench was overpowering. This time Stephen did more than gag, he retched up everything—the sandwiches he'd gulped at noon, the pancakes he had had for breakfast. As he did he coughed and moaned and cried uncontrollably, helplessly, desperate and alone. When it was over, he slouched across the clearing—as far away as he could get from the foul-smelling pit—and slumped against a tree.

On the ground beside him he noticed a furry, brownish animal about the size of a water rat. He waited to see if it would move, but it didn't. He picked up a stick and poked it, but still it didn't move. At last he reached out cautiously and took it in his hand. When he turned it over he discovered it wasn't an animal at all but a huge hank of hair and flesh, raw and bloody, torn from the hide of the defeated moose. Stephen hurled it away from him and stared at his outspread fingers. Compulsively, almost in a state of trance, he brought his bloodstained hand closer and closer to his face, but before he had a chance to smell or taste the blood, he fainted.

When Uncle Clint and Dr. Siegel finally found Stephen it was almost dusk and he was still unconscious. As Dr. Siegel brought him to, Stephen kept repeating "Roggie . . . Roggie . . ." not lovingly or longingly, but with a fierce malevolence. When they asked him what had happened, why the clearing looked the way it did, Stephen said, "I didn't do it."

"Of course not, Steve, you couldn't have," Uncle Clint remarked, "but what in the world did?"

"I didn't do it," Stephen said. After they got him on his feet and were walking back to camp, Dr. Siegel asked who Roggie was, but Stephen refused to say anything but "I didn't do it" over and over again.

"What? Do what?" the doctor and Uncle Clint asked in unison.

"I didn't do it," Stephen said, but in his heart he knew that he was lying. He knew that he had succeeded in killing Marvin Klein at last, and no amount of medicine or talk—not even the sight of Marvin himself, standing outside their pup tent, brushing out his sleeping bag and staring at him wonderingly—could convince Stephen of his innocence.

MONKEYS

Stephen rested his folded arms on the iron railing in front of the cage and watched the chimps with new awareness. As a child he had had a toy monkey named Oscar that had glass eyes, a felt face, felt hands and feet, and a body made of clean, soft, odorless plush. As a child, when Stephen went to bed at night he invariably took Oscar with him, when he went to the zoo with his father he insisted on calling every monkey Oscar, and when he encountered an organ grinder's monkey on Broadway he always presented his penny to Oscar. Even now, at the age of twelve, Stephen had a perfectly proportioned, German-made, miniature monkey, three inches tall, that he carried around with him in his trouser pocket and called Oscar II.

But today, for the first time in his life, Stephen had come to the zoo not with an adult—not with his father or mother or nurse—but with a classmate, Dennis Abrams, and he had seen monkeys that created paradoxes in his mind—monkeys he could not reconcile with Oscar. He had seen a baboon's bloodshot backside, an orangutan's distended throat pouch, a Capuchin monkey's infant penis, a rhesus monkey's fallen breasts; he had looked into the eyes of monkeys and seen the terror, fury, wisdom, wonder they contained—their cunning and contempt, weariness and wit; he had noticed little fragile hands with bony knuckles that reminded him of frog's feet, and gibbons' hands like pickpockets' hands with long and agile fingers. He had watched with fascination monkeys eating, sleeping, nursing, defecating, delousing one another, fornicating, masturbating, mimicking the visitors, and spitting in their faces; he had been delighted to see them clap their hands and keen, perform like aerialists, assume attitudes of contemplation, or be seized by fits that sent them bounding off the bars and walls as if their fur were on fire.

At this moment, as Stephen watched intently, one of the chimps hopped into a rubber tire suspended from the roof, seated itself rakishly and thrust its flat foot against the wall of the cage, setting

167

the tire in motion. The chimp, conscious of its audience—Stephen and Dennis, a little boy and a portly matron—lounged back sybaritically, grinning with exaggerated smugness and superiority.

"Look! Look, Clarence," the matron said, calling her grandson's attention to the swinging chimp. "See how nice he plays. Nice monkey, nice monkey. Make nice-monkey, Clarence."

"Clarence big boy swing in Cadillac?" Clarence asked.

"That's right, darling," the matron answered without understanding. "And look at the other one, look at his table manners, see how nice he eats. See how he peels the apple, darling, just like grandma does for Clarence." Then, looking up from her grandson and turning to Stephen, she added, "They're human, positively human."

"Come on, Stevie, this is boring," Dennis complained.

As Stephen watched the chimp cast aside the piece of tooth-scraped apple peel, he was reminded of the hands of Gussie, his mother's laundress. "No. Let's just stay another minute," Stephen said, seeing the first chimp hop off the tire, waddle to the front of the cage and squat beside a pile of feces. As if it were returning to some immemorial, unsolved riddle the chimp leaned over the feces and examined them with an expression of philosophic seriousness mixed with mild boredom. How much like that picture of Pythagoras, Stephen thought, as the chimp poked its index finger into the soft feces and began to doodle on the cement floor, glancing up only now and then to stare vacantly at Stephen or Dennis or Clarence's scandalized grandmother.

"Clarence poop a picture too!" Clarence exclaimed excitedly, clutching his groin.

"Nasty!" the grandmother hissed at the chimp. "Come on, darling, let's go and see the seals," she said as she walked away from in front of the cage and waited for Clarence to follow.

"Come on, Stevie," Dennis said.

Neither Clarence nor Stephen budged; both were too absorbed in watching the chimp raise its feces-covered finger to its nose.

"Clarence! Did you hear me, Clarence!" the grandmother called impatiently.

After smelling it a moment, the chimp drew its finger down over the surface of its enormous, coconut-shaped upper lip, pulled out its lower lip and stuck the finger into its mouth.

"Little Jack Horner, sat in a corner, eating a Christmas poop—" Clarence recited.

"Clarence!"

"That's disgusting," Dennis said, referring to the chimp, and walked away from Stephen's side and left the building.

"He stuck in his thumb and pulled out a poop . . ." Clarence continued, making himself giggle uncontrollably, but the next moment his grandmother swooped down on him.

"Now I've had enough of this! Quite enough! When I say come, I mean come!" she scolded, seizing her bawling grandson by the hand and dragging him out of the monkey house.

Left alone, Stephen reached into his trouser pocket and removed Oscar II. But somehow Oscar looked different now. He had lost all of his familiar human traits: his ability to talk, to sympathize, be sensitive, conspire, console, express affection. Whereas, prior to this moment, Stephen had always been able to minimize and even void the difference between their dimensions, now, suddenly, Oscar looked pathetically diminutive. Not only that, he looked inanimate, insensible—unreal. Stephen stuffed Oscar back into his pocket and returned his attention to the chimps. One of them was picking its nose, and Stephen was reminded of the matron's remark, "They're human, positively human." But why, he wondered, if they were human, did Mommy make such a fuss whenever he or Roggie picked his nose? Given their terms—his mother's and the matron's—wasn't Oscar II actually more human than either of these chimps? And yet hadn't Stephen just a minute ago discovered the opposite to be true: that Oscar was a toy.

"Come on, Steve," Dennis complained, rejoining his friend. "Didn't you say you have a Hebrew lesson at five?"

"What time is it?" Stephen watched Dennis remove a gold antique timepiece from his vest pocket. For some reason Dennis Abrams at the age of twelve dressed and acted like a man in his fifties. He always wore a suit and vest, white shirt, tie, and stickpin; he walked with a stoop, talked pompously, and seemed permanently anxious to conserve his strength. Often Stephen wondered why he spent so much time with Dennis when, quite obviously, he much preferred the company of other classmates such as Jimmy Reuben, Peter Bakst, and Peter Schuster.

"Four-seventeen," Dennis said, snapping the watch shut and returning it to his vest. "What did you find so fascinating in there?" he challenged, as they descended the steps toward the sea lions.

"Where?"

"In the monkey house."

"Oh, everything!"

"To see a monkey eating its own excrement! Degenerate! That's what it is, degenerate! They're neurotic, all of them. That's why I'm opposed to zoos: they make animals neurotic. I don't know why the A.S.P.C.A. permits it."

"Wouldn't monkeys do that if they weren't in the zoo?"

"Of course not! They're primates, after all, like us, like men. You don't see men doing things like that."

"Didn't you ever—" Fearful that his question might pertain exclusively to himself, might expose him to his friend as a degenerate neurotic, Stephen censored it. "Wait a minute!" he explained, taking hold of the iron fence around the sea-lion pool.

"What now?" Dennis asked with exaggerated patience.

"Let's just watch a second."

"Suit yourself. *You're* the one who's going to be late for his Hebrew lesson, not *I!*"

"How come you don't study Hebrew, Dennis?"

"I'm not going to be *bar mitzvahed.*"

"You aren't?" Stephen asked incredulously. "How come?"

"I just don't happen to believe in God," Dennis explained.

"You don't?"

"No. Do you? I mean *really?*"

Stephen didn't understand what Dennis meant by really, but he was intimidated by his friend's condescending tone. "I think I do," he faltered. "Doesn't everybody?"

"Certainly not. No informed person does—nowadays."

At this moment one of the sea lions broke the surface, and Stephen watched the length of its glistening black body revolve and ooze back out of sight. He remembered his childhood visits to the Aquarium at Battery Park—the curving dim interior, the windowed tanks, the fish, the flesh, the eels and rays and porpoises appearing, disappearing, reappearing from the depths, convolving through the green translucency as if they had no bones or joints, no other business but sensuality. What would monkeys be like if they had the sea to move in? Like porpoises? Were porpoises the monkeys of the sea? Suddenly Stephen's head was filled with an orgy of eels and seals and salamanders; and the big red rubber ball—twice as big as a water-polo ball—that floated in the swimming pool at school, gleamed at him alluringly, tempting him to mount it . . .

"Come on, Stevie," Dennis grumbled.

The words broke Stephen's reverie and he found himself staring at a red balloon held by a child on the opposite side of the pool.

As the boys strolled past the corner of the cafeteria and the empty, outdoor elephant cage, Stephen decided to ask Dennis a question that had been disturbing him greatly. "Dennis."

"What?"

But Stephen could not bring himself to articulate the question. "I don't know," he said. "Let's go through the Mall."

It was the first Friday in October and the formally trellised wisteria vines, still in leaf, arbored the promenade behind the concrete bandstand shell. "Whenever I walk through here," Dennis said, slowing down his pace, tilting his slightly oversized Roman head and clasping his hands behind his back, "I'm always reminded of Tivoli."

"Are you?"

"Now there, there's my idea of a cultivated person."

"Tivoli?"

"No, stupid. Hadrian. There were no chimps at the Villa Adriana; *that*, I can assure you. Peacocks perhaps . . . flocks of peacocks drifting in and out among the works of art. And swans perhaps, but never chimps. Not when one's entire life is dedicated to the cause of beauty."

"*I* always think of the Tower of London," Stephen said, referring to the broad cement steps that encircled the back of the bandstand shell. "Did you ever see that movie?" Stephen asked, distorting his features, hunching his shoulders, hugging the wall and limping down the steps. " 'A horse! A horse! My kingdom for a horse!' " he cried, rushing out onto the stage of the bandstand, dragging his right foot behind him.

Instead of joining his friend, Dennis went and sat on one of the hundreds of regimented benches in front of the bandstand and waited with exaggerated tolerance. "You better come down from there before you're arrested," he said soberly.

"Arrested for what?"

"Disturbing the peace, obviously. No wonder you like chimps so much," Dennis remarked, watching his friend jump to the ground, "you act just like one."

"Do I?" Stephen asked with more curiosity than resentment. "Sometimes."

"Dennis," Stephen said, sitting down next to his friend.

"What?"

"Will you tell me something?"

"Certainly."

"Promise not to tell anyone I asked—ever?"

"I promise."

"You swear?"

"Oh stop acting so infantile! I gave you my word, what more do you want?"

"Well . . . I've been wondering . . ."

"Yes. What?"

"Do you know what sperm looks like?"

Before replying, Dennis nodded his head judiciously to indicate he knew the answer. "Sperm is a white fluid, rather like milk in its consistency and color."

"White . . . ?" Stephen reflected a moment before speaking again. "How do you know?"

"How do you think? I read it in Munsom's *Fundamentals of Biology*," Dennis said, getting up and continuing their walk. Even though he had dealt with Stephen's question dispassionately, clinically, Dennis felt a need to clear the air and so he stopped for a moment in front of the solemn bust of Beethoven and Terpsichore. "Which of the symphonies do you like best?"

Stephen, who had only just begun to collect classical records that autumn and whose entire collection consisted of Brahms' *First,* Tchaikovsky's *Fourth,* Ravel's *Bolero,* and Debussy's *Clair de Lune,* took a wild guess. "The Third."

"Do you really? Of course there's no denying the power of the Third but personally I prefer the Ninth. I must play my new recording for you. Bruno Walter. Some people still insist Furtwängler does it better, but I don't happen to agree."

. . . *A white fluid rather like milk in its consistency and color* . . . White . . . white, Stephen thought, repeating the word over and over all the way home, and wondering . . . what have I been doing wrong?

"Hello, Mr. Stephen," Max, the elevator man on the G-H side of the apartment house, said.

"Hello, Max," Stephen replied politely, stepping into the walnut paneled car and walking to his usual spot in the rear left corner, diagonally opposite the operator.

"Nice weather," Max said, closing the door and starting the elevator.

"Yes." As always, Stephen's answer was followed by an awkward, interminable silence, accentuated by the motor's hum and the creaking of the cables, during which Max faced front and smacked his saliva, and Stephen stared at the dark embossed panels. Coming from the sunny street, the park, his school, into this formidable, overbearing elevator was always a difficult transition for Stephen. The ride upstairs made him anxious, self-conscious, reticent. It was like the ascent of the parachute on the parachute jump at the World's Fair, except that here, when you reached the top, there was no release: you didn't come down for hours and hours, you had to stay up there, suspended, overnight. . . . Thank God tomorrow was Saturday: *Rebecca* was at RKO. Saturday! . . . For a moment Stephen lost his breath. . . Wasn't it for tomorrow morning that Father had made the appointment with Dr. Schwartz? What if Dr. Schwartz discovered—? Stephen bit his fingernail.

"Here we are: seventeen," Max said.

"Thank you, Max." Stephen walked across the dimly-lit maroon-carpeted hall and inserted his key in G.

"Is that my baby?" Harriet said, hearing the front door close. "Where have you been? Where have you been, sweetheart?"

Harriet came out of the dining room holding two white chrysanthemums. Stephen had forgotten that tonight was Mommy's turn to entertain her family. "Nowhere."

Harriet hugged and kissed Stephen until he forcibly freed himself from her embrace. "I thought something had happened. I thought you got run over. I was just about to call the police."

"Why?" he asked defensively.

"It's five-to-five."

"Is Rabbi Pulvermacher here already?"

"No. But he will be any minute. Look at you! Look at your hair," Harriet criticized, trying to restore his pompadour.

Stephen warded off his mother's hand. "Don't."

"You better go inside and wash and put a clean shirt on— Do it now, sweetheart. You won't have time afterward. Grandpa's coming. We're having turkey and sweet potatoes. I told Annie to *bake* yours, darling. As a matter of fact I told her to bake two, so don't hold back— They're both for you. . . . What is that?" Harriet interrupted herself, noticing the bulge Oscar II made in Stephen's trousers. "What have you got in your pocket?"

"Nothing."

"Why do you say nothing? I can see—" As Harriet reached out

to investigate the bulge, Stephen turned away and walked into the dining room. "Where are you going?"

"To get another chair for the rabbi."

"I've done that already, darling. I had to give him a bridge chair tonight; we need all these in here."

The Marghab cloth was on the table. It was set for twelve with the Minton china, the crystal glasses, and the old English flatware. As if they were banderillas, Harriet thrust the last two chrysanthemums into the silver epergne, completing her arrangement. "And I've put out the pencils and paper, too—so everything's ready. All you need to do is wash and comb your hair and change your shirt. Oh, and darling, when you do, don't put that awful Roosevelt button back on."

"Why not?"

"You know how much it upsets Uncle Lloyd."

"But I want to wear it."

"Please don't, darling. For me."

"No."

"Please. Do it for Mommy."

"No!"

"Is that the thanks I get for having everything you like?—sweet potatoes, giblet gravy, stuffing. All I ever do is think of you, and this is the thanks I get. You won't even make the littlest effort. Not the littlest!" Harriet hissed, slashing the air with her hands. "You always do this to me when company's coming! Always. Well just you wait 'til your father comes home! Just you wait!" she threatened fiercely, as if she were forcing her words through a sieve. At that moment the doorbell rang. "Oh my God!" she gasped, "the rabbi! Quickly! Quickly! Go inside. Go inside. *I'll* get the door."

Stephen decided to wash now, but change his shirt *after* the lesson—that way he would be able to postpone a little longer the ordeal of facing his relatives. By the time he finished in the bathroom and was heading toward his bedroom, he overheard Harriet saying, "You don't need to tell *me*, Rabbi, I know! He's a most extraordinary child. I suppose, for the sake of modesty, I ought to say unusual—a most unusual child. Mr. Wolfe wants him to study law. We think our baby has the natural gifts to make a brilliant trial lawyer: his voice, his looks, his height, his amazing dramatic ability— He gets that from me, Rabbi. When I was seventeen—"

"I'm sorry, Rabbi," Stephen interrupted, entering the bedroom.

"Oh, there you are. We were just talking about you, lovey. Were

your ears burning? I was telling Rabbi Pulvermacher that Daddy
thinks—"

"Mommy, *please!*"

"Oh, I can take a hint," Harriet said, standing up. "Have a good
lesson, angel, and don't forget to change that shirt. I'll see you on
your way out, Rabbi."

"Thank you, Mrs. Wolfe," the rabbi said. He was a kindly but
humorless, tired, ashen-looking man in his early forties.

As usual, after he had donned his skullcap, Stephen began the
lesson by writing and reciting the Hebrew alphabet. *"Aleph, beth,
gimel, daleth, he, waw . . ."* he droned, hearing the doorbell and
realizing that the first guest had arrived. It was Aunt Milly, his
mother's sister; he recognized her singsong greeting, as the front
door slammed.

"Pay attention, Stephen."

". . . Cadhe, goph, res, sin, taw." Again the front door
slammed; this time it was Roggie.

When they were finished with the alphabet, Rabbi Pulvermacher
reviewed the prayer for wine that he had taught his pupil the week
before. Though he pretended to be reading at sight, Stephen rattled
off the words by heart. *"Baruch athah Adonai elohaynu melech
ha'olem boray pre hagoffen."* Just as they turned to another
prayer—the prayer for bread—the doorbell rang again: it was
Grandpa and Aunt Ida, Grandpa's second wife.

As always, Rabbi Pulvermacher devoted the last fifteen or
twenty minutes of the hour to the study of Jewish holidays, laws,
and customs. After four years of Sunday school, Stephen was
familiar with most of this material, but he had never before been
directly exposed to its source: the Books of Moses. Stephen had
mixed feelings about these Books. As much as he loved the stories
of Cain and Abel, Abraham and Isaac, Jacob and Esau, Joseph
and his brothers, he was bored and disturbed by the endless ex-
hortations that interrupted them.

> *Obey the commandments of the Lord thy God. . . . Thou
> shalt not kill, thou shalt not commit adultery, thou shalt not
> steal, thou shalt not bear false witness, thou shalt not covet
> thy neighbor's ass, thou shalt not: . . . transgress, abomi-
> nate, corrupt, defile, pollute, profane . . . The Lord thy God
> is a jealous God: obey Him, serve Him, fear Him, fear **His**
> anger, fear His wrath, fear His vengeance, put evil away from*

> *among you . . . . . . make atonement for thy sins, offer burnt
> offerings, sacrifice, anoint, purify. The Lord shall surely smite
> thee, ye shall surely perish, surely be punished, surely be put
> to death.*

It did not occur to Stephen to question these words; he accepted
them as sacred, and they succeeded in filling his mind and heart
with fear.

Continuing tonight from where they had left off the week before,
Rabbi Pulvermacher asked Stephen to start with Leviticus 15.
" 'And the Lord spake unto Moses and to Aaron, saying,' " Stephen commenced in a monotone, " 'Speak unto the children of
Israel, and say unto them, when any man hath a running issue out
of his flesh, because of his issue he is unclean. And this shall be his
uncleanness in his issue: whether his flesh run with his issue, or his
flesh be stopped from his issue, it is his uncleanness. Every bed,
whereon he lieth that hath the issue, is unclean: and every thing
whereon he sitteth, shall be unclean. And whosoever toucheth his
bed . . . ' " As he went on Stephen grew more and more perplexed,
until at last he stopped and asked, "Rabbi, what does issue
mean?"

"Any kind of suppuration."

"Suppuration?"

"Pus."

His teacher's answer satisfied Stephen, but only temporarily.
" 'And if any man's seed of copulation go out from him, then he
shall wash all his flesh in water, and be unclean until the even. And
every garment, and every skin, whereon is the seed of copulation,
shall be washed with water, and be unclean until the even . . .' "
. . . But that means sperm not pus, Stephen thought, trying, without raising his head, to catch a glimpse of his teacher's face, but
the rabbi's expression was inscrutable. " '. . . And if a woman
have an issue, and her issue in her flesh be blood—' " . . . Blood!
Now it's blood. Pus and sperm and blood . . . To clarify his confusion, Stephen glanced at the chapter precis: *Uncleanness of men
and women in their issues.*

"Go on, Stephen. Our time is almost up."

" '. . . And if it be on her bed, or on any thing whereon she
sitteth, when he toucheth it, he shall be unclean until the even.
And if any man lie with her at all, and her flowers be upon him, he
shall be unclean seven days; and all the bed whereon he lieth shall
be unclean. And if a woman have an issue of her blood many days

out of the time of her separation; all the days of the issue of her uncleanness shall be as the days of her separation: she shall be unclean. Every bed whereon she lieth . . .' " Once again the front door slammed. Stephen heard his father's whistle, followed by his mother's voice, "Here's the lord and master, now." . . . *The Lord thy God is a jealous God: obey Him, serve Him, fear Him, fear His anger, fear His wrath—*

"You aren't concentrating, Stephen," Rabbi Pulvermacher said impatiently.

" '. . . Thus shall ye separate the children of Israel from their uncleanness; that they die not in their uncleanness, when they defile my tabernacle that is among them. This is the law of him that hath an issue, and of him whose seed goeth from him, and is defiled therewith; and of her that is sick of her flowers, and of him that hath an issue, of the man and of the woman, and of him that lieth with her that is unclean.' "

When the lesson was over, Stephen accompanied his teacher only as far as the bedroom door and said good night. As he began to change his shirt, he heard the commingled shouts, squeals, and laughter of his family coming from the living room. After hesitating a full minute, he finally selected a red wool tie figured with foxes, put it on and tied it. Not satisfied with the knot, he undid it and retied it. Still dissatisfied, he open it again and tied it for the third time. Just as he was about to repeat this ritual, Harriet entered the room.

"What's keeping you? Everybody's here. Everybody's waiting."

"I'll be there in a second," Stephen answered irritably.

"Well please hurry, darling. I don't want the turkey to get too dry."

By the time Stephen reached the foyer, that lay like a no-man's-land between the living room and dining room, it was 6:25, and all the lamps stood engulfed in clouds of cigar and cigarette smoke. "There he is! There's my *kleine!*" Saul said.

"Always making an entrance," Roger said in an aside.

"Looks to me like you've gained more weight, young man," Uncle Lloyd commented.

"Oh, he's all right, the bruiser," Saul apologized.

"He takes after *me,*" Aunt Milly shouted.

"Come and say hello to Grandpa," Harriet said, rescuing Stephen and convoying him past his aunts and uncles to the far end of the living room where her father sat in her husband's favorite armchair.

"Hello, Grandpa." Kiss.

"Hello, Sonny," Grandpa said, pinching Stephen's cheek. "He gets bigger every time, *Gott sei dank.*"

"Hello, Aunt Ida." Kiss. Her heavily powdered flesh was as loose and soft as the throat sac of a toad.

"Hello, my darling," Aunt Ida effused. "Why don't you ever come to see me?"

"He's too busy with his schoolwork, Ida," Harriet explained curtly.

"Hello, Uncle Lloyd," Stephen said, bowing from the waist. He knew how much his father hated this habit of his of bowing instead of "shaking hands like a man," but Stephen could not help himself.

"Hello, young man," Uncle Lloyd said. "What are you doing with that Roosevelt button, trying to ruin my weekend?"

"Stevie, what did I say when you came home this evening?" Harriet asked.

"I've told him who the best man is," Saul added, "but if he wants to be stubborn and vote for Roosevelt, that's all right with me. I don't interfere with my children."

Stephen wondered why his father had used the word vote.

"Never mind," Uncle Marc said. "Don't let them tease you, Stevie. You've picked the winner."

"Will you stop corrupting the child, Marcus," Uncle Lloyd said.

"If you ask me," Aunt Pearl announced in her Smith voice, "there isn't a particle of difference between the two."

"No difference?" Saul roared. "Between the TVA—"

"If you ask *me,*" Aunt Peg put in, always eager to needle her sister-in-law, Pearl, "I'd like to see Eddie Duchin in the White House."

"That playboy!" Harriet said dismissively.

"Hello, Aunt Peg." Kiss.

"Hello, handsome," Aunt Peg flirted. "When are you going to take me dancing?"

"You should live so long, Peggy," Harriet interceded.

"Du hörst? Tanzen!" Grandpa muttered, repeating for the benefit of Aunt Ida what the *shikse* had just said.

"Hello, Aunt Pearl." Kiss. "Hello, Aunt Milly." Kiss. "Hello, Uncle Marc." Bow. "Hello, Uncle Morty." Bow.

"Dad's been telling us you've made the football team," Uncle

Morty said. Before Stephen had a chance to deny his father's fallacious report, his uncle added, "Congratulations."

"What position do they have you in?" Uncle Lloyd asked aggressively.

"Guard. Left guard," Saul boasted.

"Left *out*," Roger emended.

"What kind of position is that for a nephew of *mine?*" Uncle Lloyd sneered. "You ought to be in the backfield—quarterback! —calling the plays. The line's no place for a boy with your intelligence. You belong in the rear with the officers, not up front with the rookies."

"Oh, he's all right, the loafer," Saul said, ruffling Stephen's hair.

"Enough with the Olympic games," Grandpa said. "Tell me, Sonny, how goes the Hebrew lessons?"

"You should hear him, Pop," Saul said. "He's a real talmudic scholar. Aren't you, *kleine?*"

"Let me hear the *brucha* for wine," Grandpa said.

Before Stephen had a chance to open his mouth, his father began speaking the prayer. *"Baruch atah Adonai . . .* Come on, *kleine,"* Saul laughed uneasily, "stop teasing Grandpa. You know how it goes."

For the life of him Stephen could not remember, now, the rest of the words—the very same ones he had recited so easily an hour ago. All he could think was: *. . . The Lord shall surely smite thee . . . a white fluid rather like milk in its consistency and color . . . uncleanness of men and women in their issues . . .*

". . . *Elohaynu melech ha'olem,"* Saul continued prompting. "I tell you, Pop, he knows it as well as his own name. Come on, *kleine,* lets hear you finish with a bang."

"What seems to be the trouble, *kleine?*" Uncle Lloyd baited Stephen.

"Don't be such a *knacker,* Lloyd!" Grandpa grumbled. "Can *you* do any better, my devout, religious son?"

"Come on everybody," Harriet intervened quickly. "Dinner's ready. Come on, Pop. Come on, Ida. Dinner's served."

At dinner Stephen was much too busy overeating to speak a word. He drank his soup, ate a turkey wing, the second joint, both sweet potatoes richly buttered, two extra-large helpings of stuffing drowned in giblet gravy, two hard rolls and butter, and two thick slices of cranberry sauce. In addition Harriet donated her own roll and butter to her son, as well as two sizable pieces of turkey skin which, as she remarked, were just the way Stevie liked them: crisp! And when it came time to serve the cake, Harriet cut Stephen a double slice because she knew that chocolate was her baby's favorite.

As always, after dinner the men set up a bridge table in the foyer and played pinochle; the women retired to the living room to eat candy and gossip. As always, Roger went along with the men to kibitz; Stephen with the ladies to listen—or, more precisely, to wait until enough time had elapsed to excuse himself with propriety. As always, tonight the time dragged for Stephen. Harriet disclosed the name of a wholesale house she had discovered that sold Kislav gloves at a considerable discount. To the envy of all, Aunt Peg modeled the new "skins" (they were sables) she had just "picked up" at Bergdorf's. Not to be outshone, Aunt Milly produced the pair of diamond clips Marcus had given her for their anniversary. Immediately, Harriet put her sister down by dismissing as disreputable the immigrant from whom her brother-in-law had purchased the clips. Aunt Pearl rubbed the insult in by offering to introduce Aunt Milly to "her man" at Van Cleef's. After the ladies had finished competing over furs and jewelry, homes and servants, they turned their attention to their respective children. Since Aunt Peg and Aunt Ida were childless, they were automatically disqualified until one of them managed to bring the discussion around to some recent deaths and divorces.

At this point Stephen asked to be excused to take a bath, stood up, kissed his mother and aunts good night, and went into the foyer. Saul was triumphantly reviewing his winning hand and Uncle Lloyd was squealing with delight over some mistake Uncle Marc had made. After apologizing for interrupting the game, Stephen kissed his father and grandfather, said good night to his brother, bowed to his uncles, and backed away from the table as if he were withdrawing from royalty.

"*Kleine,*" Saul called after him. "Don't forget we go to Dr. Schwartz, first thing in the morning."

"I'll be up," Stephen said.

"*Kleine,*" Uncle Lloyd mimicked, always amused by the inappropriateness of the adjective. "Don't forget: I'm waiting to see you in the backfield with the officers."

Stephen ran the water very hot—so hot, in fact, that when he turned it off and attempted to step into the tub, he scalded his toes and had to add some cold water. When the temperature was bearable—though still very hot—he got into the tub, submerged his body up to his chin, causing the water almost to overflow, and lay back, resting his head on the rim of the tub, enjoying the heat, letting it relax and penetrate his pelvis until he felt his bowels loosen, ready to slip out of him. After washing himself, he let the water drain, leaving a small reserve of less than an eighth of an inch, and soaped himself from head to toe. As soon as he was completely lubricated, Stephen began to slide up and down in the porcelain bathtub like a toboggan, coasting down the incline, careening across the bottom and thrusting his body back again, repeating the descent over and over, creating suds and suction, caressing all the while his lathered loins in total tactile ecstasy, as he conjured up the familiar image of his father without his pajama bottoms. At last he felt the fabulous flow that seemed to issue from the base of his spine and he surrendered to its spasms.

When he opened his eyes, Stephen found himself jackknifed at the bottom of the bathtub and he reached up languidly and turned on both faucets. After he rinsed and dried himself, brushed his teeth and put on his pajamas, Stephen had to urinate and he was disappointed and disturbed to discover his specimen was yellow instead of white—not at all the color or consistency of milk. Once again he wondered, what have I been doing wrong?

Just before going to bed, Stephen decided not to carry Oscar II around with him anymore and he took the toy out of his trousers and placed it on the toyshelf in his bookcase.

In the course of the night Stephen was awakened by a severe stomach-ache—so severe, it doubled him up with cramps and made him groan aloud. When he reached the bathroom he massaged his stomach the way his mother had taught him years ago when these chronic stomach-aches had started, but it brought him no relief. With his eyes closed and his head resting on his knees, he sat moaning, absorbed by pain made more acute by the dreadful isolation pain induces, trying to defecate but unable to, wanting to vomit but unable to, wanting to die.

As if she had been waiting up for just such an eventuality, Harriet heard her baby's groans and ran from her bed to the bathroom door. "Darling! What's the matter, darling?"

"Nothing."

"I heard—"

"I'm okay."

"Are you sure?"

"Yes."

"Did you take your rhubarb and soda?"

"Yes," Stephen lied, eager to allay his mother's anxiety and be left alone.

"All right," Harriet sighed. "But I want you to take a table-spoon of milk of magnesia, too. And I want you to be sure to mention this to Dr. Schwartz tomorrow."

With some effort Stephen had managed to half-fill the specimen jar. He had undressed and donned the freshly-laundered gown. He had been measured and weighed and informed that he had grown an inch and a quarter and gained eleven pounds since last October. He had his eyes, ears, nose, and throat examined, his heart and lungs stethoscoped, his chest and back percussed, his coordination tested, and his blood pressure taken. (As always, he had most enjoyed feeling the rubber cuff inflate and squeeze his upper arm.) Finally, Dr. Schwartz had asked Stephen to remove his hospital gown and he had palpated his abdomen. At this moment, as much in an effort to delay the examination as to obey his mother, Stephen said, "I had another one of those stomach-aches last night."

"Did you," Dr. Schwartz remarked, walking around to the other side of the leather-covered table. "Does that hurt?" he asked, applying pressure to Stephen's appendix.

"A little."

The doctor pressed harder. "Now?"

"Yes."

"Hmm . . . Did mother give you a cathartic last night?"

"Cathartic?"

"A laxative: milk of magnesia or—"

"Yes, before I went back to bed."

"How large a dose?"

"A tablespoon."

"Did you have a bowel movement this morning?"

"Yes," Stephen said self-consciously.

"Does mother ever give you citrate of magnesia?"

Stephen made a face. "No, my father takes that," he answered, as if that in itself explained why he did not.

After jotting a note to himself, Dr. Schwartz returned to the table and continued the examination.

Suddenly, feeling the doctor's cold fingers probe his testes, Stephen flinched perceptibly.

"What's the matter, Stephen?"

Stephen's heart beat wildly. He could feel himself blushing. He turned away and fixed his eyes on a pair of forceps in the instrument cabinet. "Nothing."

"Why did you flinch?"

Stephen neither spoke nor looked at Dr. Schwartz. He could feel the perspiration start to trickle down his armpits.

"Did I hurt you?"

"No."

"Then why did you flinch?"

After a long silence, Stephen felt the doctor's fingers gently milk his penis once. In self-defense Stephen clamped his knees together and began to raise his thighs.

Releasing his hold, Dr. Schwartz asked slowly, "Have you been touching yourself, young man?"

Hearing this, Stephen could not breathe. His hands and feet were freezing, his heart was pounding, and the sweat ran down his sides.

"Look at me. I'm talking to you, Stephen."

Slowly, Stephen turned and saw Dr. Schwartz's bloated jowl overhanging his batwing collar, the thicket of black hairs in his dilated nostrils, his immie eyes staring sternly through his bifocals. "Touching?"

"You know what I mean. Have you been playing with yourself?"

A shiver coursed through Stephen's body. A nerve in his left eye began to twitch. Open-mouthed, he stared at Dr. Schwartz in terror.

"From your silence I infer you *have,*" the doctor said, his eyes grotesquely magnified and porcine under his thick lenses. As if to prolong Stephen's ordeal, Dr. Schwartz crossed slowly, thoughtfully to the ornate casement windows that faced Central Park. As he moved, his old-fashioned, high-topped shoes creaked. The sound seemed to Stephen like the tightening of a rack. At last the doctor turned back to the room and continued talking. "Well now, that may seem quite innocent to you at the moment, Stephen, it may even seem harmless, but let me assure you it's not! It's dangerous—unhealthy. Yes, above all, it's unhealthy. You're playing with fire, young man. If you pursue this practice—if you don't stop now, immediately, it will turn into a vice. You understand? You know what a vice is, Stephen? It's a dirty, pernicious habit that undermines your character, destroys your will, and turns you into a slave—a helpless, pathetic slave. As a matter of fact," he added, pausing solemnly, "it can even do damage to your brain tissue."

"Brain tissue?"

"I'm speaking of insanity."

"Insanity?"

"Yes, my boy. This seemingly innocent and harmless habit can render you insane." While waiting for Stephen to absorb the full impact of his words, Dr. Schwartz fingered and twirled his gold watch chain as if it were a jump-rope. "I don't want to frighten you, Stephen. I just want you to understand the possible consequences of your action. After all, you weren't given that to play with—to amuse yourself—it's not a toy. It has a serious and sacred purpose: to propagate the species. You understand? Now, I want you to promise me you'll never touch yourself again."

Stephen swallowed hard and nodded his head.

"Let me hear you say it, please."

Stephen's mouth was parched, and he had difficulty voicing the words. "I won't touch myself."

"All right. Now go inside and get dressed."

Before putting on his underwear, Stephen examined himself. How, he wondered, had Dr. Schwartz discovered it? What was different? What had changed? . . . This hair, Stephen thought, I didn't have this hair last year. Is that how he discovered it? Or is it the color? Is it the length? But it isn't any longer than a year ago. Wasn't that the purpose in the first place—to make it grow! How will I ever grow—as big as Roggie—big as Father, if I have to stop touching myself?

When Stephen was dressed he joined his brother on the commodious horsehair sofa in the waiting room. "Roggie, where is Daddy?"

"In with Dr. Schwartz."

"What are they discussing?"

"How should *I* know?" Roger asked, emphasizing his impatience by flipping the page of his magazine.

"Roggie, who's the Vice-President?"

"Garner."

"Why's he called *Vice?*"

"What exactly do they teach you at that nursery you go to? Don't you know anything?"

"But I don't understand—"

"Will you please shut up and let me read!"

Stephen waited nervously for his father and Dr. Schwartz to emerge from the doctor's study. When, at last, they did, nothing was said about their conference. Saul made no reference to it at lunch, and none was made at dinner. Consequently, Stephen had no way of knowing whether or not Dr. Schwartz had exposed his vice, but in order to keep his promise and avoid insanity, he decided not to take a bath that night.

The following morning, as always on Sundays, Saul went back to bed after breakfast to read the *Times*. When Stephen entered his parents' bedroom he found his father sprawled out on top of the bedclothes, his legs and torso characteristically exposed below his cotton pajama tops; his mother was buried under her blankets, almost completely out of sight. Stephen kissed them both, trying consciously not to notice or inspect his father's nudity; instead, he selected *The News of the Week in Review* and scanned the political cartoons. After a moment of F.D.R. and Willkie, Stephen's thoughts returned to his father and he stole a glance around the corner of the paper. The *Times* was like a screen in front of Saul's face and it gave Stephen the opportunity to ogle greedily. . . . My, Grandma, what big ears you have. The better to hear you with, my dear. My, Grandma, what a big . . . "Daddy."

"Yes, *kleine*."

"What was my report like?"

"What report?"

"Dr. Schwartz's."

"He gave you a clean bill of health. Why? What did you expect?"

"Oh, I don't know. I thought he might have said—something about my stomach-aches."

"Well, as a matter of fact—"

"*Schweig!*"

Even though the word was muffled by Harriet's pillow, Stephen heard it and knew his mother was trying to withhold or protect him from something Dr. Schwartz had said. "What, Daddy?"

"I think you're going to like this, *kleine*. The doctor said, no more laxatives. That means milk of magnesia. You don't have to take—"

"Is that *all* he said?"

"What do you mean?"

"Didn't he say anything else?"

"About what?"

"About . . ." Stephen paused. "About my weight or anything?"

"Don't be silly, darling," Harriet said, her head emerging from the bedclothes like a turtle's. "It's just a phase: baby-fat. I've told you that a hundred times. Every child goes through it."

With only this to go on, Stephen found it impossible to determine whether or not Dr. Schwartz had said anything to Saul about his vice, but he thought it likely that the doctor had. He imagined that his parents knew all about it now, and would keep a constant vigil for it. That, coupled with the threat of insanity, made Stephen skip his bath for the second successive night. Doing so demanded the exertion of considerable willpower, as Stephen proudly acknowledged to himself, "I haven't touched myself for two whole days."

On Monday, much to the surprise of his classmates and teachers, Stephen did poorly in his classwork. Though one of the brightest students in his class, today he acted like a dunce. He was inattentive and nervous, abstracted and confused. He couldn't concentrate, couldn't sit still. Every time he was called on, he asked the teacher to repeat the question, and then, only to answer incorrectly. Mr. Rankin, the history teacher, mistook Stephen's unprecedented behavior for recalcitrance and was so annoyed that he punished the entire class with an oral exam. Almost without exception, everyone called on prior to Stephen—all of his friends—answered quickly, simply, correctly—490 B.C.—Miltiades—Themistocles—Darius, but when it came Stephen's turn to name the co-commanders of the Persian army he couldn't. Before flunking him, Mr. Rankin, more in a spirit of slyness than fair play, rephrased a question he had asked earlier in the exam, but once again Stephen couldn't answer. Thereupon, flourishing his blue pencil with great satisfaction, Mr. Rankin awarded Stephen the first F he had ever received at school.

After classes, Stephen went to the locker room to undress for the pool. When he reached his row, Jimmy Reuben, who used the locker next to Stephen's, was there already and greeted him cheerfully. "Hi, Steve."

"Hello, Jim," Stephen said glumly, taking off his jacket.

"Datis and Artaphernes," Jimmy said.

"What?"

"Datis and Artaphernes."

"What are you talking about?" Stephen asked impatiently.

"The co-commanders of the Persian army."

"I know that!" Stephen protested.

"Well why didn't you say so?"

"I don't know," he said, hurling his shoe into the locker.

"What's the matter with you today, anyway?"

"I don't know!" Stephen repeated in distress.

"Come on, cheer up," Jimmy said, thrusting his forefinger into Stephen's crotch.

This playful assault was the cue for commencing what both boys referred to euphemistically as their "wrestling match." Perhaps, to the casual passer-by, it looked that way even though the whole point of the game was to get what in a legitimate match would be considered an illegal or foul hold on one's opponent and goose him mercilessly until he was aroused to erection. As soon as this state was induced in either player, the non-erect one was declared the winner and the game was over.

A split second after Jimmy had made his opening thrust, both boys, fully dressed except for their shoes and jackets, crashed to the locker room floor—their legs interlocked, their fingers intertwined —and began rolling around, struggling for supremacy. Within a minute Stephen, who was not only taller than Jimmy but fifteen pounds heavier, managed to get on top of his opponent, pin him to the floor and start to tickle his ribs which, as Stephen knew it would, made Jimmy writhe with laughter, heave his shoulder blades, and kick his legs frantically. This tickling-tactic enabled Stephen to slip his hand under Jimmy's spine, work it down under his buttocks and seize hold of his objective. In response Jimmy mobilized all his strength, arched his back and rolled Stephen over, reversing their positions, but he failed to break Stephen's grip. Instead, stimulated by the smell of Jimmy's perspiration, Stephen intensified his attack, causing Jimmy to begin to harden.

"Stop! Stop!" Jimmy laughed hysterically, but the more he pleaded and struggled, the more impulsively, obsessively Stephen persisted, until all of Jimmy's efforts to counterattack were rendered futile.

At last, when Jimmy was standing firm and stirring restlessly under Stephen's hand, Stephen panted, "Give up?"

"Give up," Jimmy conceded and the two boys separated without further struggle.

The match over, Stephen undressed, took his towel, observed the rule of showering and went upstairs to the swimming pool. As soon as he stepped through the door he saw the big red rubber ball floating at the far end of the pool and he glanced at the clock. 3:15. He knew he would have to wait until he had swum the 200-yard free style and the 100-yard breast stroke—until 3:45 at least—before he could claim the red rubber ball. But Stephen was patient. He considered the ball a reward—a reward for having to participate in these organized athletics, for being forced to swim in this overly-chlorinated water, mandatory races which he somehow never won.

"Someone get that ball out of there!" Coach Harlan shouted.

"I'll do it," Stephen volunteered eagerly, trotting down the length of the pool, scooping up the precious ball and placing it carefully on the tiled floor.

After the races were over, Stephen retrieved the ball, hugged it to his stomach and plunged into the pool. When he rose to the surface, he ducked the ball under again and forced it between his thighs, causing it to buoy him up out of the water. Keeping his balance, as if he were riding a unicycle, Stephen began to revolve the ball with his hands. The contact of the smooth wet rubber against his naked loins excited him exquisitely, and he spun the ball faster and faster until the intensity of pleasure immobilized his hands and the ball hopped out of them and he fell over backward into the water with abandon.

It did not occur to Stephen that either of these recreational activities bore any relationship to the vice against which he had been warned. He considered the wrestling matches an unspoken, private celebration between himself and Jimmy Reuben of one of nature's miracles which both of them had only recently discovered. And the water game came as a kind of recess from the airless, chalky classrooms, the uncomfortable, inhuman seats, and the sullen, sallow teachers. As far as Stephen was concerned he had not jeopardized his sanity since Friday night.

Stephen knew immediately that his father was in an irritable mood—even for a Monday. As soon as he came home, Saul began fulminating against his office and his partner, whom he called a stinking bum. When Stephen finally tore himself away from his radio and went inside to say hello, he could smell the liquor on his father's breath.

Dinner was served earlier than usual and Stephen arrived at the table last. "Which of you left his radio on?" Saul asked as soon as Stephen was seated.

"Not me," Roger boasted.

"Excuse me," Stephen said, jumping up.

"You think money grows on trees?" Saul inquired humorlessly.

"No."

"It's *my* fault," Harriet interceded. "I made him come to the table before his program was over. After all, we don't usually eat this early."

"Is it my fault if I'm hungry?" Saul grumbled.

After switching off the radio, Stephen ran back to the table and picked up his tomato juice.

"Don't gulp, darling," Harriet said, "we have nothing but time." As if to prove her point, instead of ringing for Annie when Stephen was finished, Harriet sat and waited in silence.

"What the hell are you waiting for?" Saul demanded.

"Just be patient, darling. I have to give her time to cut the meat."

"Patience. I'll give you patience. What have you got?"

"Chicken," Harriet said, ringing the bell.

"Jesus Christ," Saul complained, pushing away his water glass and the silver salt and pepper shakers as if they were alive and crowding in on him.

"It's a roaster, Saul, not broilers," Harriet explained.

"There's no water on the table," Saul announced in reprisal.

"Oh, dear. That's because I rushed her so."

"Well why did you call us if she wasn't ready?"

"Because *you* said you were hungry."

"Who said?"

"Never mind. I'll get the water," Harriet said, standing up.

"Sit down."

"But I can get it in a minute."

"Sit down, I said!" Saul commanded.

"You forgot the water, Annie," Harriet said as Annie reached for the empty tomato juice glass.

"Never mind, Annie," Saul said considerately. "No one's thirsty anyway."

"*I* am!" Harriet rebutted. "Bring the water, please!"

When Annie returned with the water pitcher, Saul covered his glass with the palm of his hand. "None for me, thanks."

"Stop that, Saul!" Harriet snapped.

"Stop what?" Saul asked innocently without removing his hand.

"Isn't this delicious, darling," Harriet said, seizing her glass and turning to Stephen. "I always say there's no water in the world like New York water."

In an effort to confirm his mother's opinion, Stephen reached for his glass, but in his eagerness he knocked it over.

"Goddamn it!" Saul exploded, cutting short Roger's laughter. "Why don't you watch what you're doing? If you don't know how to hold a glass, don't eat with us!"

"Sorry," Stephen said, trying to stem the flood with his napkin.

"Don't be silly, darling. It was just an accident. There's no harm done," Harriet assured him as she rushed into the pantry to get a dishrag.

"What do you mean, accident?" Saul demanded as soon as his wife returned. "It's *you* who egged him on. It would never have happened in the first place, if you hadn't been so stubborn. I told you not to bother. I told you I wasn't thirsty—but no! You had to have it your way. It's always the same, no matter what I do: if I say black, she says white," Saul complained, throwing up his hands, as if he were pleading his case before a supreme tribunal.

"Oh, my goodness!" Annie said, as she entered with the serving platter. "Somethin' spill?"

"That's all right. Just serve the meat please, Annie. I'll take care of this," Harriet said, spreading a clean napkin over the wet spot on the tablecloth.

"Goddamn it, Harriet, will you sit down!"

"As soon as I fin—"

"No, now!" Saul roared, forcing his wife to abandon the soggy dishrag on the sideboard and resume her seat.

"Please go on serving," Harriet said with exaggerated dignity, and Annie, who had been immobilized by the outburst, brought the platter around and offered it to Saul.

"Which is the white?" Saul asked.

"That's a piece right there, I think," Annie said, holding the platter in her trembling hands and trying as best she could to point to a piece of the breast with her nose.

"Which do you mean?"

"That's all breast, Saul, all of that along the side," Harriet interrupted, jumping up and pointing toward the platter. "That piece there—the one you have your fork on now— No, not *that* one, the piece—"

"Will you please sit down and let me help myself," Saul bristled. "Or would you prefer me to leave the table?" As soon as Annie finished serving, Saul dropped his knife and fork on his plate with a terrible clatter. "It's *dark*," he groaned.

"Oh, my God!" Harriet gasped, as if she had just received news of her father's death, and she rushed from the room calling, "Annie! Annie! Bring it back! Bring back the platter!"

"Never mind!" Saul shouted after her.

"Mr. Wolfe got the dark meat after all," Harriet continued, ignoring her husband's protest and ushering Annie back into the dining room.

"I said, never mind!"

"But, Saul, there's nothing but white meat on this platter."

"I said I didn't want it."

"Just set it down please, Annie."

"What's the matter with you, are you hard of hearing?"

"Do as I say, Annie," Harriet ordered.

"Damn you, Annie!"

"Stop it, Saul!" Harriet screamed.

"Don't tell *me* to stop!" Saul bellowed, his face and bald head turning vermilion. "Get that platter out of here!"

"That's all right," Harriet tried to comfort Annie. "It's not your fault. I'll take care of this," she said, relieving Annie of the platter and sending her back to the kitchen. "Go on, children; please don't wait for us."

"Get it out, I said!"

"How dare you talk to me that way in front of the *schwartze*," Harriet hissed. "You did it deliberately. Deliberately! You took the dark meat deliberately. Don't you think I know your tricks? Here! Here!" Harriet shouted in triumph as she stabbed a piece of breast with the serving fork and forced it onto her husband's plate. "Here's all the white meat in the world!"

"Keep it!" Saul rasped ferociously. "Keep your goddamned dinner!" he roared, shoving back his chair and hurling down his napkin. "I've had enough."

"Where are you going? Don't you dare leave this table. Come back here, Saul. Come back, I said," Harriet screamed, pursuing her husband into the foyer. "You think it's easy, feeding you? You think I've got it easy, don't you? Just lie in bed and call the butcher. 'No, not lamb, my husband doesn't like it. No, not liver. No, not veal! No, not chops! No, not chicken!' What? What? What's left? What can I give you? Steak! Steak! Steak! seven days a week like a lion," Harriet whined, her words growing more and more falsetto. "What are you doing? Put down that hat! Where are you going? You haven't eaten. Come back to the table. Please come back and eat your dinner. I'm begging you," she cried, "begging you! All right, Saul," Harriet threatened, slowly, breathily, bringing her words sharply under control, "you'll regret this. I'm warning you, you'll regret this as long as you live. If you walk through that door—" But before she had time to finish her threat, the front door slammed.

The sound of the door startled Stephen and he jumped in his chair. He could hear his mother's muffled whines—was she stifling them with her napkin?—erupting every now and then into long, frightening gasps for breath. "Go on eating, children," she called out in a strained and broken voice, as she hurried past the dining room doors and disappeared. For a moment both boys sat in silence, staring at each other.

"Roggie," Stephen whispered on the verge of tears himself, "what shall we do?"

"I don't know," Roger answered soberly. "Eat."

Stephen tried to take his brother's advice, but couldn't. In the distance he could still hear his mother's painful puling and he felt compelled to go to her.

"Where are you going?" Roger asked, but Stephen didn't answer.

After standing outside his mother's bedroom for a minute, listening to her sobs, Stephen took a deep breath and knocked gently on the door. "Mommy," he called. "Mommy," he repeated, knocking again, but his mother went on crying. Carefully, cautiously, Stephen turned the knob, opened the door and tiptoed into the blackness. "Mommy."

"Whaaa!" Harriet exclaimed, bolting from her pillow.

"It's me, Mommy, don't be scared."

"Oh, my darling."

"Can I turn the light on? I can't see."

"I'll be in in a minute, darling."

"Are you all right?" Stephen asked, inching through the darkness.

"Yes, my love. Go and finish dinner."

"All right," Stephen said, bumping into the bedstead and reaching for his mother. "But please don't cry," he pleaded, finding her at last, touching her heaving back, her hair, and kissing her on the temple.

"Oh, my angel!" Harriet wailed, rolling over and seizing Stephen violently, hugging him to her breast. "If it weren't for you, I-I'd divorce that man!"

Only after he opened his eyes and found himself doubled up at the foot of the bathtub did Stephen realize he had broken his promise to Dr. Schwartz. As soon as he rinsed himself off, he ran to the mirror on the door of the medicine chest above the sink. Still dripping wet and breathing heavily, he stared intensely at his own reflection. His pupils dilated slightly as he tried to penetrate beyond his hazel eyes, into the depths of his soul, seeking to discover there some sign of injury to his brain tissue. Tilting his head toward the light, he concentrated solely on the left eye, then the right, moving his face closer and closer to the mirror until his nose bumped the glass, and he stood back, satisfied he looked the same as ever. He hadn't changed: his face was as beautiful, his body as ugly as ever. If he really was insane or on the verge of it, at least there was no external evidence.

When he went to school on Tuesday, Stephen watched to see if anyone reacted to him differently, but no one did; and no one did at home. He was quick to realize, therefore, that as long as you continued to say "God bless you," when someone sneezed, "Excuse me," when you blew your nose at table or "Nice to meet you," when you took your leave of someone to whom you had been newly-introduced—as long as you continued to bathe every day and wear a white shirt, carry a clean handkerchief, and comb your hair, people automatically regarded you as the same polite, well-bred young gentleman they had always known. It was very much like watching your father slam out of the house and hearing your mother speak of divorce and then, the very next day, seeing them behave toward each other and their friends as if nothing of the sort had ever really happened. If no one but some hateful doctor, to whom you would never return, was aware of your vice, if there was no sign of it in your eyes or conversation, if, in fact, you were able to conceal it rather cleverly, why in the world should you give it up?

As a result of this kind of reasoning, not only did Stephen not give up his vice, he began to practice it more and more habitually.

In the spring Stephen, without consciously planning to do so, found himself visiting the zoo again, but this time he was alone. The minute he entered the monkey house he noticed that all the spectators were gathered in a tight crowd in front of one cage in the center of the building. Curious to see what was happening, he hurried toward the crowd. As he approached he realized that the expression on the faces was not of joy or amusement, but serious and solemn as if the crowd were witnessing a fire or an accident. No one was laughing or talking or jibing as they did ordinarily; everyone was standing open-mouthed and strained.

When Stephen reached the side of the crowd the only thing he was able to see was a Patas monkey, with its characteristic white mustache and blue bandit's mask, sitting on the uppermost play-bar in the cage, scratching its head. "Excuse me," Stephen said, trying to make his way through the crowd, but no one responded, no one made room, or allowed him to pass. For some reason, unintelligible to Stephen, this crowd, unlike the typical monkey-house crowd, seemed to be indifferent to children. That in itself was odd enough, but even odder was the fact that except for Stephen and an infant he had noticed sleeping in its carriage, there were no other children to be seen in the crowd. "Excuse me," Stephen repeated in a firmer tone, more intent than ever now to see what was happening inside the cage.

When, at last, he maneuvered his way through the crowd to the front of the cage, Stephen's mouth—like every other mouth around him—dropped open, his eyes bulged, and his heart began to pound. Sitting on a dark-brown bench in front of a window was another Patas monkey, masturbating. Of course, that in itself was not extraordinary—Stephen had seen monkeys masturbate before —but what startled him and held the whole crowd rapt was the size of this particular monkey's penis. The monkey needed both its small black hands to hold it—and even then it was longer than the reach of either of its arms, longer than the length of its entire body. Stephen guessed—and not at all inaccurately—it must be three feet long.

So that's the way it's supposed to happen, Stephen thought as he gazed at the spectacle. I've never done it right, never gone quite far enough. Somewhere inside me, at my center, there's a magic latch I've never touched, never found, that keeps the lid on the jack-in-the-box. If only I can find it and release it, out I'll spring! . . . as big as Roggie . . . big as Father: five feet long, maybe fifty—and then there'll be sperm. . . . No wonder I've never seen sperm.

As he stood and watched the monkey, Stephen was torn between a desire to remain and an even stronger desire to return home and practice on himself what he had witnessed. It did not occur to him to wait and watch the climax, he was much too impatient to get home.

When Stephen got home he went straight to his bathroom and locked the door. Automatically, he reached to turn on the bathtub faucet before he remembered that the monkey had not needed water, it had been sitting on a bench. For the first time Stephen realized that his pleasure did not depend for its fulfillment on a bath or lake or swimming pool, it could be experienced on land, dry land. Like an amphibian, he, too, could leave the sea behind and come upon the land. . . . After opening his fly, Stephen soaped his hand and sat down on the toilet seat, meditating on the monkey and his father.

As soon as it was over, he opened his eyes and looked down at himself expectantly, but he was disappointed. He was neither fifty feet nor five feet long; he wasn't even a fraction of an inch longer than he had been before. He had failed to make it happen, failed to find the magic latch. As he sat and watched himself diminish— almost disappear—another thought occurred to Stephen. Maybe what he had always assumed to be the end of the act was in reality only the beginning. Maybe there were phases beyond the phase he had just completed—rapturous, ecstatic phases that culminated in the colossal extension of oneself he had witnessed at the zoo. Stephen leaned back and stretched his legs, determined to go on. He tried tenaciously to arouse himself again, but failed; his body refused.

Standing up to close his fly, Stephen noticed a number of white splotches on the blue tile floor and he stooped to examine one. The stuff was sticky—like mucilage, he thought, daubing it between his fingertips. . . . Like the stuff at Potawatomi that night I heard the frenzy-call. Suddenly Stephen remembered Dennis' description of sperm: *a white fluid rather like milk in its color and consistency.* . . . But this is not like milk at all; it's mucilage. Supposing Dennis was wrong. After all, his description hadn't come from himself, from his own experience, it came from a textbook. What if the textbook had been wrong? What if sperm looked much more like mucilage than milk, and this was sperm? But then how come he had never produced it before? How could he tell it came from him? How could he prove that it was sperm? . . . There was only one sure way, Stephen decided, of finding out the answer.

The next afternoon, after locking the bathroom door, instead of closing his eyes and musing about his father as he had done the day before, Stephen watched himself as attentively as if he were a demonstration at the World's Fair. Much to his delight, within a matter of minutes he saw himself ejaculate the white stuff, and even though it happened very quickly there was time enough to collect a few drops in a glass he had smuggled out of the kitchen for that purpose.

Stephen unlocked the bathroom door and listened anxiously for Annie. At last, convinced the coast was clear, he rushed to his bedroom and placed the glass on top of his desk. It was 4:45. He knew he would have to finish his research by 5:30, before Roggie returned from school. He had less than an hour.

Stephen hurried to his brother's room and stepped across the threshold. That in itself was a violation of every law Roger had ever decreed to protect his privacy. For an instant Stephen hesitated, torn between the closet and the bookcase. What he was after was in the closet; on the other hand he was tempted to examine the group of forbidden books—*Justine, Against the Grain, The Basic Writings of Sigmund Freud, Ulysses* and *Ars Amoris*—that Roger kept concealed behind the Encyclopaedia Brittanica. . . . After all, Stephen thought, I don't get that many opportunities to look at them. . . . But not today. There isn't time, he decided, crossing to the closet and opening the door. Of all the crimes committable, Roger regarded closet-breaking as second worst—the worst, of course, was desk-snooping, an offense punishable by death.

After rummaging through ice skates, ski poles, a baseball mitt, boxing gloves, a tennis racket, drum sticks, a drummer's brush, some darts, a fez, a football helmet, a sheathed machete, a Bunsen burner, a pile of popular records, some beakers and a retort, Stephen found what he was searching for: a pea-colored, wooden box approximately the size of a medicine chest. Holding the box by its metal handle, he trotted back to his own bedroom and shut the door. Carefully, as if it were a Shinto shrine, he set the box down on his desk, flipped up the little brass hook that held its double doors in place and opened both of them at once, revealing a microscope and six glass slides.

For a moment, as he removed the microscope and one of the slides from their wooden fittings, Stephen remembered his favorite actor, Paul Muni, as Louis Pasteur, and took great pains not to smudge the surface of the slide. With some difficulty and a good deal of impatience, he managed to shake a specimen of the white stuff onto the center of the slide and insert it under the clamps. Ardently, he brought his eye down to meet the eyepiece and peered into it, but much to his surprise he saw nothing but a gray opacity. He moved his desk lamp closer and switched on the light, but that did nothing more than illuminate the void. Suddenly Stephen remembered the focusing knob and began to turn it vigorously, but in his enthusiasm he lowered the objective lens too far and sank it into the specimen. After cleaning the lens and preparing another slide, Stephen proceeded with extreme care and this time, as he twisted the knob ever so slowly, gradually the lamplit void turned into a multitude of swarming creatures.

"Polliwogs!" Stephen exclaimed, staring at the spermatozoa.— So that's what sperm looks like: a school of squirming polliwogs. Was I once a polliwog, swimming in a sea of sperm? How many polliwogs are there in a drop of sperm? Stephen tried to count the wriggling mass but lost track almost immediately. . . . More than fifty . . . more than a hundred . . . maybe a thousand, multiplied by other drops and all those other times: a million, trillion polliwogs . . . These numbers were too astronomical to grasp; so Stephen tried, instead, to contemplate the fate of a single polliwog, issuing from his penis, washing down the drain, floating through the sewers, into the Hudson and out to sea, where, as he imagined, it turned at last into a frog, swam to shore and crawled back onto land again. The cycle fascinated Stephen, and he reviewed it several times before his daydream was destroyed by a most alarming question. . . . How much sperm do we have in us? How much are we given? How much have I left? How many times can you practice this vice before it all runs out? Oh God! what if I've used up all my sperm and can never produce anymore? . . .

Stephen needed to reassure himself, but before he had a chance, he heard a knock at his bedroom door that made him flinch with fright. "Yes?" he answered artificially.

Interpreting her son's response to mean come in, Harriet opened the door and entered the room. "Hello, my pet," she said. "How come you're home so early?"

"I had some work to do," Stephen said, keeping his eye glued to the microscope.

"Oh that's my angel child," Harriet said. "Don't I get a kiss?" Without turning to look at her, Stephen raised his head high enough to enable his mother to plant her fervent lips on his cheek. The next moment he felt the weight of her arm encircle his neck and pull him toward the microscope. Realizing his mother was trying to get a glimpse of the slide, Stephen jerked his shoulders sharply. "What's the matter, darling, can't Mommy have a peek?"

"No!"

"Why not? What are you examining?"

"Mucilage."

"Mucilage?" Harriet repeated incredulously. "Are there bacteria in mucilage?"

"That's what I'm trying to find out."

"Maybe mother can help."

"Oh, Mommy, please!" Stephen begged in desperation.

"All right, darling. I won't disturb you anymore," Harriet said, picking up the glass that contained the residue of Stephen's sperm.

"What are you doing!" Stephen screamed.

"What do you mean?" Harriet said, stunned by Stephen's outburst.

"Can't you leave your hands off anything!"

"But you're finished with it, aren't you? There isn't a drop of milk left. I was only going to put it in the pantry."

"Oh."

"I don't know what kind of children I was given. I just don't know. If I live to be a hundred, I'll never understand either of you boys," Harriet said, holding the glass and leaving the room.

That night Stephen suffered another severe stomach-ache. Ever since Dr. Schwartz had raised the possibility that these might be the result of an irritated appendix and had ordered the elimination of all cathartics, Harriet had grown increasingly alarmed. She was only too aware that as a girl she had had acute appendicitis and had been rushed to the hospital in the middle of the night. Nor had she forgotten that Roger, at the age of twelve, had suffered the same ordeal. From that she concluded that appendicitis was a hereditary characteristic of the Stern family and she prevailed on

Saul to take Stephen back to Dr. Schwartz before his appendix ruptured.

"Stevie," Saul began lightly, "what do you say we pay a little visit to Dr. Schwartz this Saturday?"

On hearing the doctor's name again a chill ran over Stephen's body. "No."

"What do you mean?" Saul asked, perplexed by the finality in his son's tone.

"I don't know," Stephen apologized. "I just hate Dr. Schwartz."

"Why do you say that? What did he ever do to you?"

"Nothing."

"Then why do you hate him?"

"I don't know."

"Of course no one likes to go to the doctor, but there are times when we have no choice. You want to get rid of these tummy aches, don't you?"

"Yes."

"Well, in order to do that, we have to go see Dr. Schwartz."

"No," Stephen repeated with even more firmness than the first time, and no matter what line of reasoning Saul pursued, Stephen remained adamant. He had never resisted his father before and it frightened him to do so now, but he was even more afraid of revisiting Dr. Schwartz.

When Saul reported Stephen's stubbornness to Harriet, she was able to explain and rationalize it easily. As Harriet interpreted it, somehow the child knew intuitively that he was suffering from something more than stomach-aches and ought to see an internist. And Harriet was proved right, because when she proposed they go to see another man named Dr. Lopez, Stephen accepted readily.

Even though the X-rays revealed only the slightest inflammation, given Stephen's history of stomach-aches as well as the number of cases of appendicitis in Harriet's family, Dr. Lopez thought it best to operate, and he recommended highly a surgeon by the name of Bloom.

Dr. Bloom explained to Stephen that his appendix was a completely superfluous appendage he would never miss, and the operation as simple and safe as a manicure. Prepared in this fashion, Stephen felt completely secure, even enthusiastic. What pleased him most was the possibility that he might not recuperate in time for his *bar mitzvah*—an event which, as it grew more imminent, filled him with anxiety and dread.

Just before leaving for the hospital, Harriet, in a needless effort to buoy Stephen's spirits, said, "Do you remember, darling, from when you had your tonsils out, what it's like to take ether?"

"I remember that awful red rubber cup they clapped over—"

"I don't mean that," Harriet interrupted hastily. "I mean the dreams you had."

"Dreams?"

"Yes, my love. You know, when you take an anesthetic, all your hidden thoughts come out. All the things you really think, but never say, are spoken—just like when you're drunk, the truth comes out. Now I'll be able to discover all your inmost secrets," Harriet said in a mysterious, husky voice, hunching her shoulders and narrowing her eyes, playing the part of a gypsy. "Who you love and who you hate, why you have those moods of yours, and why, sometimes," Harriet went on, obviously upset, "you seem to be . . . so unhappy. I'll know it all, at last," she said, resuming her gypsy manner, "all the secrets of your soul."

Stephen said nothing, but unconsciously he clenched his teeth and kept them clenched until he reached the hospital. It was only when he was shown his bed that could be cranked into so many different positions, that he relaxed for the first time.

Late in the afternoon, after Stephen had met Miss O'Brien, his night nurse, changed into his hospital gown and got into his fascinating bed, a man in a white coat and trousers, carrying a small black bag, came into Stephen's room and asked Harriet to step outside for a minute. "Don't worry, darling, this nice man isn't going to hurt you," Harriet said, walking toward the half-screen door. But by the time she reached the door and laid her hand on it, she wanted some assurance from the man's own lips and added, "Are you?"

"Of course not," the man said cheerfully, opening his leather bag.

As Stephen watched his mother's legs recede down the corridor his heart began to throb. "Are you the man who gives the ether?" he asked apprehensively.

"No, no, no," the man laughed as he disappeared into the bathroom with a shaving brush and mug. "I'm just the barber."

Stephen grimaced and ran his fingers through his pompadour. "I don't need a haircut."

"Oh, yes you do," came the playful but indisputable response from the bathroom. For a moment, before the barber reappeared, Stephen listened to the sound of the shaving brush hitting against the inside of the mug and he was puzzled. "I bet this is the first time you've been shaved."

"Shaved?"

"Yes, siree," he said, pulling off Stephen's bedclothes. "Just raise your gown above the waist."

Stephen watched the barber cross to his bag and remove a pair of scissors and a safety razor.

"What's the matter, you modest?" the barber asked when he returned and saw that Stephen had not followed his instructions. 'Come on now, just lift your ass. Thataboy," he said, pulling up the hospital gown above Stephen's navel.

"What are you going to do?" Stephen said, as the barber took hold of the scissors.

"Scalp you," the barber laughed, cutting Stephen's pubic hair. "It's for the operation, so the surgeon can see where he's going."

Stephen felt like Samson—both furious and helpless to release his fury—but unlike Samson, he was wide awake and witnessing his own emasculation, allowing it to happen.

"Just lie back and enjoy yourself," the barber suggested. "This will only take a minute."

The lather was warm and Stephen liked the feel of it, until he felt the scrape of the razor. He propped himself up onto his elbows and watched the barber pull and swivel his penis.

"Not much to hold onto here," the barber cracked.

Humiliated, Stephen fell back against his pillow and shut his eyes, wanting never to see or hear or feel again.

When he was finished the barber said, "There you are, young fellow, clean as a newborn babe."

Stephen looked at himself with revulsion. Even though he had had his pubic hair only a year, this unexpected theft of it, this sudden, forced return to childhood made Stephen feel ridiculous, ashamed. Stripped of its hair, reduced in size and stature, he thought his penis looked indecent and obscene like a turkey plucked of its feathers or a poodle shorn of its coat. By shaving off his pubic hair, this wanton barber had robbed him of his maturity, his potency, his sex.

In contrast to his passivity with the barber, the following morning when the anesthetist arrived Stephen turned into a wild bronco. He thrust his feet and fists against anyone who dared to come within their range, delivering, simultaneously, a bellicose denunciation of ether. Assuming Stephen's behavior to be the result

of some bitter experience he had had with that particular anesthetic, the anesthetist tried to explain that ether was outdated and
had not been used for years, but Stephen would hear none of it.
Like a puma prepared to strike, he lay in bed and watched his day
nurse, Miss Thompson, confer with the anesthetist in whispers. At
last, much to Stephen's relief, the anesthetist left the room defeated, and Miss Thompson said, "All right, Stevie, you win. You
don't have to take an anesthetic. But how about an enema? Have
you any objections to that?"

"I hate enemas."

"So do I! But which is it to be, an anesthetic or an enema?"

"Enema, I guess," he answered listlessly. It was only after he
had received more than half the liquid that Stephen realized he
had been tricked, but the realization came too late. He had barely
begun to express his indignation before he fell asleep.

When Stephen regained consciousness, it was not Miss Thompson but Miss O'Brien, the night nurse, who was standing over him.
"How we doing, honey?" Aware of her patient's disorientation, she
added, "You're back in your room now, honey. The operation's
over. Everything's just fine."

"Over?" Stephen asked with alarm.

"Don't you believe me?"

"Did I say anything?"

"What do you mean?"

"When I was asleep."

"I guess you kicked and screamed a lot just like—"

"What?" Stephen demanded. "What did I scream?"

"I don't know exactly; I wasn't with you, honey. But it never
makes much sense."

"Was my mother with me?"

"Where?"

"In the operating room."

"Of course not."

"Oh," Stephen said, sighing profoundly, and a stream of tears
rolled down his cheeks.

"What's the matter, honey?"

"Nothing," Stephen answered brokenly. "I'm glad it's over."

Because of a slight infection that developed three days after the
operation, Stephen's incision had to be reopened. As a result, when
it finally healed, he was left with an unusually deep and unattrac-
tive scar that outlined and accentuated the bulge of his potbelly.

Almost immediately, this scar became for Stephen a symbol of his ugliness—the ugliness, evil, and vice he kept concealed beneath his polite and well-groomed surface. Sometimes, in order to remind himself of this ugliness and not to be deceived by the innocent beauty of his face, Stephen would locate his scar through the material of his trousers and rub his finger up and down its furrow. Every night and morning, when Stephen was undressed, he would stare in disgust at this furrow, this gash in his abdomen that looked, he thought, so much like the crack women had where men had balls. The over-all effect of Stephen's appendectomy was to make him loathe his body more than he had at Camp Penobscot; to make matters worse, there wasn't even the compensation of missing his *bar mitzvah.*

What troubled Stephen most about his *bar mitzvah* was the fact that it was a ceremony to celebrate his coming to manhood. He simply didn't understand how one could be a man at the age of thirteen. In his own case he was only twelve and wouldn't be thirteen until two weeks after his *bar mitzvah.* He wondered what exactly it meant to be a man. He knew his father was a man, but Stephen didn't feel or look or act like his father. He had the body of an adolescent, the penis of an infant, the crack of a woman, the vice of a lunatic, and, what's more, his pubic hair had only just begun to grow back in.

Ever since he could remember—even before he had begun to go to Sunday school—his grandfather had looked forward with great anticipation and pride to Stephen's *bar mitzvah*—that glorious day when, as Jonas Stern said repeatedly, his grandson would become a man. Two years ago, when Roger was thirteen and Stephen went to his brother's *bar mitzvah* and heard him say, "Today I am a man," Stephen had giggled uncontrollably. Now it was Stephen's turn to speak those solemn words and Roger's turn to laugh. It was Stephen's turn to endure the most dreadful stage fright of his life—to stand up in front of that congregation of feathered toques and black skull caps, of nineteenth-century aunts and uncles he had never seen before and distant cousins dressed in musical comedy colors, and pretend to read at sight a passage from the Torah that it had taken him three months to memorize in Hebrew. It was Stephen's turn to stand and pretend to be engrossed in Rabbi Berkowitz's florid sermon about maturity, responsibility, American citizenship, and Judaism in these malignant times.

As he stood there, at the altar, looking at but not listening to Rabbi Berkowitz, Stephen remembered something his mother had told him years ago, the second time he ever went to synagogue— the very synagogue in which he was standing now. In preparation for the service, she explained to him—using much the same gypsy manner she was to use again years later to describe the effects of ether—the meaning of Yom Kippur. She said it was the day on which God took cognizance of everything that had happened the previous year and determined everything that would happen in the coming one; the day on which He wrote down in a giant book all the names of those who would die and those who would live, those who would be sick and those who would be healthy, those He would smite and those He would raise up. Yom Kippur was the Day of Atonement, the day on which you fasted and begged forgiveness for your sins. But Stephen had never fasted—not only because his parents had not asked him to, but because he was only a child and ignorant of sin. But now that he was standing there in front of Rabbi Berkowitz, now that his *bar mitzvah* was very nearly over, Stephen realized what it meant to be a man. It meant that he, too, was guilty of committing sin: the sin of killing Marvin Klein, the sin of masturbation, the sin of living comfortably in America while millions of Jews, Rabbi Berkowitz said, were being exterminated in concentration camps. Now that he had become a man, Stephen knew that next Yom Kippur he, too, would have to fast.

When the ceremony was over Harriet rushed forward, hugged her son in a smothering embrace and told him through her tears how proud she was. Saul said, despite the *bar mitzvah,* Stephen was still his *kleine* and would always remain so; and Roger said, as much as he hated to admit it, Stephen had done very well. Following the immediate family, came a mob of assorted relatives and friends, offering congratulations and asking questions such as how it felt to be a man. Finally, almost at the end of the line, Jonas Stern stepped forward, his mustaches outstretched over a broad grin, and kissed his grandson on the forehead. "Stevie, come with me," he said. "Before the party, we'll take a little *spotzere.*"

Stephen felt self-conscious, walking down Broadway on this sunny Saturday noon dressed in a navy blue suit. Surreptitiously, he removed his carefully-folded handkerchief from his breast pocket and slipped it into his trousers. He felt conspicuous because he thought he looked too prosperous for the neighborhood and he felt embarrassed by his grandfather's use of an occasional Yiddish word, but even so he tried to listen attentively.

"Tell me, Stevie dear, do you know what's worse than a thief, a liar, a gangster, and cheat all rolled up in one?"

Stephen pondered his grandfather's riddle. "Hitler?"

"Ummm!" Jonas scowled, dragging down the corners of his mouth in disgust, "is that a *mommser!* But not the one I'm thinking of. No, what's worse than a thief, a liar, a gangster, and cheat —that's what's called an atheist. You know what's an atheist?"

"I think so, Grandpa."

"An atheist's a blind *schlemihl* who don't believe in God. My own son, your uncle Lloyd's an atheist. How you go on living without God, don't ask me. Ask your uncle Lloyd, he's got an answer for everything. But what that boy is doing with his life, I don't happen to call living, I call that *lady-gaying*. Thank God I won't be here when it comes time for him to answer. God don't ask that much of us. He only asks for us to believe in Him and worship Him and obey His laws and commandments. Tell me, Stevie, what's the fifth commandment?"

" 'Honor thy father and thy mother.' "

"Good boy! That's all that counts. The rest—the money and the movies and the girls—will land you in *drred*. What you did until today don't count, it's overlooked. But today you are a man, and from this day forth you are responsible to God. Love Him, Stephen—love Him lest you rouse His wrath. He's got His eye on you every minute, so behave yourself. Live a clean and righteous life and don't, for God's sake! turn into an atheist."

"I won't," Stephen assured his grandfather.

"Let me have your sacred word."

"You have my sacred word," Stephen said uneasily, after which he and his grandfather strolled back to the Community House where the *bar mitzvah* celebration was already in progress.

When Stephen entered the ballroom the two-piece band that his mother had hired for the occasion was in the middle of "Tzigeuner," and the heavily-pomaded violinist was doing his utmost to bring tears to the eyes of his listeners. At the far end of the room, facing the entrance, Stephen saw a long buffet table whose central attraction was a huge swan carved out of ice and lit from below by pink lights. Stephen remembered this swan immediately from his brother's *bar mitzvah* and realized it must be the trademark of Fanny Rosencrantz, the most sought-after caterer in New York among his mother's circle. Some of Fanny's specialties included molding cream cheese into the shape of a cauliflower, arranging slices of Nova Scotia salmon into the petals of a rose, and creating a sunburst out of a casaba melon and several pounds of impaled shrimp—all of which creations could be seen this very minute, surrounding the swan and glutting the tabletop like a superabundance of water lilies on the surface of a pond. Stephen was amused to watch his Aunt Milly hybridize a cauliflower and a rose and devour the result in a single gulp.

In the center of the room was a dance floor which was fast being cleared to make room for his father's oldest sister, Rachel, who, after drinking one champagne cocktail, was doing a combination cancan and shimmy. Stephen, who had never been exposed to his Aunt Rachel's bawdy side and expected grownups to act like grownups, was shocked by his aunt's performance. Even his father had begun to cut-up and was doing a kind of cakewalk around the periphery of the dance floor, passing out Corona Coronas that had Stephen's name and the date of his *bar mitzvah* commemorated on the cellophane.

Meanwhile, his mother, having alerted the photographer, was busy rounding up the original Wednesday Gang—the six girls with whom she had traditionally played mah-jongg before gin rummy became the vogue—and when, at last, they were assembled, she insisted that Stephen pose with them in the center of the group. But this was only the first in a series of photographs. During the next half-hour Stephen posed with his father's seven sisters, his Great-aunt Tishy and her fourth husband, Uncle Miles, his grandfather and step-grandmother, Cantor Surretzky, Rabbi Berkowitz and Rabbi Pulvermacher, and his classmates: Dennis Abrams, Jimmy Reuben, Peter Bakst, and Peter Schuster; he was also snapped in action, dancing with his cousin Bella Klein, wolfing down a parkerhouse roll and sitting on his mother's lap.

Every time he smiled for the camera, Stephen felt a twinge of guilt. He knew his smile was a lie. He knew his shining cheeks, his sparkling eyes, his lacquered hair, his spotless shirt, his well-pressed suit, and highly polished shoes were lies. He knew what neither his mother nor father nor Roggie nor Grandpa nor Rabbi Pulvermacher nor the Wednesday Gang nor his classmates—not even Jimmy Reuben!—knew: that under all the gloss there lurked an ugly, evil, vice-ridden fiend! Until today Stephen had thought that only he and Dr. Schwartz knew that. But now he realized there was someone else, someone infinitely more powerful and vengeful than Dr. Schwartz who knew his secret: there was God! . . . *The Lord shall surely smite thee!* . . . And yet hadn't Grandpa said, it's overlooked? *What you did until today, don't count, it's overlooked.* It's overlooked! . . . The words were like a panacea, filling Stephen's heart with thanks and hope. He was to be given another chance, another try. From this day forth he would be responsible to God. He would love Him. He would lead a clean and righteous life. He would never, Stephen vowed, no matter how great the temptation, touch himself again! . . .

As soon as the liveried waiters had cleared away the remains of the entrée—poached spring chicken with truffles—remarking as they did so on the gaucherie of the Jews who invariably left their truffles untouched, the band struck up "The World Is Waiting for the Sunrise," a song that Stephen had been forced to learn on the piano the year before and, consequently, hated. The grownups, on the other hand, seemed to adore the song because it made them nostalgic for a time—the period during World War I—when everything had been so much better. Even Aunt Pearl, whom Stephen considered extremely hard-boiled, led Uncle Morty onto the dance floor with tears in her eyes. By this time, however, everyone had drunk too much and was only too eager to disregard the music and demonstrate his or her own favorite step. As a result, within seconds the floor was jammed and resembled the opening minutes of a dance marathon.

At some point in the middle of "Deep Purple," Uncle Morty seized the violinist's instrument and attempted to play the cadenza from Mendelssohn's Concerto. This delighted Jonas Stern not only because his younger son, unlike Lloyd, believed in God and had chosen to play the work of an outstanding Jewish composer, but the sound of the music transported him back to a time when his wife was still alive and his sons were not estranged from him.

Overflowing with excitement and joy, Jonas called out across the floor, "Morty, play a *kazatzki!*" Morty responded immediately with an unrelieved series of ear-splitting notes. In his enthusiasm Jonas rushed out onto the dance floor, crouched on his haunches and began to fling his legs into the air faster and faster, higher and higher as his son sawed away on the fiddle.

The next moment Saul, infected by the spirit of his father-in-law, bellowed, "Hoy!" and flung himself into the hopak. This made Stephen blush and look away, but most of the other guests, as if in answer to a battle cry, began to hum and clap their hands in time with the shrill violin. Like Holy Rollers moved by the spirit of Jesus, one male after the next threw himself into the dance.

It wasn't long before Jonas Stern began to regard these new participants as competition, this *kazatzki* as a contest between the generations, and he strove to exert more energy and fling his legs out faster and higher than everyone else. Gradually, as the spectators became aware of this fact, they began to applaud him wildly and he felt compelled not only to increase his tempo but to try simultaneously to touch the toe of the leg he was extending. After accomplishing this feat successfully three times, on the fourth Jonas slipped, emitted a groan and fell onto his back, gasping.

Stephen had no idea about the seriousness of what had happened until his mother screamed, "Poppa!" and rushed to her father's side, and the rest of the guests crowded after her, murmuring among themselves, whispering, and weeping, imploring one another to please stand back and give the old man air.

Within ten days Jonas Stern was dead and most of the guests who attended Stephen's *bar mitzvah* reassembled at the West Side Funeral Chapel. Stephen came too—against his parents' wishes—and even felt compelled to disregard his father's advice and look at his grandfather's corpse.

What disturbed Stephen even more than the half-opened casket and his first general impression of death—the realization that this old man whom he had last seen in wild animation, doing the *kazatzki,* was lying now in this overstuffed and quilted jewelry box motionless, expressionless and stiff—was the fact that he found his grandfather almost unrecognizable . . . unreal. As Stephen stared at Jonas Stern's lidded, bulging eyes he realized that what really frightened him was the handiwork of the mortician: the rouge on his grandfather's lips and cheeks, the powder on his face, the tonic in his hair, the way in which his hands were crossed, the clean white shirt and tie and business suit in which he now lay dressed. Someone—or even worse, an entire crew of technicians: a make-up man, a manicurist, a hairdresser and wardrobe mistress—had handled Jonas Stern after he was dead. The thought of this violation upset Stephen so much that for a moment, until his father entered the antechamber, he stood rigid, both hands pressed against his stomach, holding back his fear.

"What's the matter, Stevie?"

"Nothing."

"I warned you not to look," Saul said.

The following morning, before the funeral service began, Stephen cried so hysterically he had to run away from his parents and hide behind a pillar in the ambulatory of the synagogue and hold onto it for support. Originally his hysteria was provoked by the sight of his mother's face as his father helped her down the aisle, but instead of subsiding when he ran away, it got worse and he began to wail not only for his mother and grandfather but for the whole human race, trapped, as it was, in the predicament of mortality. Even after the service was over and the cortège of Cadillacs was speeding triumphally through Queens, Stephen continued to cry. And, finally, at the cemetery, when the coffin began its slow, hydraulic descent into the ground and Harriet shrieked, "Poppa!" and collapsed at the edge of the grave, Stephen lost control completely and had to be led away from the burial.

That night, long after dinner was over, Stephen went into the dining room, sat down in his father's chair and stared at the twin oil portraits of Jonas and Sarah Stern. Ever since he could remember, these portraits had hung over the sideboard in the dining room of both apartments; but now, for the first time in his life, Stephen consciously examined the exaggeratedly benign portrait of his grandfather—he had never known his grandmother—which his mother had commissioned just before her marriage. While he sat absorbed in the infinite mercy of his grandfather's eyes, his mother entered the room.

Seeing Stephen transfixed with sorrow, Harriet said, "I never realized, sweetheart, how much Grandpa meant to you. But don't you worry, darling," she said, crossing behind his chair and consoling him with caresses, "he was a beautiful man and you can be sure his soul has gone to heaven."

At ten-fifteen Stephen fell into bed exhausted and switched off the light. Almost immediately—as if to counteract the day's events, to challenge or at least escape his overwhelming sense of death—he felt the need to masturbate.

Suddenly, remembering his vow, Stephen rolled over and thrust his hands under the pillow. Lying on his stomach, he began to feel the mattress pressing rhythmically against his groin. To escape the pressure, he turned over again onto his back. Now, his hands pulled open the bow of his pajama cord. Horrified, he jerked his hands away and gripped the backboard, holding tight, as if someone had grabbed him by the ankles and was trying to drag him off the bed. "I won't, I won't, I won't," he resolved, clinging to the backboard, his body writhing, wrestling against his imaginary torturer, resisting with all his strength and will. But even as he did, another torturer—a tempter this time—entered his brain, saying, "What's the use? Even if you live a clean and righteous life, once you're dead the undertaker will undress you and discover your vice."

"That doesn't count! It's overlooked!" Stephen protested.

"Don't be silly," the tempter scoffed. "Once you're defiled, you stay that way forever, you never change—so what's the use? Give in, give in . . . just one more time, just tonight. I won't tell, I promise you. No one will know, no one can hear, no one can see—not even God; He's much too busy watching murderers and thieves to be bothered with you. . . . Go on. That's it. Think of the red rubber ball. Think of Jimmy. Think of Daddy. Think of the statue of Teddy Roosevelt's horse outside the Museum. That's it. That's it. Go on," the tempter whispered, and Stephen lost his self-control.

As always, after it was over, Stephen's guilt and depression increased in direct ratio to the detumescence of his penis, so that by the time he was limp he was in a state of agony. Suddenly, through his closed eyelids, in a corner of the ceiling—or was it the sky?—Stephen saw the face of Jonas Stern again, not as he had looked in life or death, but romantically benign and glowing, the way he had been painted.

"Grandpa?" Stephen whispered, sitting up in bed and peering into the shadows. "Is that you, Grandpa?" Once again he saw his grandfather's beatific face, but this time it was far away, in a cloud above the apartment house, and Stephen had his eyes open. Automatically, he reached down and pulled up his bedclothes to hide his open pajamas. . . . He's watching me, Stephen thought. All the time I was doing it, ever since I went to bed, he's been up there watching me. Stephen lay down again, rolled over onto his stomach and pretended to fall asleep, but in his heart he knew he wasn't fooling anyone, he knew he was still being watched. He could feel his grandfather's eyes penetrate his back, he could even hear him breathing now, wheezing slightly, in the corner by the closet. He's in this bedroom with me, standing over there, hiding in the darkness. . . . Now he's moving toward my bed . . . now he's passed the door . . . passed the second closet . . . Unable to pretend sleep any longer, Stephen sprang out of bed in terror, covered his face, fell to his knees and cried out, "Oh, God! Please don't tell the others! Please, oh please, don't tell on me!"

The following September Stephen—together with his two friends, Dennis Abrams and Peter Bakst—matriculated at The Van Cortland School For Boys in Riverdale, where Roger had been studying since 1938, and started his first year of high school. By this time God had become a nightly visitor to Stephen's room. Sometimes he would come alone, sometimes in the guise of Jonas Stern or sometimes they would come together, Grandpa and the Lord. They never spoke—either to each other or to Stephen—they simply floated on the air long enough to let Stephen know that he was being watched. But since they never punished him—struck him dumb or turned him gray overnight—Stephen tried his hardest not to notice them or, at least, not to *let on* that he did. He knew that he was fooling no one. He knew that every night as soon as God and Grandpa left his room, they flew to heaven to record his sin in the Book of Judgment. He knew that he was damned already, that he would be utterly destroyed on Judgment Day. But that was too overwhelming to think about. The prospect only drove him deeper into vice, and Stephen rationalized his fall by telling himself that Judgment Day was still far off, that if he was going to have to suffer the tortures of hell when he died, he might as well try to enjoy himself now.

In this respect he had substantiated Dr. Schwartz's prophecy—at least to the extent that in failing to overcome his vice he had been turned into its slave. What had begun as a pleasurable game played in a bathtub was now a serious addiction that demanded satisfaction at almost any time or place—in fields and parks and public lavatories, in movie houses and museums, on buses and in classrooms. Instead of remaining limited to soap and water, Stephen had learned to use other lubricants such as vaseline, saliva, cold cream, hand lotion, and hair tonic; and, whereas once he had unwittingly allowed his sperm to be washed down the drain, he now collected it greedily in handkerchiefs and underwear, toilet paper and toilet tissues, disposing of it furtively. Very often he would wash out his own handkerchiefs and underwear to prevent his mother from discovering the evidence, or melt down jars of vaseline to cover up his finger prints; and once he threw a percale sheet down the apartment house incinerator because he didn't have adequate facilities to launder it himself.

In school Stephen was quick to learn—not algebra or ancient history, but how best to utilize his textbooks and his desks to subserve his vice. In study hall he would slouch down in his seat and stretch his legs until he felt the bottom of the desk press against his groin; in that position, with a textbook propped up in front of him, he would undulate his pelvis as imperceptibly as possible until he reached his climax. Or in French class when M. Renaud called on him, even as he answered, *"Oui, monsieur, vous avez quatre livres,"* Stephen would be sitting there, pressing his grammar against his groin. And even when the entire student body was called to an emergency assembly to hear President Roosevelt deliver his historic words, "Yesterday, December 7, 1941—a date which will live in infamy—," Stephen sat, using the bulk of his civics book to help him gain the relief he craved. This war, this distant war against the Nazis and, now, against the Japanese, did not harrow Stephen half as much as the war in which he found himself pitted permanently against himself, against his vice, against his parents, and his teachers, Grandpa and the Lord, his body and the fear of death.

Because of these more pressing problems, Stephen had almost forgotten Dr. Schwartz's warning about damaging his brain tissue, until one Friday afternoon in April when he was reminded of it in no uncertain terms by Mr. Garland, his General Science teacher.

Mr. Garland was a short, rotund man in his early sixties, who, except for his crew-cut white hair and bushy gray eyebrows, looked like a boy of ten. Though life had aged his stubby hands and blanched his wiry hair, it had in no way touched his face or eyes or spirit. His cheeks were still rosy and temptingly pinchable; he wore shirts with Buster Brown collars and single-breasted suits that were always several sizes too small. Sometimes he would come to school dressed in the uniform of a scoutmaster—a position he had held for over thirty years—and when he led his troop over the rocks in Van Cortlandt Park it was difficult to distinguish the master from the scouts. Even though he was officially supposed to teach the freshmen General Science and the seniors Physics, in class he would often depart from his prepared lectures to interpolate little sermons on subjects such as brotherhood, fair play, and mental hygiene. It was during one of the latter that

Stephen was forced to face again the possibility of insanity resulting from his vice.

"Boys," Mr. Garland began, pouting bitterly and perching on top of his desk like Humpty Dumpty, his legs too short to reach the floor, "today I want to talk about a very serious subject: the erogenous zones. Now this word, erogenous, comes from the Greek word *eros,* meaning love, and refers to those areas of the human body which, when stimulated, arouse the sexual appetite." This phrase provoked several titters in the classroom. "Mr. Maggin, will you please tell us all what's so funny?"

No one in the class had ever heard Mr. Garland snap at a student before, and they were quick to realize the rarity and seriousness of this occasion.

"Despite what Mr. Maggin may think, human beings happen to have a sexual appetite—just as strong as their appetite for food— and there are certain areas of the body which, when stroked, caressed, or fondled, arouse that appetite just as surely as the aroma of a juicy steak and onions arouses the salivary glands, causing the mouth to water. Even though, in looking around this classroom now, I see nothing but expressions of angelic innocence, I've worked with boys long enough to know that most of you have already discovered these zones for yourself. And let me say emphatically, there is nothing *wrong* with that discovery . . . providing, that is, you don't exploit or abuse it prematurely. Because, you see, those zones do not belong to you, they belong to your future mate, your wife, just as her erogenous zones belong to you—that, my friends, is the sacred gift of matrimony." Mr. Garland smiled cherubically and hopped down from his desk. "I think that most of you understand and accept what I'm saying. But there are some among you who disagree, who know better than I, and it is to those boys—the pathetic ones, the impatient ones, the weak and willess ones, the ones who have fallen from grace—that I wish to address myself for the remainder of this hour."

Stephen had begun to feel uneasy almost as soon as he heard the subject of Mr. Garland's sermon, but as it went on and his teacher referred to something he called "the habit," Stephen's heart began to pound; he dared not move, dared not blink for fear of calling attention to himself. And yet that was precisely what Mr. Garland sought—confession and redemption.

"Please try to understand me, boys, I am not here to condemn you, but to help you. I understand and sympathize with those of you who have fallen prey to this outrageous habit and I have nothing but compassion for you. I know—I've *seen* what it can do to boys. I've seen this habit warp their minds and weaken their bodies; I've seen it wreck their lives. I've seen boys like you— extraordinary boys with brilliant futures—suffer nervous breakdowns because of it. I've seen them sitting in asylums, helpless and inert."

. . . *It can even do damage to your brain tissue,* Dr. Schwartz had said. And now . . . *I've seen them in asylums, helpless and inert* . . . Involuntarily, Stephen raised his thumb to his teeth and began to gnaw at the nail.

"I know the stigma attached to this habit," Mr. Garland continued, almost in tears. "I know the shame and guilt its victims suffer. Naturally, I don't expect any of you to come forward now. But afterward—this afternoon, tomorrow, next week—I don't care when it is, so long as you come to me: catch me after class or in the hall or on the playing field, come to my office on the fifth floor, call me at home—my number's listed—write me a note—I swear to keep your confidence—only let me help you, let me help you fight this dread disease!" When he was finished, Mr. Garland stepped down from the lecture platform and left the classroom without looking back like Lot fleeing from Sodom.

"What did you think of that?" Dennis Abrams asked Stephen as the two boys marched stiffly down the hall toward the stairs.

"I think Garland deserves the Academy Award," Stephen said.

"No, seriously, Steve, don't you think he was a little too charitable?"

"Charitable! To whom?"

"The offenders."

"Why, what would *you* do with them?"

"Personally, I think they ought to be ostracized, sent away to some colony."

"Like lepers?" Stephen asked sarcastically, but before Dennis had a chance to answer, they were joined by Peter Bakst.

"Hey there, Stevie, how are your erogenous zones?"

"Active," Stephen said. "How are yours?"

"Rrrravenous!" Peter rasped.

"I don't understand what there is to joke about," Dennis objected. "Obviously you two missed the entire point of Mr. Garland's lecture."

"Oh, no we didn't," Peter teased. "When are you going up to the fifth floor to confess, Dennis?"

"You may think that's funny, Peter, but I don't," Dennis said.

"Look at him blush," Peter giggled, nudging Stephen.

"Guilty conscience," Stephen chimed in, hating himself for playing Peter's game, but afraid to remain silent.

"It just so happens I have a perfectly clear conscience," Dennis proclaimed, glaring at Stephen and adding maliciously, "which is a whole lot more than *you* can say. At least *I* never had occasion to ask anyone the color of sperm," he said and flounced away.

Stephen had all he could do to control his temper and restrain himself from shouting after Dennis, "The color and consistency of milk, my ass!" For an instant he remembered Marvin Klein and was ready to stalk Dennis to the ends of the earth. Instead, he made a face, exaggerating his complete incomprehension, and asked Peter, "What in hell did that mean?"

"Don't ask me," Peter said, hunching his shoulders, "I think your friend is cuckoo. I'll see you on Sunday, Steve."

"What time?" Stephen asked, remembering their date.

"Two o'clock, in front of the zoo."

"Two at the zoo," Stephen said.

"You're a poet and you don't know it," Peter said. "So long, Steve."

When Stephen got home he went straight to his room, sat down at his desk and drafted the following letter:

Dear Mr. Garland,

In class today you spoke about a certain ugly habit. You said this habit could lead someone to having a nervous breakdown or go insane. Now it just so happens that my best friend, who for obvious reasons shall remain nameless, has the habit of which you spoke. He has had it now for a year and a half. I know how hard he has tried to break it. He has prayed to God to help him. He has slept with a pair of mittens on. He has even bound his erogenous zones in a sheet, but nothing helps! He is like a soul in torment. That's how miserable he is. Do you think you could cure my friend? Is your cure some kind of medicine? Is it something I have heard about called "salt peter"? Does it hurt? Will you answer my questions by letter? I would come and talk to you in person but I don't want anyone to get the wrong idea and think it is *me* we are discussing. Sincerely, Stephen Wolfe.

In reading his letter over, Stephen decided the phrase, "who for obvious reasons shall remain nameless" sounded too suspicious and he crossed it out and substituted, "who happens to go to another school." As he read on he began to find more and more fault with the letter. The grammar, the spelling, the punctuation, the tenses—everything seemed wrong, and the more he found wrong, the more doubtful he became about mailing it. Finally, after he had unnerved himself completely, he tore the letter up and began to masturbate.

When he was finished Stephen could hear nothing but a repetition—insistent and monotonous—of the phrase . . . *I've seen them in asylums* . . . *I've seen them in asylums* . . . *I've seen them in asylums* . . . To combat this refrain and drown it out, he went to his record shelf, selected *Le Sacre du Printemps,* pulled out Side 3 and put it on the phonograph. Ever since he had seen *Fantasia,* the Stravinsky score had become his favorite composition. Despite what Disney made of it, Stephen knew this music had nothing whatsoever to do with dinosaurs. He knew it was a tone poem about insanity; he knew that someday when he went insane it would *be* just the way this music sounded. Now, listening to the insinuating flutes, the rasping fiddles, the blaring horns, the throbbing drums, Stephen kept time with his fist. Wild-eyed, he stamped around his room in circles, half-conducting, half-dancing, allowing the music to possess him.

"Stevie!"

It was not until she had shouted his name a second time at the top of her lungs and lifted the needle off the record that Stephen became aware of his mother.

"Ohhh, that Shostakovich!" she complained. "He'll drive me crazy one of these days. Dennis is on the phone. Didn't you hear me calling you?"

"No," Stephen said, going to the guest closet in the hall and picking up the extension. "Hello."

"Of course not," Harriet muttered, returning to her bedroom. "I don't know how you can hear yourself think with that racket going on!"

"Stevie?" Dennis said.

"All right, Mother, I've got it!" Stephen shouted, permanently apprehensive that Harriet eavesdropped on his conversations. "Will you please hang up in there!"

"How silly you are," Harriet remarked into the receiver, before doing as she had been told.

"I just called RKO," Dennis said. *"Kings Row* starts at 7:37. Let's meet in the lobby at 7:30."

Though Stephen had not forgotten their date, it had been made on Wednesday, before Mr. Garland had substantiated Dr. Schwartz's prophecy, before Dennis had broken his promise never to mention Stephen's question about sperm, before Stephen had tried to write that painful letter— . . . Oh, my God! he suddenly realized, I musn't leave it in the basket. I've got to get it out of there!

"Stevie, did you hear me?"

"I'm not going, Dennis," Stephen answered coldly.

"What?"

"You heard me."

"Why not?"

"Not after what you said at school."

"What did I say?"

"You know! Don't act so innocent."

"You mean after Mr. Garland's lecture?"

"That's right. You went and broke your promise—your sacred promise—"

"But I only said that because *you* said—"

"Never mind. I wouldn't go to the movies with you if you were the last person on earth."

"Oh, Stevie, stop acting so insane."

"Insane!" Stephen yelped as if he had been stepped on. "We'll see who's insane. Don't you think I know you were just trying to cover up for yourself? Don't you think I know you have the habit? Wait till Mr. Garland gets the letter I wrote about you! Just you—"

"What!"

"Just you wait!" Stephen screamed and slammed down the receiver.

As he was heading back to his bedroom, Harriet intercepted her son in the hallway. "Stevie, darling, what's the matter? Why were you shouting at Dennis like that?"

Without responding, Stephen marched past his mother.

"Stephen, I'm talking to you!"

"I heard you!"

"Well then, answer me! What's the matter?"

"Nothing! Nothing!" Stephen screamed.

"Who do you think you're talking to, one of your classmates?" Harriet demanded, following Stephen into his bedroom.

"Mother, will you please get out of here!"

"Not until you tell me what's the matter."

"Nothing, I said!"

"And I said, not to take that tone with me!"

"Will you *please* get out of here!"

"Not until—" Harriet was interrupted by the telephone ringing. "Now you just stand there until I answer that. I'm not finished with you, young man, not by a long shot!"

As soon as his mother left the room, Stephen hurried to the wastepaper basket, collected the remains of his letter to Mr. Garland, ran into the living room, seized the first box of matches in sight, made a mad dash for his bathroom and locked the door just as Harriet reached it.

"Stephen!" she said in a loud whisper, as if she was afraid of being overheard. "Stephen," she repeated, twisting the knob. "It's Dennis again; he wants to speak to you."

Holding them over the toilet bowl, one by one Stephen set fire to the yellow scraps of paper until they turned black and he dropped them into the water.

"Stephen! Did you hear me? Will you please unlock this door and come out of there! What are you doing anyway? What is that I smell? Stephen, are you smoking?"

Hearing this, Stephen jumped up and opened the window to clear the air.

"Stephen, will you answer me: are you going to talk to Dennis or aren't you? . . . Stephen! . . . Steeeeee-von!"

The quality of this last exasperated cry was so familiar to Stephen that even through the closed door he could see his mother, her face flushed, her teeth clenched, her body taut and trembling, standing like a runner with her fists drawn up to her sides, trying for the sake of Paula, the new cook, and Dennis who was still waiting on the line, to suppress the volume of her fury.

"All right," she said at last, releasing her pent-up breath and regrouping her forces. "You wait. *Just you wait.*"

Listening at the door, Stephen heard the swish of his mother's silk dress as she walked down the hall and into her bedroom to offer Dennis some apology. He knew that she'd be coming back. Quickly, he went to the toilet and flushed away the charred remains of his letter.

"Stephen," Harriet resumed collectedly. "I was supposed to be at your Aunt Milly's ten minutes ago. Everyone is waiting for me:

Daddy, Uncle Lloyd, Aunt Milly—everyone! But I'm not going to leave this house until you come out of there. Do you hear me? . . *Do you hear me?"*

"Yes."

"Then come out of there this minute!"

His mission accomplished, Stephen walked slowly, guiltily to the door, unlocked and opened it. Almost simultaneously, he saw one of his father's leather belts folded and raised in Harriet's fist; he felt it sting his upper arm.

"You! You! You!" she whined, swatting at him clumsily.

"Bitch!"

"What?" Harriet gasped. "What did you say? What did you call me? Where—"

"I hate you!" Stephen screamed, fleeing to his bedroom and locking the door.

"Come back here, you! . . . Stephen, I want you to open this door and apologize to me this minute. Where did you ever *hear* a word like that? Is that what they teach you at that school of yours? Is that what I'm spending my good money for: to be called a thing like that? To be called—" Harriet could not even bring herself to repeat the word. Instead she produced one mournful, high-pitched note—half-wail, half-bay—and sustained it for thirty seconds. "Ooooooooooooooooooooooo . . ."

Stephen had no way of knowing whether his mother was really crying or just pretending—the effects were indistinguishable. To know for certain you had to see her face, and sometimes—so convincing was her acting—even *that* was not the final test: you had to be reduced to tears yourself—genuine tears, tears of pain —before she would confess, "Don't be silly, darling. Mommy's only teasing."

Now, in order to escape the sound of her crying, to escape the guilt he was feeling, Stephen went to the phonograph and turned on *Le Sacre du Printemps* at top volume. In the course of the performance he heard his brother come home; he heard his mother pound on the door and threaten no more movies for a month; he heard her leave the house; he heard Paula announce dinner; he heard Roger shout that if he didn't come out of there that minute he had better not dare show his ugly puss ever again.

By the time the records were over, Stephen was utterly exhausted and depressed. Instead of allaying his guilt, the music had only made him feel more savage, evil, and demonic. As noiselessly as possible, he unlocked his bedroom door and slunk into the dining room. Immediately Roger, who had finished his main course and was eating his dessert, turned away abruptly and buried his nose in *Life* magazine. From that and the withering glance he received as he sat down, Stephen knew he was being given the cold shoulder or, even worse, the freeze! But despite his awareness, he ventured to speak, "Roggie."

In answer Roger spat two cherry pits onto his plate.

"Aren't you going to talk to me? . . . If I hurry we can still get to the RKO on time. It's *Kings Row*. Ann Sheridan! Don't you want to see it?"

Pointedly, Roger picked up *Life,* slid back his chair, stood up and left the room.

With a show of some annoyance, Paula served dinner. As hungry as he was, Stephen ate mechanically, listlessly. Occasionally, for company, he glanced at the portrait of his grandfather, but only for a second: the irony was too unbearable! Tonight Grandpa looked more charitable and kindly than ever before, as if he were trying to set an example—to show by contrast what it meant to lead a clean and righteous life—as if he were waiting with infinite patience for the answer to his question, "Tell me, Stevie, what's the fifth commandment?"

When he was finished, Stephen thanked Paula and left the dining room despondently. On the way to his bedroom, he stopped outside his brother's closed door. In retaliation for the Stravinsky, Roger was playing some jazz record loudly. Timidly, Stephen tapped on the door. Plaintively, he called his brother's name. "Roggie . . . Roggie . . . Please let me in. I'm sorry I acted so awful. Please forgive me, Roggie. Please let me in."

In response Roger turned up the volume on the phonograph.

". . . I sit in my chair,
I'm filled with despair,
There's no one could be so sad.

With gloom everywhere,
I sit and I stare,
I know that I'll soon go mad.

In my solitude . . ."

"Roggie . . . Roggie . . ." Stephen knew he was wasting his breath, wasting his tears: Roger was not going to open the door. In one night he had alienated his brother, cursed his mother, and lost his friend, Dennis.

Hearing Billie Holiday's refrain: "I know that I'll soon go mad," Stephen slumped away from Roger's door, down the dark hall and into his own room. There, he shut the door, undressed, got into bed, turned off the light, and plunged into his vice.

On Saturday at breakfast Saul characterized the fight between his wife and son as a "little misunderstanding," and he prevailed on Stephen to apologize. Not only did Harriet welcome the apology with tears of gratitude and professions of love, she gave her son a dollar for the movies.

In the afternoon Stephen went alone to see *Kings Row*. After buying a box of Goobers, he found a seat on the right side of the orchestra, as far from the children's section as possible. Even before the film began, during the credits, Stephen was captivated by its theme music—a simple, Sibelian melody that made his eyes brim with tears, so filled with yearning did it sound—and he knew he was going to adore *Kings Row*.

By the time the childhood sequences were over and Paris Mitchell, a boy in knickerbockers, had climbed the stile on the hill only to return, a moment later, a man in full-length trousers, the music mounting gloriously, the camera panning up his legs and body until at last it stopped and focused on the face of Robert Cummings, Stephen was completely engrossed and nervously peeling the silver foil off his empty Goober box. Never before had he identified with any leading man as he did now with Robert Cummings. In the actor's sensitive and handsome face, his earnest eyes, his sensual nose, his halting speech, his innocent and well-bred manner, Stephen saw his ideal self, he found his ideal *other*. As such: partly as himself, partly in flight from himself and pursuing the other, who, in turn, was not the other but himself as Robert Cummings, portraying yet another, Paris Mitchell, who was all of them together, Stephen left the RKO and entered eagerly the dark and morbid world of *Kings Row*. There, he devoted himself to his loving grandmother, Ouspenskaya, he befriended a wild Ronald Reagan, he studied medicine with a stern and somber Claude Rains, and fell in love with his weird and haunted daughter, Betty Field. There, he sensed something fishy about the town's G.P., Charles Coburn, so strict and cruel, and his even stricter wife,

Judith Anderson, mercilessly dominating their frail and nervous daughter, Nancy Coleman. There, as if they were his own, one by one, Stephen suffered the tragedies that overcame these lives: the death of Ouspenskaya, the murder of Betty Field, the suicide of Claude Rains, the unnecessary amputation of Ronald Reagan's legs, the revelation that Charles Coburn was a sadist. When Betty Field fled in her white organdy dress out from under the weeping willow, over the lawn, and down the hill like a sheet blown on the wind, Stephen turned cold with fright at the realization that she was insane. When Ronald Reagan searched the bedclothes frantically for his missing legs and cried out to Ann Sheridan, "Randy, where—where's the rest of me?", Stephen wept uncontrollably. When Nancy Coleman finally rebelled against her father and screamed, "I'll let the world know what you are, if it's the only thing I ever do. Tomorrow—tomorrow I'll tell everyone. I know what you are. I know all about you—and your operations!", Stephen shared her triumph fully, until Charles Coburn smacked her face, and the blow stung worse than his father's belt the night before. He didn't know precisely what any of it meant—nymphomania, infanticide, incest, sadism—but Stephen had no doubt that *Kings Row* was the most truthful representation of the world as it really *was*—a world in which everyone was hopelessly insane—that he had ever seen.

As he walked home, still very much under the spell of the movie, its score still sounding in his ears, his eyes still red, his cheeks stained with tears, the side-street seemed unbearable to Stephen. Even in the sunlight it was colorless, impersonal—nothing but brownstone, granite, macadam, cement: no meetings, no greetings, not even a cat. In order to sustain the excitement and sorrow he had felt during the movie, he began to sing its theme:

"Da dee dum!
Da dee dum!
Da dee, da dee,
Da dee dum!"

Transported by the melody, Stephen found it difficult to continue walking. Having reached the little park around Hayden Planetarium, he stopped and abandoned himself to the *Kings Row* theme. With his eyes closed, his body swaying, his voice rising and falling like a swing, he almost cried the melody:

> "Da dee dum!
> Da dee dum!
> Da dee, da dee,
> Da dee—"

"What's the matter, kid?"

Startled, Stephen opened his eyes and saw a middle-aged man with orange hair. "Nothing," he said self-consciously.

"Why are you crying?"

"I'm not," he objected. "I'm going home."

"Where is that?"

As he started to move away, Stephen felt the man grip his arm—not roughly, but firmly—trying to detain him.

"Ever been to the Planetarium?"

"Yes," he answered quickly.

"Have you seen The Destruction of the World by Fire?"

"Yes," Stephen stammered, seeing in the stranger's eyes an image of the holocaust itself, as if his pupils were lenses of the Zeiss projector. "Yes," he repeated, running away, out of the park, across Eighty-first Street and into his apartment building.

Coming from outside, the halls looked gloomy, almost black.

"Hello, Mr. Stephen," the elevator man said.

"Hello, Max."

"Nice weather."

"Yes." The motor hummed; the cables creaked.

"Here we are: seventeen."

"Thank you, Max."

"Is that my baby?" Harriet asked, hearing the front door close. "Yes."

"How was the movie, sweetheart?"

"Okay."

"Just 'okay'? . . . Doesn't Mommy get a kiss?"

Kiss. "Da dee dum! Da dee dum! Da dee, da dee, da dee dum," Stephen hummed, going to his bedroom and closing the door behind him.

That night Roger went out to a dance and Harriet and Saul had a date to play cards. Just before leaving the house, Harriet said to Stephen, "Are you sure you'll be all right, my love?"

"Yes."

"I hate to leave you all alone."

"I don't mind."

"Why don't you call up Dennis and go—?"

"I'd rather stay home and read," Stephen interrupted.

"But it isn't healthy to be by yourself all the time."

"Oh, for God's sake—!"

"All right. All right!" Harriet said, raising her hands in self-defense. "I'm going now. If you want anything, we'll be at the Saltzman's. See you in the morning, dear."

For a while Stephen tried to read *Sorrel & Son* but couldn't concentrate and tossed the book aside. At nine o'clock he turned on the radio and listened to the "Hit Parade," but for once the songs failed to soothe him and he turned the program off. He went into the kitchen, took a chicken leg from the refrigerator and devoured all the meat, but still he wasn't satisfied and made himself a peanut butter sandwich. After eating that and eating a banana, he switched off the kitchen light and began to prowl through the dark apartment, humming as he went.

> "Da dee dum!
> Da dee dum!
> Da dee, da dee,
> Da dee dum . . ."

From the window in the living room he saw the lit-up dome of Hayden Planetarium and remembered the man with orange hair.

> "Da dee dum!
> Da dee dum!
> Da dee, da dee,
> Da dee dum . . ."

In Roger's room he carefully removed the improvised snoop-detector—two paper clips!—his brother kept permanently in front of the encyclopedia on the forbidden-books shelf, and took down *The Basic Writings of Sigmund Freud*. In the index he looked up sadism. Though very little of what he read made any sense to Stephen, his research led him to other subject-headings: Masochism, Masturbation, Masturbatory impulses, Narcism (narcissism) . . . It was like having poison ivy—the moment you scratched at one spot, you had to scratch another and another and another until your entire body began to itch and erupt in running pustules, and you thought you would go insane if you didn't stop. At last, his brain a rash of words and phrases: inversion, primitive psychic mechanism, *pedicatio,* anal-erotic zone, sado-masochistic impulse—Stephen shoved the book back into place, restored the paper clips and fled into his parents' room.

There, without knowing why, even without knowing he was doing it, he suddenly began to ransack his mother's bureau. In one drawer he found a phonograph record called "Come on, Honey, Let's Make Hanky-Panky"; in another, a peach-colored, plaster ashtray in the shape of a sphinx with gigantic breasts and nipples and the head of Adolf Hitler. In his father's chifforobe, much to his surprise Stephen discovered a toy—a delightful little man with bare legs and bare shoulders, wearing a barrel instead of clothes. Curious to see the little man's entire figure, Stephen pulled the barrel off and was startled when, like a jack-in-the-box, a huge, red-tipped erection sprang out. Stunned, Stephen shoved the barrel back and replaced the toy, but before closing the drawer he spotted his father's athletic supporter.

For a moment Stephen stood undecided; then he reached into the drawer, seized the supporter and pressed its pouch against his nose. A moment later he was standing completely naked, his clothes strewn like wreckage over the purple carpet.

Suddenly, as if he were on a scavenger hunt, holding a type-written list of the items required to win, Stephen began to rush around the apartment frantically. First he put his father's jock-strap on. Then he hurried to his mother's closet, pulled out a sleeveless, black silk dress and put that on over it. In Roger's room he found a pair of tennis balls and stuffed them into the empty bodice. Next, he ran back to his mother's room, rummaged through her jewelry box, selected a rhinestone brooch and pinned it on the dress. Finally, he rushed into his parents' bathroom, flung open the medicine chest and removed his mother's mascara and lipstick.

As soon as he had the make-up on, Stephen stood back from the mirror and looked at himself admiringly. But something was wrong, something was missing . . . his hair! A hat! After combing his hair into bangs, Stephen grabbed a bath towel, wrapped it around his head like a turban and looked at himself again. This time he was rapturous. He thought of Betty Field, he thought of Robert Cummings.

> "Da dee dum!
> Da dee dum!
> Da dee, da dee,
> Da dee dum . . ."

Like a mannequin modeling a new collection, Stephen stood in front of the mirror touching the tip of his chin to his shoulder blade, placing his hand on his hip, stepping back alluringly, pivoting and peacocking until, at last, utterly entranced by what he saw, he approached the mirror seductively, lifted his skirt coquettishly, revealing his father's jockstrap, pressed his body against the glass, shut his eyes and fervently kissed the image of his own lips.

When Stephen opened his eyes again he saw the smear of lipstick on the mirror, the mascara on his lashes. Incredulous, he put his hands over his cheeks and stared bug-eyed at his own reflection. He knew that it had happened at last—just as Dr. Schwartz and Mr. Garland had predicted. A look of agony came into Stephen's eyes and twisted his mouth until his face was unrecognizable and a tortured cry escaped from his throat. "Ahhh! You're insane," he despaired, hiding his eyes from the image in the mirror. "Insane."

On Sunday Stephen met Peter Bakst, as planned, and the two boys strolled through the zoo. After looking at all the other animals—the yak with the inverted horn, the seals and bears and birds and tigers—they reached the entrance to the monkey house. Suddenly the image of the Patas monkey with its yard-long erection came to Stephen's mind and he flinched perceptibly and refused to enter. "I'll wait for you over there," he said, "in front of the cafeteria."

"Why? What's the matter, Stevie?"

"Nothing. Nothing at all. I just don't want to see the monkeys."

"But why? They're such a riot."

"No, they're not!" Stephen answered sharply. "They're disgusting and degenerate."

That night Stephen took Oscar II down from the toy shelf, petted him and put him in his trouser pocket in preparation for school the next day.

LICE

In the coach window, which was covered by a layer of soot like a cataract, Stephen caught a sudden glimpse not of the Pennsylvania landscape but of himself, holding the catalog from Midwestern University's College of Fine Arts. The reflection of his wavy hair, classic profile, prominent cheekbones, and delicate lips pleased him and made him smile. At the end of his senior year at Van Cortlandt, his classmates had voted Stephen not only Best Actor in the class (an honor almost automatically bestowed on the President of the Dramatic Club), but second Best Looking, second Most Personality. At the time he had been flattered, but now, three months later, he felt somewhat slighted. . . . I should've finished first in both those other contests, he decided.

At this moment he was distracted from his reflection by another train approaching on a parallel track thirty or forty feet away. It was traveling in the opposite direction, toward a small but nonetheless spectacular mountain that rose straight up from the side of the tracks like a fjord. Suddenly, as the engine of the second train steamed past his window, Stephen realized that it was not pulling another train at all, but his own around a huge horseshoe-shaped bend. This realization, almost a revelation, startled and disturbed him. It turned his attention away from himself and forced him to admit the world: all the other cars—the engine and the baggage car, the mail car, Pullman cars, dining car and coaches, moving past his window—and all the other passengers, other lives and destinies. Seeing a group of sailors at a table in the dining car, he thought of Roggie, soon to return from the South Pacific. He thought of the War, of Hiroshima, he thought of the dead, and felt ashamed of himself for caring whether or not he had been voted Best Looking in his class. Wasn't this brief revelatory view of the rest of the train the perfect reminder of his own despicable vanity and narcissism? . . . There is no evil worse than narcissism. The devil is a narcissist, Stephen thought, stuffing the catalog into his raincoat. . . . When I get to Midwestern, he resolved, I'm going

229

to turn over a new leaf. I'm going to be absolutely selfless . . .

As always in the early morning, Cumberland was overlaid by a heavy smog that darkened the sky and polluted the atmosphere. Oddly enough, despite the poor visibility, the darkness and the fumes, Stephen felt excited. As far as he was concerned, anything was preferable to unrelieved sunlight. He liked to think of himself as "Northern"—a word he used frequently, loosely to describe the Germano-Scandinavian aspects of his personality: his reliance on will and discipline, his need for order, his devotion to Rilke and Strindberg, his interest in morbidity, depravity, his obsession with death and duality, his love of storms, turbulent seas, solitary walks, wintertime, snow and the night. Had it been practical, he would have chosen to go to college in Stockholm or the Hebrides, but since it wasn't, Cumberland seemed a surprisingly good substitute.

As the taxi sped past Midwestern, Stephen caught his first glimpse of the campus. The big, badly-proportioned, cigar-colored buildings looked as if they might have been erected to celebrate Victoria's Jubilee. Stephen found them ugly and oppressive, and was astonished to learn, months later, that the entire University had been modeled after the Acropolis—the College of Fine Arts after the Parthenon, the College of Engineering after the Erechtheum, the School of Home Economics after the Theseum. But scarcely had he formulated his first impressions, when the taxi pulled up in front of Horatio Hall Dormitory for Men.

Stephen's suite was on the second and top floor at the rear of the building. For a moment, after opening the door, the obvious signs of occupancy made Stephen think he had entered the wrong room. A bulky orange sweater lay inside out on the seat of an easy chair; on one of two desks were some pencils, a sketch pad, a pile of art books and a framed photograph of a dark, attractive, forty-year-old woman with large, moist, fleshy lips—the kind of woman, Stephen imagined, who wore an ankle bracelet. Just as he was about to leave the room, Stephen spotted his steamer trunk and realized he had not made a mistake after all; no doubt the possessions he saw were the property of his prospective roommate.

Despite this awareness, on entering the next room, Stephen was startled to discover a naked body, backside up, sprawled out gracefully on one of two single beds. This apparition stopped Stephen dead in his tracks and made him leer—but only for an instant. Deliberately he turned away to examine the rest of the room.

Like the study which adjoined it, the bedroom walls were painted the color of cardboard. The two beds were separated by a pine night table, and there were two pine bureaus. In addition to a door that Stephen assumed led into a closet, there was another door directly in line with the one that connected the bedroom and the study.

As Stephen tiptoed toward this door, he stole another glance at the sleeping figure. He had never known anyone who slept in the nude. He himself was crazy about pajamas and just before leaving New York had bought two pairs of flannel ski pajamas with turtle necks and tight elastic cuffs. Even his father, who of all the people Stephen knew came closest to sleeping in the nude, wore pajama tops. Staring now at his unknown roommate, Stephen questioned his father's choice. If wearing pajamas was a sign of modesty, and wearing none a sign of sensuality, what did it mean to hedge the issue by wearing the tops without the bottoms? Wasn't that in some way more peculiar, more virtuous and yet more venereal, than either of the two alternatives? Hadn't it helped to turn his father—and consequently himself as well—into a griffin: all spirit, will, and aspiration above the waist, all beast below? Wasn't that the characteristic that most confused other people and even shocked them when, as often happened, things got reversed: the bottoms and the tops, the lion and the eagle? Stephen turned away stiffly from the roommate's voluptuous torso. I doubt that we're going to get on, he concluded to himself as he opened the farther door and found himself inside an antiseptic bathroom which, in turn, by still another door, led into another suite, identical to his own. Stephen had an image of two facing mirrors, reflecting infinitely a series of cardboard-colored rooms.

Just as he was closing the bathroom door, Stephen was startled by a luxurious yawn. Turning around he saw his roommate's arms and legs and torso executing an elaborate ballet of uncoiling movements.

Before Stephen had a chance to speak, the roommate yawned again, longer and louder than the first time. "Good morning," he said with unabashed intimacy.

"I hope I didn't wake you."

"No . . . no . . ." the roommate said, rubbing his scalp and kneading his face. "Had to get up, had to get up," he added in a manner that reminded Stephen of the White Rabbit. "Are you Stephen Wolfe?"

"Yes. What's your name?"

"Leonard Gottlieb," he said, his left hand exploring the top of the night table. "Do you see my glasses anywhere?"

Stephen spotted the huge horn-rimmed glasses behind the base of the lamp. "Yes."

"Thanks," Gottlieb said as he put them on and began to examine Stephen from head to toe.

To break the embarrassing silence Stephen said, "Are you in the Drama Department?"

"Yes. Are you?"

"Yes. What's your major?"

"Design." Gottlieb combed his fingers through his thick black hair. "What's yours?"

"Acting."

"That was nice of them—to put us together, I mean. You aren't a vet, are you?"

"No."

"I didn't think so."

"I'm only seventeen," Stephen said defensively, trying to justify his lack of military service. Gottlieb swung his muscular legs off the bed and sat up straight, staring at Stephen. Something about the width and thickness of his lips made Stephen realize that the woman in the photograph was Gottlieb's mother. "How old are you?"

"Twenty-one," Gottlieb said, standing up and stretching his arms until his fingers almost touched the ceiling.

Self-consciously Stephen averted his gaze, as if he, rather than Gottlieb, were standing there stark naked.

"Have you had breakfast yet?"

"Just some coffee."

"Wait for me, I'll have it with you," Gottlieb said and, without bothering to close the door, he walked into the bathroom and began to urinate.

Once again Stephen felt embarrassed and went into the study. From the window he saw a barren hill that leveled off onto a rich green plateau which, as he was later to discover, was part of a private golf course. Rather than stand around doing nothing, he decided to unpack, but no sooner had he got his trunk open than he heard Gottlieb say something in the bathroom. "What's that?"

"I said, if you have any preference about which bed or desk you want, just say so—it makes no difference to me."

"Oh no. It's fine this way."

"You haven't registered yet, have you?"

"No."

"Good. We'll do that after breakfast," Gottlieb said, arranging the waves (not just waves, really breakers, Stephen thought) in his hair.

As Stephen walked back to his trunk, Gottlieb broke into loud song:

> You better go now,
> Because I like you much to much,
> You have a way with you.
> You ought to know now,
> You've got the lips I like to touch,
> The night was gay with you . . .

Now, for the first time, Stephen realized that his roommate neither spoke, nor sang, nor yawned in a normal tone of voice—everything was amplified—and he wondered if someone in Gottlieb's family was deaf.

In the time it took Gottlieb to get ready Stephen unpacked the entire contents of his trunk, including Oscar II. He couldn't decide whether to keep the toy on his bed or out of sight. In his heart he knew he would want to have Oscar with him at night, but he was afraid of Gottlieb's ridicule. "Forgive me," he whispered, petting the monkey's head and placing him in the top drawer of the bureau, just as Gottlieb, gaudy in his orange sweater, appeared in the doorway.

"Let's go."

The main cafeteria was in a giant structure whose walls were alternately cinder block, glass, and corrugated metal, and whose ceiling was so remote that on exceptionally smoggy days it literally disappeared from sight. "This is the Hangar," Gottlieb announced as he guided Stephen toward the distant food counter. "What words can describe it?"

"Ugly," Stephen said, and Gottlieb laughed louder than the remark deserved.

"That's where the Dramats sit," Gottlieb said, pointing a long finger at two tables against the left wall. "I'll introduce you after we get our chow."

"Who are the Dramats?"

"The kids in the Drama Department," Gottlieb explained with

impatience. "Hi, gang!" he shouted as they approached the second table.

"Hello there, darling," a girl with a moon face and pig eyes called back, obviously imitating Tallulah Bankhead. The girl next to her, who was dressed in a filthy, shabby raincoat and rain hat that made her look like Garbo in *Anna Christie,* waggled her hand like a tambourine and chirped, "Hello, Mr. Gottlieb." Still another girl, with ebony bangs, arched an eyebrow, posed her hand like the head of a cobra about to strike and exclaimed, "Jungle red, Sylvia!"

Even though they seemed freakish and a little frightening, Stephen was fascinated by his classmates and eager to join them. When he did, a willowy boy, who was sitting next to the girl with bangs, asked insinuatingly, "Who's your new friend, Gottlieb?"

"This is Stephen Wolfe, everybody. Steve, this is Fu, Gum, O'Brien, Jack, Jerry, and Carmen. I feel just like Elsa Maxwell."

"If you don't stop eating pancakes, darling, you'll start looking like her, too," the girl called Gum said in her husky voice.

Stephen sat down opposite the girl in the raincoat. With her body slouched over the table, a cigarette dangling from her lips and her head at a drunken angle, she looked more than ever like Anna Christie. For a while Stephen ate in silence, aware that he was being stared at, but trying not to stare back. "I'm sorry," he said at last, "I didn't get your name."

"Frances Manchot," she drawled, the cigarette bobbing between her lips. "My friends call me Fu. And this is my roomie, Gum."

"You sound like a Chinese menu," Stephen remarked, affecting a stagey tone.

"She didn't say *sub*gum, darling," Gum declared, extricating herself from the conversation at the other end of the table and turning toward Stephen. "Just plain, ordinary, everday, American chewing gum—like Dentyne, darling." Without exchanging any signals, simultaneously the two girls nestled their heads together and broke into a singing commercial which they delivered in perfect harmony:

First you learn the whistle—then sing it—
  Dentyne chewing gum—
Dentyne chewing gum—Dentyne—Delicious—
  Refreshing.
Put the two together—then swing it—

Dentyne chewing gum—
Dentyne—so tasty you'll like it.
You will think of this little song when that
Dentyne flavor lasts so long—
Buy the bright red pack today and whistle it
on you way—Say,
You should keep your teeth white with Dentyne
chewing gum—buy—try Dentyne.

When the commercial was over, before returning to the other conversation, Gum added not as an aside to Fu but directly to Stephen, "My, but he's cute looking, isn't he?"

Stephen was charmed by Gum's theatricality, Fu's eccentricity. Compared with them he felt bourgeois, colorless, and longed to be bohemian. "Your roomie's right out of the Algonquin."

"What's the Algonquin?" Fu asked.

"A hotel in New York where a lot of famous people used to congregate—people like Dorothy Parker and Alexander Woollcott."

"Oh no, Gum's from Boston. She hates people to slur her ancestry. Her real name's Gloria Updike Morrison, but I wouldn't try tinkering with her middle name if I were you."

"Where are you from, Fu?"

"Buffalo—the birthplace of Kit Cornell," she said with irony, and once again she broke into song but this time by herself. " 'I brought culture to Buffalo in the 90's!—' " After the opening flourish Fu gagged on some phlegm and had to stop. "Oh damn! damn this drip of mine!" she said, taking out a piece of toilet paper and blowing her nose noisily. "I've had it a hundred years, but Cumberland's just the limit."

For the first time Stephen noticed a wedding band on Fu's left hand, and he felt a slight sinking sensation in his heart. "May I ask a personal question?"

"Aren't all questions personal?"

Stephen shrugged. "Are you married?"

"Married?"

"The wedding ring."

"Oh, that. To God, my dear, to God," Fu intoned. "I'm on sabbatical from the Sacred Heart. Are you?"

"What?"

"Married."

"No."

"When were you born?"

"1928."

"So was I. What month?"

"June."

"So was I!" Fu exclaimed. "What day?"

"The ninth."

"Oh damn! damn! I'm the twelfth. But we're both Gemini—that makes us very close. Maybe you're my other half—my twin."

Stephen stared at Fu's long, jutting face and Roman nose, framed by a lion's mane of wooly golden hair. Because she wore no make-up her face looked vulnerable. "I would like that."

"So would I." Suddenly a look of infinite sorrow came into Fu's eyes and she cast them down as if she were a sibyl remembering some dreadful prophecy that she had lived to see fulfilled.

"What are you thinking?" Stephen asked.

"Oh, just about my nutty family," she answered simply. "I had a great-great-granduncle who drowned a man in the Erie Canal —but he was never caught. Another one was hanged in public for being a horse thief. My father's youngest brother's in the loonybin —nothing violent—he just sits there like a corpse. A cousin of mine cut her wrists with a carving knife. My grandmother's a klepto-maniac. She lives with us. Know what she steals? My underwear. It all sounds like a Warner Brothers movie, doesn't it? But that's what I've got in my blood—all that insanity and violence—and that's what I think my twin is like: some lunatic I have to keep locked up like Mrs. Rochester. Sometimes it overwhelms me," she sighed and had to stop for a moment. "But, then, there are other times when I think of my twin as a kind of guardian angel, some-one who supports and favors me, gives me extra strength and courage. Do you ever think of yours that way?"

"No, not really," Stephen said. "Mine are enemies . . . like Cain and Abel."

Someone at the other end of the table suggested it was time to register, and everyone stood up in unison. As they straggled out of the Hangar doing everything they could to accentuate their indi-viduality, the Dramats acted like a band of gypsies come among ordinary townsfolk. "Wanta get layed?" Carmen asked a clean-cut, freshman engineer who was too embarrassed to answer. Once again Fu waggled her hand like a tambourine and called out to a complete stranger, "Hello there, duckie!" And Gum could be heard throughout the cafeteria when she rasped at Jack, "Aren't you glad you're abnormal, darling!" All of which delighted Stephen and gave him the incentive to do something he had wanted to do for years: throw his coat over his shoulders, instead of putting his arms through the sleeves.

Outside he watched Fu close her buttonless coat with a safety pin. "I'll treat you to some buttons."

"What for?" she asked.

"Your raincoat."

"Oh that!" she scoffed. "I can't be bothered."

Stephen knew she was telling the truth. He realized that the safety pin and the toilet-paper handkerchief were not merely affectations, but expediencies that enabled Fu to dedicate herself to more essential matters.

In order to register they each had to fill out eight long filing cards in quadruplicate, and Gottlieb complained it was worse than the Army. The curriculum ranged from courses with self-explanatory titles such as Voice and Speech, Acting Technique, History of the Theater and Freshman English, to more mystifying ones such as Eurythmics and Crew. "What in hell's eurythmics?" Carmen asked.

"Sounds like something to do with natural childbirth, darling."

"No, no," Gottlieb said. "It's a method of body movement. A man named Dalcroze invented it."

"Now how in the world do you know a thing like that, darling?"

"I'm interested in dance," Gottlieb explained.

"So am I," Fu announced flamboyantly, and within seconds the eight of them were paired off and waltzing over the marble floor of the Fine Arts building.

"I'm afraid I'm not very good at this," Stephen apologized to Fu.

"It doesn't matter. Just do it! Do it!" she commanded, flinging back her head in ecstasy.

Before long Stephen felt a light tap on his shoulder. Thinking someone was trying to cut in, he stopped waltzing and turned around, only to find himself face to face with Mr. Bottel, the Head of the Department.

"What in heaven's name do you think you're doing?" Mr. Bottel asked, not at all in anger but in a characteristically weary voice. "If you've got to behave like nymphs, go and do it in McKinley Park. This is a college, not a dance hall."

"Yes, Mr. Bottel," Fu said contritely.

"And, Frances," Mr. Bottel whined, "what exactly do you call that costume you've got on?"

"A raincoat, sir."

"Now really!" he objected. "You look like Little Nell."

"I'm sorry, sir, but I can't afford a new one," Fu retorted, stiffening with pride. Mr. Bottel puckered his lips cynically and walked away without another word. Noticing the worried expression on Stephen's face, Fu asked, "What's the matter?"

"Is your family really that poor?"

"Don't be silly! They've got gobs of money—three different cars. But I wasn't going to tell *him* that."

As soon as Mr. Bottel was out of sight, the other waltzers converged on Fu and Stephen. "What did he say? What did he say?"

"He threatened to throw us in irons," Fu confided hoarsely. "Starvation diet! Bread and water!"

"Mutiny! Mutiny!" someone shouted.

Stephen thought of his favorite actor, Charles Laughton as Captain Bligh. He wanted to bellow Mr. Christian! Mr. Christian! but was too inhibited.

All around them other Dramats were standing on the marble benches, posing in the niches, hugging the Doric columns, leaping up and down the hall, enacting scenes from movies, ballets, operas, plays. And upstairs in the practice rooms someone could be heard battling with "Casta diva." "It's like recess at the loony-bin," Fu remarked.

"I love it! love it!" Stephen exclaimed. "Don't you?"

"Of course. It's my life," Fu said.

After everyone had registered, Fu and Gum and the girl called O'Brien, who looked like an American Indian, announced that they were going back to the dorm to wash their hair. "See you tomorrow, Steve," Fu said.

"See you in the morning, darling," Gum said to Gottlieb. "Don't forget, I expect you to eurithe with me."

"Ta-ta," Fu called back over her shoulder.

After the girls were gone Gottlieb said, "Isn't Gum marvelous?"

"Yes. So is Fu. I think I have a crush on her," Stephen thought aloud.

"Would it interest you to double date them?"

Something about the way in which Gottlieb phrased his question

—the mere fact that it was put as a question at all rather than as a spontaneous suggestion—made Stephen wary. "I guess."

"Come on," Gottlieb said, wrapping his arm around Stephen's shoulder. "I'll show you the rest of the campus."

After touring all the buildings, they came to a large rugged park that bordered the campus on the west. "What's this called?" Stephen asked.

"McKinley Park. It runs clear down to Elmsford. We ought to go there, too. That's where the Phillips Institute is, and the library."

"Were you born in Cumberland, Lenny?"

"Nope. In Brooklyn—out near Coney. I just got here yesterday."

"Then how do you know so much about it already?"

Gottlieb smiled. "I'm a fast worker."

Nervously Stephen licked the corners of his lips and tried to smile back. "You must be."

"You better believe it. . . . Come on, I'll show you something nice."

As Stephen followed Gottlieb off the cement walk, into the trees, his roommate began to sing again:

> You better go now,
> Because I like you much too much,
> You have a way with you . . .

and Stephen grew apprehensive. It wasn't the song, exactly, that made him nervous, nor was it the idea of entering the woods, but something less specific—something in general about Gottlieb's tone and manner made Stephen feel the need to stall. "Wait! There's a chestnut tree," he shouted. There were lots of buckeyes under the boughs, and Stephen collected them greedily. As he did, he began to sing:

> In your eyes there's love,
> And the way I feel—

Realizing that he had picked up the verse from Gottlieb, Stephen broke off abruptly and turned his attention to the chestnuts. "Look at them! Look at them! Aren't they beautiful?"

"Not as beautiful as some things I can think of," Gottlieb said.

Obvious as the innuendo was, Stephen could not resist taking it up. "Such as?"

"Your profile."

Stephen was used to hearing his nose discussed—for years Roger had teasingly accused him of sharpening it in a pencil sharpener, and his classmates at Van Cortlandt had often called him Barrymore or the Great Profile—but Gottlieb's directness made him uneasy. "Thank you," he said, polishing one of the buckeyes on his sleeve.

"Where did you ever get a nose like that?"

"From my father, I guess."

"Umm . . . It's Greek, positively Greek," Gottlieb remarked, running his forefinger down the bridge.

Startled, Stephen flinched but did not turn away. His heart was filled with excitement and fear, as he stood staring blankly, waiting for Gottlieb to make the next move.

"So are your lips," Gottlieb added, removing his glasses.

"Thank you." Stephen gulped. As much as he was flattered and intrigued by Gottlieb's attention, the removal of the glasses alarmed him and he broke away. "What did you want to show me?"

"That ravine down there. Wouldn't that be a great place for a picnic?"

"I guess so," Stephen answered indifferently. "Let's go back now."

That night Stephen was exhausted and went to bed early, but couldn't sleep. By the time Gottlieb came in, Stephen had been tossing for what seemed like hours. He heard the rattle of Gottlieb's army belt buckle, heard the sound of his trousers as they dropped to the floor, and then, a moment later, landed on the seat of the easy chair. Involuntarily an image of Gottlieb's torso, naked as it had been in the morning, appeared before Stephen's inner eye. To dispel it Stephen opened his eyes and turned over onto his stomach, as Gottlieb stomped barefoot across the linoleum, into the bathroom. Stephen listened but did not move or speak. The next thing he was conscious of was being covered with a blanket. "Thank you," he mumbled, pretending to be half-asleep. Suddenly Stephen felt the weight of Gottlieb's knee depress the mattress. "What is it?"

"Don't be scared. It's only me," Gottlieb answered softly. "You kicked off your blanket."

Before Stephen could thank him again, Gottlieb sat down on the edge of the bed and lifted the blanket.

"What are you doing?"

"Getting into bed with you."

Frightened, Stephen sat up and recoiled into the corner.

"What's the matter?"

Stephen's heart was pounding too violently for him to speak. Only when he felt Gottlieb's hand touch his knee, did he manage to exclaim, "Don't!"

"What is it?" Gottlieb asked ingenuously.

"I don't— I can't—" Stephen stammered.

"Can't what?"

"I don't want to."

"Want to *what?*" Gottlieb demanded.

"Anything."

"Then why in hell did you flirt with me?"

"I didn't."

"You did!" Gottlieb insisted. "In the park this afternoon—you wanted me to kiss you. Well, didn't you? Didn't you? And this evening at dinner—"

"I'm sorry."

"You've been singing my song all day."

"What song?"

" 'You Better Go Now.' "

"I'm sorry. I didn't realize—"

"Like hell you didn't!"

"I'm sorry."

"Stop saying you're sorry."

"I'm—" Stephen began but caught himself.

"If there's one thing I can't stand, it's a cock-tease," Gottlieb grumbled and lit a cigarette. The match-light made his face look sinister.

"I'm not a—" Stephen could not bring himself to repeat the word. "I'm not."

"What *are* you then—afraid?"

"No."

"Well, what? Is it me? Do I repulse you or something?"

"No," Stephen murmured, suddenly protecting Gottlieb's feelings. "It's just . . . I'm not interested."

"Not interested!" Gottlieb jeered as he bounded up from the bed. "Whom do you think you're kidding, honey?"

From the nearness of the glowing cigarette Stephen knew that Gottlieb was standing at his bedside, waiting for an answer, but

Stephen could not speak. He felt confused and guilty, self-righteous and ashamed—sorry for himself, sorrier for Gottlieb. His body was flushed, tense, throbbing. He listened to Gottlieb's heavy breathing and waited to see what would happen next. At last, much to his relief, he saw the glowing cigarette move away, he heard Gottlieb get into his own bed, and Stephen relaxed and fell asleep almost instantly.

The next day, long before his first class was scheduled to begin, Stephen got up and went to the Hangar—not to have breakfast but to avoid Gottlieb and, almost as a corollary, to find Fu. He was avid to see Fu again, and sat down at one of the Dramat tables and waited to have breakfast with her. After waiting three-quarters of an hour, he began to wonder if something was wrong—was she sick?—but he would not eat without her. At 8:45, much to Stephen's dismay, he saw not Fu but Gottlieb, heading toward the table with his morning coffee.

"Why the hell didn't you wait for me?"

"I didn't know we had an appointment," Stephen answered coldly.

"Oh, so *that's* the way it's going to be."

As anxious as he was to shun Gottlieb, Stephen also realized they would have to live together, at least for one semester, and he tried to be more moderate. "Besides, I'm waiting for Fu."

"You mean you haven't eaten yet?"

"No."

"But the girls have breakfast in their dorm."

Without a word Stephen collected his cigarettes and stood up stiffly.

"Where you going?"

"To class."

"Wait for me," Gottlieb said, gulping his Danish. "I'll only be a sec."

"No, I'll see you there," Stephen said and left the Hangar.

To his great relief, on entering the English class, Stephen spotted Fu seated in the last row, reserving with her hand the empty desk beside her.

"We're back here," she called out.

After that, every time Stephen reached the next classroom, he found the ubiquitous Fu sitting there, saving him a seat. By the time Voice and Speech began, it was obvious to everyone, except

Miss Capeheart who taught the class, that Stephen and Fu were a "thing."

"But, Miss Manchot," Miss Capeheart pleaded in her rich, golden voice, "you don't seem to understand. I would prefer you to sit up here, beside Miss Morrison. Have you something against Miss Morrison?"

The question made Gum guffaw.

" 'Course not," Fu said impatiently. "She's my roomie."

"Your what, Miss Manchot?"

"My roommate."

"In that case, you can't have any objections. You see, I like my students to be seated alphabetically. It helps me to remember their names," Miss Capeheart confided naïvely.

"What if, instead of changing seats, I changed my name?"

"The word is *what,* Miss Manchot. *hw, hw, hw: hwhat. 'Hwhat* if I were to change my name?', not *watt,"* Miss Capeheart corrected. "We must use the voiceless bilabial glide, not the voiced sound *w.* Notice the shape of my lips, Miss Manchot, they're pursed as if I were about to whistle. *hw, hw, hwhither, hwhere, hwhy, hwhat,"* Miss Capeheart enunciated, gesturing elaborately as if she were a magician pulling a series of silk scarves out of her mouth. "Is that understood, class?" The class responded with a roar of laughter which, much to everyone's surprise, Miss Capeheart accepted good-naturedly. Despite her affected naïveté and absent-mindedness, Miss Capeheart knew exactly what she had done and why. She had changed the subject not only because she was zealously devoted to Standard American Speech, but also because she was incurably romantic and had sensed from the start Fu's reason for refusing to move. The issue was never raised again.

The last class before lunch was Eurythmics. The teacher was a small, homely but spirited German woman named Rosamund Krauss whom the upperclassmen had affectionately nicknamed Mundel. Before immigrating to America, Mundel had trained for the dance most of her life, had even danced professionally with Mary Wigman's Company. But as dedicated as she was, Mundel bore no resemblance to the popular image of the fearsome, tyrannical *régisseuse.* On the contrary, she was absolutely permissive, compassionate and loving with her students. Neither the T-shirt nor the baggy trousers she worked in could camouflage her triumphant femininity. If it came to a choice, she was always ready to sacrifice her art to life, the end to the means, the class to the individual.

Fond as they were of Mundel, the Eurythmics class made Fu and Stephen acutely self-conscious. Both of them were uncommonly tall, big-boned and slightly flabby. The relaxation and limbering-up exercises made them realize what poor condition their bodies were in, and when it came time to express themselves freely through movement, both Fu and Stephen felt cloddish and clumsy. "I feel like a freak," Stephen complained as they cavorted around the practice room.

"Me too," Fu said.

"Get Mr. Gottlieb," Stephen said, envious of Gottlieb's obvious training and ability.

"A regular Anton Dolin," Fu remarked with a Bronx accent.

"Children, children," Mundel cried in her tiny voice. "Forget that I am watching you. Forget that you are watching each other. Do not try to make your movements pretty. I do not look for prettiness. I do not look for control. First we find the river; *then* we build the dam."

Much as he wanted to follow Mundel's advice, Stephen found it impossible. Instead he resorted to an old and tested response—one he relied on whenever it came time to participate in sports or any other physical activity—buffoonery. He considered his body grotesque, and tried to make others laugh at it and overlook it by exaggerating and mocking its grotesquerie.

After the class was over and they were seated in the Hangar, Fu asked Stephen, "Why did you make such an ass of yourself?"

Stephen felt stung. "What do you mean! You said you felt like a freak, too."

"But you're not, you know," Fu said softly. "You're beautiful."

Stephen looked away.

"Don't you believe me?" she persisted

"Looks can be deceiving. You don't know what I'm like inside."

"Black as the hellhole of Calcutta?"

"Yes! If you must know," Stephen said with pride. "And you'd be smart not to get mixed up with me."

"Too late now."

"Don't say I didn't warn you."

In the afternoon the Acting majors assembled at the Workshop, a little theater in a prefabricated building behind the College of Fine Arts. There, for approximately an hour every day, a dapper, old-school Englishman named Thurston Arnold instructed the freshmen in the mechanics of acting: how to sit, to stand, to turn, and make a cross, how to light a cigarette and hold a cocktail glass. The rest of the afternoon was devoted to the more popular and meaty business of doing improvisations, exercises in sensory perception, memory of emotion, concentration and characterization —even, eventually, the performance of "scenes." Some of these classes in acting technique were taught by Mr. Bottel; others, by Gertrude Gaddis, a demoniacal but inspiring *grande dame* who once had starred on Broadway in a play by Sidney Howard. Every day, after plowing down the aisle, holding a chiffon handkerchief and a book in her hand, Miss Gaddis began her classes by reading in her breathy bass selections from the works of Stanislavsky, Boleslavsky, Gordon Craig, Robert Edmond Jones, Stark Young, or Arthur Hopkins, until her students were completely mesmerized and ready to do her bidding: shed tears for thirty minutes or transform themselves into trees and babbling brooks.

By the end of the sixth week it was generally agreed by students and faculty alike that Stephen and Fu were the most talented actors in the Freshman class. This opinion was unequivocally confirmed when they acted the final scene of *Ghosts* in the best *grand guignol* tradition and, subsequently, the Closet Scene from *Hamlet,* the Second Act of *Private Lives* and the Recognition Scene between Electra and Orestes. Finally, after too many snide and malicious references to "our own Lynn and Alfred" had begun to circulate and the class had reached a complete imbalance, both Mr. Bottel and Miss Gaddis recommended that Stephen and Fu break their unholy alliance and team up with some of their other classmates.

Naturally, Stephen and Fu were not without their detractors. Some, those who were obviously jealous, could be easily dismissed, but others posed more serious and valid objections. In Stephen's case the objections had to do with his tense, rigid, robot-like movement on stage; it was claimed that he was incapable of translating through his body the characterization he had otherwise worked out so brilliantly. In Fu's case the criticism, which came mostly from the faculty, had nothing whatsoever to do with her acting. It was directed against her outlandish way of dressing which, at least in Mr. Bottel's opinion, reflected a profound internal disorder and a shocking lack of discipline. No one, the argument ran, with as little regard for her personal appearance as Fu had, could ever hope to hold the attention of a paying audience.

Such criticism, instead of reforming her, only drove Fu to wilder extremes. No matter what the occasion—a concert at the Civic Center or a dinner at a restaurant—Fu could never be seen without her buttonless raincoat and cloche-like rain hat, and it was rumored that she slept in both. Even when the weather began to turn chilly, she refused to wear the winter coat her parents sent from Buffalo and wore, instead, several shapeless, oversized sweaters under her raincoat and a six-foot knitted muffler wrapped around her throat.

This exhibitionism of Fu's came as a great liberating force to Stephen. Ever since his early adolescence he had done everything in his power to behave like everyone else: to keep his thoughts and emotions to himself, to go unnoticed, to remain anonymous. But now, away for the first time from his middle-class environment, he was encouraged by Fu's example to become an iconoclast, and he behaved as outrageously as possible. Together, he and Fu paraded around Cumberland like Pistol and Bardolph, singing at the top of their lungs, throwing scenes on trolley cars, stealing books from libraries, eating in the street, talking at the movies, trespassing on millionaires' estates, scaring little children, and scandalizing their elders. One night they would bluff their way past the backstage doorman at the Booth Theatre to pay homage to some internationally famous but decaying star, and the next they would go to the McKinley Hotel and successfully demand to be shown Eleanora Duse's death chamber, which for the last twenty years had been opened for no one except Toscanini. By the end of November there wasn't a hotel clerk or shopkeeper, a newspaper vendor or short-order cook, a teacher or student in the vicinity of Midwestern to whom Fu and Stephen were not only familiar but infamous.

Of course they had their quiet moments too—moments when there was no one around to dish or mimic, laugh at or perform for—when they took long strolls through McKinley Park, read aloud from Shakespeare, Nietzsche, and Don Marquis (for whom their enthusiasm was so great they often addressed each other as archy and mehitabel) or went up into the hills to sit and watch the steel mills illuminate the night.

At such times Stephen would hold Fu's hand or put his arm around her waist. But he had never kissed her—had never felt the need. As far as he was concerned, he wanted only to spend every minute of his time going places and doing things with Fu, not waste it making love. Nevertheless, when it came to this subject, he often felt inadequate. Not so much because he thought Fu expected him to kiss her, but because he felt society did, song writers did, Hollywood and his classmates did; consequently Stephen expected it of himself. After all, he and Fu were "going together" and what in the world did that mean if not to be having an affair? And yet, he had only kissed five girls in his life, and those only under the most obligatory circumstances—one during a game of Post Office, another after his Senior Prom—none for the sake of pleasure. It had never, in fact, occurred to Stephen that kissing could be a pleasure; he considered it a threat, a troublesome responsibility, and challenge.

One afternoon just before Thanksgiving, while strolling through McKinley Park with Fu, Stephen spotted the ravine Gottlieb had wanted to show him his first day in Cumberland. Since then, he had never returned to the place where—as he thought about it afterward—Gottlieb had tried to make a pass at him. "Fu," Stephen said, taking her by the hand, "come with me. I want to show you something."

"What?"

"There's a ravine down there—a wonderful place for a picnic." Stephen led the way down the steep decline.

When they reached the bottom, Fu smiled and said, "You did that better than Natty Bumppo."

The bottom was much broader than it had looked from above —almost as broad as a plain. A feeble stream trickled through the area from one end to the other, bisecting it. The source of this stream was obscured by a crude stone bridge that appeared, from where Fu and Stephen were standing several hundred yards away, to be natural. "Let's go look at it," Stephen suggested, and they started up the bed of the stream, bounding from one stone to the next as if they were on a hopscotch court.

Just before they reached the bridge, Stephen stopped short abruptly. "What's the matter?" Fu asked.

"Nothing. It's just that I suddenly had the feeling I'd done all this before."

"That's what's called *déjà vu*. It happens to me all the time. That's why I believe in reincarnation. I know this is my second life, I just *know* it is! You can tell by looking at my palm."

Stephen examined the elaborate tracery that covered Fu's palm.

"Why do your hands always sweat? Why are they always so cold?"

"Nerves."

"Even now?"

Fu nodded solemnly. "I must have done something in that other life of mine—I don't know what, but something awful, something for which I have still to be punished. My mind has managed to forget what it was, but my body knows, my body remembers. This sweat you see is the sweat of a murderess, waiting to be put to death in Rome."

"Oh, Fu!" Stephen exclaimed compassionately, holding her hand and leading her under the bridge where he took her in his arms and kissed her.

After it was over Stephen realized he had not been conscious of the mechanics of the kiss: how he had held his head, where he had placed his nose, what he had done with his lips. But somehow none of that had mattered; he had been able to express everything he felt—all of his affection, the surge of his emotion—through the embrace.

"Oh, Stevie, I love you—love you so," Fu said in a trembling voice and she shut her eyes and rested her head against the arch of the bridge.

As Stephen stared at her transfigured face, two enormous tears, that looked like nectar from an apricot, oozed out from under Fu's closed lids and rolled down her cheeks. "Don't cry," he whispered.

"Oh let me. Let me cry. I haven't cried for years. I never thought I'd be able to again. Let me cry. It's good, so good. Let me cry."

Stephen waited patiently for the tears to stop. But they didn't stop; they kept on flowing, as the water did after Moses had smote the rock with his rod. And her face was like that—like that rock in Horeb: ancient and inanimate except for those tears, the tears of a dead woman, resurrected and weeping over the miracle. "What is it? What is it?" Stephen implored.

"Joy," she sobbed. "It's joy."

After the spontaneity of that first kiss, Stephen's behavior became more and more premeditated. He was eager to kiss well, to be a good lover, to convince not only Fu but himself of his passion. Above all, he was determined to disprove and rid himself forever of the taunt Gottlieb had flung at him that first night: "Whom do you think you're kidding, honey?"

At first, when Stephen walked Fu home at night, the presence of other couples outside her dorm inhibited him and he would kiss her awkwardly—not even on the lips. Then, gradually, they learned to stop along the way—in the unlit entrance to the Administration Building or the shadow of a tree—and kiss before they reached the dorm. But even then, these furtive kisses seemed studied and cerebral to Stephen—not passionate, not pleasurable.

This went on for a week or more until one night, in the middle of their kiss, Stephen felt Fu's tongue touch his lips, prod his teeth, push into his mouth. In grammar school he had heard about something called French-kissing or soul-kissing, had even thought it was the way in which children were conceived, but he had never experienced or practiced it himself. Now he felt the tip of Fu's tongue, tentative as a mosquito searching for a place to land, touch his, hesitate, flit on, alighting here and there, until it reached his palate and withdrew. Impulsively, Stephen's tongue followed Fu's, darted after it, into her mouth. There, like an otter in a pond, it slid about the surfaces, explored her teeth and gums, and playfully attacked and tagged her tongue. Then suddenly, as Stephen's tongue probed further, deeper, striving to reach, to enter Fu's throat, he felt a stirring in his groin. He was overjoyed—overjoyed, because it proved that Gottlieb had been wrong. Not only was he capable of having intercourse with Fu, he wanted to—wanted everyone to recognize him as her lover, their relationship as a love affair. But at the same time, he felt acutely self-conscious and ashamed of being aroused and was anxious to hide the fact from Fu.

"Why've you stopped?" she panted as Stephen pulled away.

"I couldn't breathe," he explained with a forced chuckle.

As their nightly kisses developed into necking sessions, this problem began to concern Stephen more and more. On the one hand, he concentrated on nothing else, was conscious of nothing else, kissed only to arouse himself and sustain his erection—as if that were his sole objective. On the other, he was so embarrassed by the phenomenon and so anxious to conceal it that he always broke away from Fu in the middle of their kisses, leaving her frustrated and himself in a state of extreme discomfort. Often, after parting for the night and finding it almost impossible to stand up straight, Stephen wondered if women suffered as much as men after necking sessions, but he was ashamed to discuss the matter. Very soon he realized he would have to do one of two things:

either consummate their love-making or stop it altogether. Stephen did not want to stop, but the alternative raised a thousand doubts and questions. First of all, would Fu be willing? Secondly, how in the world would he, who found it difficult to urinate in public, undress in front of anyone or even be seen in a bathing suit, ever be able to expose himself in front of Fu? Where would they go? What if they were caught? There were countless questions like these, but the most troublesome of all was the question of contraception.

As a child, Stephen had seen condoms in the park or floating in the Hudson—had thought, at first, that they were discarded nipples from babies' bottles but learned the truth later on, in the sixth or seventh grade, when he heard a joke about being conceived "the night the rubber broke." After that he took vicarious pleasure in the jokes and puns his classmates made on the subject and was secretly titillated every time it rained and his mother reminded him not to forget his rubbers. Sometimes when he came across a used condom in the park, if he was alone, he would poke it with a stick or roll it around under his shoe. But not until he was thirteen did he learn the brand name Trojans. In contrast to the names of boys with whom he went to high school for four years and then forgot one week after graduation, Trojans was a name that took on an instantaneous and everlasting significance.

Stephen knew that they were sold in drugstores. He had overheard men asking for them, had watched the little box being handed across the counter—but he didn't know how he would ever muster the courage to ask for them himself. One Saturday, after rehearsing for days, he went downtown, walked into a drugstore (he didn't dare go to the one near the campus where he was known) and waited shyly to be served. At last, when the clerk emerged from the prescription department, Stephen was startled to see she was a woman.

"Yes, sir, may I help you?"

"Well—er—not exactly—no. I'd like to speak to the pharmacist please."

"Surely. Just a minute."

"Yes, sir, what can I do for you?" asked the pharmacist, who looked like he might have been the subject of a Sinclair Lewis satire.

Stephen took out a scrap of paper. It was his hope or, rather, his strategy to obfuscate his real need in a long list of other superfluous toiletries. "One tube of Colgate, giant size, three bars of Palmolive, a bottle of Vaseline Hair Tonic—"

"But couldn't Miss Lacey have helped you with these?" the pharmacist asked impatiently.

"No!" Stephen said, moving further away from Miss Lacey and continuing to rattle off his list. "A tube of Palmolive Shave Cream, a box of Trojans, a pack of Pall Malls . . ."

Stephen was so relieved to get out of the drugstore alive, he decided—since he was already downtown—to do some Christmas shopping. Almost in a conscious effort to counteract his other purchase, he went into a bookstore and bought Fu *The Prophet.* When he got back to his dorm, he was so nervous about possessing the Trojans, he behaved as if they were stolen goods and hid them in his bureau. On the flyleaf of *The Prophet* he inscribed a quotation from Gibran's text: "You give but little when you give of your possessions. It is when you give of yourself that you truly give."

Shortly before Christmas, Mundel invited Stephen and Fu to her house for tea. She lived on one of those déclassé side streets in Elmsford, very near the University of Cumberland, where her husband, Herman Krauss, taught economics. Neither Fu nor Stephen had ever met Mr. Krauss before. They were greatly surprised by his enormity and sloppiness, which bordered on the gross—at least in contrast to Mundel's delicacy. He was in his shirt sleeves when they arrived and made no effort to put a jacket on or close the top button of his trousers which he had opened to relieve the pressure on his Gargantuan belly. "So you are *Schatzi's* pets, yah? She tells me you are her worst students—"

"Nein!" Mundel objected.

"—But her most beloved. It is easy to see why. Come, sit here with me, Frances. Thank God you aren't wearing the proverbial American skirt and sweater. I'm so sick of my students sticking their tits in my face—I could scream. I can't tell you how distracting! And then, when you reach for the fruit—all trussed up in those mechanical contraptions they call brassières—whack! they slap you on the wrist and call a cop. Coquettes! All of them— coquettes! A generation—a whole civilization of coquettes! Why do they do it? Why do they act that way? Can you tell me, Frances?"

Stephen was a little shocked by Herman's speech—not so much by the content, which he enjoyed, as by the fact that it had been delivered in front of Mundel. But Mundel did not seem to mind; she sat there smiling and enjoying his performance.

"I don't know," Fu said. "Maybe because they worship *two* Gods instead of one—two goddesses, I mean—the Virgin and Rita Hayworth."

"But there were two in Athens—Aphrodite as well as Artemis —and no one gave his allegiance to one in preference to the other. If so, he was destroyed in a jiffy, like Hippolytus. That's what they need of course—these sweater girls—to be pulled apart by horses."

"Either horses or their economics teacher: *nicht wahr, Herman?*"

"Never mind," Herman chided, turning back to Fu. "Before you came, *Schatzi* told me you are dressing like a garbage collector—"

"Ooch!" Mundel exclaimed. "That isn't true! Believe me, Frances, I never said—"

"—Personally I much prefer the uniform of the garbage collector to that of the average co-ed. This shirt you wear, for instance," Herman said, indicating the man's shirt Fu had on, the tails of which hung down over her jeans. "It has a sense of mystery. I cannot quite perceive your contours and yet I think they must be—how shall I say?—rapturous."

"Thank you," Fu said lightly.

"Also, I think you are not a coquette like the others, Frances. If *you* say yes to the economics teacher, I trust you mean it. Am I right, Stephen?" Stephen's speechlessness made Herman erupt into a long, lecherous laugh. "Look at him blush, *Schatzi.*"

"Hör auf, Liebling! Das ist genug."

"I haven't embarrassed you, have I, Frances?" Herman asked, taking Fu's hand into his own and patting it.

"Not at all."

"And look at this! A wedding ring! You see, *Schatzi,* a common-law marriage."

"Frances, is that true?" Mundel asked incredulously.

"Yes," Fu said. "But please don't tell the rest of the faculty."

"But how is it possible I never noticed?—I mean the wedding band?"

"I guess you were too busy looking at my stiff knees."

"Oh, stop it, Fu!" Stephen laughed. "Can't you see she's teasing you, Mundel?"

"Oh how terrible," Mundel giggled. "But I don't blame her. I blame my husband, who coaxed her on. He is incorrigible, no?"

"Yah, yah, I am incorrigible!" Herman agreed, and, as if to prove it, he jumped up, waved his arms over his head and shimmied his enormous pelvis.

"Come, my dear," Mundel said, offering Fu her hand. "Let's go and fix the tea before he corrupts us completely."

When they were out of the room, Herman sank down in the chair next to Stephen's. "I haven't offended you, have I?" he asked in an altogether different tone of voice. "Frances is a lovely girl. You are fortunate to have each other. Of course, I can tell she is still a virgin, but not like those others, not a professional. She'll be honest with you when the time comes."

Stephen's heart began to thump. Until this moment he had been enjoying himself, enjoying his host, but now he hated Herman. Somehow the remark about Fu's virginity struck Stephen as an accusation, as if Herman had seen through him and was saying, in chorus with Gottlieb, Who are you kidding, honey? What's all this nonsense about a wedding ring? Why all the pretense? You aren't fooling anyone!

"Tell me something," Herman went on, after lighting a cigarette. "What do young people do nowadays?—when they wish to sleep together, I mean. Where do they go?"

"Where did they go in the old days?" Stephen retorted.

"Ach! but that was different. Mundel had her own apartment. But Frances—"

"We manage," Stephen said with finality. Now it began to dawn on him that the disappearance of Mundel and Fu was by no means an accident but a prearranged plot of the Krauss'. His suspicion was reinforced the next moment as Herman went on talking.

"Mundel tells me that you are a gifted actor, Stephen, but she worries about your body."

"My body?"

"I mean your movements. How shall I say it? She has been observing a certain . . . constriction in your movements."

"Yes, I know. We've talked about it."

"And what do you think? Do you agree with the good Dr. Freud?"

"What do you mean?" Bridling, Stephen turned away to light a cigarette.

"That these constrictions are usually resulting from something Freud has called sexual repression—What *I* prefer to call erotic constipation. *There* we have the real American malady. Just for fun, Stephen, have you any notion, statistically I mean, what the annual sale of Ex-Lax is in the United States?"

"No."

"It's something in the billions. Shocking, yah? No wonder everybody is moving like a poker. The whole country has the cramps." Caught up in his own rhetoric, Herman went on discursively about American colonic habits, Protestant morality, the Summerfield School and Isadora Duncan, until he heard Mundel returning with the tea. Then, at last, he came quickly to the point. "Listen, Stephen," he whispered. "If ever you and Frances should want to use our house, please don't hesitate to ask. There's no one here all day, you know."

At first Stephen did not register the meaning of Herman's words. Only when it came time to leave and Herman repeated the offer, did Stephen finally comprehend what his host was saying. "Yeh— yes, I—I'll remember," he stuttered. "Look! It's begun to snow. We better hurry, Fu. Good night, Mundel. *Danke schoen.*"

"*Bitte schoen,* my dear."

"Come back soon."

"We will."

"Good night."

"Good night."

When they reached the sidewalk, Stephen sighed anxiously. "Do you know what that pig said to me?"

"Who dear?" Fu asked.

"Herman Krauss."

"No, what?"

Again Stephen breathed deeply. "Never mind. What did you and Mundel talk about in the kitchen?"

"Nothing much: jasmine tea."

"Is that all?"

"Yes. Why? Why are you so angry?"

"Never mind. It doesn't matter."

"No, Stevie. Tell me."

"I said it doesn't matter," Stephen snapped.

"But why do you call Herman a pig?"

"Because his fly was open," Stephen said sarcastically, dropping the subject. "What time are we supposed to meet Gum?"

"Six-thirty."

"It's only six. Let's go and have a drink somewhere."

Both Stephen and Fu were underage, but their height was deceptive and the bartender in the Shamrock served them without suspicion. After a minute or two of silent drinking, Stephen's resentment erupted again. "Imagine that pig talking about *Hippolytus* that way—the greatest drama ever written!—as if it were a case history. Imagine thinking Hippolytus was destroyed because he was sexually repressed—not because of Aphrodite's jealousy!"

"But he didn't say that," Fu objected.

"I'm telling you what he said to *me,* while you were in the kitchen."

"Oh."

"Sexual repression! He thinks the whole thing has to do with sexual repression. Not the gods! Not Aphrodite! Not Artemis, but *ze gut doktur Frreud und Ex-lax und Izadorra Duncan—*"

Fu laughed. "How in the world did she get into it?"

"The whole framework of the play is built around the gods— like the witches in *Macbeth*—and he talks about toilet training!"

"Oh how I wish I could've heard him."

"Let's have two more," Stephen said to the bartender.

At this, Fu waved her arms and broke into loud song. " 'Leave out the bitters; leave out the cherry—' "

"And you should've heard what he said about *you,*" Stephen went on.

"What?" she asked with interest.

" 'I can tell Frances is still a virgin, but when—' "

"What!"

"That's what he said."

Slamming down her glass, Fu exclaimed, "Why, of all the goddamn nerve! Where the fuck does he get off calling me a virgin?"

"Well, aren't you?" Stephen said accusingly, revenging himself on Herman Krauss.

Fu did not respond, and both of them lapsed into a sulky silence that lasted the rest of the cocktail hour.

At six-thirty, after they each had had two Scotches, they left the Shamrock and went across the street to the China Doll to meet Gum and Walter Cass, Gum's new boy friend. Stephen had already begun to feel the effect of the drinks when Gum asked how the tea had gone and he launched into a long, exaggerated impersonation of Herman Krauss, which everyone but Fu enjoyed enormously. Fu complained that she was hungry and asked to see the menu. Stephen was reminded of their first meeting in the Hangar when he had said the girls' names sounded like a Chinese dinner; in commemoration of that he ordered egg foo yong and roast pork, fried rice, sub gum. Gum considered the gesture adorable and clapped her hands, but Fu refused to smile. To cheer her up Stephen began to caress Fu's thigh under the table, but he only succeeded in alienating her even more. After pulling away two or three times, she reacted sternly. "Oh, behave yourself, can't you!"

In an effort to relieve the tension, Gum resorted to her most histrionic manner. "I beg your pardon, darling! To whom are you referring?"

"He knows," Fu grumbled.

After that neither Fu nor Stephen spoke another word, not even to Gum and Walter. By the time dinner was over, Gum was fit to be tied. "I don't know what the hell's eating you two, but I, for one, have had enough!" she announced. *"We're* going to the movies."

"Sorry, Gummie," Fu said in a tiny voice.

"Think nothing of it, darling, you've only ruined my life."

Stephen walked Fu back to her dorm in silence. At some point she remarked how mute the snow made everything, but Stephen refused to respond. When they reached the dorm she said, "Want to come in for a minute?"

Stephen shook his head.

"Oh, Stevie, I'm awful sorry."

"I can reject you as much as you can me."

"I know you can. You're doing it. I said I was sorry. Please forgive me."

"Never."

"I said I was sorry—what must I do?"

Stephen stared at her coldly, cruelly, refusing to speak, and Fu stared back, her enormous eyes filled with urgency and complete submission. Finally, after a prolonged silence, Stephen asked, "Well, what are you thinking?"

"I'm thinking," Fu said softly, "that I want you to take me. Not now. Not just yet. You'll know." she said, and, without another word, she turned and entered the dorm.

Two nights before the start of the Christmas vacation, Stephen and Fu put on their sweaters, mufflers, and galoshes—the snow that had begun to fall the week before, when they had had tea with Mundel, was still on the ground, and fresh snow was falling—and set out for the golf course. When they reached the top of the hill, the one behind Horatio Hall that overlooked the city, they stopped to marvel at the spectacle. The city lights—street lights, headlights, house lights, neon signs, as well as the light from the steel mills, now red, now blue, now yellow, green, fires fluctuating, flickering, fading out, flaring up again, refracted by the snow and clouds, lit up the sky, like an aurora borealis. The hum of traffic— motors, horns, sirens, whistles—shrilled through the night but distantly, mutedly, as if the sound were being transmitted from some arctic radio station. And above it all, breathing in the immaculate air, straining their necks to receive the snow, stood Stephen and Fu like Zeus and Hera standing on Olympus.

"Look there!" Fu exclaimed reverently. "There, where the light from that mill is dying. Now watch—behind us—over there—"

"Where?"

"Just be patient . . . Look! Look! See? Another furnace has begun to blast. . . . Whenever one goes out, another starts to burn more brightly."

"That's what Heraclitus said."

"What?"

" 'This world,' " Stephen quoted, " 'which is the same for all, no one of gods or men has made; but it was ever, is now, and ever shall be an ever-living Fire, with measures of it kindling, and measures going out.' "

"Yes! Yes!" Fu agreed ecstatically. "And we're part of it. Part of the trains, the mills, the night, the snow—oh, Stevie, it's too beautiful!" she cried, unable to continue for her tears.

Stephen took her in his arms and held her tightly, kissed her fervently. For once he did not move away when he began to feel aroused, but kept on kissing more and more intensively, pressing his body against hers, until he felt Fu respond—open to receive him. "Oh, my darling! Darling!" Stephen whispered. "Let's go somewhere."

"Yes! But where? Where can we go?"

"The word is *hwhere,* Miss Manchot. Hw, hw, hwere can we go?" Stephen said, mimicking Miss Capeheart.

"Oh where can we go, my love?"

"My dorm."

"No! They'll catch us—ruin everything."

"I know where . . . But we'll have to wait until tomorrow."

"Where?"

"Let me surprise you. I'll arrange everything. All right?"

"All right."

Even though it was eleven o'clock when Stephen got back to the dorm, he went to the hall telephone and called Herman Krauss. "Herman?"

"Yah?"

"I hope it's not too late—"

"Who is this?"

"Stephen Wolfe."

"Oh, so! Wait. I turn down the phonograph." Stephen lit a cigarette and listened to the music in the background. Just before it disappeared he recognized the third act trio from *Der Rosenkavalier*. "Sorry. So how are you?"

"Fine."

"And how is Frances?"

"Fine thanks. Was that Strauss?"

"*Natürlich*. The Lehmann recording. Have you ever heard it?"

"Not with Lehmann."

"Oh, but you must! You must! There's no one else."

"I'd like to." Stephen took a deep breath. "Could we come over tomorrow?"

"Certainly. Any time. Oh, wait! . . . Tomorrow . . . Tomorrow we go to the Schriebers in the evening."

"I meant the afternoon."

"The afternoon?" Herman repeated blankly, lapsing into silence. Then suddenly Stephen heard the aspirate beginnings of something that sounded like a death rattle but rapidly developed into a boisterous belly laugh. "The afternoon! Of course! Of course. I'll leave the key in the window box—you know where I mean? On the porch."

"Yes."

"In the right-hand corner."

"Thank you, Herman."

"Don't mention it. Any time. Just remember the Marschallin's advice," Herman said, and quoted several lines in German. "*Verstehst Du,* Stephen? One must do it lightly, with a light heart and light hands, hold and take, hold and let go."

"Yes," Stephen sighed. "Thank you, Herman."

"Enjoy yourselves. *Auf Wiedersehen.*"

"Good-by." Stephen hung up and went to his room. Gottlieb was there, working on a costume design. "Hi, Lenny."

"Hi, Steve."

"What's that for?" Stephen asked politely, mechanically, not really caring, wanting only to get to his bureau in the bedroom.

"A play called *Noah*. Some Master's student is doing it in the Workshop after Christmas."

"Oh," Stephen said, leaving the study. The box of Trojans was just where he had left it, rolled up in a pair of woollen socks. Swiftly, stealthily, like a squirrel unearthing its cache, Stephen took the box out, removed one of the condoms and slipped it into his wallet.

"Are you taking the train or flying on Thursday?" Gottlieb asked from the study.

"Train," Stephen said tensely as if he were committing a crime.

"What time?"

"Three forty-five." Restoring the box to its hiding-place, Stephen breathed a sigh of relief.

The next afternoon Stephen and Fu cut class and took the streetcar to Elmsford. "Where are we going?" Fu asked.

"Don't ask questions," Stephen said, enjoying his role of master.

"I won't take another step until—"

"All right. Let's go back."

"No," Fu pouted and continued walking. The sky was overcast and gray, portending further snow. As they turned briskly into Mundel's street, Fu suddenly realized where they were and stopped in her tracks. "Stevie, I don't understand. I thought—"

"Don't ask questions. Just come on."

"But I thought we were going—uh—some place to be together."

"We are."

"Where?"

"Just where you think."

"To Mundel's house?" Fu asked incredulously.

"Yes. Come on."

"Oh, no! I couldn't. I couldn't. I don't understand."

"Neither do I. But what's the difference? That's what Herman said to me last week when I got so angry."

"What did he say?"

"If ever you and Frances want to use our house, please don't—"

"For this!" she exclaimed with revulsion, as if they were planning to commit infanticide.

"Well, it's better than a hotel, isn't it?" Stephen said as he searched the window box for the key.

"How will we ever face Mundel again?"

"Come on!" he insisted, having unlocked the door and not wanting the neighbors to see them. The house was almost dark inside, but Stephen was reluctant to switch on a light. "I guess we go upstairs," he said, leading the way.

"I wish we had our own house."

"So do I; but we don't."

"Don't get nasty."

"Not nasty, just realistic," Stephen said.

Despite its small size and shabby, Grand Rapids' furniture, the room at the head of the stairs was obviously the master bedroom. "Let's see if there's another," Stephen suggested without crossing the threshold. At the end of the hall they discovered a second bedroom, even smaller than the first. On top of the white chenille bedspread, propped against the pillow, stood a massive album of *Der Rosenkavalier*. "Let's stay here."

"What's that?" Fu asked suspiciously.

"I don't know. Just some records." Stephen removed them from the bed. Even though there were curtains on the windows—an ivory gauze, yellow with age—he pulled down the shade halfway. The sky was more forbidding than ever. When he turned back into the room, he was surprised to see Fu standing in her blue jeans and brassière. . . . *zose mechanical contrapshins zey call brazearzs* . . . Not wanting to embarrass her, or himself, he sat down with his back to Fu and began to unlace his shoes. Like novices vowed to silence, they undressed without a word. The only sound in the entire house was the dry asthmatic breathing in the radiator pipes.

Stephen took off his shoes; took off his socks and trousers. As he stood aligning the creases in his trousers, he remembered his wallet—the Trojan!—and realized he would have to have it handy. Even though it was the reason for his being there in that silent, steamy, darkening room, Stephen felt embarrassed about the condom, and anxious to keep it out of sight. . . . When would he put it on? he wondered. Now? But how, if he wasn't erect? Obviously, it was meant for later . . .

As surreptitiously as possible, without so much as glancing at Fu (though he sensed her there, stretched out on the bed, waiting) Stephen placed his wallet on the night table. Suddenly he was seized with panic. Vaseline! . . . Wouldn't they need Vaseline?

Was there any in the house? Where was the bathroom? When was it supposed to be applied? By whom: him or her? . . . Stephen took off his shirt and sat down on the edge of the bed, overwhelmed with apprehensions. At last, almost in a gesture of defeat, without standing up again, he slipped off his underwear and lay down next to Fu.

For the first time since they had begun to undress, Stephen allowed himself to look at her, but he could only see her breasts —her full, enormous breasts, like the breasts of tribeswomen in the *National Geographic*. The only breasts he had ever seen before were his mother's, but even those he had seen only vaguely, veiled by the silk of her nightgown, never bared. Otherwise all his knowledge had come to him secondhand, through photographs, paintings, and sculpture. He had never even had any fantasies in anticipation of Fu's breasts—so the sight of them, the size of them, the spread and discoloration of the nipples came as a complete shock. The idea of touching them or even staring at them an instant longer repulsed Stephen and he began kissing Fu instead.

Perhaps because he was too concerned about performing well, too caught up in his own kisses, Stephen did not notice that Fu was not responding. She just lay there passively, permissively, resigned to her defloration. But Stephen went on kissing, more and more impassionedly, excitedly, until he felt himself begin to stiffen, felt Fu begin to stir, felt his sperm begin to rise in him, almost to the surface, ready to flow out of him, and—trying not to break their kiss—reached behind him for his wallet, fumbled with the Trojan, managed to get it half-unrolled, halfway on, when suddenly, unable to restrain himself another second, he realized that his hands and groin and everything was covered with semen.

Like the jackrabbit that lapses into a kind of catalepsy after ejaculation, Stephen fell away from Fu, rolled over onto his side and collapsed onto the sperm-stained spread. He was too ashamed to speak, too guilty to explain. Only after several minutes did he begin to murmur, "Forgive me. Forgive me. Forgive me. Forgive me."

Now, for the first time since lying down, Fu moved. "What's the matter, Stevie?"

"I can't go on," he confessed in agony.

When Stephen got back to his dorm he realized that he and Fu would have to exchange their Christmas presents the next day and he suddenly remembered the inscription he had written in *The Prophet*. He tried to remove the words with Gottlieb's ink eradicator, but only succeeded in making a purple mess and had to cut out the flyleaf altogether.

The next day, at noon, when school was over, Stephen handed Fu *The Prophet* without a word.

"Merry Christmas, Stevie," Fu said, giving him her present which was wrapped in the *Sun-Gazette*.

"I don't want it."

"What!"

"I said, I don't want it."

"Why not?"

"Just because I don't."

"But you haven't seen it yet."

"I don't care."

"But why? Because it's wrapped in newspaper?"

"I don't want anything from you."

"Not even a muffler? I knit you one like mine."

"What am I supposed to do with it? Hang myself!"

"Oh, Stevie," Fu said in despair. "Please, please, take it."

"I can't," he said and walked away—back to his dorm, where he picked up his valise and took a taxi to the railroad station.

Sitting on the train, watching the snow-covered countryside come and go, come and go—the scrawny trees, the frozen ponds, the fading light from a granite sky, bulging with gray, overstuffed clouds like the walls of a padded cell, Stephen felt himself part of the winter landscape. He lowered his eyes and watched the tracks streak past, a blur of steel, and, in between, a blur of weeds and dirt and gravel. In the background he heard a hum: the voices of his fellow passengers. . . . This train is never going to stop, he thought. None of us will ever be permitted to get off. None of us has a destination. We think we do. We think we know where we're going. *I* think I'm going home for Christmas. That soldier thinks he's going to his wife. That somber man, the one who has his brother's corpse in the baggage car, thinks he's taking it to Harrisburg to be buried. His brother went out West to find something— fame? Fortune? —what he found was Death. We're all like that: seeking, searching, thinking that we're going somewhere, toward something, when actually we're not. We're running away. All of us, running away, because we cannot love, cannot love, cannot love. Condemned to ride this train forever, through a winter landscape, out of nowhere, into nothing, because we cannot love. This train will never stop. . . .

After the Christmas vacation, when *Noah* was presented, everyone in the Drama Department was astonished by the beauty and brilliance of Gottlieb's sets and costumes. No one, least of all Stephen, had ever credited Gottlieb with the kind of imagination and craft he suddenly revealed. Perhaps because the actor who played the title role was so inadequate, the students lavished their enthusiasm—usually reserved for performers—on the designer, and Gottlieb became the lion of the day. The crowd around him after the performance was so deep that Stephen could not even get through to offer his congratulations and had to wait until Gottlieb came back to the dorm. "I can't tell you how much I liked it, Lenny, I never saw such costumes—such colors—they expressed the whole play. A deaf man would have understood it, just from the costumes and sets."

"Thank you, Stevie. I'd rather hear that from you than anyone."

"Why?"

"Oh . . . just because you're such a severe critic—such an intellectual. You've always made me feel like—I don't know—some kind of beast—without a brain, without a soul."

"Have I?"

"Yes."

"I'm sorry, Len."

"Don't be silly. There's nothing to be sorry about . . . now," Gottlieb said, smiling broadly. "Some of the kids and I are going up to The Greeks for dinner. Want to come along?"

"Love to."

"What about Fu?"

"What about her?" Stephen said defensively.

"Think she'd like to come too?"

"No. I think she's busy."

"Stevie, has something happened between you two?"

"Of course not. What makes you think that?"

"I don't know . . . Come on! Let's go to The Greeks."

The Greeks was a Jewish restaurant-bar with Bakelite tables, chrome-plated coat-trees, fluorescent lighting, a jukebox, and leatherette booths. By the time they reached the restaurant, Gum,

Jack, O'Brien, and Carmen were there already, drinking Daiquiris. Just to be different, Gottlieb ordered a Brandy Alexander, and Stephen, without knowing what it was, said he'd have the same. As soon as he discovered it didn't taste of alcohol, Stephen gulped his Alexander like an ice-cream soda. "What is this marvelous thing?"

"Tiger's milk," Gottlieb said mysteriously and ordered him another.

By the time Stephen finished his second drink, he felt like singing, so he got up, propelled himself to the juke box, put in a dime and pushed "You Better Go Now" twice. As the music began, he moved back toward the table enticingly, singing a deep-throated accompaniment to Billie Holiday's solo.

Hearing *his* song, Gottlieb took off his glasses deliberately—as if they were a veil that stood between him and Stephen's lips—and stared at Stephen fixedly.

Stephen acknowledged the stare by addressing most of the lyrics to Gottlieb. After the juke box had played the record twice, it stopped, but Stephen began to sing another song, "Lonely Town," as if it were a lamentation for himself. When he neared the end, the words turned into a wail, his eyes ran tears and he had to stop. Gottlieb tried to comfort him by putting his arm around Stephen's shoulder but Stephen would have none of it. "Come on, Gum!" he cried with exaggerated bravery. "Let's give 'em a chorus of 'Music, Maestro, Please!' "

The song that followed was so loud, it attracted the attention of everyone in the restaurant, including the outraged owner, who promptly threw them out. Outside, Stephen went on singing louder and more desperately, pretending to be drunker than he really was, until Gottlieb decided to take him back to the dorm.

Stephen flopped down on his bed and leaned against the wall, while Gottlieb opened Stephen's laces and removed his shoes and socks.

"Come on now, stand up," Gottlieb said.

Stephen obeyed. As Gottlieb worked to unbuckle his belt, Stephen began to sing again:

> . . . I want you so now,
> You've got the lips I love to touch
> You better go now . . .

Holding Stephen's opened belt loosely in his fingers, Gottlieb stared into Stephen's eyes. Stephen neither blinked nor looked away. Suddenly, Stephen felt Gottlieb's hands inside his waistband, drawing him closer, encircling him, seizing him by the small of the back and pulling him, holding him tight against Gottlieb's straining pelvis. Gottlieb's mouth seemed larger and more rapacious than the one that swallowed Jonah, but Stephen entered willingly and let himself be swallowed—let himself be licked and kissed and fondled until his entire body became an organ of lust, and Gottlieb lowered him onto the bed. "Please turn out the light," he said, as Gottlieb continued to undress him.

"But I want to see you."

"Please."

"All right. But why can't I see your nose? . . . Beautiful nose. . . . Beautiful eyes. . . . Beautiful lips . . . beautiful, beautiful lips. What's the matter? My beard hurt?"

"No."

"Beautiful chin . . . Beautiful chest . . ."

"Oh, Lenny, don't . . ."

"You should change to B.V.D.'s, baby, they're easier to get off."

"Don't."

"What have we here?"

"Appendicitis."

"Don't push me away."

"I hate it. "

"You're so mistaken."

"Don't do that!"

"Why not? You think it's wrong? You think I'll get the clap? Just relax . . . relax and let me love you . . ."

"No."

"Please, please, Stevie, take your hands away."

"No!"

"Oh, let me! Let me! Let me!"

"No! Come back up here!"

"You crazy fool. Why did you do that?"

"I want you here . . ."

"I should have known."

"Known what?"

"That it would be the Princeton rub or nothing."

"Is that what this is called?"

"It's nice to hear you laugh. Let me hear you laugh again: I love it. That's it, baby: laugh . . . laugh—"

"Lenny, don't—"

"Yes, yes: laugh."

"—Don't . . . don't: you're tickling me, Lenny. . . . Lenny, don't. . . . Oh, Lenny! . . . Lenny! . . . I'm—I'm—"

"Good, baby, good. . . . Tell me now, was that so painful? . . . What's the matter, Stevie? Why are you crying? . . . What is it? Please! Take that pillow off your face and talk to me—talk to me. Please stop crying, Stevie, please! . . . Where are you going? *I'll* get the towel; you stay there. . . . What are you doing? Close that window. It's freezing out. You'll catch pneumonia. Stevie, please, you're soaking wet. . . . Will you *please* pull your head back in here and let me close this window? It's *snowing* out! . . . Stevie, stop it! Stop it, please! Come back in here. . . . All right—all right: I'll get your robe."

"Oh, God . . . Oh, God . . . God, God, God, forgive me . . . please forgive me . . ."

"Here, put this on. Now tell me what's the matter?"

"Please, oh please, just leave me alone."

"But you can't stay there."

"Please!"

"All right, all right."

". . . Forgive me . . . please forgive me . . ."

The next morning Stephen was awakened by the blinding glare of sunlight reflected from the snow. So dazzling was the day, it made him disbelieve the night. Surely what he thought had happened the night before was only a dream. Yet, there was Gottlieb asleep in the other bed. Stephen frowned, put on his robe and went to the window. The sky was as blue as the Star of India, the sapphire at the Museum of Natural History. Even though he felt exhausted, Stephen was exhilarated by the sight of the snow. Looking out at it, he remembered Lakewood, where his parents had taken him and Roger for Christmas when they were children. He remembered the Georgian-style hotel, the lake, the woods, the smell of pine. He remembered riding in a horse-drawn sleigh—the graceful, curlicued runners, the restless horses snorting steam, the dip of the chassis as he mounted the step, the sealskin lap robe on the seat, the old driver who tucked him in, the crack of his coachman's whip, the sound of the sleighbells, the blinding glare, the rush of the wind, the sting of the air as they glided across the turquoise snow, breathless and faint with excitement. Thinking back on it now, Stephen did not smile at the irony but cried instead with gratitude, because he realized he had never again felt that hopeful and alive, that childlike and innocent until this morning. By some miracle this crystalline morning absolved him from the night and remitted his sin.

"What are you doing up so early?" Gottlieb asked through a yawn.

"Looking at the snow."

"But that's where we left off. How do you feel today?"

"Marvelous . . . strangely enough."

"Why is it strange?"

"Given the way I felt last night . . . You know what Thornton Wilder said? 'For what human ill does not the dawn seem to be an alleviation?' "

"What does alleviation mean?"

"Relief."

"I don't get it," Gottlieb scowled, engaged in his usual morning search for his glasses.

"Wait. I'll give them to you," Stephen said, crossing to the night table.

"Thank you, baby." For Gottlieb putting on his glasses was like washing his face to another man: not until he had was he awake and ready for the day. "There you are," he beamed, "more beautiful than ever. Don't go away. Sit down here and talk to me," he said, moving over and making room.

After hesitating a moment, Stephen sat down on the edge of the bed.

"Now tell me, what's this human ill you feel so relieved about? You mean last night?"

"Yes."

"Did you hate it that much?"

Stephen nodded.

"Oh, no you didn't, baby. You only *think* you did."

"Are you telling *me?*" Stephen challenged.

"Yes. It's that *brain* of yours—that busy, busy brain of yours, always working overtime, always judging everything. Why don't you give it a rest for a change?"

"I wish I could."

"You can. Your *body* didn't hate last night."

"Didn't it?" Stephen countered.

"No. I'm here to tell you. I know it didn't. No one who hated sex could've responded the way you did."

"I didn't respond at all."

"Didn't you? Then how do you explain this hickey?" Gottlieb asked, indicating a reddish-purple mark on the right side of his neck.

"Where'd you get that?"

"Not from Santa Claus."

"Are you implying it's from me?"

"What are you getting so touchy about? I love it, love it. I'm going to have it framed. I want more, more!"

"You're such a hedonist," Stephen said dismissively.

"What does that mean?"

"Sensualist."

"You say it as if it were a dirty word—as if you didn't have any senses of your own. Well I've got news for you, sweetheart," Gottlieb said, sitting up and laying his hand on the nape of Stephen's neck. "You're much more of a sensualist than I am. You've got a wild, low-down beast in you that you don't even know about."

"Don't I? You think you know more about me than I do?"

"Well if you know, how come you despise it so? How come you keep it in a cage and try to starve it to death?"

"That's *my* business."

"No it's not—not anymore. You see, I love that beast of yours. I think it's beautiful, beautiful and sexy, everything about it: it's sweat, it's shit, it's come—I love them all," Gottlieb asserted in a soft, husky voice, holding Stephen's face between his hands. "And I'm going to do everything in my power to win its favor, that beast of yours. I'm going to pet it and feed it and play with it every chance I get—"

"And just what am *I* supposed to do, while you two are off playing?" Stephen asked archly.

"Wait around and watch us. In between, you can teach us all those big words of yours like alleviation and hedonist, and read us all those highbrow books of yours, and tell us about all those symphonies and paintings—but now, we're going to play. Right now, this minute," Gottlieb said, moving toward Stephen's lips, "your beast and I are going for a run."

Stephen pulled back. "Oh, no you're not," he objected but before he could get away, Gottlieb caught him in a scissor hold.

"Oh, yes we are," Gottlieb laughed, hauling Stephen onto the bed and straddling his body. "Your beast and I are going to make love again, right now, here in the daylight, so that you won't call it a human ill— And you won't deceive yourself into thinking you feel marvelous because the night is over. You silly goose," he chided, bouncing on Stephen's chest. "You feel marvelous because it *isn't* over—because it's going on! It's going on." Like a closing drawbridge, Gottlieb gradually lowered himself until he was stretched out flat. "And now I'm going to show that beast of yours something it's never seen before."

"Such as?"

"The sunshine, baby."

This time, when they finished making love, Stephen did not cry. Little by little, day after day, night after night, his resistance dwindled, his shame and guilt seemed to disappear. He went around the campus with an impish gleam in his eye, singing and smiling constantly. He had his hair cut crew-style. He began to wear Lenny's clothes: his turtle-neck sweater, his tan suede jacket. Every day they gave each other gifts: books, toys, flowers, trinkets; every night they ate together: not in the Hangar but in a small Hungarian restaurant in Foxglove Hill. On the weekend they took showers together, drank Alexanders together, and went to the movies or symphony together.

By the following Monday Stephen was feeling happier than ever before. To celebrate their first week's anniversary he suggested they go "corrugating" after school. Corrugating was the name the Dramats gave to their favorite winter sport—a form of sledding in which large pieces of corrugated cardboard were used to ride on instead of sleds.

When Stephen and Lenny met at four-thirty, the sun was almost gone from the sky, leaving it the color of slate. "Guess what happened to me today," Lenny said as they mounted the hill behind the College of Fine Arts.

"What?"

"I was put on the decorations committee—for the Beaux Arts Ball."

"How marvelous! When is that?"

"In the spring—in April. Know what the theme is?"

"What?"

"The Classical World. Isn't that great?"

"Why?" Stephen asked.

"Why! Just think of the people we can go as: Damon and Pythias, Antinoüs and Hadrian, Achilles and Patroclus—"

"Orpheus and Eurydice," Stephen interjected.

"Very funny."

"I think I'll go as Diogenes or Plato."

"Like hell you will! You're going to go as Antinoüs—and like it," Lenny declared, sitting down on a piece of cardboard and pulling Stephen down in front of him between his knees.

"Will you design my costume?"

"You bet I will. And I'm going to make it as brief as the law permits."

"No. I want to wear a toga."

"Not on your life! You're going to wear a tunic," Lenny said, wrapping his arms around Stephen's waist. "And it's going to start here—and end here!'

Stephen laughed and clamped his loins together, trapping Lenny's hand between them. "I'll be arrested for indecent exposure."

"That's just what I want! No more modesty! No more Plato! No more pajamas!" Lenny exclaimed, shoving off and starting down the hill.

As they gained momentum, not only did the piece of cardboard descend with roller-coaster velocity, it began to spin like a pinwheel—since they had no means of controlling its course—and Stephen started laughing and screaming wildly. "We're going to be killed! We're going to be killed—like Ethan and Matty."

"What?" Lenny shouted.

"I said—" But before Stephen could complete the sentence, they landed on top of each other in a snow drift.

"Are you all right?" Lenny asked as soon as he caught his breath and could stand up.

"Uh-huh," Stephen murmured, lying back languidly as if he were on a beach in August.

"What were you saying before we crashed?"

"Nothing," he said, smiling up at the evening star. "I was just agreeing with you about Plato and pajamas." Stephen's words brought Lenny back down on top of him. "Don't! Don't!" Stephen objected. "Someone will see us."

"Let them! Let them! What is there to hide?"

It was not until three days later, during Mr. McCarthy's History of Theater class, that Stephen first became conscious of an itch in his groin. Mr. McCarthy was lecturing on the Chester Cycle of English mystery plays, listing their titles: *Prophetes Before ye Day of Dome, Antechriste, Domes Day* . . . when suddenly Stephen noticed he was scratching himself vigorously. As soon as he realized where the irritation was, he became self-conscious, stopped immediately and wondered if Fu, who was sitting next to him, had seen him doing it. In order to keep his hands away from himself, he put his arm around the back of Fu's seat and tried to concentrate on Mr. McCarthy's description of a medieval scenic device called a hell-mouth into whose smoke and flames the wicked were prodded by hideous, hairy devils with pitchforks. Unconsciously, compulsively, Stephen began to scratch himself again. This time, when he became aware of it, Stephen felt concerned and puzzled. I must have a rash, he thought, and remembered his mother's skin disease when he was a child.

After class he went to the men's room to examine himself, but aside from a slight inflammation, he was able to detect nothing. Off and on throughout the afternoon he tried to resist the need he felt to scratch himself, but the itching was overwhelming and he was helpless to control his hands. That night before going to bed, he examined himself again, but again he was unable to discover any evidence of a rash.

The following morning, after a good night's sleep, there were still no red spots; what's more, the itching had stopped and Stephen assumed his trouble was over. But halfway through Voice and Speech it all began again—the itching, scratching, resistance, submission, embarrassment, scratching. There must be something wrong with my underwear, he thought.

When class was over, Stephen went to the men's room again and examined his briefs. At first he noticed nothing—they weren't binding him and there was nothing wrong with the elastic or cotton. But on closer examination he discovered a mysterious deposit of tiny black specks peppered over the pouch. Stephen frowned, completely mystified. What could it be? he wondered. This confusion and concern turned into alarm when, later in the day, during Miss Gaddis' class, Stephen felt something crawl across his scrotum. "Something moved!" he said aloud.

"What, honey?" Fu asked in a whisper, trying not to disrupt the class.

Stephen did not answer. Had he just imagined it? Was it just a state of nerves or had something actually moved down there? And, if so, what was it? What was it? Stephen sat perfectly still and waited—his entire consciousness and nervous system centered on his scrotum. After a moment he felt whatever it was begin to move again—not hurriedly, not even gradually, almost imperceptibly, shifting its position as slowly but deliberately as a planet. Without asking permission, Stephen jumped to his feet and rushed out of the Workshop.

When he reached his room he locked the door and took off all his clothes. Now, for the first time he really examined his pubes exhaustively, parting the hair again and again, as if he were combing a lawn for a four-leaf clover. For a moment or two he found nothing, until he reached the area just below his appendicitis scar, and there, standing out against the soft pink flesh, he saw a black-brown spot. It was almost nondescript, unlike any measle, pock, or pimple he had ever seen—much more like a freckle, yet unmistakably alien. As he went on searching, he located other spots . . . three, four, five . . . nine—everywhere, at the root of almost every hair and over his entire scrotum, wherever he could see, Stephen kept discovering black-brown spots. "What are they?" he said in extreme agitation. Scabs? From the rash? From scratching? Stephen picked at one of the spots, but it wouldn't come off.

Suddenly, almost simultaneously, he felt and saw another spot begin to creep across his flesh. It's alive! he gasped, trying to pick it up, but the instant his nails touched the spot it became inanimate again, like a freckle or a birthmark, and Stephen couldn't get hold of it.

In a panic, he ran to the medicine chest, grabbed a pair of tweezers and began to jab and dig at the spot until he burrowed under it, pried it up, pincered it and tore it away from his flesh. What he saw between the tongs, when he held them to the light, was a writhing mass—were they limbs or feelers?—that suggested the feet tubes of a starfish or some other aquatic creature. Was it a fish or plant or sponge or what? he wondered as he began to distinguish the cockroach-colored body and stunted head from the six translucent legs that were kicking like the legs of any insect, overturned and struggling to right itself. Insect! It's some kind of insect from the sea—a sandbug or a beach flea—but how in the world did I get it? Where did it come from in the wintertime? . . .

As Stephen went on staring at the creature, studying its frantic legs, thinking exclusively in terms of tide pools and the sea, another one began to move, and he was startled to remember the sperm he had examined once, under Roger's microscope. Instantaneously, galvanically, this memory synthesized the clues. It's sperm! he cried. My own sperm, turned into these vermin, because I've sinned . . . because I can't make love the way that God intended . . . because my sperm has never reached its natural destination . . . but falls on me instead, and seeps into my hair and turns to bugs . . . biting me, because I've sinned . . .

"They're biting me!" Stephen cried out helplessly. "Eating me! sucking out my blood . . . My own babies turned to leeches and sucking out my blood, because I've sinned . . . At last I'm being punished for my sins—punished for my lust—for all those years and years I loved myself—and now! for loving Gottlieb and wallowing in scum—God has visited this plague on me. Oh, God, dear God, forgive me! Forgive me! What must I do? What must I do to regain Your love, to purify my soul?"

Stephen reached toward the pair of scissors, removed them from the medicine chest and began to cut his pubic hair. The more he cut, the more contaminated he felt, and he handled the hair as if it carried the bubonic plague, cautiously dropping the snippings into the toilet and flushing them out of sight.

When he was finished he scrubbed his hands, soaped his groin and seized his razor. Some of the hairs were still too long and snagged on the blade, sending little shocks of sharp pain through his body. Stephen waited for these shocks, welcomed them, wished that they were more intense, more acutely retributive. At the same time, he took great satisfaction in rinsing off his razor and counting the carcasses of the dead bugs floating on the surface of the soapy water.

As he drew the razor closer to his testes, he became more and more unnerved. The skin was so much more delicate now, the business of shaving so much more dangerous. He hated to have to handle himself—to see and hold that wrinkled, pimpled, purple-veined, tumescent bag, sagging there between his legs—that ugly, evil apparatus, the source of all his sins and misery. . . . If only he were rid of it!—rid of it forever; if only he could free himself forever of its tyranny—the longing and the lusting and the guilt. If only he were strong enough, brave enough to put an end to his temptations and lead a holy life. Maybe, then, God would forgive him, redeem him—if only he could cut it off . . . But suddenly Stephen's body rebelled—his bowels collapsed with fright, his heart beat violently, his hand trembled and he dropped the razor into the sink.

At six o'clock, when Lenny came home, Stephen was in bed, reading. "What's the matter, baby, are you sick?"

"No."

"Well what are you doing in bed?"

"Reading."

"Don't you remember you were supposed to come for a fitting at five?"

"Fitting?"

"For your Antinoüs costume."

"Oh, I forgot."

"Forgot!"

"I'm sorry. It doesn't matter anyway. I'm not going to the Ball."

"What do you mean?"

"Just what I said."

"What's the matter with you, Stevie? Why are you staring at me like that? This is your old Aunty Lenore. Remember me? What is it? What did I do?"

"Nothing."

"Then why are you acting this way?" Stephen didn't answer. "Come on, baby, tell me what's—"

"Keep away from me!"

"What are you saying?"

"I said, keep away. I don't want you coming near me anymore."

"You aren't serious."

"You heard me."

Lenny looked completely bewildered and began to pace back and forth between the rooms, asking all kinds of questions, which Stephen refused to answer. Finally, after a futile half-hour, he suggested that they go and eat, but Stephen wouldn't budge. "Aren't you even going to eat?"

"No."

"Why not?"

"I'm not hungry."

"You mean you're just going to go on lying there, reading that ridiculous book?"

"This ridiculous book happens to be the Bible," Stephen said superciliously.

During the next two days, Stephen read GENESIS, EXODUS, JOB, PSALMS, ECCLESIASTES, and LAMENTATIONS, and when he was

finished with those, he went to the library and took out *The Con-
fessions of St. Augustine.* In the course of both days he didn't
scratch himself once and, consequently, he assumed that God was
rewarding his penitence. But on the third day the itching resumed
—he felt the stirring and the crawling and the biting again, and
knew the bugs had come back. He found the little specks that
looked like pepper on his underwear again, discovered the black-
brown spots again and realized he had failed to kill them
all—some had escaped, had burrowed deeply into him, under his
skin, had tunneled up his anus, and no matter how he scratched or
picked or clawed at them, he would never be able to exterminate
them all—a few tough survivors would always remain to torture
him and feast on his flesh.

"I just don't understand what's the matter with you lately, Stevie
—what's come over you?" Lenny complained in exasperation.
"Why won't you let me touch you? Why do you prefer to sleep
with that stupid stuffed monkey? Why do you keep your nose stuck
in that Bible every minute?—"

"It's not the Bible, it's *St. Augustine.*"

"Why won't you talk to me? Why won't you go to the Ball?
What in hell's the matter with you?"

" 'To Carthage I came, where there sang all around me in my
ears a caldron of unholy loves.' "

"Oh, come off it!"

"No, *you* come off it!" Stephen snapped. "Just leave me alone
if you don't like it. That's all I ask, to be left alone!"

As Stephen picked up his book and continued to read, Lenny
watched Stephen scratch himself ferociously. "Stevie."

"What?"

"Have you got the crabs?"

"The what?"

"The crabs."

"I don't know what you're talking about."

"I'm talking about lice."

"Lice!"

"You've been scratching yourself so much lately, I just thought
you might—"

"Of course I don't have lice!" Stephen said self-righteously.

"Where are you going now?"

"Out," Stephen said and ran to the corner drugstore. After

fabricating a complicated story about some friend of his who had the crabs, he was sold a remedy.

When he got back to the dorm, Gottlieb was gone and Stephen read the instructions on the bottle: "Crab lice and nits. Apply gently but thoroughly on the affected hairy places. After 15 minutes wash thoroughly with soap and warm water; while still damp comb the hair with a fine comb . . ." Since he had already shaved himself, Stephen considered the rest of the instructions inapplicable and unscrewed the cap. The disinfectant smelled like gasoline and stung sorely wherever his skin was raw or broken, but he interpreted the stinging as just another form of retribution, and suffered it like a martyr.

While waiting the fifteen minutes, Stephen sat down in the bathroom and went on reading:

> To love then, and to be beloved, was sweet to me; but more when I obtained to enjoy the person I loved. I defiled, therefore, the spring of friendship with the filth of concupiscence, and I beclouded the brightness with the hell of lustfulness; and thus foul and unseemly, I would fain, through exceeding vanity, be fine and courtly. I fell headlong then into the love wherein I longed to be ensnared. My God, my Mercy, with how much gall didst Thou out of Thy great goodness besprinkle for me that sweetness? . . .

Stephen stopped and reread the phrase, ". . . out of Thy great goodness . . ." At last he understood. God had infested him with these vermin not in order to punish or destroy him, but to save his soul, to save him from himself and that caldron of unholy loves. Out of His great goodness, God had saved him!

Stephen stepped into the shower, turned on the water and watched the dead lice fall away from him like sins. Cleansed! He was being cleansed of his iniquity. Out of His infinite goodness, God was restoring him to a state of grace and Stephen wept with gratitude. "Oh, God, dear God," he cried out above the roar of the water, "thank You for Your mercy!"

During the next two months Stephen imposed a rigorous asceticism on his life. He completely abstained from alcohol and sex. (If, on waking, he discovered that he had polluted his bed during

the night, he punished himself by fasting until dinnertime.)
Though he continued to eat fish and eggs, he eliminated all meats
from his diet and considered himself a vegetarian. As much as his
wardrobe permitted, he dressed in black: black ties, black sweater,
black trousers. He gave up movies and went only to concerts. He
gave up novels and read instead Meister Eckhart, Hopkins, Ta-
gore, Pascal, Cardinal Newman, Swedenborg, and St. John of the
Cross.

As the weeks went by, Gottlieb became increasingly caught up
in preparations for the Beaux Arts Ball. The more he did, the
more Stephen disdained the whole affair. As often as his roommate
asked why he hadn't bought his ticket yet, why he hadn't come to
fit his costume, Stephen answered with the rhetorical question,
"For what? To go to Carthage? To go to Babylon? To go to
Nineveh? I've been!"

Despite this endless exchange of protests and dismissals, after
school on the evening of the Ball, Gottlieb came back to the dorm
carrying not only Hadrian's robes, but the Antinoüs costume he
had designed for Stephen. "Look what I have, Stevie."

Stephen was sitting stiffly at his desk, his back to the door,
reading PSALMS. Without even looking up, he went on mouthing the
words:

> Save me, O God, for the waters are come in even
> unto my soul.
> I am sunk in deep mire where there is no
> standing;
> I am come into deep waters—

"Aren't you even going to look?"

"At what?"

"Your costume! I decided to fit it without you. After all, I know
your measurements fairly well by now."

Turning around, Stephen saw Lenny holding a scanty white
tunic draped over one arm; on the other a white toga with purple
bands. "Why can't you take no for an answer?" he said wearily.

"Come on, Stevie. Cut the crap."

"You think I'm kidding?"

"Yes, I think you're kidding!"

"Well, I'm not."

"Why are you being so stubborn?"

"I'm not being stubborn. I just think it's a waste of time. I think—"

"I know. I know: you think it's vain. You think it's sinful. You think it's like going to Carthage. I know. I've got the message."

"Then why don't you accept it?"

"Because I've been working on this Ball for seven weeks. I worked on this costume of yours for three nights. My own time! My own money! I had to go to Bergmann's to get—"

"I'm sorry, but I didn't ask you to."

"No, you didn't ask me! You didn't ask me to buy you a ticket either!" Lenny protested, extracting one from his wallet and slapping it down on Stephen's desk.

"How much was it?"

"Never mind! It's a gift. A *gift!*" he repeated emphatically. "Something you don't know about . . . and never will."

Seeing the price marked on the ticket, Stephen took out a five-dollar bill and offered it to Lenny.

"Keep it! Keep it! I don't want it. Give it to your favorite charity!" he shouted, storming out of the room.

Long after Lenny had dressed and left for the Ball, Stephen went out for dinner. It felt like rain; the sky was overcast. It was too late to go to the Hangar, so he went to the corner drugstore and ordered a grilled cheese sandwich. Unlike other nights, there wasn't a Dramat in the place—everyone was at the Ball!—and Stephen had to eat alone. When he was finished, he strolled back toward the dorm. Along the way the signs of spring were unmistakable. Most of the porches, walks, and lawns were bordered with bright tulips. Window sills were crowded with potted geraniums and hyacinths. Everywhere forsythia and privet were in bloom. The gentle April air was saturated with the smell of loam and grass and young leaves. Its aroma was unavoidable, irresistible. It infiltrated Stephen's nostrils, stirred his heart. As he neared Horatio Hall, he began to hear the music from the Ball, intermixed with sounds of revelry: shouts and songs and laughter. In the distance through the trees he saw the Fine Arts building—every window ablaze with light—and tried to imagine the horde inside in Greek and Roman costume. It's like the Great Dionysia, he thought, before reentering the dorm. They're probably singing dithyrambs and swatting one another with giant phalluses . . .

Back in his room he tried to read *Heaven and Hell,* but the sound of the music was too distracting. As warm as it was, he got up and closed the study window. Returning to his book, he read three or four more pages before he realized that he was absorbing none of it. Like a ray of sunlight reflected in a pocket mirror by a teasing child, the white and purple toga kept catching his eye. Next to it, on the seat of the easy chair where Lenny had hurled them, were the tunic, an eye-mask and a pair of sandals.

For his own amusement Stephen decided to try on the costume. The tunic fit snugly, perfectly, there wasn't an inch of excess material. The finger-length skirt, which was split down the front and draped to overlap the crotch suggestively, exposed Stephen's legs and thighs to great advantage. He put on the sandals and tied the leather cross-lacing just below the bulge of his calf. In draping the toga he was careful to bare his left shoulder. He combed his hair into bangs and then ruffled them for the sake of virility.

At last, completely dressed, he stood in front of the mirror admiring himself and striking tragic poses. As he did, a thought occurred to Stephen: what if he were to go to the Ball not as Antinoüs but as his hero, Hippolytus? He could wear the same costume. After all, there wasn't that much difference between the Roman tunic and the Greek chiton, the toga, and the cloak. He would drape it differently: across his chest and over his left arm. No one but Lenny would recognize him once he had his eye-mask on. He could come and go unnoticed like a spy—like one of "God's spies." Yes! Yes! He would go not to participate but only to observe and pity the vanity, the folly, and corruption of his fellow men . . . So resolved, he rearranged the toga, donned the eye-mask, snatched the ticket off his desk, and left the dorm.

In order to avoid coming into the middle of the Ball, Stephen used the north entrance which brought him into the basement of the Fine Arts building. It was like entering the Polo Grounds or Madison Square Garden—the event was overhead, not yet visible but audible: the tumult and the music. Some stragglers—two girls and a boy dressed in togas—came stumbling down the hallway, arm in arm. Obviously drunk, they shouted *Salve!,* before disappearing into the men's room. Without returning their greeting, Stephen headed for the spiral staircase that connected the basement with the great Main Hall where the Ball was in progress. Much to his surprise, just as he passed the locker room and set foot on the bottom step, he was seized by acute stage fright—not at all as if he was one of God's spies, but the guest of honor, the leading player on whose shoulders the success or failure of the evening rested. To reassure himself of his anonymity, Stephen adjusted his eye-mask.

"Hello, darling."

Even with his back turned, Stephen recognized Gum's voice. For an instant he thought of climbing the stairs without answering, to make it seem like a case of mistaken identity, but the threat of facing the mob was worse than that of Gum. "Hi, Gum."

"What the hell are you doing here? I thought you took a holy vow to stay home."

"I changed my mind."

"Well come in here and help us kill this bottle," Gum said, entering the locker room.

Stephen followed. Somewhere in the maze of lockers they came upon O'Brien, limp in the arms of a boy Stephen didn't know. A bottle of Schenley's dangled from her left hand.

"Look what I found on my way back from the Forum," Gum said.

O'Brien attempted to focus her bleary eyes. "Who is it?"

"Don't you recognize the beefcake, darling? Stevie, take off that silly mask and have a drink," Gum said, relieving her friend of the bottle and handing it to Stephen.

"Well, if it isn't our own McKinley Park Hamlet," O'Brien slurred. "Have you seen the fair Ophelia lately? Her wits are gone for love of you."

"Don't be a bitch, O'Brien," Gum said quickly. "Why don't you introduce your friend? Stevie, this is Mark. Mark's an engineer."

"Hi, Mark," Stephen said.

"Don't say hello to him," O'Brien advised the engineer. "He's a louse . . . a louse."

"Drink up, darling," Gum urged Stephen.

" 'There is a willow grows aslant a brook,' " O'Brien recited, "And there, with nettles in her broken heart and daisies in her tangled hair, the fair Fu drowned."

Stephen took a long gulp from the bottle. The whiskey burned his throat and made him gag.

"Drowned . . . drowned . . . : 'Young men will do't, if they come to't; by cock they are to blame.' "

Stephen took another swig. This time, as if by capillary action, all of it went to his head.

"Come on, darling," Gum said, slipping her arm through Stephen's. "Let's get out of here!" As Stephen started to hand the bottle back to O'Brien, Gum intervened. "No! No! It's mine! Take it with you."

"By Cock they are to blame!" O'Brien shouted after them, as they left the locker room.

Before going upstairs, Gum had one last drink and told Stephen to finish the bottle. There were about five shots left and it took two gulps to down them. When he had, Stephen deposited the empty bottle under the stairs and rose to the floor above like a helium balloon cut from its ballast.

Emerging from the stairwell, he found himself in the middle of a scene that most resembled the Belshazzar's Feast sequence in *Intolerance*. Hundreds of couples dressed in everything from Greek and Roman to Assyrian costumes were swarming and dancing over the marble floor, milling up and down the broad steps that led to the dean's office. The great Main Hall was not large enough to contain them and they overflowed on one side into the vast Concert Chamber where the band was playing, and on the other into the orchestra, down the aisles and onto the stage of the Little Theater. Every column of the peristyle was wreathed with a rope of greenery. The plaster casts of Hermes, Aphrodite, Artemis and Apollo that stood in niches off the steps were crowned with gilded garlands, and, wherever possible, the decorations committee had suspended huge clusters of purple papier-mâché grapes in honor of Dionysus.

"It's like Babylon. Have you ever seen such an orgy?" Stephen said, turning to Gum, but she was gone.

In her place stood a young boy in a white cloak, which was draped over his left shoulder in such a way as to leave the right side of his body from neck to pelvis completely naked. The voluptuous mound of his firm belly was exposed to the navel. His nipple stood erect. His head was covered with a mass of wild curls that looked alive like licking flames, and his large green eyes were sorrowful. "I've never been to Babylon," he remarked.

"Oh, I'm sorry," Stephen said politely.

"For what?"

"I thought you were my friend: she was here a minute ago."

"What makes you think I'm *not* your friend?"

Stephen smiled. "What's your name?"

"Roger. What's yours?"

"Hippolytus."

"I've seen you in the halls a lot, Hippolytus."

"Have you? What department are you in?"

"Architecture."

"I'm a Dramat."

"I know."

"How do you know?"

"Ohhh, I just know," Roger said evasively. "I also know your name is Stephen."

For a moment Stephen stared deeply into Roger's soulful eyes. "You have me at a disadvantage."

"Oh, no. *I'm* the one who's at a disadvantage."

"How's that?"

"You've got that eye-mask on."

Stephen removed the mask. "Is that better?"

"Much."

"Aren't you cold, dressed like that?"

"A little."

Stephen glanced down at the swags of material that concealed the lower half of Roger's belly. "What are you wearing underneath?"

"Nothing."

"Nothing! You mean if I lifted those folds—"

"You'd see Cleopatra's Needle, yes," Roger smiled. As Stephen stood gaping, the young architect reached into the voluminous folds of his cloak and magically produced a silver flask. "Want a drink?"

"Yes," Stephen responded breathily. "Yes."

"Not here. Let's go to the men's room."

As Stephen turned to follow Roger, he heard someone shout, "Antinoüs!" It was Lenny calling from across the Hall, plowing through the crowd. Before he could escape, Stephen felt his roommate seize him from behind.

"You've come! You've come! Oh, baby, you've come!"

"Take your hands off me." Stephen snapped.

"Come now, Antinoüs. Is that any way to talk to your emperor?"

"I'm neither Antinoüs nor your subject," Stephen said. "Excuse me, but someone's waiting for me."

Suddenly, noticing how Stephen had draped his toga, Lenny groaned, "Uhhh! What have you done?"

"Where is he?" Stephen asked, scanning the crowd for Roger. "Where has he gone?"

"Just like an actor," Lenny continued, throwing up his hands. "You create something fabulous—something flattering and beautiful—and what does he do? He puts it on upside down! He wears it like a stole. A stole! Oh Léon Bakst, forgive them! Forgive them, for they know not what they do. When will actors ever learn? All they ever think about is emotion, emotion, emotion, and not one of them knows how to wear a costume!"

As Gottlieb went on lecturing, Stephen turned and walked away.

"Hey, Stevie, where are you going? Stevie! Stevie, come back here! I want to fix your costume!"

Moving as fast as possible, Stephen made his way through the crowd, rushed downstairs, ran the length of the basement and burst into the men's room, but Roger wasn't there. Turning on his heels, he started back out the door, just as Gottlieb reached it.

"What the hell's the matter with you? I want to fix your costume!"

Without stopping to explain, Stephen bolted up the north staircase—mounting the steps two at a time—and dashed down the first floor corridor until he came to the top of the marble steps above the great Main Hall.

This time, when he caught up with Stephen, Gottlieb was out of breath and irritated. "Will you stop this insane marathon and tell me who you're looking for!"

"Whom you're looking for."

"Whom you're looking for."

"No one," Stephen said, surveying the crowd for a glimpse of Roger.

"Then why did you run away?"

"Because I couldn't stand your dogma!"

"I'm sorry, Steve. I only wanted to fix your costume."

"There's nothing the matter with my costume."

"But you haven't got it on right!" Gottlieb objected. "That's not a chlamys, it's a toga! A toga. Antinoüs was Roman, not Greek."

"Thanks for the scoop. But for your information I'm here as Hippolytus."

"Who the hell is that?"

"What difference does it make? He was Greek, not Roman. A Greek who worshiped Artemis," Stephen added, staring down the steps at the goddess in her niche.

"Who's Artemis?"

"*There,* you imbecile!" Stephen barked, pointing at the statue. "The one on whom you and your committee have placed that stupid garland. Artemis, the wild one, the virgin . . . cold and heartless, pure as ice. The one who dwells on mountain peaks . . . untouched . . . untouchable . . . aloof and unapproachable. The one who roams the night alone—who roams the wilderness and woods alone except for wild beasts. Artemis: the deity of solitude, the solitary huntress, sister of Apollo, Aphrodite's opposite. The opposite of all contamination, of all corruption and carnality—of syphilis and lice! She's pure! She's clean! She's holy! She has no need for anybody's flesh. She doesn't spend her nights in filthy beds making love and breeding lice! She's free! Free—"

"Stop shouting, Stevie," Gottlieb broke in nervously. "Everybody's looking—"

"She runs with stags and wild boars among the stars!"

"Stop it, please!"

"When you offer her a garland, you don't stick it on her head," Stephen snarled, sprinting down the steps and snatching the wreath off the statue. "You lay it at her feet, like this, with reverence," he instructed, kneeling down and reciting a portion of Hippolytus' hymn:

> . . . dear lady, from a hallowed hand receive this garland for thy golden hair, for I am favored as no other man to be with thee and even speak with thee, hearing thy voice, though seeing not thine eyes.

"Stevie," Fu said softly.

For a moment it seemed to Stephen as if Artemis herself had spoken, and he raised his head expectantly.

"Gummie told me you were here. I've been looking for you everywhere."

Seeing Fu crouching down beside him, her hair upswept in a chignon, her bare arms extended toward him in an attitude of mercy, her enormous eyes welling with compassion, Stephen began to cry bitterly. "Oh, Fu! . . . Fu! . . . Fu! . . ."

"Don't," she implored in a whisper. "Don't. Let me help you up." Now, as she rose to her splendid stature, softly draped in a full-length, moss-green chiton, Fu looked like Athena, supporting the wounded Diomedes.

"Oh, Fu . . . Fu . . ."

"What do you think this is, a freak show? What are you all

staring at?" Fu scolded the crowd, as she helped Stephen to his feet. "Haven't you ever seen anyone in his cups before?"

"Is he all right?" Gottlieb asked, joining Fu and taking hold of Stephen's other arm.

"Of course he is," she answered. "Aren't you, Stevie?"

"I need a drink—Oh, God! I need a drink."

"I'll get you one," Fu said, "as soon as we sit down."

"Where'd he go? Where'd he go?" Stephen asked.

"Who, dear?" Fu asked.

"The boy with the flask."

"I don't know." Once they reached the top of the steps, Fu steered Stephen to one of the marble benches out of sight of the Ball. "Will you go and see if you can find him a drink, Gottlieb?"

"Sure, Fu."

"Try the locker room," she suggested.

When Gottlieb was out of sight, Stephen turned to Fu and took her hand. His face was wrinkled with pain. "Fu."

"Yes, cookie."

"Oh, Fu . . . Fu . . . Forgive me! Forgive me!"

"For what? For taking a couple of drinks?"

"For everything."

"Don't be silly. There's nothing to forgive."

"Oh, Fu, I love you. I love you . . . and I can't . . . I can't love anyone!"

"Why do you say that? Because of what happened before Christmas? Oh, honey bun, I don't ask for that. I never did. I can live without that. I'm satisfied—satisfied?" she interrupted herself. "—I'm overjoyed! just to be with you—just to be in your company. Don't you understand that? Whatever we do, whatever it is: go to the movies, take walks, talk, read, have lunch together— that's enough! That's all I want, all I ask. What kills me is when you cut me off. When you look right through me—" Her words made Stephen cry more pitifully. "Oh, Stevie, what is it? Tell me, tell me, darling, tell me what it is that hurts you so."

"I can't . . . I can't . . . I can't love anyone!"

"Stop saying that. Don't you realize what you've given me?" Fu paused and stared straight ahead, as if she was trying to focus on some remote landmark. When she resumed her voice was thin and husky. "When I came to Midwestern, I was a spook, a dark and twisted spook—that's all I was, all I'd ever known . . . until you crossed my path. I still don't know how it happened—why God should have been so merciful—" For a moment Fu's gratitude overwhelmed her, and she began to sob. "But there you were, that morning in the Hangar, the very first day—as soon as I set eyes on you, I *knew,* knew you were my other half, my *better* half—"

"No."

"Yes, Stevie. It's as if you were my soul," she said, almost in a state of trance, her head thrown back, her eyes glazed, her arms outstretched, the fingers spread and curled, like two bare maple boughs. "You showed me things I'd never seen before, never known, like beauty . . . love—"

"I can't love anyone."

"—You taught me what it means not to be a spook, what it means to be alive and have a beating heart—a heart that's not alone but part of every other heart, every other creature, every person, every plant. You taught me that," she whispered, "taught me I was not alone. Just by being *you,* by being alive and in this world, you made me whole, made me human. And you say you can't love."

"I can't . . . I can't . . . I can't . . ." Stephen cried. The words were automatic now. His tears flowed easily, fluently, as if to shed them was no longer painful, as if they had lost all trace of subjectivity and become a force of nature. "I can't," he repeated, standing up unsteadily and moving away from the marble bench like a sleepwalker.

Fu hurried after him. "Where are you going?"

Stephen did not answer. With the tears streaming from his open-but-unseeing eyes, he continued down the corridor, past the other marble benches, past the great Main Hall, past Miss Capeheart's room—his body moving willessly, effortlessly as if it were under a spell.

"Look, Stevie!" Fu exclaimed. "Here comes Gottlieb."

"Sorry, kids. I had to go all the way up to the fourth floor. You should see what's going on up there: it's wild, simply wild. Here's your drink, kiddo."

"No!" Fu interrupted, but before she could stop him, Stephen had drained the paper cup.

"What's the matter? What's he crying about?" Lenny asked, as Stephen moved past them, down the north stairs and into the basement.

"Nothing. He's just had one too many," Fu explained. *"Two* too many, now. We better get him home."

"We can't. It's raining out—pouring. I heard it on the skylight upstairs. Let's take him—"

"Never mind," Fu interrupted impatiently. "I'll do it myself."

"No, no, I'll help you."

When they got downstairs, Stephen was not there. Fu ran to the door and opened it. The rain was falling heavily, in drops the size of dimes.

"He can't have gone out in *that,"* Lenny observed. "He must be in the men's room."

"No! There he is!" Fu exclaimed, seeing Stephen pass under the street lamp at the end of the block. "Stevie! Stevie!" she called, running out into the rain.

"Fu! Come back here, Fu!" Lenny shouted, running after her. "Stevie! Stevie!"

Hearing his name, Stephen began running, too, running swiftly through the downpour, through the dark, away from the Ball, away from Fu, away from Lenny, across the campus, up the hillside, toward the golf course, crying and calling as he ran, "Roger! Roger! Roger!"

Far from deterring him, the rain released and rallied him, and he dashed ahead faster and faster, up the hillside higher and higher, charging wildly into the deluge, as if his ultimate destination was not the golf course but the source of the storm itself, the sky. He wanted to get away from the trees—the sheltering trees, the eaves and walls and rooftops that protected him—away from everything that stood between himself and the rain. He felt it in his hair and eyes, he felt it trickling down his cheeks, streaming down his body, refreshing and reviving him. It tasted cool and sweet, and quenched his thirst, but not enough. He needed more—needed to expose himself, immerse himself, inundate himself completely.

And so he went on running through the rain: up the hillside, up the cinder drive, past the clubhouse, past the eighteenth hole, out onto the rough—high above the city, high above the steel mills— almost flying now, gliding on the wind over the slippery grass and down the sloping fairway until he fell exhausted to the soggy ground.

Lying there, winded, panting, Stephen rolled over and surrendered to the rain, letting it pelt and splash him. He thrust back his head and opened his mouth. He spread his legs and flung out his arms. He dug his fingers into the soil—deeper and deeper into its softness, as if he were trying to make them take root. He gouged the sod with the heels of his sandals, rutting the fairway, wriggling and squirming and shouting to the heavens—beseeching the rain to purify his soul, even as he longed for it to fertilize his flesh.

RATS

As soon as the other GI's in his compartment on the troop transport, *General Houseman,* commenced their nightly poker game, Stephen went up on deck. During the day the decks were as crowded as Asbury Park, but now, after dark, there was no one, nothing but the vast starry heavens and a vivid moon, spilling down its light like so much heavy cream onto the Pacific. At last he could roam to his heart's content. At last he was alone —except, that is, for his chosen companions: Oscar II and Kierkegaard's *Fear and Trembling,* which he carried with him constantly. An hour seldom passed without his handling one of these or both; like talismans they protected him, gave him the strength and courage he needed, especially now, on his way to Japan and, more than likely, Korea.

Enthralled by the solitude, Stephen stood at the starboard rail, staring at the backwash. The vastness of the sea, the distance of the stars heightened his humility. Oddly enough, he welcomed this feeling, wanted it, wanted to feel insignificant and meaningless. It was, in fact, the reason he had come up on deck in the first place—not only to escape his fellow soldiers but to subdue something he regarded as his pride. After chow he had begun to feel miserable and lonely, homesick and afraid—emotions for which he had no patience. He judged them self-important, vain. "Vanity of vanities, saith the Preacher, vanity of vanities, all is vanity." These words were almost Stephen's motto. Let the others beef and bitch and blow off steam, not him! He knew how futile it was, how megalomaniac! to imagine oneself—one's piddling little self—at the center of the cosmos. Copernicus had long since taken care of that! No, the only way Stephen had found to survive in the army (or in life, for that matter) was to remind himself over and over that he really didn't count, that his suffering was as nothing compared to the suffering of the saints, that he must subjugate his vanity, strengthen his humility, his faith.

Feeling somewhat better now, he took from the right-hand

291

pocket of his fatigues *Fear and Trembling,* and began to study the little volume in the moonlight. Scarcely a page was left unmarked. Stephen had read the text through twice, and only resorted to it now much as a minister might dip into the PSALMS, for comfort and guidance.

" '. . . but Abraham was greater than any of these,' " he read, mouthing the precious words, " 'great through the power whose strength is weakness, great through the wisdom whose secret is foolishness, great through the hope whose expression is madness, great through the love which is hatred of oneself.' " This last phrase was underlined, and Stephen repeated it to himself several times before continuing. " '. . . the knight of faith knows how terrible it is to be born outside the universal and to go through life alone and never meet a single traveler on the road. . . . the knight of faith renounces the universal in order to become the Individual. . . . the knight of faith relies in everything on himself alone.' " Oh! how Stephen longed to achieve this ideal state, to become, like Abraham, a knight of faith.

In the distance the ship's bell rang. Stephen glanced at his wrist watch: 11 P.M. Pulling out the winder, he started to set back the hour hand but stopped. Wasn't it tonight the *General Houseman* was scheduled to cross the International Date Line? That meant his watch should be advanced—but by how much? An hour? Twenty-four? Twenty-five? Didn't they gain a day in the process? Or was it lost? Would tomorrow be Tuesday again or Thursday? He knew they were due to dock in Yokohama Saturday, but would that be three days from now or five? Feeling as much at sea as the ship itself, Stephen retired to his compartment, still holding *Fear and Trembling.*

On Saturday when Stephen came up on deck at dawn, he knew, without being told, that he was in the Orient. All around him in the harbor, through the soft gray mist, he saw the sampans, junks, and dinghies, the battened sails and colored canvas sails —red and tan and striped—the fishing nets and outriggers and awnings that comic books and movies had long ago made familiar symbols. Less familiar were the smells—a fusion of fish and brine, factory fumes and incense, sewage and smoke, herbs and oils and spicy foods, mildewed matting and rotting timber that Stephen tried, without success, to differentiate and identify. As the light intensified, the bow of mist extended, broadened to include the bay, the shore, freighters, steamers, piles, piers, warehouses, and even—in the distance, vaguely, like the negative of a photo-graph—the city itself, Yokohama. For the first time since he had left Seattle, Stephen was more expectant than afraid, more stimulated than bored.

When the *General Houseman* reached the pier, a little army band was there, just as in Seattle, but this time the musicians were much more spirited and cheerful, and they played "St. Louis Blues." After fourteen days at sea, the heat in the harbor was oppressive, and even when it began to drizzle there was no relief. With his poncho on, Stephen felt as if he were coated with cosmoline, the way his rifle had been when it was issued to him at Fort Dix, fifteen months before. Waiting to disembark, he stared at the graceful, sloping, tiled roofs of the warehouses, the bold red and black characters of the Japanese signs that towered above the buildings beyond, and tried to imagine the rest of Yokohama. But suddenly something—some darting movement down at the level of the water—distracted him, destroyed his daydream. There, under the slime-green wharf, scurrying around the piles, over the rocks and refuse, was a giant water rat. Instantly, Stephen was reminded of the only other water rat he had ever seen.

As a child, playing on the embankment of the Hudson, he had spotted one crawling among the rocks—a sleek, gray animal almost the size of an alley cat—and he had watched with fascination and revulsion, until it disappeared. Then he wondered where it had gone, where it lived, in what cave or tunnel, there, between Manhattan and the Hudson, at home in both—both the river and the city, the moist and the dry, the dark and the light—belonging to neither, but feeding off both. He had wanted to pursue it, crawl after it, into the sewers, into the slime, but he was too afraid. Instead, he went away and returned the following afternoon. For six or seven days he came back to the spot, hoping to see the rat again, but he never did, and he never mentioned it to anyone—not to Clarry or Roger or his mother.

No sooner had he disembarked than he was ordered to board a boat train, which was waiting on the pier to take the new arrivals to Camp Drake. Before the United States Army had turned it into a processing center, Camp Drake had been a Japanese military or naval academy, and the buildings—even the barracks—were the most elegant and expressive Stephen had ever seen. The plaster walls, defined and framed into bold white squares and rectangles by natural, dark wood beams were like "de Stÿl" paintings, and the massive tiled roofs, rising up, swooping down so gracefully, dramatically, creating a contrast of textures and forms, were like enormous sculptures. Surrounded by these works of art, this permanent esthetic, Stephen quickly felt its influence and was eager to experience more. But on the morning of his third day at Camp Drake, he was issued a new M-1, a bayonet and combat helmet; he heard the soldier behind him say, "Well, this is it, I guess," and the supply sergeant reply, "You better fucking-well believe it!" Late that afternoon, Stephen came out on orders, and the following day he boarded another transport, this one the *General Doyle*, bound for Korea.

As they crossed Korea Strait, the GI's traded rumors about their destination like panic-striken brokers buying in a rising market. Among the places named in the course of speculation were Inchon, Pusan, Kunsan, T'ongyong, and even Kosong, Wonsan, and Hungnam—three North Korean ports, inaccessible to United Nation forces—ports, that is, above the 38th parallel, along which line the fighting had been relatively stalemated for over a year. But no one knew his geography that well; to most GI's (including Stephen) Korea was not a country half the size of California, not even a peninsula or place, but a worthless hellhole of frozen mountains and barren waste that represented deprivation, misery, and almost certain death. As a consequence, the soldiers were much more irritable and explosive now than they had been on the *General Houseman*. But despite the step-up in their gambling, guffawing, scrapping and cursing, the war remained unreal to them, unreal to Stephen—at least, for another day or so, until the *General Doyle* approached the port of Inchon on the Yellow Sea.

Then, without warning, the generators were cut off and the ship began to float—to drift, it almost seemed—like a phantom on a barely perceptible rising tide, through a narrow channel made treacherous by a thousand natural hazards: rocks and reefs and islets that loomed up out of the mist menacingly, startlingly like Horror-House goblins, close enough to touch. All at once, as if in response to some officer's command, the GI's stopped talking and crowded to the rails. No one knew exactly what he was waiting for, watching for as the light began to wane and the fog to thicken, but everyone who could gripped the deck-rails apprehensively. Like the others, Stephen expected the sound of the enemy's artillery to shatter the unnerving silence, and he listened for it tensely. But all he could hear was the repetitious lapping of the water, all he could see was those frightful crags that drifted by like volcanic cones on the surface of the moon.

Because of the slimy mud flats, created by unusual tide conditions, the *General Doyle* had to anchor a mile or more off Inchon and the troops were ferried ashore on LSU's. By the time Stephen stepped onto the crudely built pier, it was 10 P.M. Except for some rings of lemon-colored light, cast by three or four lamps on posts, the darkness was impenetrable. None of the men had eaten since noon, and they bitched and wondered now about where in that infinite blackness they would be billeted and fed. Suddenly, even the three or four circles of lemon-colored light disappeared, leaving the men in total darkness.

Stephen looked up toward the sky expectantly, in fear of a plane, in hopes of a star, but there was neither, nothing, only blackness, indistinguishable from the blackness all around him, like the ever-expanding space in which the sleeper becomes disembodied and falls asleep. But he was not asleep. He could feel the boards beneath his boots, the pounding of his heart, the furry lump of Oscar II clutched tightly in his fist. Then suddenly he heard the tramp of many feet, marching in the distance, marching toward the waterfront, coming in cadence closer and closer, louder and louder, a thousand pairs of boots raising the dust, resounding against the earth and, louder still, against the pier, until Stephen felt the very planks beneath his feet begin to quake. As unexpectedly as the lemon-colored lights had disappeared, they came back on, and Stephen saw another group of soldiers as large as his own, standing in formation on the opposite side of the pier. As always in the Army, within seconds the two groups were in communication.

"Where you bums heading?"

"Listen to them, will you! Home! We're heading home!"

"No shit!"

"You poor slobs are our replacements."

"Lucky bastards."

"Where they sending *you?*"

"Who the hell knows."

"You'll be sor-ry!"

"What's it like? How's the chow? How's the pussy?"

"You'll be sor-ry!"

With alarming rapidity almost every member of the second group—every soldier who had come through Korea alive and was waiting now in the stifling heat and darkness to board the *General Doyle* and start back to the States—turned toward the uninitiate and began to chime in unison, "You'll be sor-ry! You'll be sor-ry!" Like a chorus in a varsity show, they all sang out, "You'll be sorry!" and Stephen thought of the words that Dante saw inscribed above the Gate of Hell.

Somewhere in the dark another train was waiting to take the new arrivals out of Inchon, but in which direction—north or south —no one knew. It was after eleven before they boarded the train, with the warning, "You'll be sor-ry!" still echoing in their ears. No one had eaten or slept for hours; everyone's nerves were shot. There were no lights in the train, or, if there were, they were not permitted to be used. The seats were made of wood, and the backs, which were not adjustable, were built at a ninety-degree angle. The space between the seats was totally inadequate, not only because it had been designed originally for legs much shorter than the average GI's, but also because the men were obliged to keep their duffel bags, rifles, and combat helmets with them. After a good deal of trial and error, Stephen managed to shove his duffel bag under the seat, straddle it, prop his rifle in the corner, cap it with his helmet, and sit down next to the window. No sooner was he settled, than he felt a hand touch his shoulder in the dark.

"Sorry. Is this one empty?"

"Yes," Stephen said, pulling up his legs and planting his boots on his duffel bag in order to make room for the soldier.

"What a ball-breaker, huh?" the soldier commented wearily, in a tone that was devoid of animosity, and gave his words a reference beyond the immediate one of the train and trip from Japan. "How the fuck did you manage it?" he asked, after struggling with his gear for a minute.

Without a word Stephen took the soldier's rifle and put it with his own.

"Thanks," the soldier said and continued to wrestle with his duffel bag.

Stephen listened to him pound and pummel the bag until, at last, he heard it being pushed under the seat . . . a broken, crippled lump, he imagined.

"Whew!" the soldier sighed, sitting down. "This seat feels good. I never thought I'd say that about a church pew."

Just then the train lurched forward and someone with a flashlight came through the car handing out C rations. A roar of approval went up from the men. In the instant the light flashed in his area, Stephen saw the labelless, brown tin cans, but he did not look at the face of his companion.

"I guess we better get used to these," the soldier said. "How the hell did you get yours open?"

"Here, let me," Stephen said.

When Stephen handed back the can, the soldier asked, "What'd you get?"

"Hamburger."

"Me too," he said, adding in a mutter, "Dog food."

By now the train had picked up speed and was swaying and joggling along like a soapbox race car in a Derby.

"Where the hell do you think we're going?"

"I don't know," Stephen said.

"Think we're going north?"

"I guess."

"To the front?"

Stephen sighed. "I don't know. . . . . I guess."

"Aren't they even gonna give us time to take a crap?"

Without answering, Stephen turned his head away and peered through the window, but there was nothing outside, nothing but blackness—not even the silhouette of a tree.

"Well, I'm gonna try and get some shut-eye," the soldier said, changing his position, shifting his weight, struggling to get comfortable. At last he settled down, his elbow rammed into Stephen's ribs, his thigh pressed hard against Stephen's.

Stephen felt cramped, but didn't move. He welcomed the soldier's thigh and elbow—the intrusion of something tangible into the void. For a moment he shut his eyes and tried to let the rocking of the car lull him to sleep, but the darkness behind his lids was almost identical to the darkness in the train, the darkness through which the train was rushing, and it gave his consciousness no relief. It's like being blind, he thought, opening his eyes again. How do the blind manage to fall asleep, unable as they are to relinquish the light, the visible? Do they fix their ears on some sound until it dies away? Do they hold some object tightly until their grip relaxes and the object falls from hand? . . .

Presently Stephen felt the soldier's head bobbing back and forth, brushing past his ear, but once again he did not move. He knew the soldier could not be asleep—who *could* be under these conditions? After a moment the soldier settled his head on Stephen's shoulder, his hand on Stephen's thigh. Stephen responded in kind: rested his head against the soldier's, placed his hand on the soldier's knee. And so they sat, their heads together, their breath on one another's cheeks, their hands on one another's flanks, touching one another, holding one another like children holding toys at night, warding off the dark and death until, at last, they fell asleep.

When the train stopped, Stephen awakened with a start. He glanced at his watch: 12:25. Though it had seemed like hours, the trip had taken less than ninety minutes. . . . Where were they now, he wondered. Beyond the window he saw a scattering of dim lights and a hint of the moon beneath a heavy haze. "At least there are some signs of life," he said aloud, but his companion didn't answer, and in the confusion of getting off the train, the soldier disappeared without a word.

Once the train had stopped, the GI's naturally assumed that they had reached their destination—at least for the night—but they were wrong. Instead, the troops were assembled in ranks and given the order to "Fo-wud, harch!" down an unlit, narrow, dusty road. As always, no one knew where he was going or how long it would take, and the prospect of having to march, even a mile, carrying one's duffel bag and rifle through this choking dust, was enough to incite an insurrection. "All right, can it! Can it! Let's have silence!" the sergeants shouted. Most of the soldiers were too exhausted to disobey, but some few continued to protest by clearing their throats of the dust and retching up their phlegm with exaggerated sound effects.

Despite the dust, which he could feel in his nostrils and taste in his mouth, Stephen was distracted by an odor that reminded him of sauerkraut. And yet he realized how much more powerful than sauerkraut it must have been in order to permeate the air and penetrate the dust, and it occurred to Stephen that he was smelling carrion. He was greatly relieved, therefore, when he looked around and noticed that the lights that he had seen from the train were coming, not from funeral pyres but the interiors of houses, filtering through rice-paper screens. He heard a woman's voice singing a lullaby and saw two men, who were obviously drunk, arguing in a doorway, and Stephen realized that he was marching through the center of a small Korean village. The dusty road led to the gates of an army base, enclosed in barbed wire, where Stephen was assigned to a tent and dropped, unconscious, onto the first cot he saw.

The next morning Stephen learned that he had spent the night in a place called Yong Dong Po, a suburb of Seoul; but before he had time to find out more, he was put on another train that took him south from Seoul to Taegu. Along the way he saw a peasant woman pulling a plow to which she was harnessed; the monolithic ruins of a Russian tank, marooned forever, in the middle of a rice paddy; a legless soldier; bands of begging ragamuffins and shoe-shine boys with teeth and eyes as fierce as rats'; the mother of three children fighting savagely with her fists to board an over-crowded train; a family of six, displaced and living on the run, its worldly possessions contained in a kerchief; and an ageless, ex-pressionless, dead-eyed man carrying a crippling load of bricks on an A-frame strapped to his back. Although Stephen had not antici-pated any of these sights and they disturbed him, they seemed like natural consequences of the war, not at all incongruous. Nor was he unprepared for the poverty of the hovels he saw—whole sec-tions of cities built completely out of tarpaper and mud, old rags and rotting staves. As a child he had seen Hoovervilles along the Hudson, and he had not forgotten them.

But what came as a complete surprise, not only because it was unexpectedly beautiful, but because Stephen had never seen any-thing remotely comparable—was the Korean landscape. It sug-gested places such as Sumer, Syria, Babylonia and Palestine—places Stephen had never seen but learned about in Sunday school and categorized collectively as "biblical." Not that the countryside contained any of the elements used to illustrate his Sunday school books—oases, desert sands, camels, palms, burnooses, cotton tents—but in some way the dryness of the dust, the daylight's glare, the straw-roofed huts, the poplars and persimmon trees, the scrubby pines twisted by survival into knots, the vast, mosaic fields of rice, the permanent horizon of protective mountains—verdant in the sunlight, magenta in the shade—the unpaved roads and thirsty rocks were suggestive, not of the Orient but of the Middle East in ancient times.

When Stephen reached Taegu, he was sent to a luxury hotel, nestled in the foothills just outside the city, and was served a turkey dinner with all the trimmings. A Korean houseboy whisked away his boots to be shined, another collected his laundry, and a third offered to take him to the company masseur, but Stephen declined. He was quartered in a large, immaculate room, so ele-gant he was not at all surprised to learn that the Emperor of Japan had often summered at this hotel before the Second World War.

After his records had been examined at Eighth Army Headquarters in Taegu, Stephen was sent on to the Second Logistical Command in Pusan, a city at the extreme southern tip of the peninsula, directly across Korea Strait from Sasebo, the Japanese port from which he had departed. At the time Stephen arrived, Pusan was the provisional capital of the Republic, and housed not only the Assembly and all the government departments and bureaus from Seoul, but also all the refugees who had fled from towns and cities farther north and swelled a population that was normally four hundred thousand to over a million. At Headquarters of the Second Logistical Command, Stephen was interviewed by a bored lieutenant who asked if he had any objections to becoming a chaplain's assistant, and when Stephen said no, he was sent to speak to a rabbi named Klingerhoff, who, as it turned out, was not seeking an assistant but a cantor to help him conduct services during the forthcoming High Holy Days. Finally, and quite arbitrarily—or so it seemed to Stephen—he was assigned permanently to the 14th MP Service Company to work in Personnel.

Parked in a jeep outside Headquarters was a corporal, dressed in a pair of fatigues which, if not actually custom made, had been tailored to his measurements and fit him like a leotard. The corporal, who looked no more than twenty, had regular features, eczematous skin and an elaborate lacquered pompadour which he took great pains to keep in place by perching his stiff fatigue cap at a cocky angle on the back of his head. In order to relieve his pent-up energy or simply to amuse himself—Stephen had difficulty deciding which—Corporal Melody had a habit of intoning intermittently a series of grunts that made him sound as if he were a claxon being played on by a jazz musician. "Onk, onk . . . onk-onk. Onk, onk . . . onk-onk."

"Excuse me," Stephen interrupted. "Are you from the 14th MP's?"

"You Corporal Wolfe?"

"Yes."

"I'm Corporal Melody," he said, removing his feet from the dashboard and turning on the ignition. "Hop in. Just throw your shit in back. . . . Don't worry about those, they're just mail bags. Onk, onk . . . onk-onk, onk . . . Where you from?"

"New York."

"Uhhh," he drawled disappointedly. "I'm from Atlanta. Onk, onk . . . onk-onk."

Stephen watched a bearded ancient, carrying a stick and wearing a stovepipe hat with a mesh crown, and a white muslin frock coat that tied over his chest in a big silk bow, start slowly across the road.

"Out of my way, *popasan,*" Melody jeered, as he drove the jeep straight toward him. In self-defense the old man raised his stick and stumbled backward. "Almost got him," the corporal laughed. "Onk, onk . . . onk-onk, onk . . ."

Stephen clenched his teeth. As they drove on he noticed that the jeep left clouds of dust in its wake, but instead of slowing down, every time Melody approached a pedestrian, he stepped on the gas, deliberately creating a dust storm.

"Nooky-nooky!" Melody shouted at a young woman, walking along the roadside. In order to protect herself from the dust, the woman covered her nose and mouth with her scarf, leaving exposed only her eyes that glared with hatred. "Man, did you see that look she gave me?"

Stephen did not answer.

"Say, you ain't exactly talkative, are you?"

Just before they reached the turnoff at the end of the road, Stephen saw a billboard on which were painted two enormous likenesses of Michele Morgan and Pierre Blanchard in *Symphonie Pastorale.* The sight of Michele Morgan's familiar and exquisite face heartened Stephen the way an image of the Holy Virgin might hearten a Roman Catholic traveling in a heathen land. Instantly it transformed Pusan from a pitiful ghetto into a fascinating metropolis. Stephen's heart sank, therefore, when they reached a primitive rotary, and Melody turned off onto a back road that led away from the city into the countryside. "Is the Company outside the city?"

"City! You call that fuckin' compost heap a city, man?"

There was just no talking to this red-neck, Stephen thought, and yet he was curious to know where in the world he was going. "Why is it called a Service Company? What does it serve?"

"Gooks!" Melody exploded. "POW's! Four thousand anti-Communist prisoner gooks—and all of 'em, cocksuckers. And I'm not just sayin' that in a manner of speakin', neither. They're fairies, all of 'em. Seven thousand slant-eyed fags, and the Army treats 'em better than *us!* Now what do you think of that? Ain't that a cryin' shame!"

"How do you know they're anti-Communists?" Stephen asked.

"Ha, ha, ha, ha! I thought you were gonna ask me how I know they're fags, and I was gonna tell you, 'Cause I made the mistake of bendin' over in front of one of 'em one day. The Army's got 'em sorted out like peaches: all the good ones—they're over here, on the mainland; the rotten ones, the commies, they're in compounds on the islands. You heard of Koje, ain't you?"

"No."

Melody broke into song, "Oooh, Koje-do and Cheju-do and little-lambs-eat-ivy, a kid'll-eat-ivy-too, wouldn't you? Onk-onk, onk, onk . . . Koje: that's the place they had them bloody riots a couple of months ago when that pinhead general got himself captured. Now that takes brains, don't it? I mean to walk into the hands of sixty thousand enemy gooks. Well, that's when they brought in Boatner. You heard of Boatner, ain't you? Calls himself the Bull. He'll be around one of these days; comes to inspect the compounds. You're gonna see a lot of brass and VIP's around this place. That's what makes it such a ball-breaker: someone's always showin' up to take a gander at them fuckin' faggots. I'd go off my rocker if I couldn't get away every day. I'm the mail clerk, you know. Corporal Richard R. Melody, RA fourteen-eighty-seven-thirty-two-forty-six. Onk, onk, onk-onk! . . What's your job?"

"Personnel."

"No shit! There's a little item I'd like you to fix up on my records."

"Sorry, I wouldn't know how. I've never worked in Personnel before."

"Shit, that don't matter. *I* know what I want, all *you* gotta do is type it in for me," Melody drawled, swerving off the road and stopping in front of a small group of Korean houses.

The first thing that attracted Stephen's eye was a large yellow sign: THIS AREA OFF LIMITS TO ALL UN PERSONNEL.

"Got some business to transact. I'll just be a minute," Melody explained, reaching under the mail bags and pulling out two cartons of Pall Malls. "The gooks, they like these best 'cause they're king-sized. These and Kools. Kools, 'cause they're mentholated. They bring twenty thousand on the black market. Make yourself at home. I'll be back in a sec."

"Is there a copy of *Stars and Stripes* in one of these?" Stephen asked, turning toward the mail bags.

"Yeah, but they're locked. What are you after, the scores? Giants lost. Red Sox lost; four to one."

"I was just wondering about the convention."

"What convention?"

"The Democrats. Have they nominated someone yet?"

"Got me," Melody said; disappearing under a slit valance that masked the entrance to one of the houses.

Stephen took out a cigarette and tried to light it but failed because his matches were wet. While the jeep was moving he had not realized how hot it was, but now he noticed that his fatigues were soaked. He could feel the sweat trickling down his neck and armpits, even as he sat perfectly still, listening to the voices and laughter that were issuing from the house Melody had entered.

"Hello, sahgee."

Stephen looked up, but saw no one and decided the voice must have come from inside.

"Hello, sahgee."

This time the words were followed by a titter of delight, and when Stephen turned he saw a little girl standing barefoot in the dust. "Hello there," he said, offering the child his hand.

The little girl didn't move. Stephen could tell she wasn't afraid, but she just stood there, staring at him walleyed and sucking in her lower lip until it disappeared. In her right fist she clutched a handful of her cotton dress, as if she were about to curtsy coyly. "Hello, sahgee."

"What's your name?"

"Nooky-nooky, have-a-yes."

For a moment Stephen thought the child had answered in Korean. "That's an awful big name for a little girl."

"Me sexy-sexy, sucky-sucky, blow-job: number hucking one."

Stephen realized she had no idea what she was saying, that she was only mimicking things she had heard or been taught inside those houses. Her expression remained irresistibly innocent. She continued to clutch her dress and stare at Stephen through her shaggy bangs, her big inquisitive eyes like two white eggs in a nest of twigs.

Impulsively, Stephen reached into his pocket for Oscar, wanting to replace the influence of adults with something childish. And yet he hesitated. He could not bring himself to part with the toy.

Instead, he pulled out a coin and offered it to the little girl. "Here."

Slowly, she toddled toward the jeep, released her dress and took the money in her hand. *"Komapsumnida,"* she said with a smile.

What she said sounded to Stephen like Can I keep it? "Yes, of course," he replied, and tears came to his eyes.

"Hi there, *sukoshi,"* Melody said, returning to the jeep.

"Hello, sahgee."

"Nooky-nooky, have-a-yes?" Melody asked.

"Number hucking one," she said, and Melody roared with laughter.

"So long, *sukoshi,"* Melody said, hopping into the jeep.

"Hello, sahgee."

As they drove away, Stephen turned to wave good-by, but the screen of dust left by the jeep was so thick he could scarcely see the little girl.

Just before they reached the company area, Melody stopped to adjust his cap in accordance with Army Regulations. This entailed his moving the peak forward from the crown of his head, over his pompadour, to within two inches of his eyebrows. "Watch-you-gonna-do?" he asked ironically. "The C.O.'s chicken-shit. Better give me your records now. He'll want to look them over with the afternoon mail."

Stephen was surprised, on entering the company area, that they passed no gates or guard or checkpoint. The compound, which was built on the side of a bald foothill at the base of a group of mountains, consisted of a dozen or more Quonset huts and half again as many rectangular buildings with corrugated metal walls and slanting roofs. A dusty, ill-defined road the color of pigskin bordered these buildings on the right and sloped up the side of the hill gradually until it reached another, much larger, area. This was enclosed by a double, barbed wire fence, eighteen or twenty feet high, and contained several hundred huts and tents. "Is that the prison?" Stephen asked.

"No," Melody said. *"This* is the prison; *that's* the guardhouse." After driving halfway up the hill, he pulled off the road and parked in front of one of the Quonsets. "Here we are. Home sweet home. The only advantage this one has is it's close to the shithouse and shower. Just drop your gear inside. There's only one vacancy—next to Leghorn—you can't miss it. Supply's down there," he added pointing to the foot of the hill. "Second building on the right. See you later."

"Thanks," Stephen said.

"Onk, onk . . . onk-onk. Onk, onk . . . onk-onk," Melody replied, driving off.

After storing his M-1 in the arms room and drawing a foot-locker, blanket, canvas cot, air mattress, and mosquito netting from Supply, Stephen returned to the Quonset hut and began to unpack. He hung his suntans and poncho on a lead pipe that ran the length of the hut along the wall behind the cots. Above this pipe was a narrow wooden shelf. Stephen was tempted to use his share of the shelf for his books, but he saw at a glance that most of the other soldiers used the space to store cookies, pretzels, and peanuts, or display photographs of their wives, mothers, and girl friends. After debating with himself, he decided against concealing his interest, and one by one he lined up neatly: *The Works of Shakespeare, A Study of History, Eleven Plays of Henrik Ibsen, Holy Bible, Science and the Modern World, T. S. Eliot's Selected Poems, Sentimental Education* and *Fifteen Decisive Battles of the World.* When this was done, he inflated his air mattress, made his bed and began to struggle with his mosquito netting. Separating the net from the sticks was as delicate and difficult as a game of diabolo but once they were untangled Stephen had no trouble erecting the sticks and suspending the hammock of netting between them. He had scarcely finished, when someone behind him asked in a rather effeminate voice, "Are you Corporal Wolfe?"

"Yes," Stephen said, turning around and seeing a tall, lithe soldier with thin hair and a needle nose.

"Colonel Clayborn is waiting to see you. I'm the colonel's secretary, Corporal Kirkland. Everybody calls me Kirk."

"I'm called Steve. Is anything the matter?"

"You mean because the colonel wants to see you?"

"Yes."

"Oh, heavens no! The colonel gives his little spiel to every new arrival. I could recite it for you now, but I don't want to spoil his fun. That's my bunk, there," Kirk said, pointing at a cot across the aisle. "Well, we better go now before the colonel has kittens."

As soon as they stepped outside into the blinding sunlight, Kirk looked up and down the road and said, almost frantically, "Quick! Quick! Let's get across while we can!" and he ran as if his pelvis was tightly bandaged. When they reached the other side Kirk explained, "Most of these drivers would just as soon run you down as not. They're Dead-End Kids, all of them. What a relief to have

someone around who can read for a change. I couldn't help noticing your books," he apologized. "Of course, PFC Leghorn reads,
but nothing very interesting, just chemistry and engineering and
such. Why these people don't even seem to know there's an election going on this year."

"Have the Democrats nominated someone yet?"

"Oh, yes." Kirk lit up as if he was about to divulge a piece of
gossip. "Stevenson."

"Who?"

"Adlai Stevenson."

"Who is that?" Stephen asked skeptically.

"The Govenor of Illinois."

Stephen lapsed into silence. He had never heard of Stevenson
and had expected someone better known. As they climbed the hill
and approached the stockade, he began to be distracted by touches
of bright color inside: South Korean flags, garlands of artificial
flowers and strips of paper bunting. "Are they having some kind of
celebration?"

"Oh, *them!*" Kirk said dismissively. "They're always celebrating
or protesting *something!* Isn't this heat unbearable? If you ask me,
it's positively tropical. I really think they ought to start issuing pith
helmets."

"How about the mosquitoes? Are they bad at night?"

"What mosquitoes? I've been here seven months and I haven't
seen one yet."

"Then why the netting?"

"Oh, that! If you ask me, it's to protect us from the rats."

"Rats?" Stephen repeated with concern.

"Here we are: HQ," Kirk said in a whisper, entering a long
building just to the right of the stockade gates. Stephen followed
him down the center aisle past nine or ten desks at which both
Americans and Koreans sat busily doing paper work. A POW
stood sprinkling the cement floor with water to keep down the
dust, his wrist-motion as graceful as a pastry chef's. At the end of
the aisle they came to a private office, and Kirk knocked gently on
its open door. "Excuse me, sir. Corporal Wolfe is here now."

"Thank you, Kirk. Kindly show him in."

"Colonel Clayborn will see you now," Kirk said, stepping aside
and winking at Stephen.

"Corporal Wolfe reporting, sir."

"At ease, Corporal."

At first glance Lieutenant Colonel Clayborn looked fifty-five or even sixty to Stephen who could only see his bald head, steel-rimmed spectacles, and gray mustache. But as soon as he looked up from Stephen's records, removed his spectacles and began to speak, the colonel exhibited an attractive, public smile which he flashed with shameless frequency, showing his yellow equine teeth. And even though he had a nervous tic that made him blink incessantly, his light blue eyes twinkled with some secret, inner mischief.

"Welcome to the 14th MP's. I'm happy to have you with us," he said in an accent that immediately revealed his Southern origin.

"Thank you, sir."

"I see from your records that you're a college man. Fine, fine. That makes what I'm about to say a whole lot easier for both of us. I think by now it should be obvious—even to a child—that this entire conflagration—I'm speakin' of Korea now—has nothin' whatsoever to do with *war*—at least as far as *I* understand the meanin' of the word. I say that, mind you, completely cognizant of the fact that, to date, more American soldiers have died fightin' over here, than died in the War Between the States. Nevertheless, what's happenin' at Panmunjom, what's happenin' right here—just outside that window there!" he said, blinking his eyes and thrusting his head toward the screen window to the left of his desk, "is somethin' I call politics. And politics, whatever you may think, will never be as honorable as war." Colonel Clayborn leaned back in his chair and paused a moment to let Stephen absorb his words. "However," he continued in a lighter vein, "since politics is what we've got, and neither you nor I is runnin' this here show, politics is what we're obliged to accept. *I* accept it, and I expect every soldier under my command to do the same. You understand me, Corporal?"

"Yes, sir."

"Now, if you'll be so kind, I'd like you to step to that window there and tell me what you see."

Since the screen was shaded from the sunlight by the eaves, Stephen had no difficulty seeing outside, but he felt at a loss to know what the colonel was after. "The stockade?" he answered hesitantly.

"Fine, fine. And what does it contain?"

"Prisoners."

"What kind of prisoners, Corporal?"

"Korean."

"What else are they?"

"Else, sir?"

"Would you call 'em POW's?"

"Yes, sir."

"Well, you'd be wrong. They're pops!"

"Pops, sir?"

"POP's: Prisoners of Politics. That's what *I* call 'em. All those men you see out there are North Korean, anti-Communists. Each and every one of 'em has sworn an oath and signed it with his blood—I mean that literally—to resist repatriation. That, as you know, if you read your newspaper, is the issue on which the truce talks are stymied now. Why? Because the mere existence of these prisoners—not to mention their extraordinary number—is a source of great embarrassment to the Reds—a poor advertisement, so to speak, for their Marxian Utopia. And that's exactly why I expect every member of this here Service Company to treat those POP's with kid gloves. Not because I have any highfalutin' regard for the Articles of the Geneva Convention—why, the commies aren't even signatories of that Convention; and certainly not because I consider any of these POP's such fine specimens of humanity—most of 'em are nothin' but ignorant slobs. But you are gonna treat 'em with kid gloves," the colonel continued softly, leaning forward and planting his hands on the desk, his fingers turned in and his arms bent at the elbows like the wings of a bat, "because we are engaged here in political combat, and that stockade you see out there is our chosen battlefield." The bat wings relaxed and reverted to human arms, as the colonel flashed his broadest smile. "Have I made myself clearly understood?"

"Yes, sir."

"Fine, fine. That will be all for now, Corporal."

As soon as Stephen stepped out of the colonel's office, Corporal Kirkland stopped him. "Psst! Corporal Wolfe."

"Yes, Kirk."

"I thought you might like to see this," he whispered, opening the middle drawer of his desk.

"What?"

"Yesterday's *Stars and Stripes*. It contains Governor Stevenson's acceptance speech."

"Why yes, thanks," Stephen said somewhat mystified but taking the newspaper and starting toward the door.

"See you at chow," Kirk called after him.

Just as Stephen emerged from Headquarters, he saw a caravan of two-ton trucks coming up the hill, raising the dust. Each truck was jammed to capacity with standing POW's, singing in chorus. The surrounding mountains—almost purple now that it was after four and the sun had begun to sink behind them—echoed the voices like acoustical shells, and the entire valley resounded with song as the trucks drove past the sally port into the stockade.

Something more than idle curiosity drew Stephen toward the barbed wire fence. As he listened to their song and watched the prisoners hop down from the trucks, his heart was filled with yearning—but whether for himself or them he did not know. He was aware that he was standing there looking *in,* exactly as he had imagined he would find the prisoners standing (on the opposite side of the fence, of course) looking out: with longing. But they were not. They were laughing, singing, shouting, straggling off in pairs, their arms around one another's necks, tickling one another, tagging one another, pulling off one another's shirts; while Stephen stood there staring enviously through the barbs of wire, as if *he* were inside and *they* were out.

Presently, from a building very near the double fence—a building marked UN ENCLOSURE NO. 17, DISPENSARY, a prisoner came out to take the afternoon air, and Stephen was immediately struck by his beauty. His head, a perfect oval, was covered by a swell of lustrous blue-black hair that hung down like a horse's mane. His eyebrows, mere suggestions of themselves, were like two brief daubs of ash above his wing-shaped eyes. His cheekbones protruded noticeably and his throat was as smooth and graceful as the trunk of a cherry tree. Stephen watched him scan the mountain tops, light a cigarette and start to stroll in his direction. When the prisoner reached the inner fence, he stopped and smiled a smile that revealed the whitest teeth, the friendliest eyes, the loveliest spirit Stephen had ever beheld.

Stephen smiled back but awkwardly, self-consciously, knowing he could never match the glory of the smile he'd been given. At the same time he suddenly became aware that he was being watched. Quite casually, he turned and saw a South Korean guard observing him attentively—not with suspicion but interest. There was something subservient, even obsequious in the guard's attitude, as if he were waiting for Stephen to give him an order or register a complaint. But instead of Stephen, it was the prisoner who spoke—some salutation or small talk in Korean—and Stephen who slinked away in silence.

When he returned the Quonset hut was empty, and, having nothing better to do, Stephen lay down on his cot and read the speech in *Stars and Stripes*. He was surprised by Stevenson's rhetoric, impressed by his intelligence and truthfulness. Who was this man? he wondered. How come he had never heard of him? Could his humility be genuine? . . . Stephen glanced at the speech again: ". . . a people whose destiny is leadership, not alone of a rich, prosperous, contented country as in the past, but of a world in ferment . . ." The phrase appealed to Stephen and he pondered it for a moment until his thoughts were interrupted by Melody's familiar onking. Now that the corporal was out of the jeep and on his feet, his noises were accompanied by a series of loose tribal dance movements.

Melody was followed in rapid succession by PFC Leghorn, a relatively quiet and intelligent young man who devoted all of his time to grooming a fanciful Turkish mustache, Private Luke Collins, a Gothic-looking fifty-year-old hillbilly, Corporal Kirkland, Corporal Salvatore Martini, a dark, kind, heavy-set boy from Jersey City who feared for his immortal soul because—as he was only too eager to confess—he suffered from the deadly sin of sloth, and Sergeant Clarence Billywood, who weighed at least two hundred and fifty pounds and had modeled himself completely on W. C. Fields with the single innovation of taking snuff.

At a quarter to six, Kirk suggested it was time for chow, and he and Stephen and Leghorn strolled down to the mess hall. Stephen followed Leghorn and preceded Kirk through the service line, which was manned exclusively by POW's. When the prisoner who was serving the vegetables tried to load Leghorn's tray with summer squash, Leghorn objected, *"Sukoshi! Sukoshi, boysan!"*

Stephen was reminded of the little girl to whom he had given the quarter. "What does *sukoshi* mean?"

"Little," Leghorn said.

"Sukoshi, please," Stephen repeated quickly, noticing that the prisoner was about to serve him not only his own portion of squash but Leghorn's as well.

The prisoner, who had tiny bead eyes, a flat broad nose, and a misshapen mouth, began to glow and gesture like a mime, bursting to communicate. "You new?" he asked enthusiastically.

"Yes."

"Me, Chang Sung Chull."

"I'm Stephen Wolfe."

Chang beamed and began circling his palm over the surface of his face. After repeating this mystical gesture three or four times, he smiled clownishly and said, "Number one."

As they walked toward the table, Stephen turned to Kirk. "What did he mean?"

"Aren't they giddy," Kirk giggled. "They rate everything from one to ten, like Kate Cameron. Only in *their* case, one is the best and ten is the worst," he explained, sitting down next to Leghorn. "I think he meant your face is number one."

"How do you say thank you in Korean?" Stephen asked.

"Komapsumnida," Kirk said, wriggling his shoulders and lowering his eyelids modestly.

Stephen set down his tray and walked back to the service line. "Chang."

"Yes, Stephen Wolfe."

"Komapsumnida."

Chang smiled from ear to ear. "Number hucking one!"

When Stephen returned to the table, he thanked Kirk again for Stevenson's speech, and Kirk asked him what he thought of it. "Number hucking one," Stephen said. "Have you read it, Leghorn?"

"Not yet."

"You ought to," Kirk suggested, and then, turning to Stephen, he said, "Have you got your voting card yet?"

"No. What's that?"

"The form you have to fill out to get your absentee ballot," Kirk explained. "Mr. Robbins has them."

"Who's he?" Stephen asked.

"The warrant officer—in charge of Personnel. You'll meet him in the morning."

At some point that seemed to Stephen like the middle of the night, he was awakened by a sharp, hollow thud. For a moment, after opening his eyes, he was confused by the eerie, unfamiliar sight of his mosquito netting in the moonlight. . . . Was it dawn? Was it fog? Was he in a hospital or underwater in a dream? What were those translucent, ghostly nests—or were they cocoons?—he had seen as a child in the uppermost branches of the birch trees in

Maine? Were they bats' nests? Birds' nests? Caterpillar tents? Hadn't they been burned and turned to smoke to save the trees? . . . The smoke of cigarettes and sinking ships. The frightening, filthy feel of spider webs breaking across your face in the dark. . . . Stephen rubbed his eyes and glanced at the luminescent face of his watch: 11:15. He had been asleep only an hour and a half; what in the world was he doing up now?

Before he was able to answer his own question, Stephen heard a crunching, gnawing noise that sounded like someone eating crackers in the dark. Was it Leghorn? Was it Luke? Stephen raised his head, hoping to discover the culprit, but all he could see was his own mosquito netting, surrounding and protecting him, isolating him like a malarial patient whose only link with reality is the noise of the jungle. Now the crunching sound seemed to be coming from somewhere closer to his bed, closer to his head, obscenely loud and voracious. As he lay there listening, trying to determine the exact source and nature of the sound, Stephen began to be aware of other sounds—rhythmic, rubbing sounds, lubricous, licking sounds, that held him transfixed, even before he was able to determine their origin and meaning. The dark beyond the borders of his netting was alive with bobbing bodies. No one was asleep, neither Luke nor Leghorn, Kirk nor Sal Martini—the pulsations of their air mattresses attested to that. Stephen lay perfectly still like an auditory voyeur, listening as the sounds intensified and their tempi increased. He heard the soldiers' breathing turn to gasps, their rhythmic rubbing turn to frenzied thumps, and the legs of their cots begin to rap the floor as their bodies bounced and tossed in spasms.

When the ruckus subsided, Stephen released his breath and tried to relax, but once again he heard the crunching sound of someone eating crackers. . . . Whoever it was, the glutton had gone on stuffing himself throughout the entire orgy in complete oblivion. By now Stephen's ears were so alert and hypersensitized, he thought he heard—between the crunches—a series of shrill peeps, but they were so high-pitched as to be almost inaudible, and he couldn't be certain they weren't hallucinatory. More than anything, he wanted to ignore the sounds and go back to sleep—most of the others had already done so, but their snoring only served to abet his insomnia.

"Onk, onk . . . onk-onk, onk. Onk, onk." Even before he heard Melody's footsteps, Stephen heard his chant. It was muted

—whether out of consideration or drunkenness, Stephen couldn't tell—and sounded like a contented sow giving suck. By the time Melody stumbled the length of the hut, flopped down on his cot and dropped one of his boots loudly to the floor, Stephen decided the mutedness had nothing whatsoever to do with consideration.

Next came Sergeant Billywood.

> . . . She'll be comin' 'round the mountain when she comes,
> When she comes,
> She'll be comin' 'round the mountain when she comes,
> She'll be—

Before the sergeant had a chance to finish the chorus, Melody dropped his second boot to the floor. "That you, Melodeee?"

"It fuckin'-well ain't the Messiah, Sargeee."

"What do you suppose happened to me tonight?" Billywood asked, stomping toward Melody with the tread of a bison.

"I've no idea," Melody drawled boredly.

"I was down the road at Ookies' place, sipping my sake like a gentleman and minding my own damn business, when all of a sudden this here little sheba-sheba shimmies up to me to ask a personal question, *'Pom-Pom,* Sahgee Billy?' *'Chotto-matte, moosemay!'* says I. 'I don't mind you getting intimate with me— you can suck my dick or give me a dose—but no one calls me Billy. The incognito's Billywood. Billywood! Clarence K. Billywood—.' "

"Oh, blow it out your ass!" Luke Collins grumbled, half asleep.

"Listen here, Jeeter Lester," Billywood retorted, "there's no call for obscenity."

> She'll be drivin' six white horses when she comes,
> When she comes . . .

It wasn't long before the lyrics turned to mush in his mouth, and Stephen heard both Billywood and his air mattress emit a great wheeze as the sergeant landed on his cot. Now, at last, except for the snoring, the Quonset hut was still—even the crunching and peeping had stopped—and Stephen fell asleep.

In the morning he was awakened by a novel reveille: the *William Tell Overture* being blasted over the stockade loudspeakers (When he went to bed the night before he had heard the *1812 Overture,* and thought it a paradoxical substitute for taps.) No one stirred but Stephen. As he sat on the edge of his cot, trying to remember and forget the elusive fragments of a troublesome dream—what had it been, that army of insects, silverfish or ticks?—Stephen noticed something on the floor behind his bed. On closer inspection he discovered five or six jagged bits of paper, and he wondered where they had come from. The mystery was solved when he stood up and saw that one of his books—*The Works of Shakespeare*—had fallen over during the night and was lying open at the title page, a considerable portion of which was missing. Scattered near the book were other bits of paper as well as some tiny black pellets that looked like the droppings of a mouse or rat. . . . A rat! Of course, Stephen thought, as he remembered what Kirk had said the day before about the netting. "It's to protect us from the rats." And there, as if to prove it, on the shelf above Leghorn's bed, next to his tin of mustache wax, were the remains of the Ritz cracker one of them had been gnawing.

After breakfast Stephen met Mr. Robbins. Considering the fact that a warrant officer is neither an officer nor a noncom but something in between the two—a little lower than lieutenant but higher than sergeant—esteemed by neither, regarded by both as some kind of curiosity to be addressed courteously, if rather dismissively, as a civilian, his status seemed to suit Mr. Robbins perfectly. Since he was too reticent and insecure to order anyone to run his errands for him, Mr. Robbins was forever trudging back and forth between Headquarters and Personnel, soliciting someone's signature or initials on some report or printed form which he himself lacked the authority to sign. In the process all of his best qualities—his thoroughness, considerateness, soft-spokenness, and patience—were completely exhausted and transformed into tight-lipped anonymity.

Instead of asking Kirk or Sal Martini to do it for him, Mr. Robbins took the time himself to teach Stephen all there was to know about the clerical maintenance of officers' records. He lugged the necessary volumes of A.R.'s and S.R.'s from Headquarters to the Personnel building and showed them to Stephen, and then, while Stephen sat comfortably at his new desk, Mr. Robbins stood for forty minutes, using his own record as a model, and explained what the various items were, how and where to make new entries, how to alter old ones, and correct mistakes. "How does that seem? Difficult?" he inquired politely when he was finished.

"I guess I'll get the hang of it," Stephen said, a little bewildered by the profusion of military abbreviations, but otherwise confident.

"I'm sure you will," Mr. Robbins said soberly, starting to close and stack the black volumes of regulations. "Don't hesitate to ask questions."

"Thank you, sir. Can I help you with those?"

"No, no. Sit still."

As soon as Mr. Robbins had left the building, the Korean boy sitting at the desk next to Stephen's stood up stiffly and extended his hand. "I am Kim Huk Sun," he said formally. "Interpreter and POW record clerk."

Stephen shook Kim's soft hand. "How do you do. I'm Stephen Wolfe."

"How do you do. You speak not like others."

"What others?"

"Other GI. I understand every word you speak. Are you teacher?"

"No."

"But you are educated man."

"Thank you."

"You go university?"

"I did."

"I go University of Seoul, now located Pusan."

"That's wonderful."

"No. Too much monies."

"Isn't it free?"

"Free?"

"Must you pay to go to school?"

"Yes. Many, many monies. In States you do not pay?"

"No," Stephen said, taking for the first time in his life pride in his country. (When he thought about it afterward, this was the moment to which Stephen traced his determination consciously to practice diplomacy during his stay in Korea.) "What do you study?"

"Political science."

"That's marvelous—the most important work there is."

Kim shook his head and brushed his coarse black hair out of his eyes. "Not good for me."

"Why not?"

"Family not rich. In Korea father must be rich for son to work in government."

"That's true in America too."

"Truman not rich."

"No."

"Lincoln not rich."

"No. I thought you meant the State Department. Is Syngman Rhee so rich?"

"Not good man," Kim said flatly, almost to himself. "Change Constitution. Block new election. Employ secret police."

"Do you think Kim Il Sung is any better?"

"No. Kim no better: different. No hope for divided Korea. China same: Mao, Chiang. Germany same: Adenauer, Ulbricht. No hope for divided world."

"How old are you, Kim?"

"Eighteen year. However, in Korea, count baby age from— from—" Kim faltered and broke off, at a loss for the English word.

"Baptism?" Stephen suggested, but retracted the word as soon as he realized its ridiculous inapplicability.

"Please: one moment," Kim said, crossing to his desk and returning with a very fat pocket-sized dictionary. "Please," he said again, pointing to the word he was after.

"Conception," Stephen enunciated carefully. "Conception."

"In Korea, count baby age from conception. When baby born, he one year old."

Pleased and charmed by the wisdom of the custom, Stephen smiled broadly, and Kim smiled back. There was something about Kim's smile that reminded Stephen of the prisoner's the day before, and he tried to discern what made it so expressive. Was it because Kim's eyeballs, like those of an Eskimo wearing a pair of snow glasses, were almost completely masked by their lids, forcing his lips and mouth to take on greater emphasis. Or was it because Korean teeth, after so many centuries of rice diet, were healthier, more dazzling and less susceptible to decay than American teeth?

"How old *you?*" Kim asked.

"Twenty-two."

"What you do in States?"

Stephen hesitated, comparing Kim's life to his own, considering the context in which this conversation of theirs was taking place —the prison camp, the prisoners, the war—and he felt ashamed and guilty about the career he'd been pursuing—whether consciously or not—for fifteen years. "I'm an actor," he said defensively. For the first time Stephen really listened to the word and realized that long before it meant one who made believe on stage or in the movies, *actor* must have surely meant one who took decisive action in the world.

"Actor," Kim repeated dreamily. "I take you theater, Pusan."

"Is there a theater downtown?"

"Yes. Woman's theater. You like?"

"I'd love to go."

"I take you. You say Shakespeare to me?"

"Recite it for you?"

"Yes. I listen. Hear sound," Kim said, tapping his ear excitedly.

"All right. Someday I'll recite it for you."

Kim shut his eyes as if he were being kissed. Stephen watched, amused and puzzled. After waiting a moment, Kim opened his eyes and commanded, "You say Shakespeare *now!*"

"Now?"

"I listen," Kim repeated, closing his eyes again.

Stephen glanced self-consciously at Sal Martini, who was sitting at the other end of the building, drinking a cup of coffee. "Go ahead, Steve. Don't be shy," Sal smiled. "It can't be worse than Melody."

Stephen recited "Of comfort no man speak." When he was finished, Kim opened his eyes and said, "I no understand."

"That makes two of us, *boysan,*" Sal exclaimed good-naturedly.

"You speak more."

"Someday, Kim," Stephen agreed. "Someday, when we're outside and I can shout my head off, I'll speak more. But you must teach me some Korean."

"I teach. We be friends."

"Yes," Stephen said, and once again he shook Kim's hand as if they were formally sealing a bargain.

By the end of the second week in August, Stephen was not only handling the officers' records with efficiency and ease, but the enlisted men's as well. In order to free Sal Martini to work full time on the prisoners' records, Mr. Robbins put Stephen in charge of the personnel section. Since getting out of Korea and back to the States was the one thing that mattered to everyone—officers and GI's alike—it was to Stephen that all of them eventually came with their questions and gripes about the rotation system. The question most frequently asked was, "How many points have I got?" But there were many others—questions about Rest and Recuperation, veterans' benefits, payroll problems, and the award of combat stripes and medals.

For reasons which no one bothered to examine, the majority of GI's were intimidated by Corporal Wolfe. Not only did he *act* superior, but something about his appearance and manner almost convinced the men he *was*. Although he wasn't muscular, he was well-proportioned, tall, and handsome. No one in the company was physically more attractive. No one was more courteous or self-controlled, conscientious or intelligent. His ability to find the answers to their questions in those forbidding, unwieldy reference books impressed the men, and they feared his brain as if it were radioactive. But even in combination, princely looks, intelligence, and gentlemanliness were not enough to intimidate an entire company. No, there was something else that made Wolfe seem so mysterious, stern, imposing, and unapproachable. Was it just his college education and "British" way of speaking? Was it his cleanliness and neatness? His abstemiousness? No one, for instance, had ever heard him curse or seen him drunk, no one had ever bumped into him at Ookies' place or, for that matter, in the company latrine. "What's with this guy? Ain't he human? Don't he ever have to shit? Don't he have to get his nuts off?" That was it, of course! The secret source of Stephen's power, the quality that made him seem untouchable, invincible, that made the men uneasy and even feel inferior, was his incorporeality. It was as if Stephen was all spirit, as if he had no needs or drives like other men, as if, precisely, he had no body.

The fact was that Stephen did everything in his power to hold himself aloof and protect his privacy. Every day, as soon as the first note of the *William Tell Overture* had sounded, he jumped out of bed, got dressed, grabbed his toilet kit, and rushed to the latrine. His toilet habits were such that he found it absolutely impossible not only to urinate but excrete in front of anyone. Part of this problem was easily solved: he simply by-passed the urinal trough at all times—even in the mornings, when no one was awake and there was no chance of his being seen, he went directly to the toilet. If, after that, someone, nonetheless, happened to come in, Stephen either waited until the intruder left or pretended to wipe himself, and came back half an hour later. Sometimes this eccentricity necessitated his visiting the latrine a dozen times a day, and gave rise to the mistaken notion that he suffered from chronic diarrhea, when, in fact, the opposite was closer to the truth.

His problem in the shower house was much the same. No matter how much anyone else admired or even envied his body, Stephen had no use for it. He detested his appendectomy scar and was falsely convinced, after careful comparative study, that his genitals were the smallest in the Army. As a consequence he stopped at nothing to conceal his nudity.

Whereas most of the men walked to the shower house naked or with their towels wrapped around their waists, Stephen went fully dressed and only undressed after he made certain it was empty. Because the others took their showers after work, between four-thirty and five or before they went on pass at seven, Stephen took his at four o'clock or nine. Furthermore, he was always careful to drape his towel over the neck of the shower next to the one he was using, so that if anyone happened to join him, he could immediately turn off the water and start to dry himself. As for "getting his nuts off," Stephen never did.

And yet, from outside, from the point of view of the men who knew nothing of Stephen's fantasies, and were constantly confronted by the hard fact of his handsomeness and stature, it was completely understandable that they should have mistaken his pathological modesty for snobbery. They assumed his hatred was directed not against himself, but them, and they interpreted it as an unwillingness to associate with them or be "one of the fellows," and someone—it was Sergeant Billywood, but Stephen never knew it, never heard it mentioned, because no one dared to say it to his face—nicknamed him "Garbo." This tag referred not only to his aloofness, but also to his habit of going off alone at dusk, up into the hills to practice Shakespeare. There wasn't a man in the company who hadn't heard the mountains reverberate his metallic voice or seen him up there in the twilight, tearing his hair, waving his arms, kneeling and rising and falling down dead. At first they thought he was engaged in some fanatic form of worship—the sight of Wolfe walking through the area with *Fear and Trembling* in his hand was not an unfamiliar one—but gradually word got round that he was an actor. Ordinarily, that would not have been enough to make the men keep their distance; on the contrary, they usually sought out the company of actors. But Garbo was not the type who clowned around or told amusing stories; like the Christ on Surgarloaf, he stood alone on top of a hill and ranted in a language that no one understood, as if he were performing exclusively for the sake of God the Father.

The other name the men called Stephen—again, of course, behind his back—was "gook lover." This stigma was used to characterize Stephen's friendship not only with the Korean interpreter who worked in Personnel, but the POW KP's who ran the chow line in the mess hall. With them Wolfe was outgoing, warm and even affectionate; whereas, with the GI's—who, after all, were fellow Americans and members of the same race—he was cool and reserved. Worst of all, perhaps, was the fact that Wolfe carried the snub to the point where he even tried to learn their language and *speak* gook.

It was just this, Stephen's interest in the Koreans and their language, that prompted Mr. Robbins to come to him with a proposal that was to change his life. "Corporal Wolfe, I have something here," he said, stirring a white piece of paper in his hand, "that I think might interest you. It's a memo from the colonel. It seems that some of the prisoners in Compound B have requested English lessons. Colonel Clayborn likes the idea, and he's prepared to go along with it, providing I can find a teacher. Well, that's the problem of course, and naturally I thought of you."

"But I don't speak a word of Korean, sir. Everyone around here thinks I speak it fluently, but that's ridiculous. I don't know a dozen words."

"You wouldn't have to speak Korean, Corporal. Apparently all these men have had at least four years of English—"

"Really?"

"What they want is a class in conversation and oral reading. You think that might interest you?"

"Yes. Very much."

"Of course, you would have to do it entirely on your own time—not during working hours. The colonel wants that clearly understood."

"That would be all right, sir. I haven't that much to do in the evenings anyway. How many classes do they want?"

"That's up to you. Two or three a week at most, I should think."

"Is there a text?"

"Text?"

"You mentioned oral reading."

"Oh, that! You know how these POW's are: they always ask for an arm and a leg: books and dictionaries and writing tablets—but of course we have no way of requisitioning such things. They'll just have to settle for conversation. That is, if you'll do it?"

"Yes, I'll do it. Gladly," Stephen said.

"Let me see, this is Friday. When would you like to start?"

"On Monday night."

"What time shall I tell them to expect you?"

"Seven o'clock."

"That's fine. Monday at 1900 hours," Mr. Robbins said, jotting down the information in his tiny, precise script on a corner of the colonel's memo.

No sooner had Mr. Robbins left than Stephen regretted not having said he would start tomorrow, Saturday. What was the point of waiting till Monday? After all, it was not as if there was any difference between one day's heat and dust, and the next. He had nothing to study, nothing to prepare. Why hadn't he said he would start tonight? Suddenly Stephen realized he had said Monday because, for the first time since he had come to the 14th MP's, he was thinking in terms of a *week*. Somehow Mr. Robbins' proposal had broken the endless circle of nameless days, the unrelieved cycle of overly-familiar faces, food, and clerical forms, the montonous, meaningless repetition of the *William Tell Overture*. The treadmill had been stopped, the squirrel cage opened! Stephen had said Monday because now, at long last, unrecorded time was over. There was to be a beginning.

On Saturday morning there were typhoon warnings. One-hundred-and-thirty-mile-an-hour winds had ripped through Okinawa and were heading straight toward Koje-do and Pusan. They were expected to strike at 2000 hours. Except for those of the prisoners who were reconstructing the viaduct on the Masan road, all work details were canceled and everyone—GI's and POW's alike—was assigned to the business of securing the stockade and company area. As if the company had been put on combat alert, Colonel Clayborn loaded his pistol, strapped on his holster and called for his jeep. Looking humorless and dour, he toured the entire area, including the stockade, making caustic comments at every stop. When he was finished, the colonel returned to Headquarters and issued an order canceling all passes and restricting everyone to the area for the night. Although the men bitched a blue streak, they dared not disobey the order because, in it, the colonel warned that he would personally conduct bed check that night. Also, since it never got dark before eight—the hour at which the typhoon was expected—he canceled the movie, and the men had no alternative but to stay indoors.

Sal Martini went to sleep. Kirk decided it was the perfect opportunity to give himself a shampoo. Leghorn used the time to measure and groom his mustache, and Stephen began to read. Sergeant Billywood organized a poker game that included himself, Melody, Collins, two men from the motor pool and the mess sergeant. Because none of the players had any money, the game, instead of being cutthroat and silent, was relaxed and boisterous. The mess sergeant took great delight in reporting that the colonel had referred to the huge kettles and caldrons in the kitchen as punchbowls. Sergeant Billywood topped the mess sergeant's story by recounting in his most inflated W. C. Fields manner what the colonel said on discovering that Billywood had sheltered all the company jeeps on the south side of the buildings next to the motor pool—that is, directly in line with the oncoming storm—instead of on the north side. Melody, who was the colonel's driver, asked what "puhvuts" were, but nobody understood the question until he explained that that's what Colonel Clayborn kept mumbling all the way through the stockade. Luke Collins then defined a puhvut as a billy goat with tits.

Stephen found it difficult to concentrate. By 1930 hours the air in the Quonset hut was so stagnant, hot, and smoky it resembled a Turkish bath—except for Sergeant Billywood, who was sniffing Copenhagen, all the players were smoking stogies. Despite the colonel's order to the contrary Stephen got up and opened the door at his end of the hut. The sky was the color of steel wool, and there was not a trace of a breeze. Stephen watched the stogie smoke to see if it would drift, but it retained its shape and position like a solid bank of snow. In the stockade some of the prisoners were singing "Onward Christian Soldiers," and Stephen wondered if the men in his class would be familiar with anything but missionary English. At 2130 the power failed, bringing the poker game to a premature end. Shortly after that, the men went to sleep. At 2230 Colonel Clayborn and Lieutenant Fry came through the hut on bed check. At each cot the colonel stopped and shined his flashlight through the mosquito netting, and Lieutenant Fry checked off the sleeper's name on a roster he was carrying. When they reached Stephen's cot, he turned his head away abruptly to protest against the light in his eyes. "Are you awake?" the colonel asked.

"Yes, sir."

"In that case will you be so kind as to latch the door behind us when we leave?"

"Yes, sir."

After hooking the door, Stephen went back to bed, but the air was stifling and he couldn't breathe. He got up again, raised the sides of his netting and tossed them in a jumble on the canopy. At 2330, just before he fell asleep, he heard the by-now familiar lubricous licking sounds of the men and the crunching of the rats.

. . . Stephen knew the MP's were asking everyone in the bar to show his pervert pass, but the Eisenhowerglass over his ID card was splintered and his photograph was missing. Behind the bar Colonel Clayborn was struggling with a huge tub of ice cubes which he emptied into the beer cooler with a deafening din . . .

Stephen opened his eyes and heard the rain on the roof. Amplified by the corrugated metal, the torrents seemed to be lapidating the Quonset hut, and he wondered how long the roof could possibly hold up. The wind, like a giant football player, was hurling its brawn against the walls, rattling the doors, backing off and charging in again. Its impact made the building quake and created a pressure in Stephen's ears. He swallowed and thought about the protection of the surrounding mountains. But that was no consolation because he realized now that he had confused the words typhoon and tornado; instead of being blown away, the hut was going to be crushed from above like so much scrap metal under a compression press.

As Stephen waited for the wind to burst the little lead hook and eye he had latched before he went to sleep, he suddenly recoiled in fright. A piece of the ceiling had fallen on the canopy over his cot. He wanted to rush outside before the hut collapsed, but the falling board startled him so he couldn't move. Then, just as suddenly as it had landed, the board—the thing!—began to stir, to squirm, to scramble in the sagging net, and Stephen started to howl. "Yahhh! Yahhh! Yahhh!"

"What is it?"

"What the hell?"

"What is it?"

"Someone turn the lights on!"

"Yahhh! Yahhh!"

"The power's dead."

"Tell me! Tell me what it is!" Sergeant Billywood demanded. "Tell me!"

Stephen heard the insistent voice, but it was not until the sergeant seized him by the shoulders and began to shake him violently that Stephen saw the crisscross of flashlight beams, realized he was standing in the center of the hut and came to his senses. "In my netting. Something's caught," he panted hoarsely, and all the flashlights were focused on his cot.

Even before Kirk had a chance to exclaim it squeamishly, Stephen saw the rat for himself. Except for its snout and incisors, that protruded through a hole it had ripped or gnawed in the bottom of the canopy, it was hopelessly tangled and ensnared in the netting. The flashlight beams were reflected in one black, ferocious eye.

"Jesus Christ! Is that all!" Collins scoffed. "It ain't a mountain lion, Corporal." Stephen watched Collins stride toward the netting, stretch out his arms the length of the cot, grab the canopy in both his hands and lift it off its uprights. Then, as if he was folding a blanket, he brought the two ends of the netting toward the center of his chest, gathered them together and clutched them in his right fist. Aware of both his audience and the tumult of the storm, Collins addressed the rat stentorially, "Better start praying, bugger!" Like a child carrying a bag of candy, he meandered slowly into the center aisle, swinging his booty boastfully. As he moved, the flashlights trailed him. When he reached the end of the Quonset, he gripped the netting in both hands, wound up like a batter and began to smash the netted rat against the wall.

If there were any sounds other than the pounding—any squeaks or squeals—they were drowned out by the storm. Everyone watched enrapt as Collins went on smashing the rat until its blood —black in the yellow flashlight beams—spattered the gray transite wall, and Melody began to onk orgiastically. When the slaughter was over, Collins casually tossed the corpse outside, and everyone went back to sleep.

The rain continued through the night, and when the men got up on Sunday morning it was still raining. Though by no means a typhoon—at its worst, the wind velocity was less than 70 miles an hour—the storm had done some damage. In addition to the power lines, more than twenty of the prisoners' tents were down, the company's switchboard had exploded, and the supply room was flooded. At the same time, much to everyone's relief, the rain had settled the dust and dispelled the heat. But the relief was only temporary. Gradually, as the rain continued to fall all day and night Sunday and all day Monday, it began to transform the dust into a new and in some ways worse discomfort: mud.

By the time Stephen set out for his English class on Monday night, there were streams and puddles everywhere, and the hillside ran with a rich brown gravy. The rain had stopped at five, and massive clouds sailed across the sky, grouping and regrouping like a fleet on maneuvers. As Stephen climbed the hill, the wind made his poncho billow out like Bismarck's cape, and he felt as if he were at the summit of the world, the heavens within hands' reach. The guard at the sally port recognized Stephen and let him pass without question. "Which is Compound B?" Stephen asked.

"First one on the right."

The mud inside the stockade was even softer, deeper than outside, and Stephen's combat boots sank into it up to the ankles, and made sucking noises as he moved. When he reached the gate of Compound B, he was surprised to see Chang Sung Chull, the KP from the mess hall, waiting on the other side. "Hi, Chang."

"Good night, Stephen Wolfe," he said smiling broadly.

"What are you doing here?"

"Wait for *sonsaeng*. Take to English class."

"*I'm* the teacher, Chang."

"Yes! Yes!" he said, smiling and nodding. "Number one GI. Make PW *tochsan* happy. Come!" he said, turning and leading the way like a beadle. "I take you class."

As they trudged through the mud between the rows of huts and tents, Chang kept whistling three high notes that sounded like the call of a cardinal. In response, the prisoners kept raising their tent flaps or coming to the doors of their huts. Soon Stephen realized the whistles were some kind of signal or fanfare to announce his arrival, and it seemed to him like that inevitable moment in every jungle movie he had ever seen when the white explorer is brought into the native village and taken to the chief. Except that now there were no drum beats, no suspicion or hostility, only curiosity and various expressions of friendliness—smiles, nods, even some applause—and Stephen felt unworthy.

When they reached their destination, a squad tent, separate but not different from the rest, Chang pulled aside the flap and held it up for Stephen. Even before he was able to register clearly the number of prisoners seated around the conference table, the class rose in a body, faced Stephen and bowed from the waist. For an instant Stephen thought of objecting to the custom on the grounds that it seemed undemocratic—after all, this was an English class, and students in the West did not bow to their teachers. At the same time, he felt embarrassed and despite his objections, returned the bow, not only out of courtesy but in order to hide his blushes. In doing so the custom became real to him. At once it bound him to his students in mutual humility, compassion, and respect; Stephen felt conjoined with them at this specific time and place for a purpose that suddenly took on a serious, devout significance.

"Thank you," he said almost inaudibly. After the exchange of bows, the class sat down. "I am very grateful to be here with you," Stephen continued slowly, looking around the tent. The three oil lamps that had been placed at regular intervals down the length of the conference table gave off a sooty smoke like smudge pots, but very little light. Stephen had difficulty seeing all the faces—especially those in the shadows beyond the periphery of the table—but he guessed that altogether there were forty men in the tent. "Do you understand?" he asked. No one answered. Stephen realized the silence had more to do with shyness than noncomprehension, and he tried to break it by repeating his question in Korean. "Please," he said, extending his hand toward the man on his right, *"Ihae hasimnikaa?"*

Instantly the class relaxed and expressed its understanding and approval. "Yes! Yes!" they exclaimed, and they smiled and whispered among themselves, repeating for those who had missed it what the *sonsaeng* had said. When the class settled down, the prisoner to whom Stephen had addressed his question said with difficulty, "We understand. PW also much grateful for teacher."

Stephen's fingers coiled into fists as he tried to restrain his tears. "Thank you," he said. "Instead of PW and GI, I would like us to call each other by name. My name is Stephen Wolfe. What is yours?"

"I, Pak Man Kap."

Stephen knew he ought to stop and call Pak's attention to his omission of the verb, but he hadn't the heart to do it. For one thing, he appreciated the struggle behind Pak's simple, tenuous words, and was anxious not to discourage him. For another, the fact that they were talking, communicating with each other, meant more to

Stephen than the grammatical correctness of what was being said; and he realized, there and then, that he was going to make a dreadful teacher. "Pak, what did you do before the war? What was your profession?"

"Profession?"

"What kind of work did you do?"

Pak did not understand and could not answer until one of his neighbors coached him in Korean. *"Ne, ne,"* he said, turning back to Stephen. "I profession, carpenter. Build table. Bench."

Despite Pak's modesty and limited English, Stephen realized he was not speaking abstractly. He was referring specifically to the conference table on which Stephen's elbows were resting at this moment, and to the benches on which the class was sitting. Of course, Stephen had noticed the table before, but had taken it for granted. Perhaps, if instead of being a sturdy, beautifully finished and oiled piece of furniture, it had been more primitive—four or five rough planks laid across two shaky wooden trestles—Stephen would have realized it was handmade and remarked on it earlier. But it was just the expertness of Pak's craftsmanship that had deceived him. "You *made* this table!" he exclaimed incredulously.

"Yes. I make."

"It's very beautiful," Stephen said, drawing the flat of his palm admiringly over its satin surface. "You made these benches?"

"Yes. I make."

"And this chair?" he added, springing up from the armchair —almost a throne—in which he had been sitting. "Did you make this chair, too?"

"Yes. I make."

All at once it dawned on Stephen that everything—except for the tent itself—everything he saw around him: the benches, table, chair, ashtrays, even the oil lamps had been made by the prisoners, and he was wonderstruck. "I admire you . . . so much," he said, speaking not only to Pak but the entire class. "And this? Who made this?" he asked eagerly, holding up an ashtray that had been hammered out of a Schlitz beer can. "Who is the tinsmith?"

"I, tinsmith, Teacher," someone on the opposite side of the table giggled.

"What is your name?"

"I, Kim Hi Yong."

After speaking to Kim and Chu Fun Loo, a barber, Lee Song Su, a farmer, and Mung Cho Ho, a student, Stephen noticed for the first time the presence of a child in the class. He was sitting in the shadows at the far end of the tent, obstructed by the row of men sitting in front of him at the table. "What is your name, please?" Stephen asked, standing up.

"I, Bak Dal Mook."

"No, no. I'm sorry," Stephen said. "I meant the little boy behind you." Bak understood and leaned to one side, out of the way. "Yes. Thank you. What is your name, please?"

The little boy curled his delicate lips, and his eyebrows fluttered like a fledgling's wings, but he did not speak.

"He is name, O Hi Seong. He do not speak English, Teacher."

Stephen was not certain who had answered for the boy. He only knew that the gentle voice had come from the same general vicinity, and he directed his next question to the shadows. "How old is he?"

"He is twelve year old, Teacher," the unknown speaker answered.

Stephen remembered what his friend Kim had told him about the Korean method of computing age, and he realized that O Hi Seong was only eleven. He thought of himself at that age . . . puberty, Potawatomi, the war it had been, a war without warfare— but *this* war was real; this camp, a real prison; this child, a real POW . . . "What is he doing here?" Stephen cried out.

Although he had addressed his adjuration to the heavens, it was not God but the unknown speaker who answered Stephen. "He help me in dispensary."

The speaker's calm, matter-of-fact tone plus the look of embarrassment on most of the students' faces made Stephen regain his composure. "You speak English very well," he said, trying to penetrate the shadows. "I'm afraid I can't see you. Isn't there room for you at the table?" Immediately, by squeezing to the right and left, the men on the bench at the opposite end of the table made room for the man and the boy. "That's fine. Thank you."

As soon as he stepped into the circle of light, Stephen recognized the man. It was the prisoner who had smiled at him the day of his arrival. And there it was again! that resplendent smile, outshining the oil lamps on the table and filling the gloom with affirmation and promise like a white hyacinth in March. "Thank you," the prisoner said, sitting down and speaking not only for himself but the child who looked frightened.

"Please explain to O that nothing is wrong. I am happy he is here and look forward to the day when we can speak in English together." As he said this Stephen watched the prisoner's face for some sign of recognition, but if there was any it was not discernible. His face was so open and unmasked, so direct and outgoing, that its permanent expression was one of recognition. Even that first afternoon—over a month ago—it had seemed to Stephen like the face of a very close friend who had come to meet him at an airport after a long separation.

When he finished translating Stephen's remarks for O, the prisoner said, "He say, thank you very much, Teacher."

"What is your name?" Stephen asked.

"My name is Pak Sun Bo."

"Like my friend here," Stephen said, gesturing toward the carpenter. "You have the same first name." This observation brought giggles not only from the two Paks, but most of the class. "Why is that funny?"

"Pak is not first name, Teacher," Pak Sun Bo explained. "Korean first name, not first name like GI first name, first name, last name, last name—" Obviously, to his own ears, what Pak was saying sounded like doggerel; it made him laugh so hard he could not finish.

"No. No. I understand you perfectly," Stephen said, trying to keep a straight face. "In Korean my name would be Wolfe Stephen. I understand. You said O helped you in the dispensary. Are you a doctor?"

"Yes. I am doctor."

"In that case, to differentiate between you and my friend the carpenter, I will call you Dr. Pak." For some inexplicable reason, this remark produced pandemonium. The titters and giggles of the last few minutes erupted now in uncontrollable laughter, and the students rocked back and forth and slapped their thighs until the tears ran down their cheeks. Though he hadn't the vaguest notion what was funny, Stephen laughed too—so hard, he had to hold his stomach, so hard his legs became weak and he collapsed into the throne chair.

When, at last, the laughter subsided, Stephen decided to change the subject—if only to give his lungs and ribs a rest. "Have you heard about Mexico's new proposal to the UN?" he asked, referring to the Assembly's latest effort to break the truce-talks deadlock. (Mexico had suggested a plan whereby all those prisoners of war who so desired would be given temporary residence in neutral nations under arrangements that would permit the prisoners to live and work.) As Stephen was later to discover, there was no proposal, however insignificant, that had any bearing whatsoever on their fate, about which the prisoners were not thoroughly informed. Somehow they knew before the newspapers what was happening in the UN, Panmunjom, Pusan, Pyongyang, Peking, Moscow, Washington, Tokyo, New Delhi and Geneva. In this case they were not only aware of Mexico's proposal but violently opposed to it, and the mood of the class changed radically. The men scowled and grumbled and shifted their weight. "What's the matter? Tell me what you think," Stephen insisted.

"May I say to you frankly, Teacher?" Dr. Pak inquired politely.

"Of course! I *want* you to!"

"Mexico proposal, anti-man: send fish on land, bird in water. We are Korea! Not Brazil. Not India. Korea!"

"I understand. You're right—absolutely! But what is the solution?"

"Kill Communists!" Lee Song Su, the farmer, exhorted, and the class agreed with him. "Yes! Yes!" they growled. "Kill Communists!"

"*Who* should kill the Communists?" Stephen asked impatiently. "Chiang Kai-shek!"

"*We* kill!" Chu Fun Loo exclaimed.

"Yes! Yes!" the class joined in. "We kill! Free us out of prison! We kill! We no fear!"

Stephen imagined a group of pro-Communist prisoners on Kojedo having the same discussion, but reaching the opposite conclusion: Kill imperialists! "No," he objected. "That what's been happening for two years, and nothing's been accomplished. We're right back where we started. There must be a truce."

"No want truce! Want unify Korea!"

"So do I!"

"Teacher," the student, Mung Cho Ho, said, leaning forward with a look of sly impudence. "How you unify Korea without kill Communists?"

"Through the UN."

"But UN opposed to Communists. Why you here, if UN no oppose?"

"Why you fight?" Pak joined in.

"The UN is opposed to Communist aggression—to the crossing of the 38th parallel. It wants to restore—"

"We no want parallel!" Lee shouted, pounding the table. "We want North Korea! North Korea, South Korea, same! Communists—Communists—" At a loss for the English words, Lee lapsed into his native tongue and delivered a long, blistering tirade that left him purple in the face.

When it was over, the student Mung translated the gist of Lee's sentiments. "Lee say, North Korean people same South Korean people. Same face, same history, same custom, same language—"

"Yes, I understand," Stephen interrupted.

"Communist, *not* same," Mung continued. "Communism come from Rooshia. Rooshia partition country, partition family, partition heart, brain."

At the mention of Russia the class broke into an uproar. The students beat the table with their fists, and once again there were cries of Kill Communists! Kill Stalin! Kill Rooshians!

"But Russia was not the only nation that signed the Potsdam Declaration," Stephen objected. "The United States did! So did China and Great Britain. They're all to blame."

"What matter blame?" Dr. Pak interjected. Although it wasn't clear to Stephen at the moment, he realized afterward that by speaking quickly the doctor had probably averted a riot in the class. "What matter blame?" he repeated softly. "Potsdam is seven year in past. We are now."

"Exactly!" Stephen agreed. "And the issue now is how to end the war."

"No, Teacher," Dr. Pak said firmly. "Excuse me to contradict you, but war or peace not issue. Issue: independence." He spoke the word conclusively, as if it clarified and summed up everything. "Intention, Potsdam Declaration: Korea independence. Intention, Moscow Agreement, same: end Japanese domination, gain Korea independence. But what happen? Japanese go away, Rooshians come. Pyongyang, Moscow become to same. Rooshian teacher, Rooshian doctor, Rooshian soldier, Rooshian engineer. Korea has not independence. Without independence, what matter peace?"

"It matters to O! How can a child grow up in a prison camp?"

"How can child grow outside?" Dr. Pak asked gently. "Mother: North Korea—maybe she is dead. Father, take in army—maybe he is prisoner, maybe he is dead. What should boy do?"

A shudder ran through Stephen's body. "I don't know," he stammered. "I don't know."

"Here, boy grow, live, become to man—same as we do. How

boy become to man under Communists? Boy become to Communist under Communists."

Once again, like the leader of a Greek chorus, Lee began to shout, Kill Communists! and Stephen was relieved to hear the first notes of the *1812 Overture*. "It's nine o'clock already. I have to go."

"When you will come again?" Dr. Pak asked eagerly.

"Wednesday. I'll come at eighteen-thirty. That will give us more time," Stephen said, standing up.

Immediately the class rose, too. *"Su-yoil, Su-yoil:* Wednesday, Wednesday," the word went round, and the men nodded with satisfaction.

"I want to thank you for this evening—even though I feel a little guilty. We have spent all our time talking, not studying English. On Wednesday I would like to try something else. I would like to spend half the evening conversing and the other half reading. How do you feel about that?"

After talking it over at great length among themselves, Dr. Pak spoke for the class. "Class consider proposal excellent, Teacher. But class wonder how possible to read without book."

Stephen laughed. "It's not possible. I was just about to ask you that: the name of the reader you requested from Colonel Clayborn."

"It call *National English Reader-Fourth Series.* Can Teacher find?" Dr. Pak asked hopefully.

"Teacher will try." It was not until Dr. Pak grinned knowingly that Stephen realized he had answered in the third person, as if he was dealing with a child, and a look of amused understanding and intimacy passed between them. "Good night," Stephen said.

"Good night, Teacher," the class said.

As he stepped out of the tent, the impact of the cool air made Stephen aware how overheated and excited he was. Not only his perspiration but all of him—his breath, nerves, heart—seemed to be evaporating in the night, and he had to stand still a moment to assure his balance. He threw back his head and looked at the sky. It was turbid, swollen, overbearing. And yet for Stephen it had the effect of one of those sharp, crystalline, star-studded skies that comes at the end of a stifling summer as a welcome sign of autumn. He felt refreshed and clarified, vital and purposive. The glutinous mud that tried to suck him under with every step he took seemed feeble and incongruous by comparison.

Just as he reached the gate of the compound, Stephen was startled to hear again those halting, heartening words, "Good night, Teacher." He turned and saw Dr. Pak, O, Lee, Mr. Pak, Chu, Chang, Mung—most of the class—standing in the yellow floodlight, smiling. They had followed him silently, devotedly all the way from the squad tent as if he were the Pied Piper. "Good night," Stephen said. "I wish it was Wednesday already."

"Good night, Teacher."

When he got back, all the lights in the Quonset hut were on but it was empty. The men were either at the movies or in town. Stephen felt both disappointed and relieved that there was no one there with whom to share his experience. Returning from the stockade reminded him of the way he had felt every time he returned to Fort Dix after a weekend in New York. It was like leading a double life. But to Stephen, the two worlds between which he moved seemed so disparate, so irreconcilable, they canceled each other out, expatriating him from both.

The following morning, before starting work, Stephen went to Headquarters to speak to Mr. Robbins. "Sir, can I get a voting card from you?"

"Voting card?" the warrant officer asked absent-mindedly. "Oh yes, yes. I'd forgotten," he said, pulling out the bottom drawer of his desk. "No one but Kirk's requested one."

"Not even the officers?"

Stephen watched the intimation of a sneer begin to puff up Mr. Robbins' freckled cheeks, but it vanished in an instant. "No, not even the officers," he repeated ironically. "Oh, by the way, how did your English class go last night?"

"Wonderfully," Stephen beamed, and he took the voting card and went next door to his office.

After greeting Kim cheerfully, Stephen said, "Have you ever heard of the *National English Reader?*"

"Of course," Kim said. "I had in school."

"Where can I buy it?"

"Pusan."

"Will you take me to the store?"

"Yes. Not far from parent house. I take."

"Can we go this evening?"

"Yes," Kim said. "After work, I take."

The International Market covered four or five hillside blocks in downtown Pusan. Some of it indoors, some of it out, some permanent, some temporary, the market was a maze of muddy streets, lanes, aisles, alleys, byways, and arcades that intervolved through a chaos of counters, carts, sheds, shops, stalls, tents and lean-tos. For its boundaries it took the medieval-looking stone wall of an embassy or temple on the south and the barbed wire fence around a military installation to the north. On top of the embassy wall were displayed great overblown melons, pears, peppers, cabbages, cucumbers, tomatoes, radishes and celery, all of which were two or three times normal size. When Stephen asked why they were so large, Kim explained, not without considerable embarrassment, that the Korean farmers fertilized their crops with human manure. On the fence to the north, hung in neat rows and looking like tobacco leaves, were dried carp, flounders, snappers, squids and eels, as well as strings of ortolans and whole smoked ducks. In the market place, between the wall and fence, thrown together with no attempt at logic—or so it seemed to Stephen—were books and bolts of cotton, American toiletries and Japanese cameras, sticky-looking bean cakes and dainty rubber slippers with turned-up toes, caged canaries and crickets, musical instruments, bins of grain, archery equipment, eyeglasses and Chinese ravioli. No matter how carefully one chose his steps, indoors as well as out, omnipresent was the mud like blackstrap molasses underfoot, while in the air floated the sharp, inescapable aroma of dung and rotten vegetables.

"What *is* that smell?" Stephen asked, recognizing in it strong traces of the stench he had mistaken for carrion his first night in Korea.

"That *kimshee,*" Kim explained. "Korea national food. Layer cabbage, layer turnip, layer radish, layer meat, layer what you fancy; put in urn, size of boy, stand one year, become to pickle before eat." Stephen winced at the thought. "You no like?"

"I don't know, Kim. I'll have to try it," Stephen said, stopping, as he had done every step of the way, in front of a stall that attracted his attention. "Kim—"

"Come, Stephen," Kim interrupted. "Bookstore not much far, top of hill."

"What kind of shop is this?" Stephen asked, staring at two stuffed birds—an owl and a hawk—displayed on a crude wooden counter. Next to the hawk were several large glass jars that contained snakes, toads, the wing of a starling, a skinned rabbit, and some unrecognizable entrails, all preserved in formaldehyde.

"Come. We go bookstore," Kim said impatiently.

"Wait a minute, Kim. I want to look."

"No. We late," Kim insisted, tugging at Stephen's sleeve. "Book-store soon close."

"Can't you even tell me what this place is?"

"I no know English," Kim said evasively. "Come!"

"Haven't you your dictionary?" Without speaking, Kim frowned, took out his dictionary, flipped through its pages and pointed to the word "pharmacy." "You mean to say these animals are medicines?"

"Why you so much interest?" Kim demanded.

"It's fascinating," Stephen said, squatting to examine the jars more closely. "What is this?" he asked, pointing at an entrail.

"I no know," Kim said without looking.

Stephen glanced at the shriveled husk of the white-haired woman who was sitting motionless and cross-legged on a platform behind the counter. "Can't you ask the owner?"

With obvious reluctance and resentment, Kim did as he was told. In response the woman, almost in a state of trance, moved her lips mechanically and croaked an endless answer in a voice that did not seem to be her own but a voice from the dead medi-ated spiritualistically. "She say, that liver from monkey."

Stephen had to resist the impulse to seize the jar in both hands, instead he ogled as if it was filled with jelly beans and he was six years old. "Monkey liver," he whispered rhapsodically. "What's it for? What does it cure?"

"I go now," Kim threatened.

"Please," Stephen begged. "Can't you wait a second? What's the matter with you anyway?" Kim stiffened but did not answer. Ste-phen knew his friend was exasperated, but he could not pull him-self away from the jar. Just below the monkey's liver, at the very bottom of the jar, limply curving with the wall, its pelage dark and sleek in the formaldehyde was the tailless, phallic body of a rat. . . . 'But in a sieve I'll thither sail, And, like a rat without a tail, I'll do, and I'll do, and I'll do.' . . . All of a sudden Stephen realized that the old woman was a witch, and he stole another glance at her, wondering what sort of talisman was tied to the end of the thong she wore around her withered neck. Why were her hands so masculine and youthful? What witchcraft could she work with these animals and entrails? . . . Potency? Fertility? Rejuve-nation? Were those the powers of this priapic rat? . . . "Kim, how do you say rat in Korean?"

"I no know."

"A simple word like rat!"

"Chwi," Kim said, so quickly and begrudgingly it sounded as if he was spitting.

"What?"

"Chwi. Like sound rat make: *chwi."*

Hearing the word, the witch began to croak again. When she was done Stephen asked, "What did she say?"

"She say, you want buy rat?"

Stephen hesitated, tempted, but only for a second. "No," he said, "but thank her."

"I no thank! I no stay! Good-by, Stephen!"

For the first time it occurred to Stephen that Kim's family might be waiting for him. "I'm sorry, Kim," he said, catching up to his friend. "Are you late for dinner?"

"No late," he said moodily.

"Then why did you act that way? Why are you so upset?"

"No upset. Angry!"

"Why?"

"Hate pharmacy. Reflect ignorance of people. Only superstition. Hate superstition! Make me shame I Korean."

"Why? Don't you believe in witches?" Stephen asked playfully.

"No! *You* believe?"

"I don't know."

"Pharmacy lady no witch: business woman! Like other business woman in market: wait for customer. Only she no sell necessary produce. Sell superstition. Live off ignorance of people. I hate! You no agree?"

"Yes," Stephen said soberly.

"Why then you so much interest?"

"I don't know," Stephen shrugged.

"You no ignorant! You educated man."

Stephen considered Kim's protest carefully, seriously, but was unable to justify or explain his behavior. He did not understand it himself. "I guess some part of me must still be living in the Dark Ages. I'm sorry, Kim . . . sorry to annoy you—disappoint you. Let's go and buy the books."

The *National English Reader-Fourth Series* contained five of Aesop's fables, and stories by Tolstoy, Mansfield, Balzac, and Chekhov. Except for "Bliss" none of the stories had been written in English and the translations were abominable. That, plus the fact that not one American author was represented, irritated Stephen greatly. Nevertheless, it seemed better than nothing, and he bought the dealer's entire stock: a dozen copies.

At some point in the night the rain resumed and it continued all through Wednesday. When it came time for Stephen to go to his class, he put the books under his poncho, not only to protect but to conceal them. The mud was worse than it had been on Monday, and his combat boots sank into it up to the third set of shoe lace eyes. Once again, when he reached the gate of Compound B, Chang was waiting for him.

"Good night, Stephen Wolfe."

"Chang, why are you waiting in the rain? There's no need. I remember the way."

"No same classroom. Classroom change. New classroom. I take," he said, scurrying over the surface of the mud as if he had no gravity.

"Why has the classroom been changed?" Stephen asked, trying without success to keep up with his guide.

"*Tochsan* student."

"More than last time?"

"Many, many."

"Why is that? Why are there more?"

"Student speak of *sonsaeng*. Everywhere, student tell of *sonsaeng*. Other PW listen, hear, want to see with own eye: come class."

Stephen felt both flattered and self-conscious but said nothing. After a minute they reached the dispensary—the one from which Dr. Pak had emerged that first afternoon—and Chang tugged open its warped wooden door. Unlike the squad tent, the dispensary was electrified, and Stephen had no difficulty seeing. As he entered, no less than seventy men stood up and bowed. With the rain dripping down his face, Stephen clutched the books to his stomach and bowed back. "Good evening," he said, straightening up.

"Good evening, Teacher."

Slowly, carefully, Stephen raised the front of his poncho, revealing the books. But now, in relation to the size of the class, the number of books seemed pitifully inadequate, and he placed them on the table with embarrassment. "I'm afraid there are too many of us— or too few of them," he apologized, turning away to take off his poncho. As Stephen molted the wet garment, the silence of the students seemed to confirm his misgiving.

It was not until he put his poncho aside and returned to the table that he saw how mistaken he was. Far from being disappointed or dissatisfied, the class was overwhelmed by the books. Mung held the tips of his thick stubby fingers over his gaping mouth, Pak Man Kap hung his head to conceal his emotion; like a cat, Lee stretched his body toward the books as if they were a sparrow, Chang's usually funny face looked reverent, O sat grinning and Dr. Pak stared wide-eyed, wavering between tears and laughter. "Let's try to do the best we can," Stephen suggested, starting to hand out the books, making certain that none went to the newcomers—the curiosity seekers—but only to the men he knew.

"Teacher," Dr. Pak interrupted, "PW forget what new book like. All time PW dream of past: boyhood, mother, brother, home, school, Pyongyang, trolley car—time before war. But past is only dream, in mind; not real. What is real is prison, war, riot, torture, death. PW forget what new book like. Now Teacher bring new book into prison. PW see, remember," he said, tapping his temple. "New book is clean; not torn, not dirt, not grease . . . not dream. New book real. Make boyhood real—time before war, real. PW grateful to Teacher."

"For me . . . it is the same," Stephen said slowly, referring not to the books but to the emotion he felt and shared with Dr. Pak.

When the books were distributed, Stephen asked those who had received copies to turn to the table of contents. Of the authors represented, Aesop, Tolstoy, and Chekhov were known to the students, and Stephen was pleased. He attributed their ignorance of Balzac to the vicissitudes of literary fashion, and of Katherine Mansfield to her relatively minor position. But gradually, as the discussion became more general, Stephen began to be aware of a radical imbalance. Whereas every student was conversant with the works of Gorky, Pushkin, Tolstoy, Turgenev, Gogol, Andreyev, Dostoyevsky, Chekhov, Simonov and Sholokhov; almost no one had ever heard—not to mention read—a single word of Homer, Dante, Shakespeare or Goethe. They were casualties of the cold war. The fables of Aesop were admissible only because their author had been a slave, oppressed like the proletariat; Tolstoy's aristocratic heritage was overlooked because of his land reforms, Dostoyevsky's Christianity, because of his poverty.

Stephen was furious. Angrily, he boasted of America where books were printed regardless of their origin or point of view,

where the works of Marx were as readily available as those of
Thomas Jefferson. But there was no argument: the class agreed
with him. Surely, they said, that was one of the reasons they refused to be repatriated.

With that question settled and out of the way, they turned to the
fable, *The Wolves and the Sheep:*

> Once on a time, the Wolves sent an embassy to the Sheep,
> desiring that there might be peace between them for the time
> to come. "Why?" said they, "should we be forever waging
> this deadly strife? Those wicked Dogs are the cause of all;
> they are incessantly barking at us, and provoking us. Send
> them away and there will be no longer any obstacle to our
> eternal friendship and peace."
>
> The Silly Sheep listened, the Dogs were dismissed, and the
> flock, thus deprived of their best protectors, became an easy
> prey to their treacherous enemy.

The translation discouraged Stephen to the point of despair, and
he tried to explain how stilted and unintelligible it was. But the
students were eager to practice their pronunciation, and, reluctantly, Stephen called on different ones to read aloud. When they
were finished, he asked others whom they thought the wolves represented, and without exception the answer was, The Rooshians.
The dogs were the UN forces and, of course, the Koreans were
the sheep.

When it came to questions of vocabulary, Stephen refused to
resort to the two or three pocket dictionaries in the class. Instead,
he relied on his imagination and pantomimic ability to act out the
answers. By placing his throne chair in the narrow aisle between
the last row of students and the wall of the dispensary, and repeatedly failing to circumvent it, he illustrated "obstacle." By enlisting
the help of the little boy, O, and stealthily creeping up behind him,
he dramatized "easy prey." Thus Stephen turned the boring business of vocabulary into an entertaining charade.

After the first hour was over, Stephen asked the men to put aside
their books, and he opened the conversation period with some
casual questions about the rain and the monsoon season. Despite
his intention to keep the discussion uncontroversial, it rapidly
turned to world affairs and the subject of the American elections.
Stephen was not surprised that the prisoners were better informed

and more partisan than the average GI. The overwhelming majority favored Eisenhower. They felt the time had come for a world-wide counterrevolution. Mankind was ready, waiting! they said. All that was needed was the proper leader—a man of strength, decisiveness, courage, action, in short, a hero like Eisenhower—to "wipe out Rooshians!"

Stephen objected. What was needed was not a warrior but a man of intelligence and vision, a man with a sense of history. He wanted to say more. He wanted to stress the need for a leader who would dare to differentiate between libertarianism and totalitarianism, between Socialism and Communism, who would dare to work for the welfare, rather than control, of the entire human race, but Stephen was too diffident. Even the few remarks he did make were tentative and bloodless compared to those of the prisoners, and the contrast disturbed him profoundly. Why, he wondered, was their involvement so much more passionate than his own? After all, they had no vote, no vested interest, and yet they were as sanguinary about the American elections as they had been about the Mexican proposal; whereas, he was reticent and shy. What accounted for this difference in their attitudes? Were they, the prisoners, endowed with so much more intelligence and passion than Stephen? Surely he was capable of thinking and feeling as deeply as they. No, the difference lay elsewhere—in the realm of commitment and engagement—in the degree of self-conviction. For some reason these men, who had been stripped of everything, who were nothing but a bunch of names and numbers on a prison roster, were, nonetheless, convinced that who they were and what they thought and felt and did was of the utmost importance in the world. And so they were; so they had become! Despite their imprisonment, their homelessness, their condition of absolute uncertainty, despite the global super-Powers that were trying every second to manipulate and control their lives, these prisoners, had, for months and months, successfully obstructed a settlement of the Korean war. And they had done so, solely by means of an heroic self-assertion, with no other weapons than themselves: their reason and their bodies. What accounted for such courage? Stephen wondered. Where did it come from? What was its source? If not God, then who or what empowered a man to pit his featherweight against the onslaught of reality, and not only not be overcome, but stand and leave his mark? As Stephen looked around the class at

Pak Man Kap's pugnacious jaw, Mung's wild head of hair, Lee's alert and smoldering eyes, seeking to discover there the answer to his question, the lights went out.

The failure of Pusan's power was a common occurrence, and the men laughed and made jokes about it as they lit the oil lamps. Since it was already twenty to nine, Stephen decided to end the class. With various expressions of disappointment, the students said good night and filed out of the dispensary. From the sound of the rain on the roof Stephen could tell it was falling harder now than it had all day. He was not surprised to find his poncho still wet inside. It felt like the yellow oilskin in which the first-aid kits had been wrapped at Penobscot and he remembered with revulsion his trip to Lobster Pond

When his head emerged from the poncho, Stephen was startled to see Dr. Pak standing in front of him like Florence Nightingale with an oil lamp in his hand. Because it was coming from below, the flickering light cast unflattering shadows, and Stephen realized that Dr. Pak was older than he had thought. It was hard to tell exactly, but Stephen guessed that he was somewhere between thirty and thirty-five.

"Will Teacher stay? Take tea with Pak?"

Stephen glanced at his watch and was about to refuse when he noticed the look of disappointment in Dr. Pak's eyes. "Yes. Teacher," he said teasingly, "would love to stay."

Like a ripple on the surface of a pond, a smile appeared on the doctor's lips and began to spread in ever-enlarging circles until it reached the extremities of his face, and even his hairline, his ears, and Adam's apple seemed to be smiling. "Come please, Teacher," he said, starting to walk toward the opposite end of the building, holding the lamp to light the way.

"Why don't you call me Stephen?"

"Not proper. How would sound for student to call teacher Stephen? No respect. Teacher call student doctor."

"What if I were to call you by your first name—if I called you Bo?"

Dr. Pak giggled. "Bo is name reserve for mother—sometimes wife say Bo, but friend say Sun Bo."

"All right. Then I'll say Sun Bo."

"Thank you, Teacher."

"No. Now you must say Stephen."

"What matter what *tongue* say?" Pak shrugged. "Sentiment in heart what matter."

In its construction and layout the dispensary was identical to Headquarters. It consisted of one enormous workroom—the area in which the English class had been held—and one much smaller, private room at the far end of the building. Just outside this room, which was the counterpart of Colonel Clayborn's office, against the wall were a counter and sink as well as the shelves and cabinets in which the medicines and instruments were stored. There were no beds; prisoners sick enough to be hospitalized were sent to Pusan.

When he reached the counter, Dr. Pak set the oil lamp down and started to speak rapidly in Korean. Stephen, who had thought they were alone, was surprised. After a moment, the little boy, O, appeared in the doorway of the private room, bowed to Stephen and began to scurry about the dispensary, fetching a small tripod, filling a tin can with water, lighting an alcohol lamp. At the same time Dr. Pak was busy transferring tea leaves from a canister into three aluminum canteen cups. From the meticulous, inequitable way he apportioned them—dropping a tiny pinch in two of the cups and twice as much in the third—Stephen could tell how precious the tea leaves were. "Please," he objected. "You must be fair."

Dr. Pak looked puzzled. "Fair?"

"You mustn't give me more than you give yourself."

"How is that possible?" he asked ironically, raising his delicate eyebrows. "Teacher give book, give English class; doctor give cup of tea. How not fair?" Stephen conceded the point with a smile. Dr. Pak turned to O. From his gestures Stephen could tell he was giving the boy instructions about the tea. When he was finished, the doctor picked up the oil lamp and led Stephen into the smaller room, which was furnished with an army cot, a desk, and chair. "Please, sit," he said, indicating the cot.

"Is this where you sleep, Sun Bo?" Stephen asked, taking off his poncho.

"No. I sleep in hut. Orderly sleep here."

"Is O the orderly?"

"Tonight—every night someone different."

Despite its starkness, the room seemed cozy in the rain and Stephen relaxed and took out his cigarettes. "Would you like one?"

"Please, yes," Dr. Pak said, selecting one with as much care as if he were drawing a straw to determine his fate. Stephen struck a match. Like a swan the doctor stretched his long neck toward the light and cupped his hands around Stephen's, bringing the match closer.

"You said a man's wife sometimes calls her husband by his first name," Stephen said, lighting his own cigarette. "Are you married, Sun Bo?"

"Yes, I marry," he said, savoring the smoke.

"Have you a picture of your wife?"

"No. I have no picture."

"Does your wife live in Pyongyang?"

"No. Wife dead."

In the silence the rain on the tin roof sounded like hailstones.

"Are *you* marry, Stephen?"

"No, Sun Bo." Stephen was relieved by the sight of O carrying two of the canteen cups. "Oh, good," he said. "I'm very thirsty." After handing one cup to Stephen and the other to Dr. Pak, O went out again to fetch the third. The tea was still too hot to drink, but Stephen warmed his hands on the cup. When O returned, he went and stood beside the doctor's chair, and Dr. Pak put his arm around the boy's waist. In response O wrapped his arm around the doctor's shoulders and leaned his weight against the doctor's body. The way their bodies fit together was so complementary and intimate, Stephen could not help remarking, "You look like father and son."

"You think?" Dr. Pak asked with interest.

"Just the way you are this minute—not all the time. I don't mean you look alike."

O was curious to know what was being said, and Dr. Pak explained with gusto. When he understood, O giggled impishly, placed his hand on the crown of his head and pulled it down over his cropped hair until his palm hid his face completely, and his nose peeked throught his middle fingers like the nose of a caged raccoon.

"Would you like that?" Stephen asked O. "Would you like Dr. Pak to be your father?"

As soon as Dr. Pak had translated Stephen's question, O giggled again and answered in Korean. "He say, yes, he would like," Dr. Pak reported, trying to refrain from giggling himself.

Stephen could tell they were in cahoots—withholding, hiding something, some secret that endowed both his questions and their answers with a delicious double meaning, known only to themselves. Had he stumbled on the truth? he wondered. Were they actually father and son? . . . While the three of them sat noisily sipping the bitter tea, Stephen began to search in vain for family resemblances. Whereas O's hair was cropped, his eyes contemplative and sorrowful, his nose flat, his lips thick and sensual, his neck short, and the over-all shape of his head—from which his ears stood out like the handles on a soup cup—round; Dr. Pak's head was oval, his hair soft and pensile, his eyes gleeful, the bridge of his nose straight and raised, his lips delicate, and his neck unusually long.

As Stephen continued to observe them, the doctor caught O's head in the crook of his elbow, playfully pulled him into the space between his spread thighs, and wrapped his arm around the child's stomach. From his catlike grin and half-closed eyes, it was obvious to Stephen that O was in a state of ecstasy. He let himself go completely, slumping like a rag doll, blissfully secure in the knowledge that Dr. Pak would not let him fall. Now Stephen's thoughts took a different turn. In place of O and Dr. Pak, he saw himself and Uncle Hank. But he had never been like that—like a ferry come to berth—between Uncle Hank's massive thighs. They had never gone that far. They had just held hands sometimes or sat together side by side. Stephen tried to resist his next thought, but in suppressing it he realized it was too late—one could not suppress a thought that one had not already had. Is it possible they're lovers? No. No. It's evil-minded, monstrous! Stephen thought. This lovely man is not a lecher, a fiend. This little boy is not a Giton. Yet look how much he's enjoying himself. Wasn't that exactly what *I* wanted at Potawatomi? What I longed and yearned for! What if Uncle Hank had not had what's-her-name to go to? What if he had been confined like this, like Dr. Pak? But Pak is married—at least he *was,* poor man. What's the matter with me! Stephen reproved himself impatiently. I must be depraved. It's obvious they're father and son.

At this moment, O butted Dr. Pak in the groin with his backside, provoking a playfully erotic melee. What if they're *both?* Stephen wondered, watching the doctor slip his hand inside the seat of O's trousers. Not only father and son, but lovers, too! This idea, which seemed to Stephen an absolute aberration, had scarcely crossed his mind, when the stockade loudspeakers began to blast the *1812 Overture* and he seized the opportunity to flee. "I must go now!" he said, standing up.

Out of respect for Stephen, Dr. Pak rose, too. "But Teacher have not finish tea." Like a commuter late for his train, Stephen gulped the rest of the tea. "When you come again?"

"Oh, gosh. I forgot to say, didn't I? Friday. I'll come on Friday. Will you tell the others?" Stephen asked, picking up his poncho.

"I will tell."

"Goodnight, Sun Bo. Goodnight, O."

"Goodnight, Teacher."

"Thank you for the tea."

On leaving the stockade, instead of going to his Quonset hut or the movies, Stephen went to his desk in Personnel to type a letter.

Sep 10, 1952

Dear Brother:

Many thanks for your lovely letter and the issue of *Life* with *The Old Man and the Sea,* both of which arrived today. Is it really true the odds have begun to favor Eisenhower? Do the voters really think that if there were several million ROK soldiers available to replace GI's the Democrats would refuse to use them? The implication is that the Democrats are deliberately killing off American men, whereas the truth is just the opposite. For almost a year now the Democrats have been doing precisely what Eisenhower boasts he will do, if elected. If only I were in a position to work for Stevenson!

I had such a marvelous English class tonight—so challenging and stimulating. I'm not a very good teacher—too subjective and dogmatic. My teaching is merely an expression of my own personality, but oh how much I enjoy it! And the prisoners! The prisoners are like heroic children: petulant, playful, giggly, noble, brave—utterly irresistible. There is one, a doctor, who is the most civilized, sensitive, and sympathetic man I've ever met. I wish I could remember half the things he said tonight. Do I begin to sound like Mr. Chips? Well, that's the way it is, I guess. Sometimes darker, more disturbing, but nonetheless Mr. Chips. Strangely enough I begin to dread the day when I'll have to leave. (Do you realize I have only seven months to go before discharge?)

Will you explain that to Mother, Rog? Try to convince her how lucky I am. I've tried and tried. I've told her I couldn't be safer or happier anywhere in the Army (least of all in the States!) but she refuses to believe me. Her letters are fraught with worry and concern—even depression. Again and again I've tried to express my belief in what the UN is doing here, but she prefers not to listen. She prefers to dwell in the twilight of her own imagination. Why? What can her imagination possibly tell her about Korea? Why won't she accept what I say on good faith? Why won't she accept my being here? Though I'm afraid to do so, I almost believe Korea is a thing to die for! Not the Pentagon! Not the Kremlin, but Korea!

The rain continues without let-up. Soon the earth will be as it was before creation. Who knows? That just might be the answer—: to start all over again out of the rat-infested slime. Good night, Rog, and love,

Stevie

The next morning at breakfast, when Stephen came through the chow line, Chang grinned elfishly and handed him a folded piece of paper. "What is this?" Stephen asked, glancing at the outside flap which was delicately decorated with watercolored chrysanthemums and South Korean flags.

"Stephen read," Chang urged, almost unable to contain his delight.

Stephen lifted the flap. Inside, written in the most painstaking English script, was the following message:

> You are cordially invite to attend humble festivity in celebration of Full Moon 15 August to be held on Thursday 18 September in Compound B at 2000 hour. Your truly, Pak Sun Bo, POW student, English class.

Stephen smiled and put the invitation in his pocket. "Thank you, Chang."

"You come, Stephen?"

"Of course!"

"Number one!"

"But why is the full moon of August fifteenth celebrated on September eighteenth?"

"Moon calendar," Chang explained.

"Oh, I see. Is it a religious holiday?"

"No. Like GI four July: anniversary end Japanese occupation. You know?"

"Yes, I understand. I'll be there. Will you thank Dr. Pak for me?"

"Yes. I thank."

On September 18, after twelve consecutive days of rain that turned the crust of the earth into seventeen inches of semi-jelled chocolate pudding, the sun came out. With it came the native women dressed in their silk and cotton finery—fuchsia, yellow, cobalt blue—to celebrate the holiday. While the men sat indoors drinking, the women sang and danced outside, their ribbons, scarves, and sashes fluttering, flying in the sunlight until the countryside resembled a preserve of tropical birds. By nightfall many old men were lying face down and unconscious in the mud along the roadside, but the festivities continued as the moon began to rise. Like the shield of Achilles, flung into the firmament, the full moon dominated and outshone all the stars and planets, dimming them to obscurity.

As soon as Stephen saw the moon, he was enthralled and could not look away. Like a lover, helplessly enslaved, he fixed his eyes on its face and followed it up the slippery hillside, through the sally port and into the stockade. He did not return the greeting of the GI guard at the gate or the salutes of the South Korean guards inside, but passed them by somnambulistically, oblivious to everything but the bewitching luminosity of the moon. It was not until he reached the gate of Compound B and heard Chang speak his name, that the spell was broken.

Unlike the two previous occasions on which Chang had acted as guide, tonight, instead of turning to the right as soon as Stephen entered, Chang turned to the left, leading him farther and farther away from the company area, up the hill and into the heart of the compound. "Where are we going, Chang?" Stephen asked after a minute or two.

"PW hut," Chang answered. "We come soon."

From outside, the hut looked the same as the dispensary or Headquarters. It was the same size and had the same kind of corrugated metal walls and peaked roof, but the interior was different. A center aisle, six feet wide, ran the length of the building from the front door to the rear wall. No attempt whatsoever had been made to cover this aisle with flooring or even duck-boards. It was solid dirt (now turned to mud in the wake of the monsoon)—the very ground on which the building stood. On either side of the aisle was a raised wooden platform, eight feet wide and two feet high. These two platforms were covered with crude hemp matting and constituted the prisoners' sleeping area.

When Stephen entered, the men, who had been lying down or sitting cross-legged, jumped to their feet and bowed. "Oh, no," Stephen objected. "Not tonight! This is a holiday, not a class. Please don't get up."

Pak Man Kap, who, like the others, was in his stocking feet, padded over to the edge of the platform. "Welcome to PW home, Teacher."

"Thank you, Mr. Pak. I'm very happy to be here." Seeing the neat row of boots and shoes lined up in the muddy aisle, Stephen sat down on the platform to remove his own.

Pak Man Kap looked mystified. "How you know Korea custom?"

"I see," Stephen shrugged, nodding toward the aisle. When his combat boots were off, Stephen raised his legs onto the platform, stood up and followed Pak. Most of the men were sitting in a group on the same side of the hut; the other platform, the one on the right, was vacant except for two or three men lying in the shadows. Stephen greeted everyone he knew—Chu, Lee, Mung, O, Dr. Pak—and was introduced to a tailor named Nun Do Wan and to an exceptionally tall, elegant-looking young mechanic named Ha Yung Koo, who helped Sergeant Billywood in the motor pool.

When the introductions were over, Stephen sat down next to Chang, who, much to his surprise, was holding a guitar in his hands. "How marvelous!" Stephen said. "Where in the world did you get it?"

"Koje-do. GI cowboy throw away. You play, Stephen?"

"No," Stephen said, noticing that the strings of the instrument had been replaced with wires.

"How you say in English?" Chang asked, flourishing the instrument.

"Guitar."

When Chang repeated the word it sounded like catarrh and Stephen could not help but smile. "Why you smile?"

"I want to hear you play. Will you, Chang?"

"Yes. I play catarrh for Stephen. Song I play call—" Chang was unable to translate the title into English and turned to Dr. Pak for assistance.

"Song is call 'Fisherman Wife,' Teacher."

Because of the wires, the chords sounded tinny and shrill, and forced Chang's voice high above its normal register. As he sang his voice became increasingly plaintive, his expression increasingly pained, until his forehead looked as wrinkled as a walnut and his tiny eyes filled with tears.

Seeing that Stephen did not understand the song, Dr. Pak scrambled over to him on his haunches. "Will I tell you story?" he asked in a whisper.

"Please."

"After bad storm, young wife of fisherman wait on shore for husband. Sky has many cloud. Air is cold. Sea is very rough. Toe of woman dig in sand while she wait. Nighttime come. No moon. No star. No husband. Woman build fire on beach for husband to see—guide boat. Woman remember warm of husband body. She see husband face in flame of fire. Suddenly wave from ocean put out fire. No more light. No more warm. No more husband. Woman know she wait in vain."

When Dr. Pak finished, Stephen shivered, but whether in response to the story, the tears in Chang's eyes, or the sensation of the doctor's hot breath against his ear, Stephen did not know. "Thank you, Sun Bo," he whispered.

After the guitar solo, other instruments appeared. O took a harmonica out of his pocket and Ha Yung Koo produced a home-made drum. At a signal from the latter, all the men, except for the three musicians, jumped to their feet and bounded over the aisle like mountain goats. Now the second platform became a stage and the one on which Stephen sat, the orchestra. Within seconds the men paired off in a circle facing one another, their right arms held gracefully aloft, their left arms planted rakishly on their hips, waiting for the music to begin. Fundamentally, the dance was simple. It consisted of a stamping of both feet, followed by three hops to the right and three to the left, but the men executed the steps with great aplomb and style. They held their heads haughtily and their stamping resounded loud and sharply against the wooden platform. Though their eyes, which were focused on the floor, never met and their right arms never interlocked, their shoulders touched suggestively at every turn. Occasionally, in accompaniment with his stamping, one of the men would let out an impassioned cry that

sounded as if it issued from his bowels. These cries not only increased the tempo but spurred the dancers on to more and more
dynamic and exaggerated movements, until the entire group looked
like a flock of courting herons.

When it was over, Stephen applauded energetically, and the men
laughed and combed the hair out of their glowing eyes. For an
encore they all joined hands and did a round dance, rotating clock-
wise and then counterclockwise, over and over, faster and faster,
until they were exhausted, and the circle fell apart, and the men
straggled back to Stephen's platform, laughing and perspiring.
"That was wonderful! Just wonderful," Stephen said.

"No. We have no right instrument," Mung protested, sitting
down next to Stephen. When he was comfortable, his friend, Ha
Yung Koo, lay down perpendicular to Mung and rested his head
on Mung's winded stomach. Gradually, the others settled down in
pairs—some lying front to back, some side by side, some crawling
under blankets or sitting cross-legged, their arms around one another's shoulders. Only Dr. Pak remained standing.

"Why don't you sit down with us?" Stephen asked.

"I will. One moment, please," he explained, disappearing into
the shadows and returning with an airtight canister that made a
hollow pop when he pulled off its lid. "Please, Teacher, you take
some," he said, offering the can to Stephen.

The aroma was so overpowering it made Stephen gag. But he
tried to camouflage his reaction by blowing his nose and pretending he had sneezed. "What is it?" he asked politely, still holding his
handkerchief to his nose and peering at the stinking, grayish-brown
strips that looked like pieces of oak bark.

"Dry fish."

"What kind of fish?"

No one knew the English name so Dr. Pak handed Stephen the
canister while he looked up the word in his pocket dictionary. Just
as Stephen was on the verge of helping himself, the doctor exclaimed triumphantly, "Squid!"

"Ohhh," Stephen drawled squeamishly.

"You like?"

"Oh, yes," he replied, taking as small a piece as he could find
and handing back the canister. After their guest was served, the
men passed the squid among themselves, tearing off pieces and
popping them into their mouths with relish. Though it took every
bit of courage he could muster, Stephen did the same. The squid

was rubbery and fibrous, and tasted even worse than it smelled. As hard as he tried, Stephen could not swallow it and he had no choice but to imitate his hosts who were chewing the fish vigorously, grinning all the while.

When Dr. Pak returned, Mung and Ha moved over, making room for him next to Stephen. "Squid like chewing gum, yes?"

"No," Stephen laughed, almost choking on the fishy juices trickling down his throat.

Following the squid, Lee came forward with a bottle of sake in one hand and a canteen cup in the other. The sight of the wine made the men jubilant and they smacked their lips and commented excitedly. After pouring some into the cup for Stephen, Lee passed the bottle around, and each man took a swig.

"Why do I get mine in a cup?" Stephen complained.

"You no like?" Lee asked.

"Yes. But I want to have it the same as you."

"What you mean?"

"I want it from the bottle."

When, at last, he understood, Lee handed Stephen the bottle, and everyone applauded as he drank. The taste of the sake was spoiled by the squid, but once it was down, it burned in Stephen's stomach and made him feel a little lightheaded. "That's good," he said to Dr. Pak.

"You would like more?"

"Yes," Stephen answered spontaneously. "But only if everyone else has had some."

"Please, drink from cup now," the doctor suggested.

Stephen had forgotten about the cup which he had set aside in front of him. "Will you share it with me?"

"Yes, I will share," Dr. Pak nodded, raising the cup to his lips. As soon as he had finished taking a sip, the doctor handed the cup to Stephen. While they were drinking, O began to play the harmonica. It sounded sad, and Stephen listened dreamily as he sipped the wine and then passed it on to Dr. Pak who, in turn, took a sip and passed it back to Stephen. And so it went, back and forth, until the cup was drained and Stephen felt vibrant, warm.

Suddenly, as if the time that had elapsed between the round dance and the present moment was merely an interlude, Mung and Ha Yung Koo jumped to their feet, stripped off their shirts and rolled up the legs of their trousers well above their knees. Mung's body, though somewhat flabby, looked extremely powerful. He had a thick neck, broad shoulders, large hands and highly developed calves. Ha was a good deal taller and more muscular than his friend, but very much lighter. "What are they going to do?" Stephen asked, turning to Dr. Pak.

"Exhibition." The doctor's simple answer sounded ambiguous to Stephen and left him both curious and slightly apprehensive. All the men began to drag their blankets toward the front of the platform to get a better view. Dr. Pak moved too. "Come," he said to Stephen, taking hold of a blanket.

For a moment Stephen didn't move. Instead, while the doctor had his back turned, Stephen took the opportunity to spit out his cud of squid. Then, feeling much relieved, he went and joined his friend. With all the men stretched out on their sides, chewing their squid and lounging on their elbows, Stephen thought the scene resembled the end of a Roman banquet. And he was hardly wrong because in the next moment Mung and Ha let out a savage cry and leaped across the aisle, landing face to face on the opposite platform, their hands on one another's naked shoulders, their heads rammed together like gladiators ready for the contest.

What followed was part wrestling match, part acrobatics, part kabuki dance and part a performance of living statues. Sometimes Mung and Ha, their bodies interlocked, would roll the length of the platform so rapidly that Stephen could not differentiate between them; sometimes they would stop and sustain a classical tableau for thirty or forty seconds; or Mung, his hands and feet touching the floor, would arch his back upside down and hold the position while his partner slithered in slow motion over and under his torso and out through his legs like a serpent. Depending on the moment, the audience rooted violently for its favorite or leaned back and grunted its approval.

Though less demonstrative, Stephen was even more excited than his hosts. Not only did the "exhibition" satisfy his dramatic and esthetic instincts, it aroused his senses. As often as he swallowed, his mouth kept filling with saliva, and he could feel his heartbeats. At first he attributed the excitement to the sake. But gradually, as he began to study the voluptuous ripples of Mung's stomach flesh, and his breathing grew heavier, and he noticed how hard he was biting his knuckle, Stephen realized that what he was experiencing was lust.

Surreptitiously, he glanced at Dr. Pak. The doctor had his back to Stephen and was lying on his side, leaning on his elbow, his cheek couched on his palm, his knees drawn up in front of him, the line of his spine and buttocks and thighs, a lovely curve. All the other men were in the same or similar positions, but in couples, their bodies nestled front to back, fitted together without the smallest gap between them, as only the bodies of lovers can be. Stephen alone was in a sitting position—consciously assumed from the start of the match—his legs crossed, his back stiff, holding himself aloof.

"Why you do not lie down, Stephen?" the doctor whispered over his shoulder, his hair falling back attractively with the movement of his head.

Without answering, Stephen pivoted his body, stretched out his legs and lay down on his left side, facing Dr. Pak. He wanted to wrap his arms around the doctor's waist, the way Lee's were wrapped around Chu, Pak Man Kap's around Kim, Nun's around Chang—but Stephen didn't dare. Not only was the doctor married, but he respected Stephen. So did the others. He was their teacher. Their relationship was based on that. What would they think if he suddenly debauched himself in front of them? After all, it was one thing to make a point of drinking from the same bottle and quite another— And what would the colonel think? What would happen if Colonel Clayborn came in and found him there like that, not only in the prisoners' sleeping quarters but in a compromised position? He'd be disgraced, called a pervert, court-martialed, dishonorably discharged! He'd lose his citizenship, his vote—his all-important vote for Stevenson! Thank God it was five to nine!

As Stephen was thinking these thoughts, Dr. Pak backed his buttocks into Stephen's lap and, with his left arm, reached around Stephen's body and pulled it up close against his own. Stephen's heart beat violently as he looked around to see if he was being watched. Everyone's eyes were fixed on Ha and Mung. Slowly, tentatively, Stephen reached out and rested his hand on Dr. Pak's hip. Once again the doctor looked back over his shoulder and his lovely hair fell away from his forhead as he smiled radiantly. Now Stephen's arm encircled the doctor's body, hugging him hard, and his lips fell on the doctor's neck. But even as he did so, the first notes of Tschaikovsky's Overture blasted his lips away. Like a crab Stephen began to sidle backward on the platform.

"No!" Dr. Pak implored. "You stay!"

"I'm sorry, Sun Bo, I can't. I can't. I'll see you in class tomorrow," he whispered. "Thank you for everything. Please don't get up! Please don't stop!" With that, Stephen put on his boots as rapidly and inconspicuously as possible and hurried out of the hut.

That night Stephen had great difficulty falling asleep. Like a teletype and wirephoto service at a time of international crisis, his brain produced a flood of words and images, impossible to stem. As he tossed in bed, he remonstrated with himself for running away. Surely Sun Bo would misconstrue his rude departure and think that Stephen was rejecting him. What else *could* he think? He couldn't possibly know how unsure Stephen felt, how inhibited he felt in front of the others—however charming and relaxed they were about their sexuality—how afraid he was of being caught. Surely Sun Bo would misinterpret it and think that Stephen felt contemptuous not only of the country and the customs—had Sun Bo seen him spit out the squid?—but the race. Racially superior! A free, white, American in contrast to a gook—a filthy, yellow gook! What if he thought that? Or what if he thought that Stephen had refused to stay because of protocol—because Stephen was the guard and Sun Bo the prisoner? The captor and the captive! Is that possible? Stephen wondered, rolling over restlessly. Is it possible I go to them that way—with that attitude: safe and secure in the knowledge that they're POW's? Am I magnanimous only because I can afford to be? Because I know ahead of time that I can come and go as I please, can draw the line whenever I choose—as I did tonight! To go to their quarters, to take off my boots, to eat their food and drink their wine, to lie with them and watch their show, to wrap my arms around Sun Bo and kiss his neck and then cry, No! You've made a mistake. I was only teasing. I'm not really one of you! Not a gook! Not a queer! Not a POW. You seem to forget, I'm a soldier in the UN forces. A citizen of the United States. It's nine o'clock and I must go—back to my company, back to my kind . . . But when I do, when I'm here, here in this hut, what happens? Sal says, Why don't we go to the USO? And I say, No. Sorry, Sal. I'd like to, but I can't tonight. I have to teach. Or Kirk suggests we go to the movies—*The Marrying Kind* with Judy Holliday whom I adore—and I refuse, because I have a class. I have a class! Can't you understand that, Kirk? Sal? Leghorn? What's the matter with you guys? Can't you understand that though I eat and sleep and work with you, and though I speak your language, I'm not really one of you. You've made a mistake! I belong in there—in that stockade!—with *them*. My heart's in there with them.

And yet, Stephen thought, opening his eyes and seeing the empty barracks, the empty beds, the truth is that I'm neither! Neither gook nor GI, neither here nor there, fish nor fowl, straight nor queer, prisoner nor free! I'm neither one nor both but in between . . . without myself . . . partitioned, like Korea. . . .

The next night Stephen lingered after class. "I'm sorry about last night, Sun Bo."

"Sorry?"

"For running away like that—so abruptly. I scarcely thanked you."

"Celebration was not as should be," Dr. Pak apologized. "Not proper celebration."

"Don't be silly! It was wonderful."

"No. Should be rice, fish, meat, vegetable, and bean cake, cider, apple, pear."

"What are you saying! The sake was marvelous. So was the squid. I loved the dancing and Chang's song and the exhibition—"

"Teacher generous to say."

"No! I'm not being generous. I mean it! Please don't think I ran away because it wasn't good enough. I ran away—because—" Stephen looked down at the dispensary floor. "—because I was confused."

"Why you are confuse?"

"Can we sit inside, Sun Bo?" Stephen asked hesitantly. "In the little room?"

"Yes, please. Come. I make tea."

"No. Please don't bother."

"No bother. You sit. I will come. One minute."

When Stephen entered the small back room, he saw Mung stretched out comfortably on the cot. He was reading *A Farewell to Arms,* which Stephen had bought for him in Pusan.

"Hi, Mung. Are you the orderly tonight?"

"Yes. I disorderly orderly," he punned with glee, ruffling his hair until it looked like a golliwog's.

"You're such a clown."

"No. I slob," he grinned, tucking in his shirttail.

"Do you like that book?"

"Very much. Italy, Korea: same-same."

"In what way?"

"Mud . . . war . . . hospital . . ."

"Yes. Except that here there's no Catherine Barkley."

"What we need Catherine for?" Mung asked rhetorically. "Let's go to bed!"

Stephen swallowed hard. "What?"

"Come to bed, darling. Let's go back to bed, darling. When we go to bed, darling?" At last Stephen realized the words were meant to parody Hemingway's, and he relaxed and laughed with Mung. "Oh, my darling, dearest, dear heart, sweetheart, dear love—" By the time he was finished, Mung was literally doubled up with laughter. His knees were touching his chin and he was hugging his legs tightly to keep from rolling off the cot. "I crazy in love with you!" he wailed, quoting Hemingway again and wheezing with laughter.

"You're just plain crazy," Stephen said. "I've just finished reading Hemingway's new book. It's beautiful—even better than that one. If I can get hold of enough copies, I'd like to use it in our English class. As a text, I mean, instead of the *National Reader.*"

"What new book about, war?"

"No. It's about going to bed."

"Going to bed!" Mung repeated, screaming with laughter and kicking his feet. "Who you go to bed with, Stephen?"

"No one."

"Why no one?"

"It's not about going to bed, you fool," Stephen said impatiently. "It's about a fisherman, an old fisherman, who catches a marlin."

"What is marlin?"

"A fish. A giant deep-sea fish with a sword sticking out of its head. You know what I mean?"

"Yes. Like man, when he make love."

"No. Out of its head! Its *head,* I said, you incurable lecher!"

As Stephen went on telling Mung about *The Old Man and the Sea,* he heard the first notes of the *1812 Overture,* but he did not move. At the same time, Dr. Pak came in with the tea and stood in the doorway listening. He looked moody and troubled. "It's really about man's struggle with nature . . . with life . . ." Stephen continued. "His dignity and pride . . . his limitations. You see, in order to catch the marlin, the old man has to go out too far, and he loses his catch to the sharks."

When Stephen finished, Dr. Pak who was still standing, holding the two canteen cups, said, "You do not hear Tschaikovsky music?"

"Yes. I heard it."

"You do not go away tonight?"

Stephen looked deeply into the doctor's anxious eyes. "No," he said in a thin, hushed voice. "I'd like to stay awhile—if that's all right with you."

Dr. Pak responded with a smile so broad the pink of his upper gums appeared, and his eyes were reduced to slits. After handing Stephen one of the cups, he turned to Mung and spoke rapidly in Korean. When the doctor was finished, Mung put on his boots, picked up *A Farewell to Arms,* made a feint at Stephen's crotch and said, "Good night, dear heart."

"Good night, you nut," Stephen said. He looked at his watch: 9:07. The dispensary door slammed as Mung went out. Stephen was startled by the noise. His heart began to pound. He could feel his intestines turning to water, his mouth going dry. Sun Bo was sitting on the cot holding his canteen cup in both hands and staring at Stephen. Stephen stared back, overcome with desire. More than ever he was struck by Sun Bo's beauty. He wanted to get up and go to the cot. He wanted to take Sun Bo in his arms and kiss him on the lips and plunge his hands in Sun Bo's hair—but Stephen could not move, his body would not let him. No matter what he thought he wanted, his body disagreed, his body was in terror! By now his insides had collapsed completely, his mouth was parched and tasted foul. He hadn't enough saliva to enable him to talk, much less to kiss. How could he think of approaching Sun Bo with breath like this, stinking of tobacco? How could he begin to make love to him with this rebellious body? This ugly, fat, disgusting body! Stephen took a sip of tea to wet his lips, but no sooner had he swallowed it than he felt the need to urinate. "Oh Christ!" he complained, standing up unsteadily. "Excuse me."

"Where you go?"

"Outside. I'll be back in a minute." Stephen went around to the far side of the building—the side that could not be seen from the company area—but when he got there he could not urinate. No matter how hard he tried, nothing happened. He was furious. Once again he berated his rebellious body. He wanted to be rid of it! Rid of its inadequacy, its perversity, its tyranny! He wanted a body that would do as it was told—a sexual organ that wouldn't shrivel up and disappear as soon as it was touched or called upon to function. Like Kierkegaard, he wanted to be done with it, and become a Knight of Faith, "great through the love which is hatred of oneself."

Stephen heaved a sigh and looked up toward the heavens. The moon was as full and bright as it had been the night before. As he stood, staring at its light, longing to be fused with it, transmuted into spirit, his body relaxed and he began to urinate. With great relief he shut his eyes and let it flow, listening with pleasure. But suddenly he felt someone's arms encircle him from behind. "Whaaa!" he flinched.

"I think you go away," Sun Bo whispered, not releasing his hold.

"Oh, you frightened me."

"I am sorry."

"Please go back. I'll be through in a minute."

"No, I wait. You finish."

"How can I, with you standing there?"

"I help."

"What are you doing? No, Sun Bo."

"Yes. I help."

"Please, Sun Bo. Someone will see."

"No one see."

"They will."

"No one care, but me."

"Stop it, please! Oh, please, Sun Bo! Not here!"

"Why not here?"

"It shouldn't be like this."

"How should be?"

"Together . . . I want you, too. I want . . ."

"Later, Stephen."

". . . Oh, Sun Bo . . ."

When he was finished, Sun Bo escorted Stephen back into the dispensary. Inside, in the light, he turned and smiled innocently, intimately, with great satisfaction.

Stephen returned the smile. Completely relaxed now, he stood starring at Sun Bo with unabashed love. After a moment he offered Sun Bo his hand, and Sun Bo took it. For more than a minute they stood that way, in silence, facing one another, not quite holding hands nor yet shaking them, but simply making contact—their hands performing what their eyes expressed. Then Stephen led Sun Bo to the small back room and took him in his arms. There was no shortage of saliva now, no feeling of dissolution in Stephen's bowels, and the pounding of his heart resulted not from fear but passion. "Oh, how I wanted to do that last night."

"Why you did not?"

"I was too self-conscious."

"Self-conscious?"

"Ashamed," Stephen explained.

"Why shame?"

"I—I don't know—the other men."

"Other men?"

"Mung and Lee and Chang—"

"They do not object."

"I know. It's *me,* I'm just not used to that."

"To other man?"

"Yes."

"Before now, you have only woman?"

The misunderstanding made Stephen laugh. "No, no. I mean I'm not used to other men watching."

"Oh-ho. That is what makes you shame?"

"Not ashamed exactly—inhibited."

Sun Bo looked pensive. Stephen assumed it was because his friend was unfamiliar with the word, but just as he was about to explain the meaning, Sun Bo began to speak. "On Koje, Stephen, I see man beat other man with club. I see man beat other man with whip made from barb wire. I see man punish other man with bayonet, cut off organ. I see man bury other man alive. I see many man tie to ground and stample on by other man with boots . . . to death . . . When I see that, I feel shame . . . I cry. But when I see man make love to other man—" Sun Bo shrugged—"I laugh."

Stephen was touched and filled with pity. He wanted to make up for the atrocities Sun Bo had seen, the evil he had suffered—all the evil in the world. But there was no need. The laughter of which Sun Bo had spoken was on his lips this moment, and Stephen had only to affirm it with a kiss. This kiss, which lasted several minutes, impelled their bodies to the cot. There, Sun Bo pulled Stephen down on top of him and they went on kissing. As long as their love-play was limited to kissing and caressing, Stephen participated with gusto, but the moment Sun Bo started to unbuckle Stephen's belt, Stephen became self-conscious and asked his friend to turn off the light.

"Why turn off?"

"Please, Sun Bo."

Sun Bo smiled archly. "Modesty?"

"I guess."

"Suppose to be opposite—no, Stephen?" he asked with affected innocence. "Korea suppose to be modest; GI, bold."

"Really? Why don't you turn off the lights and we'll see?" Stephen retorted. And Sun Bo accepted the challenge.

After they had finished making love, Stephen kissed Sun Bo good-by and promised to return the following night. It was five to ten, and Stephen felt extremely anxious about being stopped and questioned by the GI guard at the sally port. But his anxiety was unfounded. When Stephen reached the gate, the guard did nothing more than smile and say good night. If he entertained any suspicions about Stephen's late departure, the guard, like a well-trained doorman, kept them to himself.

Stephen was much too impatient to wait until Saturday night to see Sun Bo again. At noon he went to the dispensary just to say hello. At 3:15, on the pretext of filing some papers, he went to Headquarters. The files were directly in front of the screen windows that faced the dispensary, and Stephen took his time in the hope that he would see Sun Bo come out for a stroll the way he had two months ago, the day of his arrival, but Sun Bo never did. At six o'clock, after gulping his dinner, Stephen entered the stockade. He did not come out again until 10:15.

On Sunday, as always, Stephen had the whole day off. It was a perfect autumn day. The air was cool and dry, the sun bright and hot, and there was not a cloud in the sky. As if it had never been otherwise, the earth was solid again, without a trace of mud. Afternoon sick call for the prisoners was not yet over, and Stephen sat down and waited while Sun Bo attended to his last three patients. Stephen was pleased but not the least surprised to see how gently, humanly Sun Bo dealt with their complaints. Nothing about his manner suggested the professional man; he was intimate, warm, and personally concerned.

When he was finished, Sun Bo walked over to Stephen. "I am sorry to keep you waiting."

"Don't be silly. I enjoyed myself. Are you finished now?"

"Yes."

"Do you have to stay?"

"No. Assistant will stay now; Sun Bo will stay tonight—with Stephen."

Stephen expressed his approval of the plan by staring at Sun Bo intimately and caressing his cheek. "Where can we go now?"

"Hut."

"Can't we stay outside awhile? It's such a beautiful day."

"Yes. We can go to recreation area."

The recreation area was in the northeast corner of the compound on the borderline between the foothills and the mountains at the rear of the stockade. Most of the flat ground in the area was given over to a volleyball court on which, at the moment Stephen and Sun Bo approached, there was a furious game in progress. What the players lacked in height, they made up for in agility and wiliness. The way the Koreans played the game, it moved as fast as *jai alai,* and was full of split-second turns, tricky passes, and Fred Astaire footwork. To the right of the volleyball court was a horseshoe pit around which two six-man teams were engaged in a heated tournament. To the left was a small but delicately beautiful pine grove that stood like an oasis within the confines of the stockade. Stephen had never seen or even suspected the existence of this grove; it was situated in a dell, hidden from sight by the last rows of prisoners' huts.

In the center of the grove, seated on a backless bench and playing the same instruments Stephen had heard them play the night of the party, were Chang and O. But today, instead of folk music, they were playing a popular song, "China Nights"; and instead of a round dance the prisoners, in couples, were shuffling slowly, loosely over the pine-needle-covered ground, moving in and out among the trees, doing a fox trot. At the periphery of the grove a group of stags stood watching the dancers. Nearby two men were sitting on the ground playing *chon gee,* a variant of chess. Others were simply lying down, stretched out on their backs, listening to the music. In the alleyway between the stockade's double fence, a South Korean guard was squatting on his haunches, smoking a hand-rolled cigarette and watching the prisoners with envy.

Stephen and Sun Bo joined the group of stags. As fascinated as he was by what he saw, Stephen felt self-conscious and wanted to remain in the background. But as soon as the prisoners became aware of his presence, they stepped aside deferentially, forcing him and Sun Bo to the front of the group. When they reached the edge of the dance floor, Sun Bo said, "We will dance."

"No, Sun Bo."

"Why no?"

"I don't know how," Stephen lied.

"I show you."

"No. Please. Let's just watch," he said firmly. Stephen was reluctant to dance for two reasons. In the first place he was conscious again of the barrier between himself and the prisoners—the captor and the captives. And, more important, he never liked to dance with anyone, at any time, under any circumstances. No sooner did he step onto a dance floor than he felt foolish, his muscles tightened, and he became stiff and awkward.

But Stephen had scarcely refused to dance when Chang Sung Chull spotted him and, without interrupting his guitar-playing, shouted out, "Number hucking one!" Chang's hearty recognition attracted everyone's attention. Instantly, heads began to turn, hands to wave, broad smiles to appear. Lee and Chu danced over to where Stephen was standing to say hello. So, too, did Pak and Kim, Mung and Ha. Other students from the English class followed suit. At last, never one to be left out of anything, Chang stopped playing, put down his guitar, and ran over to shake Stephen's hand. Taking the lead from Chang, O pocketed his harmonica and did the same. Even the dancers who did not know the *sonsaeng* personally had heard about him from their friends and were eager now to see this exceptional and celebrated GI for themselves. It wasn't long, therefore, before the entire grove was empty and everyone was crowding around Stephen with curiosity or affection.

"Please don't stop," he protested. "Please go on. Chang! O! Please go on playing."

"You dance, Stephen?" Chang asked, but his words were not really a question. They were a proposition, a bargain, by which he meant, if you dance, we'll play.

Stephen realized that if he refused now, with everybody watching, the prisoners would certainly be disappointed—even insulted. There would be no way of explaining. He would have to leave the grove immediately. He would have to stop this whole masquerade —equality! fraternity! democracy!—and confine his relationship with the prisoners to a strictly formal basis. If he refused now, he would have to admit, not only to them but to himself, that he was only slumming. "Yes. I'll dance," he said, taking Sun Bo's hand.

Obviously elated, Chang and O ran back to the bench and took up their instruments. As a tribute to their guest they played the only American song they knew, "Body and Soul," and everyone resumed dancing.

Only Stephen and Sun Bo stood still. Stephen shifted his weight self-consciously. Since he had never danced with a man before, he had never anticipated the problem that now confronted him: was he expected to lead or to follow? The question left him frowning.

"What the matter, Stephen?"

"Do you mind if I lead?" he asked, realizing that he didn't know how to follow.

"Lead?" Sun Bo looked puzzled.

Stephen was at a loss to explain. "Never mind. Let's just dance," he said, wrapping his arms around his friend. As always on the dance floor, Stephen felt constricted, clumsy, rhythmless— repeating over and over the only step he knew, the box-step. Occasionally, to relieve the monotony, he would move in the opposite direction, counterclockwise, but since his lead was far from firm, he invariably tread on Sun Bo's toes. "Sorry," he apologized, feeling more and more like a stiff in contrast to the prisoners who swayed and dipped and spun with enviable freedom. He took no pleasure in the feel of Sun Bo's body or the smell of Sun Bo's hair; he was much too conscious of his own awkwardness and the grace of the other dancers. "Sorry," he said again.

Dismissing the apology, Sun Bo moved his hand down onto Stephen's buttock and squeezed.

Stephen scowled. More than self-conscious, Sun Bo's gesture made him angry, and Stephen had to restrain his impulse to shove the hand away. Gradually, as he glanced around the grove, he began to feel contempt for the prisoners. Forgetting that he had the same difficulties with a female partner, Stephen blamed his discomfort on the fact that he was dancing with a man. No wonder he felt cloddish, no wonder he kept stumbling and stepping on Sun Bo's toes—men had not been meant to dance together. It's unnatural, he said to himself. That's what it is, he decided in his father's voice, unnatural. No wonder there's all this confusion about following and leading. That never happens with a girl—it couldn't! The whole thing's predetermined, simple, as simple as the sexes: the man leads, the woman follows, man is active, woman passive . . . In his mind's eye, Stephen saw a couple copulating; they were face to face, the man on top, the woman under him. Yes, yes, he concluded, dancing's just a metaphor, a metaphor for sex—no wonder it's impossible for men . . .

And yet he had only to observe the other couples—Lee and Chu, Pak and Kim, Mung and Ha—to realize how untrue this conclusion was. No man and woman could have been more attuned, more responsive to each other than Lee and Chu. Indeed they danced as if they were man and woman, as if no biological barrier existed. There was no awkwardness between them, no stumbling or stiffness, no question as to who should lead or follow —Lee took the lead, Chu followed. And now that he considered it, the whole arrangement made perfect sense to Stephen. He could not imagine it otherwise, could not imagine Lee adopting the woman's role, Chu performing the man's. The same held true for all the couples—in every case the larger, stronger, more demonstrative of the two men took the lead. This observation brought Stephen back to his earlier conclusion that dancing was a metaphor for sex. Then, quite suddenly, he acknowledged something he had known for years—but only vaguely, indirectly, through books and jokes and slang. He remembered a thesis he had read at college whose point was that Shakespeare could not have been homosexual because of the absence from the plays of buttock imagery, remembered the gist of all the jokes he had ever heard in shower rooms, remembered Sun Bo backing into his lap at the party, and the way in which the other prisoners had lain together, and all at once Stephen realized that these men made love in a manner different from any he had ever known.

"Why do you stop, Stephen?"

Stephen shook his head, as if in a daze. "Sorry," he said, continuing to dance. So that was why he and Sun Bo had such difficulty dancing together, because neither of them took the woman's role, their roles were not defined. How could they be? The thought of making love *that* way was inconceivable to Stephen. Not only did it seem filthy and repugnant, he imagined it would be painful. Of course it would! Painful and humiliating. No, no, it was out of the question: he could never take the woman's role. . . . But then neither could Sun Bo. After all, Sun Bo had been married, had made love as a man to his wife; he couldn't suddenly reverse himself, couldn't suddenly become feminine and passive. When you came right down to it, he wasn't even queer. It was only circumstances—this prison, the war, the death of his wife—that made him seem that way. Under normal conditions, he would no more have chosen to dance with a man—

"Why you are so silent, Stephen?"

"I don't know—just thinking."

"What you are thinking?"

Stephen sighed. "How different things would be if—if you weren't here—in this prison, I mean—if there were no war, if your wife were still alive and you were living in Pyongyang."

"If no war, if not PW, if wife still alive—" Sun Bo repeated with irony. "You speak like good mother who has nothing but rice for family to eat. Mother say, 'Oh, if only we have egg and anchovy and meat.' Plenty rice, but mother-talk make everbody dissatisfy, everybody hungry. You understand?" he chuckled. "There *is* war, wife *is* dead. I *am* here. I *am* PW. That is as world is. I cannot imagine otherwise. To imagine otherwise make me miserable, make me crazy maybe."

Now, as if to break the mood or change the subject, Sun Bo removed his hands from Stephen's buttocks (placing one on Stephen's shoulder blade, the other at his waist), thrust his pelvis forward assertively, and began to conduct Stephen over the pine needles in a two-step. The transition was so abrupt that before Stephen realized what was happening, they were halfway across the grove. "I'm following," he laughed, "following."

"What, Stephen?"

"Nothing! Go on, go on." Relieved of the responsibility of leading, Stephen relaxed and began to enjoy himself. He liked the idea of Sun Bo taking charge of him this way, it made him feel submissive and secure. He shut his eyes and let himself be moved about at Sun Bo's will. For the first time since they had started dancing, Stephen was conscious of nothing but the sound of the music (just when "Body and Soul" had ended and this Oriental tune had begun, he could not have said) and the feel of Sun Bo's body, pressing hard against his own. Now it was Stephen's turn to take hold of Sun Bo's buttocks. In response Sun Bo nibbled Stephen's neck. This so excited Stephen, his hands began to knead Sun Bo, who, in turn, tickled Stephen with his tongue. They were scarcely dancing now, just standing in place, hugging one another, swaying with the music and rubbing thighs, until each of them felt the other begin to stir, to stiffen. Then suddenly Sun Bo began to move again, quite rapidly (or so it seemed to Stephen, who did not want to break his reverie by opening his eyes) in a straight line for a considerable distance. Only when he felt Sun Bo let go of him, did Stephen look and see that they had left the grove behind. "Why are we stopping? Where are we going?"

"Hut."

Though Stephen went with Sun Bo willingly, even eagerly, as they walked along in silence, his doubts reawakened. By letting Sun Bo take the lead, hadn't Stephen as good as accepted (if only by default) the woman's role? Wasn't that what Sun Bo had in mind right now, this minute, as they headed toward his sleeping quarters? Hadn't Sun Bo taken the lead from the start? Hadn't he made the first move (the night of the party)—made *all* the moves, in fact, just as if he were pursuing a girl? And hadn't Stephen responded that way: modestly, coquettishly, as if indeed he were a girl, a hipless slip of a thing like Chu instead of a big, strapping fellow, a head taller than Sun Bo and thirty pounds heavier? By all rights it was he, Stephen, who should have made the advances, who should have smiled at Sun Bo right off, that first afternoon outside the dispensary, who should have made a pass at him as soon as Sun Bo invited him to tea— Oh, but he hadn't!—so what was the use of thinking about it now?—hadn't made a single pass, hadn't even been able to take the lead in the dance, couldn't! couldn't take the masculine role, didn't want the feminine role, was good for nothing but the Princeton rub—so why on earth was he leading Sun Bo on like this, following him into his hut?

The hut was empty except for one man who was asleep on the platform just to the right of the front entrance. The only source of light was the doorways at either end of the building, but the doors were open and it was light enough inside to see. Sun Bo's bedding was in the far corner, diagonally opposite the sleeping prisoner. Even before Stephen reached the end of the aisle, Sun Bo had slipped off his rubber shoes and stood waiting on the platform. "We can't stay here," Stephen whispered.

"Why not?"

"What if he wakes up? What if someone comes?"

"No one come. No one care."

"*I* care."

"Why?"

"Because I—because—"

"Because we cannot turn off light?" Sun Bo asked wryly.

"Not only that."

"Dispensary has more light, Stephen. You take off boots now, please."

Reluctantly, Stephen sat down on the edge of the platform and began to unlace his boots. As he pulled the first one off, he heard the rattle of Sun Bo's GI buckle and he knew his friend was getting undressed. By the time his second boot was off and Stephen turned around, he saw Sun Bo naked, crawling on his hands and knees, spreading out the blanket. To Stephen's eyes, Sun Bo's build seemed somewhat irregular—perhaps because he was extremely low-waisted. His head and trunk accounted for almost two-thirds of his height, his legs for the remainder. But aside from that his body was beautifully proportioned and youthful-looking. His limbs were muscular, his shoulders broad, his hips slight, his buttocks firm. Stephen decided his youthful, almost boyish appearance was due to the fact that except for his groin and armpits, there wasn't a single hair on Sun Bo's body.

When the bed was ready, Sun Bo lay down. His knees were slightly raised and he leaned back on his elbows like an Inca statue. "Why you do not undress, Stephen?"

Without a word, Stephen opened his belt and unbuttoned his fly. Slowly, he took off his trousers, folded them neatly and put them aside. Slowly, he removed his shirt and undershirt. With his socks and undershorts still on, he walked over to the bedding and tried to crawl under the blanket.

"No," Sun Bo objected. "We remain on top. There is other blanket if Stephen cold."

Stephen was, in fact, shivering, but not from the cold; his discomfort was the result partly of anticipation, partly of anxiety. No longer was he ruminating on his sexual "role," there was the more immediate problem now of shame. "Yes, please, Sun Bo," he stammered, meaning he would like the second blanket.

Sun Bo did not understand. Quickly, he sat up and kneeled on his haunches next to Stephen; deftly, he began to unbutton Stephen's undershorts. But before he was able to finish, Stephen intercepted Sun Bo's hands and held them tightly. "Why you stop me, Stephen?" Stephen neither spoke nor released his grip. "Each time, you try to stop me. Why? Why you pull away? Why you ask to turn off light? You wish me not to have desire for you—not to see you, not to touch! Why? What is wrong with me?"

Stephen released Sun Bo's wrists and turned his head away. "Not you. Not you, Sun Bo. It's *me!*"

"What you mean?"

"It has nothing to do with you."

"How nothing? It is *I* you are with."

"It wouldn't matter whom I was with, I'd act the same."

"Why?"

"I can't explain, Sun Bo."

"Please. You try, Stephen. You look at me now, please."

Stephen turned and saw Sun Bo. The sight of him brought tears to Stephen's eyes, and he covered his face contritely. "Oh, Sun Bo!"

"Why you weep?"

"You! . . you're . . . so beautiful."

"You are also beautiful, Stephen."

"No, I'm not! That's just the point. When I ask you to turn off the lights, it's because—because I don't want you to see me—"

"Yes, yes, I understand. But why? Why you do not want me to see? What you want to hide?"

". . . Myself . . ."

"Why you want to hide self?"

"Because-because—I guess, because I'm ugly."

Half-amused, half-amazed, Sun Bo reached out and touched Stephen's cheek. "Ugly?"

"Not my face, Sun Bo, my body—they're not the same."

"Face and body—?"

"Please don't laugh."

"How is possible to have beautiful face, ugly body—as if face and body separate? I do not love only face."

"You've never seen my body."

After considering this absurd-sounding statement for a moment, Sun Bo realized it was true and nodded perspicaciously. "You show me, please."

"No."

"Why not?"

Stephen hunched his shoulders. From his pained expression one might have thought he was being tortured. "I can't," he despaired.

"You forget I am doctor, Stephen. Every day PW come to dispensary: physical examination. I see body of man—many man. Some man wound in abdomen. Some man wound in leg. Some man finger missing. Some man have no nose. But no man shame to show me body. Why you have shame, Stephen?"

Stephen knew his position was indefensible. Without a word he opened the bottom button of his undershorts and stood up. As the shorts fell to the floor, he tensed his stomach muscles, held his breath. Had he been Hester Prynne with all of Salem watching him, he could not have felt more humiliated. He looked aside, looked up at the ceiling, kept turning his head, as if he was tracking a fly. He wanted to lose consciousness, to disappear, to die. Then suddenly he felt Sun Bo touch his appendicitis scar. Stephen flinched.

"What is name in English for this surgery?"

"Appendectomy."

"Ap-pen-dectomy?"

"Yes."

"Appendectomy not serious," Sun Bo stated flatly.

"No."

"Scar from appendectomy, reason you hate body?"

"One reason, yes."

"And other reason?"

Since he himself was so acutely conscious of it, Stephen naturally assumed that what he considered his genital inferiority would be only too conspicuous to Sun Bo. By dropping his shorts he thought he had exposed himself completely—not just his flesh but all of him, the inmost secrets of his soul. There he stood! His nakedness said everything—what more was there to say?

"What is other reason?" Sun Bo persisted.

"Isn't it obvious?"

"Obvious?"

"Can't you see!" Stephen exclaimed impatiently, and he thrust both hands downward, so that his outturned palms framed his groin.

"See what?"

"Oh, let's forget it!" he said, crossing his legs and sitting down Oriental-style.

"No! I do not forget," Sun Bo retorted angrily. "You tell me!"

Stephen had never seen Sun Bo lose his temper, had never even suspected his friend of having one; as a consequence he struggled, now, to control his own. "What is there to tell?"

"Reason you hate body."

"Just look! Look!"

Sun Bo was bewildered.

"Here!" Stephen protested, gesturing toward his groin again.

But still Sun Bo did not see, did not comprehend. He looked nonplussed. Hopelessly he shook his head, causing the hair to fall into his eyes. Nervously he combed it aside, as if to clear his vision. "I am sorry, Stephen. My English is too poor: I do not understand."

"Your English." Stephen hung his head. "It has nothing to do with your English, Sun Bo. Your English is perfect. It's *me!* me again. I haven't said yet what I mean—haven't begun. I can't! can't bring myself to say it." Oh, but he knew he would have to now. He felt compelled, compelled to speak, to confess to Sun Bo what he, Stephen, could scarcely bear to admit to himself. "It's just—that I—" he began but stopped to lick his lips. The effort was excruciating, humiliating, and he buried his face in his hands. "Don't you see—" he started over but instantly broke off again, trying to restrain himself: to hold his breath, hold back his tears, hold his tongue; but neither words nor tears nor breath would be restrained and all broke loose at once. "How small I am!"

"Small?"

"Kleine," he added to himself. "The *Kleine, kleine, kleine* . . ."

"You mean here, Stephen?"

"Don't," he objected, pushing Sun Bo's hand away.

"Organ small?"

"Yes."

"Oh, but we make big," Sun Bo offered jovially.

The joke fell flat. Irritated, Stephen moved away and crawled under the blanket. "I knew you wouldn't understand."

After a moment Sun Bo followed and laid his hand tenderly on Stephen's. "You are foolish man." Stephen looked up—his eyes full of resentment—but said nothing. "Foolish to say organ small. Organ *not* small."

"It is."

"What the matter with you, Stephen?" The corners of his mouth betrayed Sun Bo's impatience. "You wish for organ size of skyscraper? Ha-ha. One you have is plenty big—I know, I have experience. There is nothing wrong with one you have. Healthy, strong, able to perform. No disfigurement. No blood in urine. No retention. No, no," he chuckled, "one you have is excellent, believe me. If sometime it is small, that because of fear. Organ same as turtle-throat: pull away in fear. If you have fear: someone come, someone see—organ disappear. Or if you have shame of body, if you say, face is beautiful but body ugly—organ understand (very, very sensitive), organ feel despise and disappear. This," Sun Bo said, indicating his penis, "and this," he added, touching his temple, "are not separate, cannot be. This and this are unity, like night and day, sun and moon—one not possible without other. If separate, then something wrong: there is strife, there is war, like here, like in Korea." A sudden thought brought a twinkle to Sun Bo's eye and he smiled knowingly. "Stephen also in partition. You know what you must do, dear friend?"

"What?" Stephen played along.

"You must call UN into emergency session. UN will vote to stop war, send ambassador to Stephen. Ambassador is name Pak Sun Bo. Ambassador say, What is matter with you? Why you fight against self? You are splendid man: splendid brain, splendid body. Why do you allow partition? There should be no partition! Partition just in mind—not really there, not really exist. You understand? Imaginary! Arbitrary! Partition make man weak. End partition! Become strong, free, independent man."

"Oh yes, Mr. Ambassador, I agree—we're in absolute agreement. But how-how do you suggest I go about it?"

"To begin, do not despise body, Stephen. Man in world in body, yes? Without body, no world—man lose place in world. Man lose self. Man lose other man, without body. I do not speak now of Pak Sun Bo," he quickly added, "but *all* man, yes?"

"Yes."

"When other man see Stephen, and he say Stephen beautiful, he love Stephen—Stephen must believe, not say I am ugly. Not possible for Stephen to see self. Other man know better. Other man can prove Stephen wrong by making love with Stephen." Lapsing into silence, Sun Bo stared at Stephen searchingly, then lifted the corner of the blanket. "Yes?"

This time, Stephen realized, the "yes" meant more than do you understand; it was a proposition. It meant: may I come under the blanket, too? may I demonstrate what I've been saying? "Oh, yes! Sun Bo, yes!" he exclaimed, sitting up and taking the doctor in his arms.

Despite Sun Bo's express desire to affirm Stephen's body, it was Stephen who seized the initiative—Stephen whose tongue invaded Sun Bo's mouth almost to the uvula, Stephen whose fingers explored and caressed Sun Bo's armpits, nipples, thighs, Stephen whose lips found their way to Sun Bo's groin, and whose teeth nibbled Sun Bo's bottom. This was not the first time he had taken the initiative with Sun Bo (or with others, for that matter), he often did—once he was in bed and the lights were out. In part his passion spurred him on, in part he did it to protect himself: to prevent the other person from discovering his shame. But with Sun Bo he had already exposed himself, there was no longer any need to hide his shame. With Sun Bo he wanted only to express his love—and love to Stephen's mind meant just one thing: *giving,* giving selflessly, totally, without anticipation of return. It meant pleasing someone else—serving him, stimulating him, satisfying him—regardless of oneself. If in the process you had to debase yourself or sacrifice your own satisfaction for the sake of his—so much the better! so much more profound the love. There was only one thing to be avoided—avoided at all costs—*taking.* Taking was the antithesis of love.

As a result of this doctrinaire attitude, Stephen's love-making, however effective, lacked spontaneity, lacked playfulness; it was deliberate and willed. But all the willpower in the world is useless without the knowledge to implement it. And so, having seized the initiative, having aroused himself and Sun Bo to the limits of foreplay, Stephen suddenly found himself at a loss to continue. He didn't know how! didn't know what Sun Bo expected—except that when he, Stephen, tried to complete the act in the only way he knew, Sun Bo pulled Stephen's head abruptly from between his legs, turned over onto his side and backed into Stephen's lap, just as he had done the night of the party.

Now all the thoughts Stephen had while dancing, all those disturbing notions about sexual roles and positions, began to nag him again. He couldn't believe that Sun Bo meant for him to take the "masculine role"—and yet there he was, forcefully pressing his buttocks into Stephen's groin, his cheeks like a mouth striving to ingest Stephen's manhood. But then, quite suddenly, mysteriously, Stephen felt the hunger too! felt it in his bowels, felt it in his groin. Somehow all the resistance and repugnance he had experienced in the pine-grove disappeared, and in his loins he, too, wanted what Sun Bo wanted. But still he didn't know how! And even when Sun Bo attempted to assist him, Stephen couldn't manage it—the whole thing seemed impossible.

"Wait," Sun Bo whispered, and he crept away into the shadows.

Stephen could hear him rummaging through a knapsack, fiddling with something, opening some kind of tin, but he didn't look, didn't want to see what Sun Bo was up to, just lay there with his eyes shut, waiting, waiting.

At last Sun Bo returned and assumed his former position: his back to Stephen's front. Wrapping his free arm around Stephen's waist, he pulled him closer, hugging him like a bear. But still Stephen waited. "Please, now," Sun Bo said, moving his hand to Stephen's groin, "you enter me."

As if he was about to dive into a freezing pond, Stephen drew a deep breath and mustered all his will. Sun Bo groaned. "Am I hurting you?" Stephen asked with alarm, ready to withdraw.

"Ani, ani," Sun Bo panted, striving for an even greater union.

And now, at last, Stephen stopped observing himself, observing Sun Bo, stopped wondering what to do next, stopped worrying about roles, stopped doubting, stopped denying, stopped thinking altogether. At last he was released—released from his great constricting self, his self-opposing self with all its isolating power and power to negate, its eccentricities and handicaps, willfulness and vainglory—released to join Sun Bo, experience Sun Bo (and, thus, himself) more intimately and fully than he ever had before.

But just before the consummation, Sun Bo exclaimed in Korean something Stephen didn't understand, and groaned again. More than a groan, it was a growl this time, an attenuated growl, so convulsed and startling, Stephen had no doubt his friend was in pain. "I'm hurting you!"

The denial came not from Sun Bo's lips, but from his straining torso, from his clutching hands; and presently Stephen was surprised to hear himself growling, too.

When Sun Bo regained his breath he began to chuckle. Gradually the chuckles multiplied, growing louder, faster, more aspirated and out-of-control, until Sun Bo was shaking with laughter.

The laughter was contagious, and Stephen laughed awhile, too, before he thought to ask, "What's so funny?"

"Am I—am I—" Fits of laughter made Sun Bo inarticulate. "Am I—" he repeated helplessly. "Am I—" he tried again. At last he got the words out. "Am I hurting you?" he guffawed, quoting Stephen.

"What's so funny about that?"

Sun Bo covered his face with his hands; he was laughing much too hard to answer. "Hurting me!" he sputtered, almost doubled up with laughter. "Broken leg hurt. Bullet wound hurt. Love-making do not hurt."

Now, for the first time in his life, Stephen did not resent being teased, and he, too, began to laugh—laugh at himself with Sun Bo.

When their laughter subsided Sun Bo said, "You never make love that way before?"

"No."

"You like?"

"Like!" Now it was Stephen's turn to laugh at Sun Bo. "Yes, I like. I like very much," he mimicked. "And you? How about you?" he said, changing his tone. "Do you like?"

"Oh, yes!"

"But how-how can you?" he asked, not in judgment of the fact that Sun Bo had assumed the "passive role," but worried now that his friend had not been gratified. "How can you?" he persisted, adding, as if to explain everything, "You didn't come."

"Come?"

"You weren't satisfied."

"What you mean?" Sun Bo objected. "I am satisfy."

There was no arguing the point; Stephen had to take Sun Bo's word for it. Nevertheless, he was completely mystified—mystified because he could in no way account for Sun Bo's satisfaction. He did not understand it physiologically. "How? I don't understand how?"

For a moment Sun Bo didn't answer. Then, assuming that Stephen was referring back to the problem he had raised earlier, Sun Bo emitted a knowing "Oh" and petted Stephen's penis. "You still think you are small?"

The question took Stephen by surprise, and he laughed again. "No, Sun Bo, no." But suddenly his laughter turned into tears—tears of relief and gratitude—and he hugged Sun Bo. *"Komap-sumnida, komapsumnida."*

Nestled in the crook of Stephen's elbow, Sun Bo nuzzled Stephen's arm.

Now, utterly at ease and content, the two men lapsed into a kind of luxurious slumber. But presently Stephen became aware of a series of high-pitched, squeaking sounds overhead:

. . . chwi . . . chwi . . . chwi . . .

It took him a moment to identify the noise, but when he did, he was not afraid. He did not sit up or even stir, but only remarked quite matter-of-factly, "Rats."

"What?" Sun Bo drawled, half-asleep.

"Chwi, Sun Bo, *chwi."*

"Ne, chwi. How you know that word, Stephen?"

"Oh, I know a lot of things," he answered playfully.

"Soon they will be gone."

"They don't bother me," Stephen said, remembering the night of the typhoon, and he squeezed Sun Bo gratefully and added, "Now." But Sun Bo had dozed off.

Relaxed as he was, Stephen was too stimulated to sleep. He kept thinking about Sun Bo and wondering if he really had been satisfied or if he was only saying that to pacify Stephen. Like the chattering of the rats, his doubts grew more and more persistent. Of only one thing was he certain: Sun Bo had not had an orgasm —so how could he claim to be satisfied? Obviously he was lying. Unless, somehow, it was possible to have an orgasm internally . . . an anal orgasm. Was there such a thing?

In time this question came to plague Stephen. He could think of nothing else. Day by day he mulled it over in his mind. Night by night he scrutinized Sun Bo's responses. Often they seemed more intense, more extreme than his own, but Stephen had no way of knowing for certain, no empirical evidence. The only way of proving it, he finally decided, was to experience the "passive role" himself. He had to! simply had to find out for himself, to know if Sun Bo was telling the truth. His curiosity consumed him. And yet, in some ways, it was more than curiosity. Now he absolutely longed for that which just the week before had most repulsed and frightened him—he longed to take the "woman's role," to feel Sun Bo fulfilled inside of him, to take as totally as he had given.

And so, the following Sunday, Stephen asked Sun Bo if he would mind reversing roles. Sun Bo was only too delighted. Stephen could scarcely contain himself with anticipation. But when the moment came, the pain was even worse than he had imagined, and Stephen cried out, "No! Sun Bo, no! I can't. I can't. I'm sorry."

"Do not be sorry, Stephen. It do not matter."

"It does! It matters more than anything. I don't know what's wrong with me—wrong with this body."

"Again too small? No, dear friend, it has not to do with body. Your body want, but brain refuse, brain not ready. One day brain will no more shame, brain will want; then body know, body open up like flower: permit Sun Bo to enter."

"Oh, Sun Bo, I hope so. I hope so."
"It will happen, Stephen."

On Monday morning at 0615 hours Stephen was awakened not by reveille but by the cold. Overnight—or so it seemed to Stephen, who was covered by only one blanket—the bracing cool of autumn had given way to the bitterness of winter. As he lay, huddling in bed, he remembered a directive he had seen a month ago on Mr. Robbins' desk; it had ordered the replacement of all tents and the complete winterizing of all prisoners' huts before a single stove could be issued to the GI's. . . . At least Sun Bo would be warm, he thought, and the thought brought Stephen's own body some relief. Fortunately for the GI's the men were scheduled—that very afternoon—to turn in their suntans and mosquito netting in exchange for winter gear. Though the timing was perfect, Stephen wondered about the rats. Without protection from the netting— Suddenly, forgetting the cold completely, he sat up in bed. Much to his surprise Stephen realized now that he had neither seen nor heard the rats for several nights. Had they gone away or had he just been sleeping better lately? No, they must have gone; he remembered Sun Bo saying that: "Soon they will be gone." But where? Did they simply disappear and die in winter like flies or migrate south like birds? But they couldn't go farther south than Pusan—except into the sea. No, most likely their disappearance was due to the doors being closed. The men had begun to close the doors at night against the cold, and the rats could no longer get in. That was the reason. It had to be, Stephen decided, after glancing at the shelf and seeing Leghorn's habitual box of crackers there, untouched. They couldn't get in!

Still sitting up, Stephen looked at Luke and Leghorn, and then across the aisle at Melody and Kirk. Melody was onking, even in his sleep. Stephen foresaw the commotion they would make getting up, shivering and bitching and cursing the gooks for having stoves while they froze their asses off. Stephen was amused, and smiled at the prospect—whereas, two weeks ago he would have frowned. They weren't such a bad lot after all, he thought, despite the fact that none of them intended to vote. Not even Leghorn! He could understand Melody and Luke, but Leghorn! In Leghorn's case it was laziness, sheer laziness. The same was true of Sal and Sergeant

Billywood: they were just plain lazy, all of them. Lazy, he repeated, mulling the word over in his mind and rubbing his forehead in anticipation of a brainstorm. Since most of the GI's were
too lazy to vote, what if he, Stephen, were to do it *for* them? He
didn't exactly mean vote, but fill out their cards, and then pretend
(or at least imply) that it was mandatory for the men to sign
them.

Stephen liked the idea and decided to act on it immediately. As
soon as breakfast was over, he went to see Mr. Robbins and said
he had received several requests for voting cards. Mr. Robbins was
too preoccupied to consider the matter carefully. Without thinking,
he pulled out the bottom drawer of his desk and handed Stephen a
stack of cards. Stephen snatched them greedily and hurried back to
Personnel. There, with the aid of the enlisted men's records, he
typed up voting cards not only for every man in his Quonset hut
but for several in the motor pool as well.

The first test of his scheme came later in the morning, when
Luke Collins stormed into the office. Collins was enraged by a
dispute he'd been having with Melody. "Let me see my records,
Corporal!" he demanded, slapping his fatigue cap down on Stephen's desk.

"Sure. What's the matter, Luke?"

"Medals! I want to know what medals they give me for being in
this hellhole."

"Well, now, let's see, Luke. So far you've been awarded two:
the Korean Service Medal with one bronze star, and the United
Nations Service Medal."

"That's what I thought!" Collins exclaimed, spitting on the floor.
"That's what I said! But that fuckin' Melody—"

"Oh, well, you know Melody," Stephen said.

"I'm gonna award that motherfucker the Purple Heart before I
get finished with him," Collins grumbled, seizing his fatigue cap
and starting toward the door.

"Oh, by the way, Luke," Stephen remarked quickly but
casually, "while you're here, you might as well sign your voting
card."

"My *what?*"

"Your voting card."

"What's that? What's that?" Collins asked suspiciously.

"Oh, it's just a form you have to send to Nashville in order to
get your absentee ballot. Here it is," Stephen said, handing Collins

the white card. "It's all ready; all you have to do is sign it."

"What I want with an absentee ballot?"

"You need it to vote, you can't vote without one."

"Who the fuck wants to vote?"

Stephen was stymied for a second and stared at Collins stupidly. "You do, don't you?"

"Me? Are you kiddin', son! I ain't voted but once in forty-seven years—and that time only 'cause Mr. Roosevelt paid me."

"Well no one's going to pay you this time!" Stephen snapped impatiently.

"That's what I figured; and that's why I ain't gonna vote."

"You make it sound like some kind of penalty, Luke."

"As far as I'm concerned, it is."

At that moment, staring at the supercilious and stubborn expression on Collins' face, Stephen remembered the man's cruelty and courage the night he had pulverized the rat. "Well, if that's the way you feel about it, why don't you start walking north and give yourself up to the Communists? *They* won't make you vote!"

"Ain't no one gonna make Luke Collins vote."

"*I* am, Luke." Stephen was no less surprised than Collins by the incontestability of his tone. "What do you think you're doing here in the first place?" he demanded. "Why do you think you were sent to Korea?"

"Got me," Collins confessed, somewhat quashed by Stephen's outburst.

"To vote! That's why you were sent; you're here to vote!" Stephen decreed. "Come on now. Here's a pencil. Sign your name."

Like an intimidated child, Collins took the pencil in his large, leathery hand. Because he wetted the point before making each letter, it took him more than a minute to execute his signature. When he was done, he asked obediently, "What now?"

"That's all, Luke. That's all there is to it," Stephen smiled pleasantly. "You don't even need to worry about mailing it. I'll take care of that."

"Thanks, Corporal."

"Don't mention it. Oh, and Luke, when you see Melody, just tell him that his voting card is ready. He can come by and sign it any time this afternoon."

After his experience with Collins, Stephen decided to approach the problem somewhat differently: he would treat it as a routine

matter, about which there could be no possible question. Consequently, at noontime Stephen went around to everyone in the barracks and said, "You haven't signed your voting card yet." Although his tone was matter-of-fact, it contained a slight trace of
reprehension, as if he were Captain Warren saying, "You haven't
had your yellow fever shot yet."

Before returning to work in the afternoon, he paid another visit
to Mr. Robbins.

"Sir, I'm out of voting cards."

Mr. Robbins grimaced. "Out?"

"Yes, sir."

"But that was quite a stack I handed you this morning."

"Yes, I know, sir."

"And you mean to say you've used them up?"

"Yes, sir. I just handed out the last one before lunch."

"To whom?"

"Private Collins."

"Collins!" the warrant officer repeated incredulously.

"Quite frankly, sir, it surprised me, too. But suddenly the men
seem passionately interested."

"You don't say," Mr. Robbins mused. "Hmm. Well, here are
some more," he said, handing Stephen half a dozen cards.

"Sir, why don't I just take the whole lot? That way I won't have
to keep bothering you."

From the ruminative expression on his face, Stephen knew that
Mr. Robbins was reviewing the hundreds of directives that had
crossed his desk in the last few months, trying to recall if any of
them contained the slightest reason why he should not accede to
Stephen's suggestion. "Very well," he said at last. "That will be all
right, I think. Help yourself."

"Thank you, sir."

Stephen was so elated by the success of his mission, he almost
floated down the hillside and into Personnel. After greeting Kim he
sat down at his desk and uncovered the typewriter. Starting alphabetically, he took the enlisted men's records and typed up voting
cards for everyone from Antonio through Nosselson. Occasionally,
in the course of the afternoon, one of the men from Stephen's hut
wandered in to sign his card, but otherwise he worked without a
break until five o'clock.

When he saw what time it was, Stephen realized he had missed
his shower. That is, he knew that if he wanted his customary

privacy in the shower house, he would have to wait until eight or nine o'clock. But today was Monday. He had an English class at six-thirty, and, after that, he would want to stay with Sun Bo . . .

Now for the first time since he had come to Korea—since he had entered the Army in fact—Stephen decided to take his shower with everyone else. Like everyone else, he undressed in his hut, wrapped his towel around his waist, walked to the shower house and waited in line impatiently. When, at last, it came Stephen's turn to shower, he had to forego his habit of taking his towel with him and draping it over the adjacent showerhead; instead, like everyone else, he left it on the bench outside.

At first he felt extremely self-conscious and welcomed the veil of steam in the room. Had he been given a choice, Stephen would have taken one of the corner showers where, if you faced the walls you could enjoy at least a modicum of privacy—but none of the corner showers was free. The only other means of preserving one's modesty was to put a lot of soap on quickly—which Stephen did. But even as he did so, as his soapy hands slid over his slippery flesh and the hot water began to relax his muscles—he remembered some of the things Sun Bo had said in the last two weeks and Stephen was emboldened. Despite his will to disembodiment, despite his history of self-estrangement, self-denial, self-abuse, Stephen's body understood what had happened in relation to Sun Bo, and through that understanding had emerged from its spectrality. As never before, Stephen was aware of himself standing, here and now, in this shower room, his legs astride, his feet against the duckboards, his body occupying—even claiming!—a particular extent of space between Sergeant Antonio on the one side and Sal Martini on the other. Not only had Sun Bo affirmed the handsomeness of Stephen's body but, in doing so, he had given it location. "Hi, Sal," Stephen said warmly.

"Hey, Steve. I didn't realize it was you. Did you finish off those voting cards?"

"Not quite. I will tomorrow."

"Want to have chow?"

"Sure, Sal. I'll be through in a minute. I just want to talk to Antonio for a second," Stephen said, turning toward the mess sergeant. "Sergeant."

"Yeah."

"My name's Wolfe."

"Yeah, I know: Personnel."

"Tomorrow sometime, when you get a chance, I'd like you to come by the office. Your voting card is ready."

"Voting card?"

"There's nothing to frown about; it's just a form."

"For what?"

"I'll explain tomorrow, when I see you. And tell the rest of your men to do the same. Everybody has to sign one."

"Oh! It's for everybody!" Antonio said, obviously relieved. "Sure thing, Wolfe. I'll be there."

By Tuesday afternoon Stephen had typed up voting cards for every enlisted man in the company. But even then—even after he had done that much of the labor for them, the men were apathetic. Only those whom he had approached personally, bothered to sign their cards; the rest were much too busy. After waiting all day Wednesday for the men to come to him, on Thursday morning Stephen decided to go to them.

Except for the stockade guards, whose irregular hours and erratic shifts made them more elusive than anyone else, Stephen had little difficulty collecting most of the signatures; by the weekend he had tracked down even the guards. That left only the officers. At first he felt somewhat apprehensive about approaching them, but once he overcame his fear, Stephen found the officers more submissive than the enlisted men, and was able, with the help of Kirk, to obtain the colonel's signature—a feat which gave him a sense of satisfaction and brought to a close his one-man registration drive.

And yet, as time went by and Stephen grew increasingly impatient for the ballots to arrive, he came to realize that his motives were more partisan than he had originally suspected. Not only did he want the men to vote, he wanted them to vote for Stevenson. He regretted his haste and indiscrimination. He wished he had overlooked typing up voting cards for men like the colonel and Sergeant Antonio who, he felt sure, favored Eisenhower. But the damage was done. His only course of action now was to start compaigning actively for the candidate of his choice.

To that end Stephen suddenly became positively gregarious—so much so that the GI's began to wonder what had come over Garbo. Every meal found him sitting at a different table in the mess hall, chatting with a different group of men. Every evening found him under a different showerhead in the shower house, every morning shaving at a different mirror; but always questioning, persuading, arguing, coercing.

And afterward he would go back to his office, take out the records of the men he had approached and mark them with a tiny $\checkmark$ or x or ?. By the time he had contacted most of the company, Stephen was overjoyed to discover that the $\checkmark$'s outnumbered the x's almost two to one, and he began to concentrate on the ?'s. He saw to it that these "undecideds" were given preferential treatment by the prisoners who manned the chow line and by those who ran the barbershop, the tailor shop, the laundry. He even stooped to making certain minor changes on their records in return for their assurance of a vote for Stevenson. And when, at last, he received his own ballot, Stephen began to hang around the mail room, watching for the ballots of other soldiers and taking the recipients aside for one final "little talk."

By election day Stephen had imbued most of the GI's and even some of the prisoners with his own feelings of anxiety, excitement, and suspense. As soon as the Armed Forces Radio began to broadcast the returns at 1000 hours, all Army business stopped. In Headquarters and the stockade, in the Quonset huts and mess hall, motor pool and mail room, the men congregated around loudspeakers and portables, listening intently. Despite Eisenhower's early edge of 500,000 votes, there were no returns from New York, Pennsylvania, California, or Texas, and Stephen's hopes remained high. He refused to budge from the radio in Personnel, even for lunch. At 1446 hours the announcer took his listeners to Stevenson headquarters for a concession of defeat. When the Governor appeared to read his statement, some woman in the Illinois audience cried No! No!, and Stephen in Korea did the same. That night for the first time since he had begun, Stephen was too upset to teach his English class. It was not until Friday that he could bring himself to return to the stockade.

As always, when Stephen entered the dispensary, the class stood up and bowed. For a moment the prisoners' lowered heads seemed to Stephen to express their sympathy for Adlai Stevenson's defeat, and he felt ashamed of the American electorate, as if the voters had betrayed not only themselves but these men. "I'm sorry," he said, bowing back. "Forgive me for not coming last time. I-I wasn't feeling well. I guess by now you know who our next President is."

"Yes. Yes," the men responded. "We have many hope. He will come Korea. He will wipe out Rooshians! He will save free world!"

Stephen resented the overconfidence and smugness of the prisoners, but seeing the hope in their eyes, he supressed his anger. "You mustn't expect too much."

"He will not come? He will not keep promise?"

"Oh, yes, I'm sure he'll come." Hearing this, the men beamed and nodded their approval—even Sun Bo did. "It's just that you mustn't expect miracles. After all, he's only human," Stephen said somewhat bitterly, and he wondered if Eisenhower could possibly be aware of his messianic image.

"Eisenhower great soldier, great statesman—"

Stephen was in no mood for politics, so he cut the discussion short by opening the *National English Reader*. On finding the place, he was suddenly reminded that the class had almost finished the reader. There were only a half a dozen pages left. For over a month Stephen had been meaning to go to Pusan to buy or borrow as many copies as he could find of the issue of *Life* containing *The Old Man and the Sea,* but he had been too busy. Now he made a mental note to attend to the matter on Sunday without fail.

After the class was over, Stephen stayed on to talk to Sun Bo, whom he had not seen since Monday. "I missed you . . . so much."

"I, too, Stephen. You were sick?"

"No . . . just depressed."

"Depressed?"

"Unhappy."

"Why unhappy?"

"Over the election."

"I am sorry, Stephen. I know how much defeat of Stevenson mean to you."

There was something patronizing in Sun Bo's tone that irritated Stephen. "Not only to me! to *you,* Sun Bo, to all of us."

"Perhaps."

Stephen shook his head in despair. "There's no perhaps about it," he said. "You just don't understand, Sun Bo: the *loss,* the stupid, stupid—" Stephen could not finish for his tears, sobbing so bitterly he had to bury his face in his hands. "How could they? How *could* they?" he cried out against his countrymen.

Taking Stephen in his arms, Sun Bo tried to console him. "We must wait to see what Eisenhower do."

"What is there to see!" he retorted savagely. "You want to see the Seventh Fleet removed? You want to see Chiang Kai-shek unleashed?"

Sun Bo sat a moment, deep in thought. Then he went to his desk and picked up the dictionary. As soon as he found the word he was after, he pronounced it aloud. "Con-sis-tent?"

"Consistent, yes."

"It would, perhaps, be more consistent of your government, more true."

"What would?"

"Removal of Seventh Fleet."

"What!" Dumbfounded, Stephen stared at his friend. "You don't know what you're saying. You sound like General MacArthur."

"MacArthur," Sun Bo echoed with a mitigating shrug. "I do not say right or wrong, but I think MacArthur honorable man."

This statement brought Stephen to his feet. "Honorable!"

"Yes, I think."

"Oh please! please!" Stephen said, repulsing Sun Bo with his palms as if his friend were a wasp.

"Where you go, Stephen?"

"Away. Away. I can't stay here," he said, hurrying out of the back room into the dispensary.

"Why you cannot stay?"

"You-you, you're—" he stammered, not wanting to speak the word on the tip of his tongue. But Stephen could not help himself. "Fascist! Fascist!" he shouted and ran into the night.

By the following morning Stephen very much regretted his hysterical outburst, and was feeling rather guilty. At the same time he was still disturbed by Sun Bo's political attitudes. He did not expect his friend to grasp the distinction of Adlai Stevenson, but to call MacArthur an honorable man, to wish for the removal of the Seventh Fleet—

Since it was Saturday, no English class was scheduled. At 1830 hours, as soon as he had finished dinner, Stephen went to the dispensary and settled down with Sun Bo on the cot in the back room. After apologizing for the way he had acted, Stephen picked up the conversation where he left off the night before. "But still, Sun Bo, there's something I don't understand. Do you really think it would be better if the United States withdrew its fleet from Formosa Strait? You think Truman should have let MacArthur cross the Yalu?"

"No. I do not say better. What I say last night—" Sun Bo stopped and knit his brows. "Och! now I forget word again."

"Consistent."

"Consistent, yes; and also true, more true: that is what I say last night."

"But why? Why would it be more truthful?"

"That very difficult to answer, Stephen. You must know Korea history, and also Korea geography to understand."

"I *do* know the geography, Sun Bo."

"Geography make Korea much important to many nation. Not just now, today, but since end of prior century, China, Russia, Japan have much interest in Korea. Also, England, France, U.S., interest in Korea—selfish interest, yes?"

"I understand."

"For thirty-five year, until surrender, end of Second World War, Japan occupy Korea, rule Korea. Korea colony of Japan. But after war, December 1945, Russia and U.S. hold Moscow Conference: agree to establish independent, democratic Korea government. Not *two* government," he added bitterly, "one Pyongyang, one Seoul —but one government for entire country. You understand?"

"Yes."

"Independent Korea government: that is what people want, what people wait for all of life. But, then, it do not happen. What happen is Cold War. Russia forget promise to unify Korea. U.S. forget. Instead, Russia and U.S. build army, build industry, build power—make two separate country, enemy country, until there is war, and only hope for unify Korea is UN."

"But the UN didn't send us here to unify Korea. They sent us because the North Koreans crossed the 38th parallel. Isn't that right? Isn't that the reason the UN entered the war? to restore the status—the two zones?"

"I do not know now why UN enter war," Sun Bo answered wearily, as if discussion were futile. "That is great confusion. In 1947 UN endorse independent, unify Korea. When UN enter war, 1950, Korea people remember that, remember Moscow Conference. For first time since 1945, Korea people hope again for unify Korea. That is what MacArthur try to do. That is why I call

MacArthur honorable man: he try to unify Korea, not restore two zone, two separate country like Truman. That confusion in Truman mind."

"But MacArthur wanted to do much more than that. He wanted to extend the war to China." Sun Bo nodded in agreement. "Well, do you—do you think that's right, Sun Bo? You think he should've been allowed to cross the Yalu?"

"How I know, Stephen?" he rejoined. "We return to point where we begin: many nation interest in Korea. *All* I know," he said with passion, "is that division must end! Country must be unify, must be free—free from outside interference, free from other nation selfish interest. Otherwise, no hope for Korea."

Though unconvinced about MacArthur, Stephen found the rest of Sun Bo's argument irrefutable. Ever since his arrival in Korea, Stephen had accepted without question the partition of the country. Now, for the first time, he realized that the separate zones were not inevitable, but some preternatural condition imposed upon Korea from outside. The war had not resulted from a simple act of aggression—aggression was merely a symptom, partition was the cause. After all, what Sun Bo wanted for his country was not so different from what Stephen wanted for himself: integrity. "You're right, Sun Bo. I must've been mad last night, to say those things. Forgive me, please."

"Yes, Stephen."

"I love you, Sun Bo."

"I, too, Stephen."

Now, more than ever, Stephen wanted to give himself to Sun Bo. What better way to express his faith, his trust, he thought, than by taking the "passive role." It would be a kind of gesture— the *beau geste* of his love, and he wanted more than anything to make that gesture now. But once again he failed—failed because it meant too much, because his impulse was too conscious. He realized and regretted that. Nevertheless, when their love-making was done, Stephen felt utterly relaxed and satisfied, united with Sun Bo, and suddenly a thought occurred to him. "Sun Bo."

"Yes."

"Tomorrow, I have to go to Pusan—to get new readers for the class. Would you like to come with me?"

Sun Bo sat up. "To Pusan!"

"Yes."

"You are crazy, Stephen?"

"Why?"

"You forget I am PW?"

"No," Stephen chuckled, amused by the look of confoundment on his friend's face. "How could I forget?"

"How I go to Pusan?"

"In a jeep, with me."

"You are crazy, Stephen," Sun Bo concluded, lying down again.

Stephen was delighted by Sun Bo's skepticism. "No, I'm not. What's the problem?"

"Tell me, Stephen, how I go past guard?"

"With me. The guards all know me. They won't stop us. I doubt they'll even realize you're a prisoner. It's not as if you wore a uniform. You dress the same as Kim, that friend of mine, the interpreter. I really doubt the guards will ever know the difference. You know that joke about the GI's not being able to tell one gook from another." Though silent now, Sun Bo still looked skeptical. To further assure him, Stephen added, "After all, it's not as if we weren't coming back."

"But who will take charge of dispensary, Stephen?"

"Mung or Lee or—whoever the orderly is."

"And if emergency arise?"

"They'll get the doctor from another compound."

"But then I be in trouble."

"Don't be silly. They'll cover up for you." When the idea first occurred to him, Stephen hadn't realized just how radical it was; now that he did, the prospect tempted and excited him more than ever. "Please, Sun Bo. Please say you'll come." From the look on Sun Bo's face, Stephen could tell he was struggling with his conscience. "Please."

"All right," he sighed at last. "I come."

Greatly pleased, Stephen laughed and hugged Sun Bo. "Good! We'll leave right after lunch."

By Sunday noon everything was ready for the outing. Stephen had finished lunch, put on his o.d.'s, transferred Oscar to his overcoat, and signed out for the day, jotting down as his anticipated time of return, the latest possible hour: 2200. After parking the jeep obtained from Sergeant Billywood in front of Personnel, Stephen got out and walked, carefree and humming, toward the stockade. But as he approached the guard at the sally port, his confidence collapsed, and he heaved an anxious sigh. He must be mad, he thought, planning to take a prisoner out of the stockade without orders. If he was caught, he would surely be court-martialed. And yet, having practically twisted Sun Bo's arm, he couldn't very well call off the trip now . . .

"Hi, Wolfe," the guard greeted Stephen.

"Oh, hi, Kallish."

"You working today?"

"Yeah: a pisser, isn't it," Stephen griped, hoping to allay the guard's suspicions.

Before entering the dispensary, it occurred to Stephen that he ought to coach Sun Bo to keep his eyes on the ground and his mouth shut until they got past Kallish. But he didn't want to unnerve his friend, so he acted nonchalant. "Are you ready, Sun Bo?"

"Yes, Stephen."

"Is sick call over?"

"Yes."

Noticing that Sun Bo had no overcoat, Stephen said, "Will you be warm enough like that?"

"I think."

"All right. The jeep is parked in front of my office."

The distance from the door of the dispensary to the sally port was less than a hundred yards, but to Stephen it seemed miles. Holding his breath, he walked in silence, his legs stiff, his back erect, his heart pounding.

Sun Bo sensed the tension. "You are sure there will be no trouble, Stephen?"

"Yes," he answered curtly, not wanting Kallish to see them conversing. But Stephen's apprehensions proved unnecessary. To his great relief, when they reached the gate, Kallish wasn't there. The guard had stepped into the sentry box for a smoke, and Stephen and Sun Bo walked past without a word. But even then, even with the stockade behind them, Stephen still felt jittery. On the pretext of having to attend to some last-minute work, he ducked into his office in hopes of not being seen when they got into the jeep. "I'll just be a minute, Sun Bo."

"This is where you work, Stephen?"

"Yes," he said, busying himself with some papers from his in-and-out box.

"This is your desk?"

"Yes."

"This is your typewriter?"

Surprised by all the questions, Stephen glanced up at his friend. Sun Bo looked bemused. He was fingering the typewriter keys dreamily. Then suddenly it dawned on Stephen that Sun Bo had not set foot outside the stockade for at least a year. Though physically the same as the dispensary, the personnel building was not within the confines of the prison, and that made all the difference. At that moment, had they been transported to Stephen's apartment in New York, Sun Bo could not have been more affected. To express his sympathy, Stephen reached out and stroked Sun Bo's fingers, and then kissed his hand. "We can go now," he said softly.

After making certain that the coast was clear, they got into the jeep and started down the hill. For Stephen the fear that they might be discovered made the descent almost as convulsive as it would have been on the roller coaster at Coney Island. But once again his fears were unfounded. They reached the bottom without passing a soul, and drove out of the company area onto the Pusan road as easily as if they had done it every day of their lives. "You see," Stephen sighed, "I told you there was nothing to worry about."

It was a magnificent afternoon: crisp and clear and sunny, not a single cloud in the cerulean sky. The terraced fields that graduated toward the mountains, the mountains toward the sky, filled Stephen with a sense of latitude, and he stepped on the accelerator. Like so many shaving brushes left in the sun to dry, the leafless aspens along the roadside receded in a rush. The cool wind caught Sun Bo's hair, pulling it straight back from his forehead, as if he were swimming underwater. He was smiling broadly now, his sunlit face alive with excitement, his dark eyes dancing with the landscape. Stephen smiled, too, experiencing with no less intensity than his friend, Sun Bo's sudden freedom.

When they reached the rotary that led to the city, Stephen slowed down, not only in compliance with the speed limit but because he was aware of Sun Bo's great excitement. Like a child at a three-ring circus Sun Bo tried to look in all directions at once—at the countless civilians crisscrossing the streets, at the buses, two-ton army trucks and Chevrolets, at all the shops and buildings. "Do you know the city, Sun Bo?"

"No. I only see once, very little, when I come from Koje."

"It's wonderful, isn't it."

"Yes. Yes, wonderful," Sun Bo agreed almost with awe. "It is like New York, Stephen?"

"Not exactly." Stephen smiled to himself as they drove past an ancient, wearing a white muslin frock coat and one of those stovepipe hats with a mesh crown. "Why does he wear that kind of hat, Sun Bo? Does it mean something?"

"Keong kam."

"What?"

"Wise man," Sun Bo explained. "Net allow wise-thought to escape into world."

From time to time, seeing a look of particular pleasure on Sun Bo's face or hearing him chuckle aloud, Stephen would ask the cause. "Beauty parlor," came the reply, or "Frenchy movie," or "U.S. automobile."

On one such occasion the answer to the question was, "Woman theater," and Stephen promptly stepped on the brake. "Where?" he asked with interest.

Sun Bo pointed at a rather large, dilapidated wooden structure across the street.

"When I first came to Pusan," Stephen recalled, "Kim promised to take me there, but he never has. What sort of play are they doing, Sun Bo?"

"Golden Pig: famous play."

"You know it?"

"Yes, I know—everybody know. You should see, Stephen."

"Do they perform it every night?"

"No. Only Sunday—"

"Tonight?"

"In afternoon."

"This afternoon! Maybe if we get finished in time—" Stephen thought aloud. "What time does it start?"

Squinting, Sun Bo studied the billboard on the opposite side of the road. "Fourteen hundred hour."

Stephen glanced at his watch: an hour and twenty minutes till curtain time. With luck they could make it! "Would you like to go, Sun Bo?"

As if to say, Are you serious! Sun Bo grinned from ear to ear.

"Should we get the tickets now?"

Sun Bo's smile suddenly vanished.

"What's the matter?"

"I have not money, Stephen."

"You don't?" Stephen said with a straight face. "What a shame." Then he punched Sun Bo playfully and laughed. "You're with a rich American, stupid! What about the tickets?"

"Plenty time for ticket."

Spurred on by the incentive of going to theater, in less than an hour Stephen managed to buy, beg or steal from two service clubs, four MP companies and the black market, seventeen copies of the September 1 issue of *Life*. Compared with the dozen readers the class had been using for three months, the number of magazines seemed superabundant, and both Stephen and Sun Bo were more than satisfied. After carefully concealing them under the seats of the jeep, they returned to the theater in plenty of time for the performance.

The auditorium was extremely modest. There was no balcony, the curtain was little more than a wine-colored rag and the seats, mere wooden bleachers, were placed so close together, Stephen had no leg room. If he sat forward his knees jabbed into the ribs of the rich lady in front of him; if he sat back he himself was poked in the base of the spine, and when he pulled in his legs and sat perfectly erect, free from physical contact with anyone, the people behind him complained he was too tall. To make matters even more uncomfortable, both smoking and eating were permitted in the theater, and the air was foul and hot. In the aisles men were hawking ice-cakes and cider. At the front of the house, just behind the orchestra pit, a mob of boys and girls ran riot in the children's section. Since they were admitted for half-price, the children were given no choice but the floor, on which they rolled about, giggling, kicking and screaming, to the great irritation of their elders. One old man in particular, a *keong kam* in the first row, was so infuriated by the horseplay that he finally stood up, raised his stick and brought it down with a resounding smack onto the skull of a schoolboy. The child's stunned expression and sudden flood of tears made the audience roar with laughter.

Never in his life had Stephen seen the likes of it—except, perhaps, for Lodge at Potawatomi. Though interested, he was terribly uncomfortable now and beginning to regret having come. He and Sun Bo could have stayed outdoors in the sunshine. They could have gone for a drive or just strolled around the city, instead of wasting their day in this cramped and vile-smelling trap. But Sun Bo

was obviously enjoying himself, so Stephen tried to hide his displeasure. "Tell me about the play," he said. "What is the story?"
"Story concern princess, name of Moon. She—she—" Sun Bo floundered. "Not yet marry. How you say time before marry?"
"Engaged."
"Engage, yes. Moon engage with prince, name of Sun—"
"Like you, Sun Bo."
"No, no," he giggled, blushing, "like in sky. Evil, jealous Woman make Sun think Moon unfaithful. Moon is not unfaithful, Sun only imagine so. In anger he call Moon prostitute, and destroy engage—"
"Engagement."
"Engagement. Now evil Woman carry Moon away to mountain: cave of Golden Pig. Golden Pig is demon. You understand?"
"Yes."
"Golden Pig make prisoner of Moon. Then Sun begin to realize mistake. He go after Moon, to cave of Golden Pig. There he battle demon, kill demon, free Moon from prison. At end, Sun and Moon return to palace—" Before he could finish, a gong sounded. A temporary hush came over the audience and the house lights went out abruptly. Sun Bo inched forward on his seat. "Play have happy end," he summed up in a whisper, as the curtains parted.

Having expected little more than an amateur performance, Stephen was greatly surprised by the artistry with which *The Golden Pig* was produced and acted. Out of nothing: some scraps of paper, wire, rags, gunny sacking and cardboard, the designer had fashioned the most elaborate, colorful castles, mountains, caves, and throne chambers. Though the scenery was too operatic for Stephen's taste, he could not help respecting the inventiveness, even genius that had gone into its creation. The same was true of the costumes and, to a lesser degree (for lack of equipment), the lighting.

But what interested and excited Stephen most was the conventions of the theater. Whenever, in the course of the drama, the emotion became too intense for words, a little orchestra took over and the actors broke into song. As far as Stephen could tell, this orchestra, which was not in the orchestra pit but offstage, consisted of a giant razzle-dazzle, a drum and one or two stringed instruments. It produced terrible sounds—crashing, rasping, rending sounds that Stephen had never before heard, but had sometimes, in states of extreme agitation, *felt*. That was its purpose: not, as in

Verdi, to interpret and characterize, abet and advance the action through music, but the opposite: to stop the action and put the screws on the audience, to make the audience not only understand but *feel* what the hero or heroine was feeling at a given moment of exultation or agony. It was at these moments that the actors were forced, not only by the dramatic context but by the orchestra itself—goading and tormenting them—to abandon spoken dialogue for long, whining arias. One such aria, sung by Moon, just after Sun had accused her of being a prostitute, lasted ten or fifteen minutes and was one of the most beautifully controlled and touching pieces of acting Stephen had ever seen.

As he watched the actress who was portraying Moon perform this difficult aria which demanded, simultaneously, a highly developed pantomimic skill, virtuoso vocal range, and the ability to express emotions larger than life, Stephen began to think about his own career with new awareness. Hadn't he always, at Midwestern and even before, at Penobscot and Potawatomi, acted out of a need to express his own emotion, with the peculiar result that he performed better by himself—rehearsing in a room alone—than in front of an audience? As soon as he stepped in front of an audience, his body tensed, he was overcome by guilt and his performance suffered. But it wasn't only audiences that hindered Stephen, his fellow actors did. They restricted and inhibited him; invariably, they interfered with his preconception of a role. The truth of the matter was that Stephen always gave his best performance not on opening night, early in the run or even during rehearsals, but at the first reading, after weeks of solitary preparation. . . . Why? he wondered. Why did he prefer soliloquies to dialogue? Why did he most prefer to climb a hill alone and shout against the wind or rain some speech from *Richard II* for the exclusive gratification of himself and the Unknown? Wasn't that a complete perversion of what it means to be an actor? A colossal piece of arrogance and self-delusion—the very definition of the amateur! Now, suddenly, sitting there beside Sun Bo, watching this Korean actress, Stephen longed to get up on the stage and perform, not for himself, but an audience; not in order for himself to experience his own emotion but to allow others to experience it. He suddenly realized that while in Korea he had undergone a mysterious transition: his entire thinking had changed—not only his thinking, his being, his body had changed. All his life he had been inside himself, blindly; now, though still inside, thinking his own thoughts, he was able, at the same time, to transcend and see himself, much as he was seeing this gifted actress playing Moon. All his life he had been alone inside a room, rehearsing; now he was out, and eager to join his fellow actors and perform before an audience. Somehow he had lost his fear, his stage fright—his permanent, day-to-day life-fright—and he was impatient now to go to work. After years and years of reacting to being acted upon, at last Stephen felt he was ready to become an actor.

Actually, Stephen could not have said for certain just when the idea to give Sun Bo his freedom first entered his mind—while leaving the stockade or in the personnel office or as Sun Bo was telling the story of the play; perhaps it had been there much longer than that—but he knew without a doubt the moment it had become conscious. It was in the Second Act when Sun, in order to rescue Moon, had to slay the Golden Pig. It was then, while the orchestra brought to a crescendo its infernal din and the prince plunged his gleaming sword into the demon's chest and the audience grunted appropriately, that the idea came to Stephen in a flash as blinding as the magnesium flash in which the Golden Pig vanished from the stage. From that moment on he could think of nothing but letting Sun Bo escape. Throughout the denouement, the wedding scene, he wrestled with the problem. At first the prospect terrified him. He considered Kallish, considered the colonel, considered the likelihood of being court-martialed, imprisoned himself, and the effect that such an eventuality would have on his family, his future. The consequences made his insides collapse. But gradually he began to rationalize the matter. There was always the possibility that Kallish hadn't seen them leave the stockade, and that he would either forget about Stephen's initial entrance or deem it too routine to mention. But even if he did, even if, in time, Sun Bo's escape were linked to Stephen, of what could Stephen be accused? The misdemeanor of taking a prisoner out of the stockade? The gross negligence of allowing his escape? Perhaps. But only that, nothing more. Surely no tribunal could ever find him guilty of premeditation or convict him as an accomplice to the crime. There was even reason to suppose that such an escape would not be judged a crime. After all, these anti-Communists were no ordinary prisoners. The authorities were in sympathy with them—witness the truce-talks deadlock over their repatriation. How many times, in fact, had Syngman Rhee himself threatened to liberate the anti-Communist PW's! . . . Such thoughts as these minimized the consequences and strengthened Stephen's nerve until, at last, he put aside all consideration of himself. In the final analysis what mattered was Sun Bo—nothing else! Not all the army rules and regulations put together meant half as much to Stephen as Sun Bo's fate.

To reassure himself, Stephen glanced at his friend out of the corner of his eye. Sun Bo was crying in response to what was happening on stage: the wedding celebration. As if they, too, were being wedded, Stephen covered Sun Bo's hand with his own. But suddenly, in the light of their imminent separation, this precious contact seemed almost unbearable to Stephen, and he had to bite the shoulder of his Eisenhower jacket to keep from bawling.

When the play was over, Stephen applauded enthusiastically. But the minute the house lights came on, he left the theater.

"What the matter, Stephen?" Sun Bo asked, hurrying after him. "You do not like play?"

"I have to talk to you," Stephen said with urgency.

Sun Bo got into the jeep. "Yes, Stephen?"

"Not here." It was after five now, and though still daylight, the sky had clouded over and there was a chill in the air. "Indoors. Someplace quiet."

"Coffeehouse?"

"You know of one?"

"Wait. I will ask."

The coffeehouse was on a hilltop just above the International Market, and it overlooked the harbor. Though Sun Bo had said it was the most famous one in Pusan, Stephen was unprepared for its elegance. The walls, dove gray trimmed in white, were hung with postimpressionist paintings. On every table there was a white cloth, as well as a little vase of button chrysanthemums. Most of the customers were more richly dressed than any Koreans Stephen had seen. Many of the men sported woollen overcoats and ivory cigarette holders, some of the women carried muffs or modest fur pieces—all were engaged in animated conversation.

As Stephen and Sun Bo entered, a couple got up from a window-side table, and Stephen sat down at once. The view of the harbor was panoramic. Though he had had to stay in second gear all the way up the hill, Stephen hadn't realized just how far above sea level he had driven. Now, the port with its guardian mountains on the one side and on the other its vast network of railroad yards, finger-like piers, fishing fleets, and freighters spread out below him, an ant kingdom. To the west he could see the entire city, to the south, beyond the basin of the harbor, beyond the perimeter of volcanic-looking mountains, Korea Strait. The spectacle made Stephen feel at once infinitesimal and Olympian. "Isn't it something," he sighed, draping his overcoat over the back of the chair.

"Yes, beautiful," Sun Bo said, but all the wonder and delight that had set his face aglow until this minute were gone now, and he looked soulful, sad.

"What's the matter?"

"Hospital ship," he replied, staring out the window.

Stephen followed Sun Bo's gaze. Anchored in the center of the harbor was a sizable steamer, painted white with huge red crosses, and flying the Swedish flag. "What about it?"

"On Koje there is no hospital," Sun Bo explained. "Seriously injure patient or seriously sick must be remove from island to hospital ship."

Just as Stephen was about to ask what the ship was doing there in Pusan, thirty miles from its mission, a helicopter hummed out of the southwest, hovered over the bow of the ship and, then, landed on the forward deck, delivering into the hands of two waiting attendants, a body on a litter. Stephen turned back to his friend. "You mean, that man they've just unloaded was brought all the way from Koje?"

"Yes," Sun Bo sighed. "Prisoner, like me."

"Chinese?"

"No, Korean."

"But pro-Communist?"

"Maybe. Maybe not. Maybe anti-Communist, punish by kangaroo court. I do not know."

It was beginning to grow dark outside, and the weariness in Sun Bo's voice, the sorrow in his eyes, seemed to complement the twilight, as if something in his spirit, too, like the day, was waning.

Stephen guessed at what it was. "Did you once work on that ship, Sun Bo—as a doctor I mean?"

"No. But I dispatch many, many man . . ." The rest of the sentence trailed off into thought, which, judging by Sun Bo's expression, was bitter and painful. To break the mood he signaled for the waitress. "I am sorry, Stephen: I detest to remember Koje."

"I understand."

"What you like to drink?" he asked as the waitress appeared.

"What do you suggest?"

"You like chocolate?"

"Yes."

While Sun Bo was ordering, Stephen stared out the window at the lights that were beginning to come on in the railroad yard, aboard the hospital ship and the freighters—sharp little pinpoints far below, like moonlight reflected in the water at the bottom of a well. The magical sight filled Stephen with fervor. "Sun Bo," he said softly, breathily, almost trembling, "I want to tell you something. When I do, I don't want you to answer right away. I want you to think about it, carefully. All right?"

"All right."

When Stephen opened his mouth to speak again, there were no words, nothing but a terrible quivering suspension of breath. To calm his nerves he lit a cigarette. Only with effort was he able, at last, to produce his voice. "I'm not going to take you back to the stockade tonight," he whispered.

Sun Bo knit his brows but said nothing.

"I'm going to give you whatever money I have and leave you here in Pusan—not for just the night but forever . . . free. You understand?" It was apparent from the frown on Sun Bo's face that he did not understand. "I'm going to pretend that you escaped—that is, if it ever comes to that, if I'm ever questioned. I'll just say you ran away."

After a long pause Sun Bo said, "Why you wish for me to run away, Stephen?"

"Not run away. I wish for—I want—I just want you to be able to live like everyone else, like all these people here," he added, looking around the coffeehouse, "out of that stockade."

Lost in thought Sun Bo helped himself to one of Stephen's cigarettes. "May I?"

"Of course."

"And you are prepared to be in trouble yourself, so that I may—?"

"Please, Sun Bo," Stephen interrupted, "you mustn't think of me. Nothing will happen to me, I promise you. You must believe that."

"You are uncommon man, Stephen, uncommon friend."

These simple words both touched and embarrassed Stephen, and he was almost relieved to see the waitress with their order. After they were served, Stephen toasted his friend and then took a sip of the chocolate. It was much too sweet for his taste, but Sun Bo obviously adored it. Like a little boy he grinned from ear to ear, smacked his lips and licked the corners of his mouth. "Just think, tomorrow you can have another."

Sun Bo looked puzzled. "What do you say, Stephen?"

"Tomorrow you can have another."

"How possible?"

"Just by coming back, here, to this coffeehouse."

It took a moment for Sun Bo to understand, and then he giggled somewhat nervously, until his giggles gave way to an impish grin. "What make you think Pusan better than stockade for me?"

"Oh, come on, Sun Bo!"

"No, truly, Stephen."

"You would only need to have seen your face just now, when you tasted the chocolate, to answer that."

"Chocolate very good, but I know nobody in Pusan."

"Then go to Seoul, go to Taegu—it doesn't matter where."

"I have no work in Seoul."

"Surely they need doctors there."

"Not more than PW need."

"No, but—" Stephen stopped, confounded. "You mean, you'd rather stay in prison?"

Almost without deliberation Sun Bo said, "I think."

The only way Stephen had of accounting for the perversity of this response, was to interpret it as an effort on Sun Bo's part to protect him. "How can I convince you that nothing will happen to me? nothing serious. Please don't think about me, Sun Bo."

"I do not think about you."

"Then how can you say you'd prefer the stockade?"

Sun Bo avoided Stephen's gaze. "I have reason."

"What? what reason? Your friends? Politics? What?"

"I am sorry, Stephen, I cannot say."

"Why not? Don't you trust me? What could be so—?"

"I trust you more than any man I know, but still I cannot say."

The finality of Sun Bo's tone left no room for further questions, and Stephen lapsed into a moody silence.

"You have disappointment, Stephen?"

"A little, I guess."

"I am sorry."

"Don't be sorry. It's just that I wanted so much—I don't know—to do that, to give you—"

"Once again *to give?*" Sun Bo said with irony. "No, Stephen, you give me everything. There is nothing more to give. Because I am PW, there is-is—" At a loss for the word he demonstrated with his hands.

"Imbalance."

"Imbalance, yes. In our friendship there is imbalance. You give everything: English class, book, theater, chocolate—even in love-making, it is you who give. I, also, wish to give."

If the catalog of gifts had not included love-making, Stephen could have easily dismissed it. But since he himself had so many doubts in that area, Sun Bo's statement sounded like an accusation. "Oh, Sun Bo, don't you know how much I want you?"

"Want me?"

"To make love to me, I mean."

Sun Bo smiled. "I would like."

For a long time the two men stared at one another lingeringly, until their eyes brought about a fusion of their beings, and their hands reached out across the table. But Stephen felt self-conscious in this public place. "Can't we go somewhere else?"

"I will ask," Sun Bo said and went in search of the manager.

It was night now and the harbor lights cast an irresistible spell. As he gazed out the window at the hospital ship, Stephen dreamed of taking a voyage with Sun Bo—the two of them alone forever on an ocean liner . . .

"I hear of restaurant," Sun Bo said, coming back to the table.

"But I don't want to be with a lot of people," Stephen objected.

"No, Stephen, only us."

"Only us? What kind of a restaurant is that?"

"Come. I will take you."

Leaving a dollar in GI scrip, Stephen stood up and followed Sun Bo into the night. The air was cold. "Is it far?" he asked, concerned that Sun Bo had no overcoat.

"No. Very near."

"Don't we need to take the jeep?"

"No."

"You better come under here then with me," Stephen said, wrapping his overcoat around Sun Bo's shoulders.

From outside, the restaurant, which occupied the second floor of a two-storey building, looked terribly unpromising, not at all what

Stephen had in mind. In order to get to it, they had to mount, single-file, a flight of stairs so rickety and perilous it seemed more like a ladder than a staircase. But once they reached the landing, Stephen and Sun Bo were welcomed by a very chic proprietress who led them down a narrow passage, past several *shoji* screens on which were cast the lively shadows of other customers—all drinking, laughing, singing—to a warmly lit, private dining room.

The simplicity and cleanliness of the room took Stephen by surprise. Apart from the floor mats and a burnished, black lacquer table, the only other furnishing was something against the far wall that looked, at first, like a large divan extending the width of the room, but on closer examination proved to be a sumptuous brocaded mattress on which was scattered more than a dozen soft silk pillows. From the distance came the strangely soothing glottal sounds of an Oriental tune.

Following Sun Bo's example, Stephen left his overcoat and boots in the hall, walked across the room and sat down cross-legged on the mattress. As soon as they were seated the proprietress began plumping and arranging the pillows behind them, while she spoke to Sun Bo in Korean.

After a minute or two Sun Bo turned to Stephen. "You would like sake?"

"More than anything . . . almost."

"And to eat?"

"Can't we wait?"

"Yes, but food must be prepare," Sun Bo explained. "If we order now, food will come in hour."

Stephen stole a glance at his watch. Much to his relief it was only 6:25. There was plenty of time. The prospect of spending the next hour there on that divan, drinking sake with Sun Bo, filled him with ardor. "You order for both of us, all right?"

"All right. You are hungry?"

"No, but I think I will be," he said suggestively, "an hour from now."

It took Sun Bo and the proprietress what seemed to Stephen an eternity to plan the menu, but finally they finished. After thanking them repeatedly, the woman bowed out of the room and closed the screen behind her.

The instant she was gone Stephen flung his arms around Sun Bo and kissed him.

"You like restaurant?"

"I love it. But surely it's not a restaurant."

"What you mean?"

"Surely it's a brothel."

"Brothel?"

"A house of prostitution."

Sun Bo roared with laughter.

"No, really," Stephen insisted. "That woman's not a restaurateur, she's a madam. You saw all those rings on her fingers, didn't you? She's as rich as Midas. And that music. And this bed—it has to be a brothel!"

"No, no, restaurant," Sun Bo objected through his laughter.

"You can't fool me. She's gone to get the girls. They're going to give us baths and things."

The more Stephen teased, the more Sun Bo laughed, laughed until he was limp with laughter and fell back helplessly onto the pillows.

At this moment the screen was slid aside again, not by the proprietress but by a very shy young girl, carrying a lacquer tray.

"You see," Stephen whispered, "what did I tell you!"

Though he tried to keep a straight face, Sun Bo couldn't, and he had to bury his head in one of the pillows.

The waitress paid no attention. Like the prop man in *The Golden Pig,* who was dressed in black and was assumed, therefore, by the audience to be invisible, she went about her business, moving the table closer to the bedside and setting down the tray. From the tray she took a graceful china sake bottle, two tiny cups, and a lacquer plate which contained two washcloths, neatly rolled.

By this point Sun Bo had regained his composure enough to speak to the waitress. When he was finished the girl withdrew from the room, bowing as she went.

"What did you say to her?" Stephen asked.

"I say, Please do not return until food will be ready."

"And will she obey?"

"Of course," Sun Bo said, picking up one of the washcloths and wiping his face and hands.

Stephen did the same. The cloth was not only damp and hot but scented with mint. He held it to his face a long time, until his muscles relaxed completely and he was almost intoxicated by the fumes. "Oh, that feels good," he sighed, removing the cloth from his eyes.

Sun Bo was holding the sake bottle. "Please, you take up cup now, Stephen. We will drink in Korea manner."

As Stephen complied he suddenly noticed that the bottle was

embossed with a little open-mouthed bird. "What's that, the spout?"

"No. Be patient please." After instructing Stephen how to hold the cup, Sun Bo coiled his hand around Stephen's, so that their wrists were interlocked, and then tipped the bottle back until the wine began to flow. As it did, the little bird commenced to whistle.

"Oh! it's a nightingale. How wonderful!"

"You drink now, Stephen. But take care not to break chain of hand."

Stretching his neck, Stephen drained the cup. The ceremony delighted him, and he was eager to hear the nightingale again. "Now you, Sun Bo. Do we use the other cup?"

"No. Same cup."

"That's nice." Though he handled the bottle with a lot less finesse than his friend, Stephen was proud of himself for spilling only a small amount of the wine. Once again the nightingale sang, and Sun Bo downed his drink in a breath.

By the end of the third round the nightingale had begun to lose its voice. Both men were feeling the effects of the sake. Stephen took off his jacket and lounged back on the bed. Sun Bo stretched out beside him.

"You're sure no one will come?" Stephen asked.

Sun Bo answered with a kiss.

Instantly Stephen was aroused. Without a word Sun Bo sat up on his haunches and started to undress him. For once Stephen did not object to the lights being on. He enjoyed seeing the look of intense concentration on Sun Bo's face, the passion in his eyes, as he undid Stephen's buttons with remarkable dexterity.

When Stephen was naked Sun Bo took off his own clothes and lay down on his side, facing Stephen. For a long time they kissed —kissed until their kisses seemed inadequate. Then Stephen pulled Sun Bo on top of him and murmured in his ear, "Oh my love, come into me. Please, please come into me." But scarcely had the words left his mouth, than Stephen realized there was no lubricant in the room—nothing! nothing but some lukewarm sake—and his heart sank.

But Sun Bo was not deterred. Slipping away from Stephen's lips, he began to kiss him on the neck, the nipples, the navel, the thighs, until Stephen felt almost galvanized, and Sun Bo turned him over tenderly and penetrated Stephen with his tongue.

So exciting was the sensation, Stephen made no effort to resist.

All he could do was moan—his moans becoming more and more audible as his excitement increased. And when, in response, Sun Bo embraced him from behind, attempting to come into him, Stephen tried consciously to relax.

"No, no," Sun Bo whispered, "do not force."

Stephen bit the pillow to keep from crying out. But even as he did, he understood at last that it was not a matter of submission or surrender but of self-assertion—of actively laying claim to Sun Bo, wanting him, demanding him—and his teeth released the pillow, as he took Sun Bo into himself, shouting out triumphantly, "Yes! yes! yes!"

At the same moment all of Stephen's questions about the "passive" partner's satisfaction were answered by Sun Bo, who licked his hand and took hold of Stephen.

Unable to restrain himself, Stephen began to grunt. Some part of him, his consciousness, that seemed just now outside himself, was shocked by the sounds he produced. In their volume and ferocity they were reminiscent of the moose at Lobster Pond, the lions at the zoo. But as he neared his climax the grunts diminished, grew more staccato, breathy, until, for one split second, there was no sound at all, no breath, and Stephen thought his heart had stopped, before he heard himself let out a long ecstatic cry. Then, somewhere toward the end of it, this cry turned abruptly into laughter—loud orgiastic laughter that seemed to issue from his bowels. It was uncontrollable, he simply could not stop. And so he laughed and laughed and went on laughing, and as he did he suddenly remembered the myth of Zarathustra, about whom it was said that when he was born, instead of crying, he burst into laughter. Stephen had never fully understood the myth before, but now he did—now, in the midst of his ecstatic joy, he realized he was being born.

For a long time afterward Stephen felt too spent to move. It was only the sound of the waitress, tapping on the screen, that finally brought him to his feet. Then, even though Sun Bo instructed her to wait outside, Stephen dressed as if the restaurant were on fire, and when they let the waitress in, he felt convinced she knew their secret, but Stephen was much too happy and too ravenous to care.

Luckily Sun Bo had ordered a banquet—beef and pork and red snapper, all of which were served in little lacquer boxes. Stephen was enchanted. He did not even attempt to use the chopsticks, but used his fingers instead. When he was finished his hands and face were covered with sauce, and the waitress had to bring another washcloth.

By then it was 8:30, and Stephen was beginning to feel somewhat anxious about going back. So he paid the bill, tipping the waitress extravagantly, had Sun Bo convey his compliments to the "madam," and left the restaurant.

The air outside seemed freezing. To keep his hands warm, Stephen put them in his pockets. He had forgotten about Oscar, and for a moment was at a loss to identify the object encountered by his right hand. When at last he realized what it was, the toy left him indifferent. Somehow it seemed extraneous now, a lifeless threadbare lump of plush—nothing more—and he regretted not having given Oscar to that little girl six months ago.

As they neared the bottom of the hill, Stephen was surprised to see the market still open. All the lights were on and the streets were as crowded as they had been at midday. "Shall we see if we can find some more copies of the magazine?"

"No, Stephen, we have plenty."

Because the shoppers disregarded the road, Stephen had to drive very carefully, slowly. As he inched the jeep through the crowd, he suddenly saw a familiar sight: the apothecary shop. On the spur of the moment he pulled over to the side of the road and parked. "I'll just be a minute."

"Truly, Stephen," Sun Bo said, following his friend, "we have plenty magazine."

"I'm not going to buy anymore."

"Then what do you wish?"

Shrugging off the question, Stephen approached the stall. There was the witch, just as he had left her, sitting cross-legged on her platform. There on the counter were the stuffed birds and the huge glass jars filled with their magical medicaments. There were the snakes and toads, the flayed rabbit, and the monkey liver. There was the priapic rat, eternal in formaldehyde.

From his pocket Stephen took out Oscar and placed him on the counter. Seeing this, the witch began to croak.

"What did she say, Sun Bo?"

"She ask what you wish."

"Tell her I want nothing—just to make her a present of this toy."

From the scowl on her shriveled face and the harshness of her tone, Stephen could tell how much his gesture had angered the witch. "What did she say this time?"

"Let us go now, Stephen."

"What's the matter? Did she curse me?"

"Let us go," Sun Bo repeated.

Leaving Oscar on the counter, Stephen walked back to the jeep.

"Tell me what she said, Sun Bo."

"She think you play joke on her. Joke make her furious. She suggest you give toy to child."

Stephen could hear her croaking still. He smiled to himself and started the jeep.

"Why you do that, Stephen?"

"I don't know," he answered winsomely. "It's much too complicated to explain. We'd better hurry now," he added, leaving the market and turning onto the road back to the company area, which they reached a little after 2100 hours.

Stephen was scheduled to leave Korea at the end of the second week in February, but he hadn't the heart to tell Sun Bo. He could scarcely face the fact himself. Every time it crossed his mind he became dejected. Every time he stayed with Sun Bo the thought of February came between them, as if he were an adulterer trying to conceal his marriage from his mistress. Tonight! you must tell him tonight, he would say to himself, only to put it off another time. And so he procrastinated for weeks and weeks until, one day, it was January 30, and Stephen could procrastinate no longer.

After the Friday-night class, he asked Sun Bo to make some tea. When it was ready they went into the back room, settled down on the cot, and Stephen told Sun Bo his news.

For a long time Sun Bo sat in silence, staring into his canteen cup as if into the flames of a fire. When at last he spoke, all he said was, "I regret."

Though Stephen observed the look of sorrow in Sun Bo's eyes, he was nonetheless disappointed by his friend's reaction. His own tears were so close to the surface, Stephen found it difficult to accept Sun Bo's impassivity, but said nothing. Neither of them spoke again, in fact, until it came time for Stephen to leave.

Then Sun Bo said, "Please, you bring spoon tomorrow, Stephen."

"A spoon, Sun Bo?"

"From mess hall."

"Yes, I understand but why? What for?"

"Surprise."

This ambiguous response reminded Stephen of the night of the celebration, when Sun Bo explained Mung's disrobing by the one word: Exhibition. "What kind of surprise?" he asked suspiciously.

"If I reveal surprise," Sun Bo retorted, "surprise will not surprise."

Stephen laughed. "All right. I'll bring the spoon tomorrow."

The purpose of the spoon remained a mystery for two weeks until, the night before his departure, Stephen went to the dispensary to teach the final English class. By then he was so distressed he had virtually forgotten about the spoon. He could think of nothing but the impending separation from Sun Bo and from his students. He had so much wanted to finish *The Old Man and the Sea* before he went away, but even that, like everything else, would have to be left up in the air. Yet Stephen realized what a mistake it would be to give in to his sorrow now, and so he tried to conduct the class like any other.

The prisoners, too, behaved as if it were just another Friday night. There wasn't the slightest hint of sadness on any of their faces. They had grown to adore Hemingway, and all of them vied with one another to be called on to read aloud.

Only when the class was over did Stephen feel compelled to speak of his departure. "I think you know, without my saying—" he began softly, hesitantly, but lost his voice and had to turn away to hide his tears. It was only the whispers of the class that forced him to control himself.

Urged on by his classmates, Pak Man Kap stood up and said, "Please, you wait please, Teacher." As Pak disappeared into the back room, the men began to squirm in their seats and to beam as if they would burst with excitement. When at last Pak returned he was holding a white bundle, which he brought to the front of the room.

"No, no," Stephen protested under his breath, even before he saw what the bundle contained or heard the little presentation speech that Pak had prepared.

"We, student of Compound B English class, wish to express gratitude to beloved teacher."

Stephen knew he would bawl if Pak said one more word, but

fortunately the speech was over. "Thank you," he sighed, taking the bundle and putting it down on the seat of his chair.

Now, the whole class rose in unison and crowded forward to watch Stephen open the gift. Much to his embarrassment the bundle, like Santa Claus' sack, contained not one but seven presents. There was a polished brass buckle, monogrammed SW; a watercolor of a woman on a swing, suspended from a weeping willow; a woodcut of a tiger engraved not on wood but on a rubber sole; an ornately tooled leather belt; a pyrography of a lonely mountain crag crowned by a single pine. The white nylon square (cut no doubt from a parachute), in which the gifts had been wrapped, was itself a present—a sizable scarf, decorated with South Korean flags and signed in Roman letters by every member of the class. Finally, there was a paper scroll, tied with a strand of purple wool, that looked like a diploma.

From the way in which the men craned their necks the moment Stephen picked it up, he understood that they were much more interested in his response to the scroll than to ary of the other presents. "What's this?" he said, undoing the wool.

The question provoked some titters but no reply, so Stephen unrolled the scroll. Printed in an exquisite hand, the message read as follows:

From student Compound B English Class to esteem Teacher:
Before Teacher come to Prison Camp, PW have life of indolence, decadence, monotony. No purpose to PW life. Man eat, man sleep, man work. Sometime sport event, sometime sing, but in general no constructive program. Then Commanding Colonel is generous to send Teacher to PW. PW learn much from Teacher about difficult English language. PW learn to read in English from Aesop, Tolstoy, Mansfield, Balzac, Chekhov, and also US own great Hemingway. English Class eradicate temptation to indolence, decadence, monotony indigenous to PW life. English Class have meaning to PW as much as rice and fuel for fire. English Class make PW heart rejoice.

But English Class not alone reason for rejoice. More important reason for rejoice is Teacher. Teacher Stephen Wolfe is great Democratic man like Abraham Lincoln and Franklin Roosevelt. Also he is wise man, kind man, gentle man. In short Teacher is best man PW meet in lifetime. PW will never forget.

By the time he finished reading, Stephen had stained the testimonial with his tears. His hands and legs were trembling so, he had to sit down. When he tried to say thank you, the words caught in his throat, and he hung his head.

The next thing he was conscious of was the sound of a harmonica. Looking up, Stephen saw the little boy, O Hi Seong, playing. At a signal from Pak, the class came to stiff attention and began to sing "Auld Lang Syne."

Even under ordinary circumstances the song seldom failed to reduce Stephen to tears; on this occasion he had to grip the arms of the chair and clench his teeth to keep from becoming hysterical. On the other hand the Scottish words posed problems for the prisoners, and there were moments when Stephen didn't know whether to laugh or cry, whether to sing along or be silent, whether to express his appreciation by standing up or remaining seated—didn't know what to do in order to get through the endless chorus.

At last the song was over. Stephen stood up shakily. Looking around the room at all the smiling faces, he tried to smile, too, but couldn't. He, too, wanted to tell the men how much the English class had meant to him, to offer them *his* testimonial, but couldn't. He wanted to go up to each man individually and shake his hand and say good-by, but couldn't. All he could do was blurt out, "I'll never forget you either," and flee into the back room.

Stephen was lying face down on the cot, trying to muffle his sobs in the blanket, when he felt Sun Bo stroke him on the head.

"What the matter, Stephen?"

"Hold me! please, just hold me!"

The contact of their bodies made Stephen sob even more. At the pit of his stomach he felt a void, as if some essential part of him that gave him his solidity had been removed, robbed! and he could not stop weeping over the loss. But finally the paroxysm ended, and Stephen opened his eyes. He felt cried-out, so much so that he couldn't even raise his hand to wipe away his tears.

Sun Bo did it for him.

"Thank you," he sighed. "I don't know what came over me."

"You are better now?"

"Yes."

"Then I have surprise."

"No, no, please. I couldn't take another surprise."

"Wait," Sun Bo said, ignoring Stephen's protest and going to the desk.

The stealth with which Sun Bo removed whatever it was from the drawer and concealed it in his hand, aroused Stephen's curiosity. "What is it?"

"I thought you could not take."

Stephen grinned. "Must I shut my eyes?"

Sun Bo didn't understand. "How you will see with eye shut?"

"Show me then."

Sun Bo sat down and opened his hand. In the center of his palm he held a silver ring.

Stephen picked it up with care. The ring was in the shape of two clasped hands. On one side of the band, designed to represent an arm, was inscribed the name Sun Bo, on the other, Stephen.

"You remember spoon from mess hall?"

Stephen nodded.

"Spoon now ring," Sun Bo explained. "Why you do not put it on? I know you do not like luxury, but ring not luxury. Ring mean to represent friendship between Stephen and Sun Bo."

Stephen tried to put the ring on his third finger but it wouldn't fit, so he put it on his pinky. "I'll never take it off, Sun Bo. Never, never."

"You weep again," Sun Bo observed.

"I'm sorry, sorry."

"Why you weep?"

"Because-because—" Stephen stammered, squeezing the ring as if to keep the hands from coming unclasped, "because I have to leave you."

"Yes, of course," Sun Bo said matter-of-factly. "You are not like little boy, like son, who must rely on me."

"No, I know, but— Son?" Stephen interrupted himself.

Sun Bo shifted his gaze.

"Why did you say son?"

"I only make example, Stephen. Come, I will walk with you to compound gate."

Stephen did not move. "Sun Bo?"

"Yes."

"That night in Pusan, you said there was some reason why you couldn't leave the stockade."

"I tell you reason: no life for me in Pusan."

"But you said there was some *other* reason—"

"No!"

"Yes, something that you couldn't say. Can't you tell me now?"

As Sun Bo stared at Stephen, all expression left his face. "I think you know."

"That O is your son," Stephen whispered.

"How you know that, Stephen?"

"I didn't know exactly, I—I just suspected."

"You must speak of it to no one!"

"Of course not."

"No one know but you, no GI," he added. "In truth, O is name of mother. Name of boy, same as me: Pak."

"I'll never say a word, I swear." For a full minute Stephen stood in silence, staring at Sun Bo. His love and admiration seemed too enormous to articulate; he could only shake his head. "I don't know what to say."

"There is not more to say . . . except good-by."

"Good-by, Sun Bo." Stephen hugged him tightly. "I love you . . . love you . . . so much."

"I, too, Stephen."

Mustering all his courage, Stephen collected his presents and started toward the door. Sun Bo followed. "No. Please don't come to the gate with me."

"You prefer?"

"Yes—no—it's not that I prefer—it's just—Good-by," he said, darting out the door.

Leaning against the deck rail, twisting the silver ring on his little finger and watching the shrieking gulls patrol the churning wake, Stephen felt both overjoyed and sorrowful, as the troop transport, *General Miller,* steamed through the Golden Gate. Joyful to be home again, to see his family and friends again, and soon to begin his career; sorrowful, not only because he had lost Sun Bo and left Korea, but also because he had lost something of himself. What it was, he could not say, but from the way in which he gazed down at the emerald water, Stephen seemed to know by instinct that he had lost it in the sea. Part of him—some central part, some fiercely personal, yet antenatal, even prehistoric part he would have thought he could not live without—was drifting, drowning there below the opaque surface, even as the rest of him was being borne back to the Pacific Coast . . .

Suddenly, just overhead, like a gigantic metal sea fan, dazzling in the sunlight, Stephen saw the underspanning of the Golden Gate Bridge. A little army band was on the pier again as the *General Miller* docked, and Stephen stepped off the ship, away from the water, away from the ocean, down the gangplank, onto the land.